A Woman of Courage

RITA BRADSHAW

A Woman of Courage

MACMILLAN

First published 2023 by Macmillan
an imprint of Pan Macmillan
The Smithson, 6 Briset Street, London ECIM 5NR
EU representative: Macmillan Publishers Ireland Ltd, 1st Floor,
The Liffey Trust Centre, 117–126 Sheriff Street Upper,
Dublin 1, DOI YC43
Associated companies throughout the world
www.panmacmillan.com

ISBN 978-1-0350-0031-9

1 3 5 7 9 8 6 4 2

A CIP catalogue record for this book is available from the British Library.

Typeset by Palimpsest Book Production Ltd, Falkirk, Stirlingshire
Printed and bound by CPI Group (UK) Ltd, Croydon, CRO 4YY

Visit **www.panmacmillan.com** to read more about all our books
and to buy them. You will also find features, author interviews and
news of any author events, and you can sign up for e-newsletters
so that you're always first to hear about our new releases.

For our beautiful furry baby, Muffin.
You were infinitely precious and unique, little man, and we loved you beyond words. Your passing has left us broken-hearted, and with a Muffin-shaped hole in our lives that can never be filled.

Acknowledgements

The research needed for this book was quite intensive, and although the internet was as helpful as ever, the following books deserve a special mention:

The Gilded Age in New York, 1870–1910,
   by Esther Crain

*Immigrant Women in the Land of Dollars: Life
   and Culture on the Lower East Side, 1890–1925,*
   by Elizabeth Ewen

*Picturing New York: Photographs from the Museum of
   Modern Art,* curated by Sarah Hermanson Meister

*Island of Hope: The Story of Ellis Island and the
   Journey to America,* by Martin W. Sandler

Immigration to New York, edited by William Pencak,
   Selma Berrol and Randall M. Miller

Contents

PART ONE

Toby

1890

Chapter One

'Now remember what I said and be careful, hinny, all right? Keep to the streets where the gas lamps are and no taking shortcuts through them dark alleys.'

Josie Gray smiled at her mother, nodding her head. 'Don't worry, Mam, I never do. Toby said he'd meet me out tonight and walk me home, by the way.'

Maggie patted her daughter's arm. 'Did he? That's good,' she said, but the worried expression didn't lift. Her eldest daughter was such a beauty, that was the thing, with her great green eyes and mass of curly chestnut hair. Josie was a good girl, no doubt about that, but in Sunderland's labyrinth of passageways and back lanes there were plenty of dark corners where things were known to go on. The East End was bad enough in daylight but once night fell it was no place for a young girl on her own. However, Ralph said Josie had to work at the Fiddler's Elbow and that was that.

'I'll be fine, Mam.' Josie touched her mother's lined cheek before she pulled on her coat and hat. Not for the world would she worry her mother more by admitting she always scurried along with her heart in her mouth until she reached the public house where her father had arranged for her to sing each night. She hated to be out on the streets after dark. The dockside dollies would be plying their trade and drunken sailors thought nothing of making a grab for you as you walked past. Her two older brothers, Toby and Joe, had shown her some moves to defend herself if she was accosted, but had emphasized that the first thing to do if she was attacked was to scream her head off.

'Bite and kick and try to bring your knee up into their privates,' Toby had said, 'but scream too. Whatever you do, don't freeze in fright, lass. They'll likely panic and let you go if you make enough racket.'

Dear Toby, Josie thought, as she left the house in Long Bank close to the docks. The Bank joined High Street and Low Street and the stink from the kipper-curing factory coloured the air summer and winter. She knew her brothers worried about her like their mam, but her da couldn't care less. He'd had her singing in the East End pubs since she was knee high to a grasshopper, and now, at fifteen, she could earn more money than Toby and Joe did working at the docks. Money was all that mattered to her father but like Toby said, it didn't matter enough for their da to go out to work himself. He was forever complaining of a bad back, but if it suited him he was as sprightly as the next fellow.

It was sleeting in the raw wind as she made her way

towards the Fiddler's Elbow and the November night was miserable. For once there were no bairns playing or women gossiping on their doorsteps. Years ago the old river-mouth settlement of Sunderland's East End had been the place where the wealthy and influential residents of the town had built their fine houses, but when they'd left the busy commercial area to reside in the more fashionable and quieter Bishopwearmouth, the working class had taken over. Beautiful three-storey houses built for wealthy merchants and shipbuilders had fallen into rat-infested slums where whole families lived in one room and the outside privy and tap was used by twenty or thirty folk. Now the smell of poverty and decay was the order of the day.

It only took Josie a few minutes to reach the Fiddler's Elbow. It was one of many notorious public houses in the East End and a frequent haunt of the dockside dollies. Most evenings she had to sing there from seven o'clock until after midnight. Her father had come to an agreement with the landlord – George Mullen – some years ago and had told her she should count herself lucky to have regular employment when she hadn't even left school. On the first night she had made the mistake of slipping outside into the pub's courtyard for a breath of fresh air and had found several women obliging their customers. She'd scampered back inside, shocked to the core. It had been then she'd understood why the Fiddler's Elbow and some of the other pubs were called whore markets, but overall she didn't mind working there. George Mullen might be rough and ready but he looked out for her and wouldn't tolerate any of his customers taking any liberties with her; neither would his wife, Ada, who was big and blowsy and could put the fear of God into even the most awkward drunkard.

When she pushed open the heavy studded front door of the pub the noise hit her. The enormous interior was dimly lit by flickering gas lights and the smell of beer and smoke hung in the air. There was the normal crowd of folk inside, a good number of them sailors and dock workers, and the level of conversation was deafening. The only time the din died down was when she sang and then the regulars would make sure she could be heard.

She made her way through the tables and chairs towards the bar where George and Ada, along with their two daughters, who were younger versions of their mother, were busy serving customers. The Fiddler's Elbow was a popular pub with the locals and George and Ada turned a blind eye to the goings-on in the courtyard and other nefarious activities that took place in dark corners. If smuggled goods or drugs changed hands it was nothing to do with them; they had a living to earn after all.

A couple of the young local lads called out to Josie as she passed but she just smiled in reply and kept walking. She had never had a beau and wasn't in any hurry to acquire one, and the thought of marriage held no appeal whatsoever. From what she'd seen, it seemed that once a lass got wed it meant having one bairn after another as regular as clockwork and living in fear of the rent man for the rest of your life, like her mam and everyone else she knew. It didn't appeal.

Ada Mullen smiled at the girl she thought of as pretty as a picture. She had a soft spot for Josie; the lass was reliable and not mouthy like some of the types they got in the pub. Furthermore, she felt sorry for her having a father like Ralph Gray; as far as she knew the man had never done a day's honest work and would sell his own grandmother if the price was right.

'There's a fresh pot of tea in the back,' she said as Josie reached her. 'Go an' have a cup before you start, lass, an' warm yourself up. I've left a couple of teacakes out an' all an' a slab of butter.'

'Aw, thank you, Mrs Mullen.' Josie's mouth was already watering; she was always hungry. It was rare her brothers got a full week each at the docks – often it was just three or four shifts and even with what she brought in money was always tight. Her mother could stretch a penny to two but with her three younger sisters to feed besides the rest of them and the rent to pay each week they were forever robbing Peter to pay Paul. She had never spoken of what it was like at home to Mrs Mullen but she felt the publican's wife knew anyway. There were no secrets in the East End.

Ada shook her head to herself as Josie disappeared into the corridor behind the bar. *Poor little beggar*, she thought for the umpteenth time. The lass was as thin as a lath and always looked half-starved, but at least she could make sure the bairn filled her stomach when she was here of a night, which was something.

She caught her husband's eye and he, reading her mind, shook his head too before turning back to his customers.

He knew his wife was fond of Josie and she was a nice little lass after all, but the bairn was one of many such undernourished youngsters hereabouts. At least Josie was lucky inasmuch as she had something special that might set her apart in the future. Her voice was exceptional; with a bit of training from someone who knew about such things she could go far. He'd said as much to Ada, hoping to comfort her when she was worrying about the girl, but his wife had merely shaken her head and said sourly, 'With a da like Ralph Gray? He'd never let her pay out a penny to better herself as long as she's keeping him in beer and baccy money. The man's a parasite, a leech, an' you know it. And his poor wife – Maggie must have given birth to thirteen or fourteen bairns in her time and only six of 'em alive, and I'm amazed she's managed to rear that many with a ne'er-do-well of a husband like him. For two pins I'd refuse to serve him when he comes in here an' tell him to clear off home an' give the money to his wife.'

'You'll do no such thing,' George had replied, faintly alarmed. Where would they be if his wife started getting a conscience about such things? 'His money is as good as the next man's and it's up to him an' Maggie to sort out their own going-on.'

That conversation had been a few weeks ago when the weather hadn't been so bad, but it had curbed his tongue when Ada had come back from the market earlier today with a thick winter coat for Josie. Instead of objecting as he might have done, he'd nodded when his wife had said, 'That coat Josie's wearing is threadbare and the sleeves are halfway up her arms; she'll be no good for custom if she gets a chill and loses her voice. I saw this going cheap on Hutton's stall at the market. It can do for an early Christmas present for the lass.'

Reginald Hutton's stall had a reputation for being more expensive than most; he dealt in better-quality second-hand clothing and his prices reflected this. Cheap wasn't a word George would have associated with Hutton. He hadn't pointed this out to his wife, however, neither had he remarked that to his knowledge they weren't in the habit of giving Christmas presents to their staff apart from a few extra pennies in their wage packets. If buying the bairn a coat kept Ada happy and stopped any further talk about turning paying customers away then he was all for it.

When after a few moments he looked to where his wife had been standing and saw she was gone, he smiled to himself. Ada had been itching to give the coat to the lass and he'd had a private bet with himself that she wouldn't be able to wait until closing time.

In the pub's big kitchen, Josie was staring in wonder at the olive-green coat with a white fur collar that Ada had just presented her with. She found herself stammering as she said, 'But I – I can't accept th-this, Mrs Mullen.'

'Of course you can, hinny.' Ada was highly gratified at the girl's reaction. 'It's your Christmas present from Mr Mullen and myself like I said. All right? There's snow forecast so I thought you might as well have it now been's I'd got it. Try it on and make sure it fits.'

In a daze, Josie slipped off the old brown coat that had already been somewhat the worse for wear when her mother had picked it up at the market three years ago and put on the new one. It felt as though she was being enfolded in a warm blanket and she stroked the soft collar as she said huskily, 'I don't know how to thank you, Mrs Mullen. It's beautiful, just beautiful.'

Ada beamed. 'My pleasure, lass. You look right bonny, I must say.' In truth, she was taken aback at just how much the coat had transformed the girl. She'd always thought that Josie was a pretty little thing but now she realized the lass was a child no longer and she was going to be a stunningly lovely woman. Of course, she told herself in the next breath, Josie's beauty would be wasted round these parts. Girls got old before their time and even the bonniest of lassies ended up haggard and work-worn. It would be a shame in this case, a crying shame.

'Take it off and have a sup tea and finish your teacakes,' she said briskly, her face betraying none of the disquiet her thoughts had produced. 'Come through when you're ready but there's no rush, hinny. Fred's not here yet.'

Josie nodded. Fred was an ancient, gnarled little gnome of a man who accompanied her on the pub's battered piano in return for as much beer as he could drink, the occasional packet of baccy for his beloved pipe and a spot of food now and again. This arrangement meant he was often three sheets to the wind by the end of an evening but as it didn't affect his playing no one cared.

Once Ada bustled off, Josie sat in the relative peace

of the kitchen. The hubbub from the main room of the pub filtered through now and again – laughter and voices and the occasional shouting – but she loved her moments in the kitchen. It was always as warm as toast courtesy of the huge black range that was kept going winter and summer, and Ada and her daughters – Dora and May – kept it as clean as a new pin. The pub's cat, a fat tabby with golden eyes, was curled up on the thick clippy mat in front of the fire, and Josie stroked it for a moment or two. It purred contentedly before dozing off again as she reached for her mug of tea.

The cat was a bone of contention between the publican and his wife. Ada had acquired it as a kitten when the little scrap of nothing had turned up in the courtyard one winter's night, soaked and shivering. She'd insisted on bringing it into the warm, saying it would pay its way by keeping the mice down once it grew, but when it had become obvious it was no mouser she'd refused to get rid of the animal, telling her husband that she'd as soon kick him out as the cat.

Ada's 'couple' of teacakes had been a plateful, and Josie ate the lot before making her way into the big smoke-filled room in which she sang. She felt comfortably full for once. Fred had arrived and was sitting at the piano supping his first tankard of ale. He smiled at her as she joined him, revealing his brown rotting teeth. 'How do, lass?'

It was his normal greeting and as he put the empty tankard on the top of the shabby piano and set about lighting his pipe, Josie smiled at him. She liked Fred. He'd lost his wife to the fever some years before and lived with one of his daughters but she didn't like having him underfoot. The Fiddler's Elbow was the old man's refuge.

She climbed onto the upturned box next to the piano and immediately the room quietened a little. Even the dockside dollies sitting at tables or on sailors' laps lowered their voices, and if they didn't George's regulars would make sure they did. Some of the inns and licensed premises in the better part of Sunderland would charge 'wet money' if any entertainment was offered. This was so called because the fee charged on admission was returnable by drink. When George had made the decision to employ Josie he'd known such a charge wouldn't wash with his rough-and-ready clientele in the East End, so he had agreed to pay her a very small fee each week but have a hat on the piano into which his customers could throw coins to show their appreciation. Within a few weeks his gamble to take the girl on six nights a week had proved a success. Word had spread and his customers had nearly doubled; furthermore being close to the docks brought in the sailors and they were the ones with money in their pockets. The sight of a young girl singing about true love or mother love, or idyllic villages with thatched cottages and roses at the door, seemed to appeal more to men far away from home than the suggestive, risqué songs, although Josie was adept at both. 'Silver Threads Among the Gold' always brought a good response, along with 'A Flower from Mother's Grave' and 'My Dearest Heart'.

As always happened when she began to sing, Josie forgot about her surroundings. The room reeking of smoke and beer and unwashed humanity, the buzz of noise and the fact that she was being stared at by umpteen pairs of eyes faded away as she started the evening with 'Rescue the Perishing', a hymn the sailors always seemed to like. Her voice rose pure and unfaltering with a sweetness made more poignant by her faded old dress and lovely face. Even George and Ada and their daughters stopped what they were doing for a minute or two, leaning on the counter and listening quietly.

She sang another hymn before going into a rendition of 'Grandfather's Clock' and then a couple of rousing Irish songs that had the customers' feet tapping, before the slower 'I'll Take You Home Again, Kathleen'. She normally had a break and a drink of water after half a dozen or so songs – the heavy smoky air made her throat dry.

Walking across to the bar she stood with Ada and the others, sipping the glass of water as she watched the publican's daughters laugh and joke with the customers. The two girls were younger editions of their gregarious mother and she found herself envying their confidence and quick repartee. Shy by nature, when she wasn't singing and lost in that other world, she felt too self-conscious to engage in banter, although there were one or two regulars she felt comfortable with.

One was in tonight. Hans was a sea captain from Norway, a tall dark-haired man with vivid blue eyes. She knew he had a wife whom he missed when he was away and that they had seven children, the oldest a young man who accompanied him on his voyages. She had been surprised when he'd first told her he was from Norway. She had always assumed that men from that part of the world were fair-skinned with blonde hair – certainly the ones who drank in the Fiddler's Elbow tended to be – but as she had got to know Hans better he'd told her that although his father was Norwegian his mother was from Italy.

She smiled at him now as he came to get drinks from the bar and he winked at her, leaning further over the counter as he said in his heavy accent, 'And how is my little songbird this evening?'

Jules, Hans's son, had joined his father and before she could reply, Jules said proudly, 'It was a boy, Joo-see.' His wife had been expecting their first child on the previous visit.

'Oh, that's wonderful, Jules. Congratulations.'

'Not so wonderful. This makes me a grandfather, yes? An old man.' Hans wrinkled his nose but his grin conveyed the pride he felt in his firstborn. He had once confided to Josie that Jules was the most like him of all his children, both in looks and temperament, and it would have been clear to a blind man that the young man was the apple of his father's eye.

'You're far from an old man, Hans.'

'You think so? That is good. I like this.' His teeth gleamed white in his olive-skinned face as he smiled. 'It is true I was just a – how do you say in your English? – whippersnipper when Jules was born.'

'It's whippersnapper,' said Josie, laughing.

'Yes, whippersnapper.' Hans paid for the drinks he had bought for his men, who were sitting at a large table at the back of the room, and as Jules carried them over, he said in a lower voice, 'He misses Kristina, his wife, and the boy, and this trip will be a long one as another cargo was waiting for us when we unloaded yesterday which is bound for America. So' – he shrugged in a way that betrayed his Italian roots – 'there we must go. Jules is not happy about this.'

'Oh, I'm sorry, Hans.'

'I tell him this is the life of a sailor, the life you have chosen, and he shakes his head.' Hans's blue eyes narrowed. 'But the sea is in his blood, like it is in mine. You cannot escape your destiny, Joo-see. You remember this, yes? If you try it will find you.'

'I'll remember.'

They talked for a few moments more before she walked back to the piano. There were already a number of coins in the hat which Fred always kept an eye on if she took a break. She had tried many times to get the old man to take a share of the money but he always refused, insisting that the beer and baccy and bags of chitterlings that Ada kept him supplied with were all he wanted. As she resumed her position on the box, someone called out, 'How about "Sweet Mary Ann", lass?'

She nodded, but for once her mind was only half on what she was singing as she began the song. Hans's talk of destiny had left her feeling strangely unsettled. She knew full well that if she didn't marry in the future, as a spinster she'd be expected to live with her parents and care for them in their dotage. She would happily look after her mother, but the thought of doing the same for her father in his old age was as unattractive as marriage. According to Hans, your destiny would always find you, which meant in effect you couldn't break free from it.

Did she believe that? she asked herself as she finished the song. She wasn't sure. If it was true then it was terribly unfair. If whatever a man or woman did to better themselves or strive for a new life was pointless, then it was all useless. It took free choice away and she didn't think God was like that. And then she put the matter to one side. It was only Hans's opinion, after all, and as such not necessarily true.

The evening progressed the same as any other. When Hans and his party left, the Norwegian came up to the piano and placed a number of coins into the hat. He was always generous for the short time he was in port, but tonight he must have given her ten shillings or more. She had just finished a rendition of 'My Dearest Heart', which she knew he liked, and he smiled at her as he said, 'Beautiful, my little songbird. I would like you to get something for yourself tomorrow, yes? I do not like to think that all that you earn is taken by your father.'

'Thank you, Hans,' she said softly, but she knew her earnings would disappear as soon as she got home – her da would be waiting with his hand out. 'When do you leave for America?'

'First light.'

She nodded. Most of the sailors from the big ships and cargo boats only stayed in port for two or three days.

'Take care, Joo-see,' he said in his broken English, patting her cheek before turning away and joining Jules and the others.

Her eyes followed him as he left the pub and it was then that she noticed a man sitting at a table at the side of the room. His chair was leaning against the wall, tilted in such a way that he had his boots on the table in a relaxed pose, but his eyes were fixed on her with unnerving intensity. In the brief moments before turning away she saw he was very good-looking and dressed like a gentleman. This was unusual in the Fiddler's Elbow. It wasn't the sort of place that gentlemen frequented.

Now that she had become aware of him she had to restrain the desire to glance his way again as she began to sing, but as the song ended she let herself look quickly for a moment and saw that his eyes were still on her. Flushing, she said to Fred she was having a break and walked over to the bar.

'Here, hinny.' Ada had her drink of water ready as she joined the others behind the counter.

She waited a minute or two till there was a lull in serving customers, and then took Ada aside. 'Who's that man? The one sitting by the wall who's dressed so well?'

She didn't look his way as she spoke but Ada seemed to know who she meant because she said straight away, 'That's Adam McGuigan, lass. He's the youngest of the McGuigan brothers and you don't want anything to do with them.'

'The McGuigans?' Josie's eyes opened wider. Everyone in the East End knew the name. The family had acquired their considerable wealth by dubious means – extortion, gambling dens, smuggling and other criminal activities. They owned a good number of run-down tenement properties in the East End and beyond, and had a reputation for being ruthless landlords. No one was foolish enough to cross the McGuigans, not unless they wanted to end up in a back alley somewhere with their throats cut.

'They don't often come in here,' Ada continued quietly, 'although a couple of the older brothers might occasionally but I haven't seen Adam for years. His mam sent him to a private school by all accounts and he thinks he's a cut above the rest of us.' She smiled sourly. The McGuigans lived in the better part of Sunderland in fine houses and drove about in carriages but to her mind they were still scum. Not that she would dare to express such an opinion – you never knew who was listening and walls had ears. She'd got nothing against folk bettering themselves, she told herself as she resumed her position serving customers at the bar, but to do so by trampling your fellow man into the mire didn't sit right. The grandfather, Edgar McGuigan, had been a wrong un' all right but not in the same way as his son and now the brothers.

Josie took her time drinking the glass of water. When she joined Fred again she could feel Adam McGuigan's gaze although she didn't look in his direction. It was after George called closing time and she finished her last song that Adam walked over to her, his companions remaining at their table. He was tall and even more handsome close to, his wavy black hair and deep brown eyes making her heart race.

'Hello,' he said softly. 'You're Josie, aren't you.'

She nodded, unable to speak, partly through fear of the family's reputation but mostly because his good looks had taken her breath away. As she stared at him he reached in his pocket and took out a gold sovereign, dropping it into the hat. 'You sing beautifully.' His voice was deep and although his accent was strongly North-East he used his words like the middle-class would, she thought dazedly. She had never received a sovereign before and this, combined with the sheer presence of him, had her tongue-tied.

'How old are you, Josie?' he said even more softly.

Somehow she managed to stammer, 'Fif-fifteen.'

He nodded, his gaze wandering over her chestnut curls and creamy skin before resting on her mouth for a moment. When his eyes met hers again they were smiling. 'I thought you might be even younger.'

Her wits were returning and with them the knowledge that there was something too intimate about their conversation. She straightened, and now her voice was cool when she said, 'Thank you for the sovereign but you shouldn't have given so much.'

His smile widened. 'I think I should. I have had the most enjoyable evening, thanks to you.'

When in the next moment Toby appeared at her elbow Josie didn't know if she was relieved or disappointed. Her brother's face was straight and his voice was cold as he nodded at Adam McGuigan before saying, 'Are you ready, lass?'

Adam's eyes had narrowed and now she said hastily, perhaps too hastily she realized afterwards, 'This is my brother Toby,' before turning from him and saying to Toby, 'I'll just get my coat from the kitchen,' as she lifted the hat off the piano.

Adam McGuigan had gone when she returned and Toby was standing talking to Ada and George. She didn't let herself acknowledge that the feeling that swept over her was disappointment that Adam wouldn't see her in the beautiful new coat. The sovereign he had given her along with Hans's money and the normal contributions from other customers meant her takings for the night were more than she had ever earned before, and as she had counted the coins in the kitchen her mind had been racing. *Dare she give her mother the bulk of the money without her father knowing?* she'd asked herself. She could give him the rest in line with what he'd be expecting. It would mean her mam could pay the back rent off – they were always weeks in arrears – and perhaps stock up the cupboard with food for once. It would help her mam but her da would knock her into next weekend if he found out. She just didn't know what to do. Nevertheless, the coins jingling in her pocket made her face bright as she joined her brother, smiling as she said, 'Look what Mr and Mrs Mullen bought me for Christmas, Toby. A new coat.'

There had been an expression on Toby's face that she couldn't put a name to when he had seen her walking towards him, but it cleared as he turned to the Mullens, saying, 'That's right kind of you both. It's grand, bonny.'

'Our pleasure, lad.' Ada's voice was warm. 'She deserves it and she looks a picture, doesn't she.'

'Aye, aye, she does that.'

Josie stared at her brother. What was wrong? He'd said the right thing but something was amiss. Surely he didn't mind about the coat? Not only would it mean she'd be warm and snug for once but Ellen could have her old one.

The weather had cleared while she'd been in the pub and the black night was high and star-filled as they walked outside. It was bitterly cold. She pulled the fur collar closely round her neck as she said, 'What's the matter, Toby? You don't object to Mr and Mrs Mullen buying me a Christmas present, do you?'

He'd taken her arm because the earlier sleet had frozen on the pavements and they were like glass in places. Now he stopped, turning her to face him. 'Of course I don't. I'm pleased for you.'

Josie lifted up the old coat she'd got over one arm. 'Ellen can have this and that'll help things and—'

'I told you, it's not about the coat.'

'So there is something? Tell me.'

'It's him, McGuigan. What were you doing talking to him?'

'What do you mean? I have to talk to the customers if they talk to me and give me money.'

'And McGuigan? What did he give you?'

In spite of herself she flushed as she said, 'A sovereign

as it happens and Hans was in and he gave me ten shillings or more so—'

'A sovereign?' They had begun walking again but now Toby stopped again, drawing her to a halt. 'A *sovereign*? And you accepted it?'

'Of course I accepted it.' She pulled her arm away, nettled at his tone. 'It's why I'm in there singing every night, isn't it? To earn money.'

'Aye, and I've never liked that as you know, but I thought with the Mullens keeping an eye on you it'd be all right.'

'It *is* all right.' Her momentary irritation had faded at the sight of his concerned face. Of all her siblings she was the closest to Toby. There was over four years between them and Joe was the second eldest at seventeen, but she'd never had the bond with him that she had with Toby. 'Really, it is.' She slipped her arm through his again. 'It was the first time that Adam McGuigan has been in – ask Mrs Mullen if you don't believe me – and he'll probably never come in again.'

Toby didn't look convinced. 'What did he say to you?'

'Just that he'd had a nice evening and liked the songs I'd sung, that's all.' She didn't think it wise to mention the conversation about her age.

They walked on a few steps in silence before Toby said, 'Look, lass, you know me an' Joe work at the docks and the McGuigans have got their fingers in the pie there same as other places. He might look as though butter wouldn't melt in his mouth with his fine clothes an' all but the whole family's bad. Bruce, the eldest brother, he walks about as though he owns the town and maybe he does in a way. Anyway, what I'm saying is they're all tarred with the same brush and they're dangerous.'

She nodded. 'I still couldn't not take the sovereign,' she said in small voice.

'Oh, I know, I know.' He hugged her to him for a moment. 'I'm sorry but seeing him talking to you like that . . .'

He didn't go on and she didn't want him to; he was spoiling what had been a special night and not just because she had been given the coat. Adam McGuigan had looked nice, not like Toby was saying. His brothers might be bad but he'd just looked— She couldn't find a word to describe how he had looked and gave up trying. 'Anyway, you like my coat then?' she said, forcing a smile.

Not for the world would he reveal the shock he had felt when he had first seen her in it and thought McGuigan had bought it. She was so bonny, that was the thing. Too bonny to be singing in the Fiddler's Elbow with the types you got in there, although he had to admit he'd never thought of one of the McGuigans being interested in her. And Adam McGuigan *was* interested. He'd seen it in the man's face in the moment before the pair of them had known he was there. 'You look lovely, lass, and it's a grand coat,' he said with as much enthusiasm as he could muster, and as her face relaxed and her smile widened, his worry increased. Aye, she was too bonny by half and the coat made her look different, older. Something in his guts told him there was trouble ahead.

Chapter Two

Adam McGuigan was without his cronies when he pushed open the door of the Fiddler's Elbow the following evening. He hadn't wanted company. His eyes immediately searched for the young girl who had occupied his every waking moment and when he saw her talking to the old pianist he let out his breath in a silent sigh. She was as beautiful as he remembered, more so if anything. That Titian hair, it was as though light radiated from it.

He stood for a moment before walking over to the table he'd occupied the night before, which happened to be free even though the pub was crowded. He caught the eye of one of the barmaids and when she came to his side he ordered a bottle of whisky. He knew by the girl's manner she had recognized who he was – she was edgy, nervous – and he smiled as she scurried off. He liked the power the McGuigan name afforded him.

His gaze went back to the girl at the piano. He knew a great deal more about her than he had the night before. He'd had one of Bruce's lackeys make some enquiries;

Larry was a dab hand at finding out information and he had a way with him that made people trust him, often to their cost.

Her name was Josie Gray and according to Larry she really was as shy and innocent as she appeared, despite working in this dive. Not that that would bother him normally. He'd had his fair share of women since the age of fourteen, ten years ago, when his brother Bruce had arranged for him to be 'broken in', as Bruce had put it, as his birthday present.

His eyes narrowed. The girl had only been a couple of years older than him but she'd been on the game since she was a child. She'd known everything there was about pleasing a customer. But although women of that type were good for one thing, he wouldn't want to be seen with them in daylight. And he had a fancy to court Miss Josie Gray. Properly.

The barmaid returned with his whisky and a glass and he paid her, throwing in a good tip without taking his eyes off the girl at the piano. Everything about her enthralled him. According to Larry the family lived in Long Bank and he'd been amazed when he'd found that out. It seemed impossible that anything so lovely could come from that quarter. The rent men they employed always had trouble collecting from the streets near the docks; the scum of the earth lived there. He rarely ventured into the East End himself, although Bruce and a couple of his other brothers who had business that was best done under the cover of darkness were familiar with the area. If it hadn't been for the fact that one of his pals had suggested slumming it for a laugh, he would never have seen Josie.

He poured himself a drink and knocked it back in one before filling his glass again, noticing how when the piano struck the first note the noise died down considerably. She began to sing, but her voice gripped him less than the sheer beauty of her. Despite her faded frock and lack of adornment she was the epitome of loveliness, he thought, unaware that he was holding his breath until he let it out in a shuddering sigh. He wanted her, but not like one of his usual dalliances. Josie Gray was special.

The brother hadn't liked him though. His eyes narrowed. But he could be dealt with. Larry had told him her two older brothers worked at the docks and Bruce could see to it they toed the line. The risk of finding themselves blacklisted should bring them to heel, along with making it clear that if they played ball with the McGuigans they'd suddenly find they worked a full week at good money.

He settled back in his chair, emptying his glass. As Josie finished the song – a plaintive melody about lost love – she glanced in his direction. Their eyes met for a moment before she broke the contact, but not before he had registered how the colour rose in her cheeks and how flustered she appeared as she began to sing again.

She liked him, he told himself. He'd seen it in her face before she'd dropped her gaze. He was used to the female sex finding him attractive; some because of his looks or wealth or perhaps a combination of both, and others because they were intrigued by the influence and weight of the McGuigan name. He had noticed the night before that Josie took a break now and again, and he wondered if she would come across to his table when she stopped singing. Perversely, a part of him would be disappointed if she did. It would relegate her to being like all the others and he felt she was different.

He waited, more het up than he would have thought possible, and when after a few more songs she bent and said something to the old man at the piano and then walked towards the bar, he relaxed back in his chair. He continued to watch her as she talked to the publican's wife and the barmaids for a few minutes. She didn't look his way, nor did she glance at him when she resumed singing, but he knew she was just as aware of him as he was of her.

He'd had a few more glasses of whisky when Bruce slid into the seat beside him some time later. 'Thought I might find you in here after Larry had a word in my ear. What the hell are you about, man?'

'If Larry's been shooting his mouth off you've probably got a good idea,' Adam snapped angrily, annoyed the man had reported back to Bruce and even more put out that his brother had seen fit to turn up here. He was a grown man for crying out loud, not a youth still wet behind the ears. 'Not that it's any of your business, I might add.'

Ignoring that, Bruce looked across the smoky room. 'Is that her?'

'Now look, Bruce—'

'Is that her?'

'Aye, that's her. Josie Gray.'

'And Larry said she's a bit lass from Long Bank. Have you gone out of your mind? Mam'd have a fit if she got wind of this. She's got that councillor's daughter in mind for you, you know that, and you can't afford to be seen messing about with anyone else. Are you as gone on her as Larry thinks?'

'I've never had any intention of getting involved with Bernice Chapman. I can't stand her or her toadying father.' Bruce had got half the local council in the palm of his hand, and especially Eustace Chapman, who regularly pocketed the generous bribes Bruce gave him to look the other way on dodgy business dealings. His daughter was a pretty, simpering young lass and had made it clear she carried a torch for Adam; their mother had been delighted about this. She thought the Chapmans were a cut above and had a fancy for her favourite son to marry well.

'Aye, well, Bernice Chapman aside, a lass from Long Bank?'

'Our grandfather was born not far from there.'

'And he got out when he could an' all and wiped the stink off his boots.'

'Oh, come on, Bruce. Do you seriously think that the folk round here are fooled by the fact that we live in big houses and could buy and sell them a thousand times over? They know where we came from sure enough even if they wouldn't dare point it out.' Adam loved his eldest brother, perhaps more than anyone in his life thus far, and he respected him too as head of the McGuigan clan. However, he wasn't frightened of Bruce like everyone else was. At forty-four years of age Bruce was twenty years older than him and had always been more of a father figure since their da had died umpteen years before. His other brothers – David, who was forty, Philip a year younger, and the twins, Mick and Rory, who were thirty-seven – were a tough bunch, but Bruce was tougher. His authority was never questioned, not even by their mother.

Adam himself had been what his mother fondly called a 'late surprise'. She'd fallen for him long after she'd imagined her childbearing days were over, but after the initial shock she had apparently been over the moon. When he'd arrived with a shock of dark curls and great brown eyes she had pampered and spoiled him as she had never done with her other sons, but funnily enough there'd been no resentment from them. Bruce in particular had indulged his youngest brother from when Adam could toddle.

Bruce poured a good measure of whisky into Adam's glass and knocked it back before saying, 'Aye, well, Mam doesn't think like that and don't you ever suggest it to her either.'

'Of course I wouldn't.' His mother's ability to see life through rose-coloured glasses had always amazed him, however. From an early age he had been aware that the 'family business' as she called it was one of varied and mostly illegal enterprises. True, the houses they owned and rented out were above board, but little else was. And he knew there was good reason for folk to be frightened of the McGuigans, and of Bruce especially. He had been about sixteen when he'd seen his brother beat the manager of one of their gambling dens to a pulp over missing cash. When, white-faced and feeling queasy, he had asked Bruce why he'd reacted so violently over a few pounds, his brother had taken him aside and told him that the beating was in the form of a warning to others who might be under the illusion that they could cheat the McGuigans.

'Give 'em an inch and they'll take a mile,' Bruce had said unemotionally as two of his men had carried the unfortunate individual out into the street and dumped him there. 'It's human nature, lad. And no one makes a monkey out of a McGuigan.'

Adam looked at his brother now. In appearance Bruce took after their father – all the brothers did apart from him. His dark good looks came from his mother whereas Bruce and the others were big, thickset men with solid muscled bodies and rough-hewn faces. Adam had been the only one of them to go to a small select school in Newcastle where he had received a good education which included a smattering of Latin, and after he had left school at eighteen there had been talk of him going to university but here he'd put his foot down. He didn't want further years of studying, he wanted to be with his family. His mother and Bruce had tried to persuade him to go but he had been adamant, so he and Bruce had reached a compromise. He would be inducted into the family business but not involved in all of it. His strong points were more on the academic side and he'd excelled in all things mathematical. Therefore the running of the property side could be his, along with checking that their accountant – a foxy little man – didn't cheat them and their accounts could stand inspection from the law if necessary. It had worked fine.

'Bruce, I like her.' He reached for his glass which Bruce had seconded and filled it. 'And by all accounts she's a nice lass, an innocent.'

'Growing up in Long Bank?' Bruce shook his head.

'You know what I mean. She might be worldly wise in some ways but she's never had a lad.'

'You can't be sure of even that.'

'I'd bet my life on it.'

Bruce swore softly under his breath. He had never seen Adam like this over a lass. Their mam would throw a blue fit. She'd had high hopes of him marrying into the upper echelons of Sunderland society. Not only was Adam her blue-eyed boy but he gave an air of respectability to the McGuigan name which he knew she craved. She was a funny mixture, was their mam – hard as nails at times and possessed of an iron will which even he found intimidating, but where Adam was concerned she was as soft as clarts. And she wanted him to rise in the world.

'Bruce, stand with me on this. It'll make all the difference with Mam if you back me. Anyway, I haven't even asked Josie out yet. She might say no. Certainly her brother was none too keen on me.'

'Her brother?'

'Aye, he came to collect her last night when I was talking to her and if looks could kill I'd be six foot under. Larry found out he works at the docks with another brother and he knew who I was for sure.'

Bruce's eyes narrowed. It was one thing for him to object to Adam's interest in the lass; quite another for the disapproval to come from her family. 'Is that so?' he said softly. 'Well, maybe a word in his shell-like wouldn't go amiss.'

'Leave it. Don't do anything for now,' Adam said hastily. He knew what his brother's 'little words' could lead to and he didn't want the man to end up at the bottom of the river with his throat cut. Not yet anyway. He might not be a problem. After all, everyone had their price.

Bruce took the glass of whisky Adam handed him and drank it in two gulps before he stood up, flexing his broad shoulders. He was dressed well – all the McGuigans bought their clothes in the best establishments – but his tweed suit and pearl-buttoned waistcoat only accentuated his bullet-shaped head and craggy features.

He looked across to where Josie was singing. She was a beauty all right, he thought to himself. Dressed in the right clothes she could look the part. His own wife and the wives of his brothers were working-class lassies too, but even when they were dressed up to the nines on a night out their roots showed. Course, none of them were stunners, not like this girl. She'd have to stop this singing lark if Adam took up with her though; their mam wouldn't tolerate that.

'Just take it nice and slow, lad,' he said flatly, 'and keep it from Mam for the time being. You don't know the lass and this could be something or nothing.'

Adam nodded eagerly. If he had Bruce onside everything would be a whole lot easier because this was going to be something for sure. 'Aye, thanks, man.'

He grinned up at his brother and Bruce returned a reluctant smile, shaking his head. 'Remember, you're the one holding all the cards, not her. Act like a McGuigan rather than a lovelorn puppy.'

Adam's grin widened. 'I can't help it.'

Bruce groaned softly. Whichever way this went it wouldn't be plain sailing and for once he felt it was something outside of his control. That didn't sit well. He'd been hoping that Adam would have been content to have this girl on the side; he could have arranged that. According to Larry, the father was scum, the kind of seedy little individual who could easily be bought and who'd be open to a deal for his daughter. Now he realized that wasn't what Adam had in mind at all. 'Aye, well, like I said, go easy till you know what you're letting yourself in for, man. Some lassies are not what they seem.'

Even as Bruce spoke he knew he was preaching to the converted – if anyone knew about lassies it was their Adam, he thought ruefully. From a young lad he'd noticed them and the girls had certainly fallen over themselves to get noticed too.

He slapped his brother on the back before making his way out of the pub. A couple of his henchmen were kicking their heels waiting for him. He rarely went anywhere alone; he had far too many enemies and in the East End it would be asking for trouble. That was why he'd come here tonight; he didn't like the idea of Adam hanging around this girl without backup.

He called to one of the men, who was built like a brick

outhouse. 'Go in the pub and keep an eye on Adam,' he said quietly, slipping him a few bob. 'But make sure he doesn't clock you. Don't leave him till he's home, all right?' It was one thing for Adam to slum it in the company of some of his pals, quite another for him to be in this quarter without protection.

He had been interested to see this girl who'd got his brother so hot under the collar, but having seen her he felt more disturbed than ever. A common floozy with an eye to the main chance was one thing, but Josie Gray didn't fit that description. Of course, she could be cleverer than most of her type, and with a father like she'd got . . .

'Right you are, boss.' Bruce's bodyguard's eyes lit up. Sitting drinking a few glasses of beer and a spot of babysitting was a darn sight more agreeable than most of the jobs he was called upon to do by Bruce McGuigan.

It was nigh on closing time when Adam sought Josie out. Despite the whisky he'd poured down his throat he was steady on his feet. He had been drinking since he was a lad; all his brothers were heavy drinkers and his tolerance to alcohol was high. In a repeat of the previous evening he dropped a sovereign into the hat as he said softly, 'Hello again.'

'Hello.' She felt painfully shy. She had been vitally aware of him all night but hadn't dared to look his way.

'I'm Adam. Adam McGuigan.' He knew someone would have told her who he was but he wanted to set the ball rolling. 'And you are Josie Gray. I confess I've asked about you. Do you mind?'

She stared at him, pink staining her cheeks. He was so handsome, she thought breathlessly. 'No, I – I suppose not.'

'Good.' He smiled, showing perfect white teeth. 'In that case may I walk you home?'

'My brother's coming for me.' That made her sound like a child and she added, her blush deepening, 'He – he worries about me walking back late at night.'

'Very commendable.' He nodded approvingly. 'If I had a sister I would be exactly the same. The streets are no place for a young woman once darkness falls.'

He had a lovely voice, Josie thought through her hot embarrassment. It was deep and warm and gentle. Yes, gentle. It belied all the bad things she'd heard about him – well, not him exactly, she corrected herself. More the McGuigans in general. She didn't believe he was like his brothers. She liked his voice and she liked him in spite of what Toby would say. Nevertheless, the thought of her brother made her gather the hat from the piano and say hurriedly, 'I – I need to go and get my things from the kitchen.'

'Of course.' Adam sensed her discomfiture and the reason for it; her brother had made it very plain the night before how he felt about him and no doubt he had warned her off. Keeping the annoyance from showing in his voice, he said quietly, 'I'll say goodnight then.'

'Goodnight.' *Had she offended him?* she asked herself

wretchedly as she turned away. He probably wouldn't come in again.

By the time she reached the kitchen she almost felt like crying and she told herself not to be so soft. A man like him – and he was a man, he must be a good few years older than her – wouldn't be really interested in someone like her anyway. Adam McGuigan must be able to pick and choose his lassies, after all; he was so good-looking and wealthy too. She had picked May's brains about him when Ada was otherwise occupied, and the girl had told her that although all the other brothers were married with houses of their own, Adam still lived with his mother in a big house overlooking Barnes Park. 'They all live close to each other in lovely great properties,' May had whispered. 'Like mansions they are. Don't let anyone tell you that crime doesn't pay, lass.' She'd dug Josie in the ribs with a knowing wink. 'Rolling in it, they are. You'd be in clover if you reeled in Adam McGuigan.' Like her mother she had noticed Adam's interest the night before.

'He wouldn't want me,' Josie had said quickly.

May hadn't contradicted this, saying instead, and some-what wistfully, 'He's so good-looking, isn't he. Not like most men hereabouts. Half of 'em have got faces like battered plucks, my Wilf included.' She'd giggled. May was courting a beefy docker who supplemented his income by taking part in organized fist fights, most of which he lost.

Josie sighed as she pulled on her coat, tipping the contents of the hat into her pocket before leaving the kitchen. George had called for the last reluctant customers to drink up some minutes before and the pub was almost empty. Ada and her daughters were bustling about clearing used glasses and wiping tables and George was standing talking to Toby who'd arrived while she was in the kitchen. There was no sign of Adam McGuigan and she hoped he'd gone before Toby had seen him.

The two men stopped talking as she approached and Toby nodded goodbye to the landlord before taking her arm. 'Let's away,' he said flatly.

Immediately her heart sank. He'd either seen Adam or Mr Mullen had told him Adam had been in.

Once outside in the bitterly cold night they walked in silence for a few yards before Toby said tersely, 'So McGuigan's still sniffing around, is he?'

'He wasn't sniffing,' she said indignantly. It made Adam sound like a dog. 'He came in for a drink, I suppose, like lots of others.'

'Don't be naive. He came in to see you and you know it. George said he didn't take his eyes off you all night. Did he give you money again?'

He made it seem as though she was no better than one of the dock dollies and now she pulled her arm from his, rounding on him with a mixture of hurt and anger in her voice as she said, 'We had this out last night. I'm there to sing for money, Toby, whether you like it or not.'

'I *don't* like it, I never have.'

'Well, take that up with Da, not me.'

'I have, more than once.'

'And you got short shrift no doubt so what's the point

in discussing it? What I earn keeps us all going, you know it does. I'm not saying you and Joe don't do your bit but you can't always get shifts and when you do you never know from one week to the next how many. If I worked in a factory or a laundry or in service I wouldn't get half of what I earn now, and Mam can barely manage as it is. She lives her life worrying about putting food on the table and the three little ones can't help yet, apart from going to the tip and getting cinders for the fire now and again and you don't like them doing that either.'

'The tip's no place for bairns, same as the Fiddler's Elbow is no place for you.'

Irritated now as well as angry, Josie said sharply, 'Needs must and while we're talking like this you make everything ten times harder acting the way you do.'

She flounced off, nearly going headlong on the icy pavement, and when Toby took her arm again saying gruffly, 'Calm down, calm down, you'll break your neck,' she ignored him.

They had gone a few steps before he said, his tone appeasing now, 'I'm sorry, lass. I didn't mean you'd done anything wrong if that's how it sounded but I'm sick of Da's skiving and sitting on his backside all day long. And Mam doesn't say anything, she lets him get away with blue murder.'

'She's worn out, Toby. Can't you see that? She's got no fight left, only blind acceptance.' She turned to look at him under the flickering light of a gas lamp and what she saw in his face made her voice soft as she said, 'I know you worry about us all but it is what it is. And the littl'uns love going to the tip with the other bairns and coming home with bucketfuls of cinders. They think it's a game.'

'And what about you? Do you think it's a game having to sing for a pub full of drunken sailors and having blokes like Adam McGuigan giving you the eye? Don't tell me you enjoy that because I know how shy you've been from a little bairn.'

'It's not as bad as you're painting.' She reached up and touched his face. 'It's really not, Toby. Mr and Mrs Mullen look out for me and most of the customers are nice. You get a few of the other sort but that's the same anywhere. And to be honest, when I'm singing I sort of forget about where I am.'

'Aye, well, that's as maybe, but I'd rather you not be there and I can't help that.'

'I know.'

She was feeling tender towards him now but this feeling evaporated when he said, 'I saw Adam McGuigan leaving as I walked in and told him I didn't want him pestering you.'

'You didn't!'

'Aye, I did. You're fifteen, Josie, and he's a grown man of twenty-odd.'

She was about to let fly at him but then she asked herself what was the point? Toby saw things in black and white and as far as he was concerned all the McGuigans were tarred with the same brush. So instead of raising her voice she said quietly, 'He didn't pester me, as you put it – in fact, he only said two words as he was leaving.' She didn't mention the sovereign. She had already decided she would give that straight to her mam and tell her to keep quiet about it. 'And now can we talk about something else other than me singing and Adam McGuigan and the rest of it?'

'Aye, all right.' Truth be told, he was relieved she had taken him warning McGuigan off as well as she had. Lassies of her age were susceptible to a handsome face and silver tongue. 'Well, how about this? Teresa's mam's invited me round for Sunday tea.'

'No.' Josie stared at him in amazement, Adam temporarily forgotten. Toby had been courting Teresa O'Leary for over six months but with her family being staunch Catholics and them being Chapel, Teresa's mam had said that Toby would never set foot in their house. This was a turn-up for the books. The barrier between a Catholic and a Chapelite was greater than any social divide, but the pair were fair gone on each other and despite pressure from her family Teresa had refused to give Toby up.

'Aye.' Toby grinned at her. 'Teresa reckons her mam's hoping I'll convert.'

'And would you?'

'Not a chance. Teresa knows that. And between us, she's fed up with her mam and the church and the priests in particular. She says Father Owen and Father O'Brien have scarcely been off the doorstep since she took up with me and her mam's scared to death of them – they all are except Teresa. The power them priests have over folk is diabolical if you ask me.'

'Well, just don't say that on Sunday.'

'No fear.' He chuckled. 'I value me kneecaps and you know what nasty bits of work her da and brothers are. No, if the subject of church comes up I'll be – what's the word? – oh aye, non-committal.'

'Just make sure you are.' Josie was really worried now. The O'Leary menfolk were known for two things – one, being as thick as two short planks, and the second, being a mite too handy with their fists. One of the brothers had been sent down the line for putting a man in hospital some years ago, a fact the rest of the family were proud of. Teresa despaired of them. 'Are you sure you have to go?' This felt as though Toby would be walking into the lion's den.

'Aye, I do. Teresa'd be upset if I didn't, but don't concern yourself, lass. I've already said the same to Mam. I can be as tactful as the next bloke if I put my mind to it.'

Josie thought her mam would have doubted this and she did too. Her brother didn't have a subtle bone in his body.

They had reached Long Bank, and turned off into the back lane. The once prestige houses were no more. In Josie's building a family of eight lived in the two attic rooms and below them in what had once been three bedrooms were the Turner clan. Mr and Mrs Turner lived in one room and their two married sons and their families in the other two. Josie had often wondered what the house had been like in its heyday with just one family occupying it; lovely, she supposed.

They occupied the ground floor. The front room had been divided by a ceiling-to-floor curtain, and her parents slept on a mattress in one half and she and her sisters top-and-tailing on another mattress in the other half. Her brothers slept on a pallet bed in the kitchen which was propped against one wall in the daytime. She'd always envied them – at least the kitchen was warm.

The old kitchen table and bench seats took up a considerable amount of room and when they were all together it was a squeeze. Nevertheless, Josie counted herself fortunate to live downstairs. Not only did it mean that they didn't have to haul buckets of water from the tap in the yard up the steep stairs, but the kitchen boasted a big blackleaded range which was far superior to a small fire or paraffin stoves.

Josie could put up with the bugs under the wallpaper against which her mother fought a constant battle, along with the resident mice which sometimes ran across their bedding in the middle of the night; she could even tolerate the cold and being hungry most of the time, but it was the privy in the yard she really hated. The lavatory was shared by all the occupants of the house and although her mother did her best to keep it clean, the other housewives weren't so particular. Sometimes the contents would practically reach the top of the seat by the time the scavengers came with their long shovels to empty it. Flies abounded in the summer when the stench was at its worst and even in the winter months it could stink to high heaven.

Josie had been tremendously grateful when Ada Mullen

had had a word with her after she had begun singing at the Fiddler's Elbow and told her she was welcome to use the family's private lavatory that was situated just outside the kitchen in its own small walled yard, as opposed to the one for customers in the pub's courtyard. The scrubbed bricks on the floor, the whitewashed walls and the white wooden seat extending across the breadth were always clean, and the privy rarely smelled – Mrs Mullen saw to that with fresh ashes down the hole daily. There was always plenty of newspaper cut into squares and the bolt on the door was sound and strong.

As Toby now opened the door of the house they could hear the wail of a baby. The Turners' fifth grandchild was a sickly child and cried all day and night. Toby heaved a sigh. 'Why can't they shut it up, it drives me barmy,' he grumbled to Josie with a marked lack of sympathy. 'Five nights on the trot it's been screaming.'

'Perhaps the poor little thing is hungry?' The child's mother was a thin scrap of a woman with big eyes in a shrunken skull of a face.

'I don't care. I just want some sleep.' Still grumbling to himself, Toby made off for the kitchen.

Josie opened the door to the front room quietly. Her parents and sisters were asleep. She undressed quickly in the freezing air, keeping her underclothes on. She had separated the sovereign from the other coins before entering the room and now she slid it inside the bodice of her shift between her breasts before wriggling under the covers beside Ellen, trying to avoid Kate and Nelly's feet. She knew her father would go through her coat pockets in the morning and take every penny of her earnings.

Once she was lying in bed she began to warm up a little. That was the good part of sharing a mattress with her three sisters – they were rarely cold. She shut her eyes and in the blackness against her lids she saw pictured in vivid detail Adam's face when he had talked to her. He had been so nice, she thought wretchedly, and Toby had been so horrible to him by all accounts. Whatever had he thought when her brother had told him to stay away from her? Would he assume she'd told Toby to say something? She squirmed in mortification and then became still as Ellen stirred at the side of her.

Well, she had known it could come to nothing, hadn't she? Not because of Toby but with Adam being so handsome and rich and everything. What would he think if he came here? The answer made her screw up her eyes as though in pain. So perhaps Toby's intervention was all for the best.

She bit down hard on her bottom lip, telling herself she was daft. She had only spoken to him twice and here she was feeling as though she had lost something when it had never been hers in the first place. Yet he *had* asked to walk her home and the way he had looked at her . . .

It took her a long while before she fell asleep and even then she awoke every hour or so before falling into another uneasy slumber, the sound of the Turner infant far less disturbing than her thoughts.

Chapter Three

Across on the other side of town – which could have been another world, so far removed was it from the squalid area close to the docks – Adam McGuigan was also awake. His bedroom was big enough to have swallowed the downstairs of the house in Long Bank whole, and the glowing fire in the ornate fireplace meant the room was as warm as toast. Although his bed was a large four-poster, it didn't dwarf the beautifully decorated surroundings. A custom-made wardrobe filled almost one entire wall and two big leather armchairs and a small table stood in the bay of the window with bookcases filled with volumes either side. A bathroom and a dressing room completed the suite.

The luxury of his surroundings rarely registered on Adam; he had been born into it and couldn't imagine anything else. He dressed as a man of means and their excellent cook and two maids meant he lived and ate in comfort. He was well aware of the McGuigan crime empire that financed their wealth even though Bruce made sure he had little to do with it, but running the property side of the family's interests satisfied his desire to be part of the organization. He had never been denied anything in his life which was why Toby Gray's warning to stay away from his sister had him beside himself with rage.

He was sitting in one of the armchairs staring out into the blackness of the night which mirrored his thoughts, a glass of brandy from the half-empty bottle on the table in his hand.

Who the hell did Gray think he was, talking to him like that? He knocked back the brandy and poured himself another glass. The man was just a docker, a nobody, damn him. He ground his teeth, remembering the way Josie's brother had looked at him – as though he was muck under his boots. Well, no one told him what to do, least of all East End scum.

Slamming the glass onto the table he stood up and began to pace the room, the nasty temper that rarely surfaced, for the simple reason that he was hardly ever thwarted, making his face livid with anger.

He'd show Toby Gray who was boss. He'd have a word with Bruce tomorrow and let his brother set his dogs on the man. He should have let him do it the other day when Bruce had suggested it. It would have to be a permanent solution; he didn't want Gray being able to suggest to his sister that he was responsible because one thing was certain, he was going to have her and he wouldn't let hell or high water stand in his way.

The decision made, he walked back to the table and finished the glass of brandy before falling into bed, there to sleep like a baby.

Bruce McGuigan settled back in his chair in his book-lined study. He had never read any of the leather-bound volumes but they created the kind of impression he liked to make if any of his business associates came to the house. The residence was in the same gracious, quiet street as his mother's house and two of his brothers, and the other two only lived a short distance away. He believed in keeping the family tight.

He stared at Adam, who was sprawled in an armchair to one side of the beautifully inlaid walnut desk, kicking his foot moodily against the wood.

'Stop that,' he said mildly, and as his brother straightened, he added, 'Consider Gray dealt with.' Adam had just explained the events of the night before.

'You understand it can't be traced back to me?'

'Perfectly.'

'I thought an accident at the docks maybe?'

'Leave the details to me – the less you know the better. I take it you are still set on this girl?' Bruce loved his brother, perhaps more than his own children whom he considered had a lot of his wife's side of the family in them, but unlike their mother he wasn't blind to Adam's faults. This lass hadn't fallen at his feet like the others and not only that but the brother had fuelled the flames of Adam's desire by warning him off her.

Adam nodded. 'She's the one for me. I know Mam won't like it—'

'That's an understatement.'

'But I intend to court her and marry her when she's sixteen.'

'What if she doesn't want *you*?'

'She will.'

It was spoken with supreme confidence and now Bruce laughed. 'Aye, I dare say.'

'With the brother gone it'll leave a clear path.'

Bruce nodded. 'I'll get Larry to find out a bit about him. All we know is he works at the docks with the other brother, isn't it? You haven't had a run-in with the younger one too?'

'I've never even seen him.'

'Aye, all right. Well, for the time being I'd advise you to stay well clear of the Fiddler's Elbow, at least till the job's done. Then you can go in all sympathy and understanding with a shoulder for her to cry on and use some of the McGuigan charm.' He grinned. 'Not that the rest of us are abundant in that department.'

Adam smiled for the first time since his confrontation with Toby Gray. 'A bit of sweet talk can work wonders.'

'You should know.' Bruce's smile broadened before he said, 'Well, I've got business to deal with. I'm meeting Chapman in twenty minutes. His lass is going to be none too pleased when she finds out your affections are elsewhere.'

Adam shrugged. He didn't give a fig about Bernice

Chapman. His mother had had the family round for dinner a couple of times and the girl's open adoration of him had been flattering but slightly irritating. He stood up as he said, 'I'll leave you to it and – Bruce?'

'Aye?'

'Thanks, man.'

'What else are brothers for if not to assist the path of true love?' Bruce said sardonically. 'Just make sure you leave me out of it when you tell Mam about her, that's all. I've enough on my plate at the moment and I don't need a whole lot of aggravation from her. You'll be on your own there.'

'I can handle Mam.' Adam sauntered to the door and opened it, raising his hand before he disappeared into the hall.

Bruce stared after him for a moment or two. Aye, Adam could handle their mam like he did every other female. She might throw a blue fit initially but she'd come round. His eyes narrowed as he thought about Toby Gray; this was going to have to be handled more carefully than usual – he couldn't risk the sister suspecting Adam had anything to do with it. But he'd find a way, he always did when problems presented themselves. He'd get Larry sniffing around – the man was useless as one of his heavies, being small and slight with a boyish, pretty face, but he had a way of ferreting out information that was second to none. And once he knew all there was to know regarding Gray he would decide how best to do what needed to be done.

His wife appeared in the doorway, her voice expressionless as she said, 'Adam looked more cheerful when he left than when he arrived.' She had no doubt that her brother-in-law had been after something, and of course he'd have got it from Bruce. 'What did he want?'

'Nothing you need to worry your head about.'

Phyllis stared at her husband for a moment before turning away. She was an attractive woman with dark brown hair and large blue eyes, but any claim to beauty had been spoiled by her prominent nose. She had been a shop girl when Bruce had first seen her and begun courting her, having decided it was time to further the image of respectability by getting married. On her part, she'd been grateful to find herself brought into the McGuigan fold with the privileges of wealth it afforded, and even in their courting days she'd learned to ask no questions and keep her mouth shut about anything she might hear. They rubbed along fairly well on the whole; he had his small empire to take care of and she had her beautiful home and most of all her four children, who were the joy of her life.

She had always been careful not to betray her resentment of Adam's place in her husband's affections. It hadn't bothered her before her two sons were born, but as the boys had grown she had often thought that if Bruce had given half as much attention to their needs as he did to Adam's his relationship with his offspring would have been better. It was different with their daughters – girls naturally cleaved to their mother, she told herself – but her husband's lack of interest in his boys, which verged on indifference, hurt her. She wouldn't have dared to raise the matter with Bruce though. Like everyone else, she was frightened of him.

Phyllis stood for a moment in the wood-panelled hall before walking through a door which led into a corridor off which the large kitchen and the servants' quarters were situated. They employed a resident cook and maid, along with a young gardener who also doubled as coachman and took care of the two horses. Norman lived above the stables, and Phyllis knew he was courting their maid, Cissy. Her relationship with the staff had always been informal, although she had to be careful when Bruce was at home. He disapproved of familiarity with the servants. She supposed in part that was because he had been brought up with domestics and followed his mother's lead in dealing with them. Her mother-in-law was uppity in Phyllis's opinion.

She knew Bruce would hit the roof if he found out she chatted to the cook and maid as friends most of the time, but she needed company and people of her own kind. She had been brought up in a little two-up, two-down terrace in Bishopwearmouth and her father was a docker with no ambitions to be anything else. Besides which, she had to admit she liked to hear all the gossip that Annie, the cook, obtained from her two sisters, who lived in the East End. She learned more from Annie about the McGuigans' activities than she ever did from Bruce.

Annie was rolling out the pastry for an apple pie as she walked into the kitchen; she was an excellent cook and could rise to producing elaborate dishes when they entertained, although Phyllis preferred plainer, more wholesome food on a day-to-day level. Cissy was scraping the carcass of a chicken preparatory to mincing the meat to make patties for lunch, and both cook and maid looked up and smiled at her entrance, saying, 'Good morning, ma'am.'

They were always careful not to take liberties with regard to the mistress's informality although both thought she was no better than them at heart, being from working-class stock. Still, as Annie had said more than once, some of them who had risen from the ranks, so to speak, were the most high and mighty of all.

'Good morning.' Phyllis pulled out a chair from under the large kitchen table and sat down with a little sigh. She would have liked to do a little baking herself – she had been a dab hand at cakes and scones before she had got wed – but she knew it wouldn't be the done thing in Annie's eyes, let alone Bruce's. 'I think it's time we had a cup of tea, don't you.'

'Right you are, ma'am.'

The three of them often had a cuppa together about this time of the morning but always kept an ear cocked for Bruce if he hadn't already left the house. It was rare he ventured into this part but just in case, Annie always placed her menu book and pencil on the table so it appeared as though the mistress was going through the meals with her. Cissy always drank her tea standing by the kitchen door so she could hear anyone approaching.

It was a system that had evolved naturally without any one of them suggesting it but it always warmed Phyllis's heart. Annie and Cissy were on her side. Why it was a question of sides she never let herself dwell on.

Once she was sipping her tea, Phyllis said, 'Adam didn't seem happy when he called round this morning.'

It could have been a casual observation but all three understood she was asking if they knew anything she didn't.

'Well, ma'am, Norman was playing cards last night with Larry and some of the others.' Annie sniffed here – she disapproved of Cissy's beau getting too friendly with what she called McGuigan's thugs. Not that she had any cause for complaint regarding the master – she was paid well and her room was comfortable enough – but coming from the East End as she had she was fully aware of what the McGuigans were: gangsters by any other name. 'And Norman told Cissy that Larry had let slip that the master's brother's got his eye on a young lass from Long Bank who sings in the Fiddler's Elbow. It might be something to do with that? I can't imagine Mrs McGuigan would be pleased about it if she's heard.'

Phyllis stared at her cook. That was an understatement. Her mother-in-law would be hopping mad. Sadie McGuigan was very much the matriarch of the family and although she gave the appearance of being a motherly Italian mamma, there was nothing warm and soft about Sadie. She was as hard as nails. But Adam was her Achilles heel. In fact, where her youngest son was concerned, Sadie was plain daft, and Phyllis knew she had plans for him marrying well because Bruce had told her so. With this in mind, she said quietly, 'Oh, dear, no, she wouldn't be pleased at all, Annie.'

'According to Norman, they've all been trying to keep it quiet from their mam but you know how folk talk. Perhaps she's found out and there's been a bit of a do?'

'Perhaps.' Phyllis nodded. Larry had told Norman and he had told Cissy and she'd told Annie – that was how gossip spread; it made life a bit more interesting after all.

As Annie poured her another cup of tea and the talk turned to other matters, part of Phyllis's mind continued to mull over what she'd been told about Adam and this girl. Was he serious about the lass? she wondered. He had certainly looked out of sorts when he'd arrived at the house earlier. She couldn't ask Bruce about it but she could pop round and see her sister-in-law later. Hilda was married to Bruce's brother David, and theirs was a love match. David talked about most things with his wife, as he should, she thought bitterly. She had always envied them their evident closeness.

Her curiosity well and truly aroused, Phyllis finished her tea and left the kitchen. The study was empty; Bruce had clearly gone for the morning and so she put on her hat and coat and walked the two hundred yards or so to her sister-in-law's house.

By the time she emerged from her chat with Hilda, who didn't like their mother-in-law any more than she did and had been all agog about the potential bombshell in their midst, she knew that Josie Gray was a young lass of fifteen whose family lived hand to mouth, and that the girl's older brother had rubbed Adam up the wrong way. 'You can imagine how that went down,' Hilda had said, her eyes bright with excitement, 'and your Bruce is none too pleased about it either. Dave said he wouldn't want to be in the lad's shoes if he doesn't start playing ball pretty quick.'

'But surely Adam would blot his copybook with the girl if he did anything to hurt her brother?' Phyllis had protested.

Hilda had shrugged. 'I'm only saying what Dave said and you know our lot. They're not used to anyone getting in their way and if they do . . .' She had shrugged again.

Oh, yes, she knew 'our lot', Phyllis thought as she walked along the gracious, tree-lined street to her own house. She stopped at the end of the wide pebbled drive and gazed at the large detached building in front of her. It was built of natural stone and it had a dark slate roof and the front door and window frames were the same charcoal colour. The house was framed by two mature elm trees and the grounds at the back of the property were nicely landscaped with a row of evergreen fir trees hiding the stable block at the far end. She had been overawed when Bruce had brought her to view it a few weeks before their wedding. He had already bought it for their matrimonial home by then and hadn't asked her opinion on the matter, although she understood Sadie had gone along to see it.

Perhaps that was the reason it had never really felt like her home? she asked herself as she walked up the drive in the first snowflakes that were beginning to fall from a leaden sky, although she had felt more settled after her first bairn had been born. Children made a house a home after all.

Once inside the house she walked along to the long L-shaped conservatory at the rear of it. She liked this room, mostly because she had organized the building of it and had furnished it how she had wanted. It looked out onto the grounds and with the wood-burning stove she'd had installed was warm both winter and summer. Cissy lit the fire in there every morning, knowing her mistress would spend at least part of the day reading or sewing in the conservatory.

Phyllis walked across to the floor-to-ceiling French doors and stood looking out. The snow was coming down in big fat flakes and already there was a dusting on the trees and bushes, but she wasn't really seeing the garden, she was thinking about this young girl, Josie. She hoped the lass's brother had enough influence over her for her not to get entangled with Adam. He might seem different to his brothers with his exceptional good looks and the charm he could turn on and off like a tap, but he had the same vicious temper as all the McGuigans along with a supreme sense of his own importance which both his mother and Bruce had fostered through the years. No, she wouldn't wish Adam on anyone, least of all a young lass of fifteen.

Chapter Four

'So, how do I look?'

Josie smiled at Toby but it was their mother who said, 'You look grand, lad, but just you watch it with that O'Leary bunch. I wouldn't trust any of them as far as I could throw 'em, especially when they've had a drink.'

'It's Sunday tea, Mam.'

'Aye, an' I dare bet they were wetting their whistles in some pub or other earlier when they came out of Mass. Straight out of church and into the pubs, that's the O'Learys.'

Toby pulled his overcoat on over his brown Sunday suit. Both had been bought second-hand from the market and although the overcoat was a reasonable fit, the suit shoulders were too tight and the sleeves a little short. Because the suit was only brought out once a week for chapel it didn't normally matter, but Josie could tell his appearance was adding to the nerves Toby was trying to hide.

It was just the three of them in the kitchen. Ralph Gray was snoring his head off in the front room and Joe had disappeared off with some pals straight after Sunday dinner.

The younger girls were playing in the back lane with some other bairns despite the snow that was falling. It was only three o'clock but it could have been gone five as the light had vanished earlier than usual and the kitchen was lit only by the glow of the fire. Her mother never lit the oil lamp until it was impossible to see; every penny counted.

Her voice soft, Josie said, 'Toby, you look grand like Mam said and Teresa will be pleased you've made the effort. Just praise her mam's spread whatever it's like and don't drink your tea out of the saucer,' she added with an impish grin. This was a habit of his and she was always telling him off about it.

He chuckled, his face relaxing. 'No fear. I'll be the model of decorum.'

Maggie snorted. She'd been livid when Teresa's mother had dared to ban her son from the O'Leary house. 'Huh! You're a cut above them Irish scum, my lad, and don't you forget it.' Not that she had anything against Toby's lass; she was fond of her and the girl had a sensible head on her shoulders. The rest of the family were a different kettle of fish though.

Toby and Josie exchanged a smile; their mam had been very vocal about Bridget O'Leary. He gave her a brief hug as he said, 'Now, now, don't get on your high horse.'

The show of affection was unusual and Maggie's pleasure sounded in her voice when she said, 'Go on then if you're going and mind you keep your wits about you.'

Once it was just the two of them, Josie smiled at her mother. 'Fancy a cup of tea, Mam?'

'Aye, that'd be nice, lass.' It was rare she got to sit for a few minutes in the day and as she watched her daughter mashing the tea, she said softly, 'You're a good girl, hinny.' The two sovereigns that Josie had slipped her on the quiet had been a godsend. For the first time in years she was up to date with the rent and had even been able to salt away a few shillings for Christmas in a hidey-hole at the back of the range that Ralph knew nothing about. It had made all the difference; she felt that at last things might be looking up. Shutting her eyes with a little sigh, she leaned her head back against the hard wood of the settle.

Josie placed a cup of tea in front of her mother but didn't interrupt her doze. Sitting down, she looked at the snowflakes through the small kitchen window and allowed her thoughts free rein. Adam hadn't come to the Fiddler's Elbow the last couple of nights, and although she told herself there was absolutely no reason why he should, she felt disappointed. And let down. Which was stupid, daft.

She took a sip of tea, wincing as it burned her mouth. Had Toby put him off or wasn't he interested in her after all? He must have his pick of lassies, he was so handsome. And nice. She didn't care what people said about the McGuigans, Adam was nice. Different to the rest of them.

The kitchen was quiet and warm with an unusual air of cosiness about it, but it didn't settle her mind. She felt restless and all at odds with herself. She walked over to the ancient spotted mirror and peered at her dim reflection, wishing she was two or three years older. Adam might like her then. She'd buy some grips and put her hair up, she decided suddenly. It was high time and that would make her look less like a bairn. She wished her bust was bigger; she'd started her monthlies earlier in the year and her mam had said her figure would develop after that but her breasts were still small. Most of the girls she'd gone to school with had lovely busts.

Her mother stirred and opened her eyes, reaching for her cup of tea, and as Josie joined her she told herself she had to forget about Adam McGuigan. She had only met him twice and he wouldn't be interested in a lass from Long Bank anyway. It had been a pipe dream, nothing more, and she would probably never run into him again.

Nevertheless, later that evening as she got ready for work she found her heart was fluttering with a mixture of hope and excitement. He might be there tonight, she told herself as she prepared to leave the house. She would like him to see her in her new coat if nothing else.

Toby was whistling to himself as he strode along. The meeting with Teresa's nearest and dearest had gone better than he had expected. Partly, he had to admit, because he had chickened out and hinted that he might be prepared to turn. He had no intention of doing so, but if it kept things sweet with Bridget O'Leary and the rest of them for a while it was all to the good. Teresa had known what he was doing, he'd seen it in her twinkling eyes. He grinned to himself. They'd make a go of it, him and

Teresa, even if they married in a register office, which would alienate her mother for good.

It had been snowing steadily all day and it was thick underfoot, but unlike most people he knew he didn't mind the snow. True, it made life that much more difficult and caused problems at the docks when it was really bad, but he loved the clean purity of it and the way it made even the meanest streets different for a while until it turned into grey slush. It was beautiful when it first fell, magical.

He shook his head at himself, feeling embarrassed by his thoughts. He was thinking like a bit lass, but he felt happy tonight. The situation with Teresa's family had been weighing heavy, not for himself but for Teresa. Her mam had certainly put a good spread on though, not that he'd say that at home with things being so tight and his mam doing her best each mealtime. All the O'Leary menfolk were in work, that was the thing, so Bridget could afford to splash out a bit.

He hadn't been aware that he was being followed, not until a voice behind him shouted, 'Gray? Toby Gray, is it?'

He turned, taking in the three big bullet-headed men and realizing the snow must have muffled their footsteps. 'Who's asking?'

They surrounded him and increased his rising apprehension, which didn't diminish when one said, 'That's not very friendly.'

'What do you want?' He tried to keep the fear out of his voice. They'd chosen to make themselves known as he'd taken a shortcut home through a back alley near

Bodlewell Lane and now he wished he'd kept to the main streets with their gas lamps.

'It's like this. You've upset someone important, which was a silly thing to do, wasn't it? But perhaps you think you're a clever beggar. Do you? Do you think you're canny?'

It had dawned on him what this was about. If he'd upset someone it could only be Adam McGuigan. 'No, I don't think I'm canny,' he said, licking his lips, which were suddenly dry.

'Neither do I, lad. But you've put this someone to a bit of trouble having to keep tabs on you and find out what you're about. Been to the O'Learys' to have tea with your lass's lot. Nice tea, was it?'

How on earth did they know that? But then he'd told a few of the blokes at the docks he worked with – it hadn't been a secret and at the back of his mind he'd thought if Teresa's da and brothers started on him he could say there were plenty of folk who knew where he was the night. He didn't reply but he mentally prepared himself for what was going to happen; they were going to duff him up.

'I said, was it a nice tea?'

'Aye, all right.'

'That's good, isn't it?' The man glanced at the other two, who didn't move a muscle of their faces. 'The condemned man ate a hearty meal.' He grinned, turning back to Toby as he added, 'Ever heard of that expression?'

Again Toby said nothing.

'Now if you'd kept quiet before instead of shooting

your gob off we wouldn't be having this conversation, would we? But no, you had to play the big man in front of your sister.'

So it *was* Adam McGuigan but then he'd known that, hadn't he. These three had McGuigan thugs written all over them. 'I was just looking out for her, that's all. You'd do the same for your sister.'

'Oh, no, lad, I wouldn't. Unlike you I've got me head screwed on the right way and know when to keep my trap shut.'

He stared at them and now the fear swept over him, turning his bowels to water, but in the next instant the man who had been doing the talking motioned with his head to the other two and they caught him as he turned to run. He was aware of being lifted right off his feet by one of the men as another punched him in the jaw. He was striking out to the left and the right and kicking for all he was worth, but it was like a child having a tantrum whilst being held by a far superior, fully grown adult. Another great fist hit him again, breaking his nose, and then he was on the ground and now they were using their big hobnailed boots on him.

He was screaming – he could hear his screams through the pain as the boots pounded into his torso and groin and legs – but then one hit him full on his head and from that point he didn't know any more. He didn't feel it as the three of them continued to use him like a football, the steel caps on their boots breaking bones and splitting his skull open.

They were panting when they finally stood away from the lifeless figure on the ground. The snow around it was scarlet. They bent and rubbed their boots clean with handfuls of snow before the speaker said shortly, 'Job done.' He cast one more glance at the body and then the three of them turned and walked back the way they had come.

Josie stood at the open door of the Fiddler's Elbow peering out into the dark street. It was half an hour after the last customer had gone and the night was quiet and still. Ada joined her, saying, 'Still no sign of Toby, lass?'

'No.' Josie had become increasingly fearful and it was reflected in her voice when she said, 'He'd never be this late, Mrs Mullen. Something's happened.'

'Aw now, hinny, don't work yourself into a lather. Look, Mr Mullen'll see you home and ten to one you'll find Toby's fell asleep whilst waiting for the time to come and collect you.'

Josie shook her head. 'He wouldn't.' She pulled the collar of her coat more closely round her neck. 'Don't bother Mr Mullen, it's not far and I'll be all right.' So saying, she stepped down into the street and began walking as swiftly as the icy, snow-covered pavements would allow, her heart pounding with sick dread.

Toby would have come for her unless something had prevented him, she told herself, and he *had* gone to tea with the O'Learys. Had he got into a fight with Teresa's brothers? But surely someone would have gone and told her mam if that was so, and if Toby was hurt, Joe would have come and met her? Toby would insist on that.

Halfway home she slipped and fell hard onto her bottom, jarring her coccyx, but it wasn't the pain that had her fighting back tears. She had a terrible feeling on her.

As soon as she reached home, she went straight along the hall into the kitchen. As her eyes adjusted to the near blackness she could see just one hump in the pallet bed. Stepping out of the kitchen again she opened the door that led into the yard holding the privy. Perhaps Toby had eaten something that disagreed with him and had the skitters? If he couldn't get off the lavatory that would explain why he hadn't come to meet her.

The privy was empty and as her last hope died Josie gave a little sob. Something had happened.

She scurried back into the house and shook Joe awake. It took a moment or two – her brother was a deep sleeper. Joe immediately realized the gravity of the situation; Toby would never let Josie down. Unless he was doing a night shift he always met her out of the pub, even if he'd had a skinful himself. 'Get Mam in here,' he whispered. He didn't have to tell Josie not to wake their da; they both knew he wouldn't stir himself.

Once Maggie was in the kitchen she lit the oil lamp and her face was grim. She looked at Josie who, her voice thick with unshed tears, said, 'What should we do, Mam?'

'First thing is to knock up the O'Learys and find out what time he left there.' Maggie didn't say, 'And find out if there was a fight,' but Josie and Joe knew what she meant. 'I'll go.'

'No, Mam.' Joe put out his hand towards his mother. 'You stay here with Josie in case he comes back. I'll go.'

'I'm coming with you,' Josie said in a voice that brooked no argument.

Five minutes later they were hurrying through the warren of streets and alleyways to Woodbine Street where the O'Learys lived. The street of two-up two-down terraced houses was in total blackness when they arrived, and as Joe hammered on the front door the sound seemed to reverberate through Josie's head.

It was Silas O'Leary, Teresa's father, who opened the door, and his initial '*What the hell*?' moderated as his bleary gaze took in Josie and Joe. A couple of his sons and Teresa had come up behind their father, and it was Teresa who said, 'What's wrong?' as she looked at their faces.

'It's Toby.' Josie's voice was shaking. 'He's not come home.'

'What?' Silas opened the door wider as he said, 'Come in, come in.'

As he led the way into the kitchen the rest of the family joined them, yawning and blinking, and Josie was aware of the smell of stale beer. Had Teresa's brothers got drunk and attacked Toby? She wouldn't put it past them but how did you word asking something like that?

Joe had no such reticence. 'Like Josie said, Toby's not been home since he came here earlier. Do you know anything about it? Was there a disagreement?'

'Now look here, lad—'

Teresa cut across her father's voice as she said, 'He was fine when he left here, Joe, I promise you. He said he was going home for a kip before he went to meet Josie.'

'What time did he leave?'

'About nine, just before,' one of the brothers put in. 'We'd had a few beers and played a game of cards and before you ask, it was a friendly game, all right? No aggro.'

'Everything was fine,' Teresa said to Josie. 'Really. The lads and Da carried on drinking and me an' Mam went to bed.'

'So they could have gone out and you wouldn't know?' Joe looked straight at Silas. 'Did you? Did you follow Toby?'

'What are you suggesting—?'

Silas raised his hand and the brother who had spoken fell silent. 'Look, lass,' he said directly to Josie, ignoring Joe, who had squared up at the brother's belligerent tone, 'if Toby's run into a spot of bother it's nowt to do with us, I swear it. We've not left the house all night. Have you been to the Infirmary?'

'The Infirmary?' Josie said dazedly. She was feeling weak, faint and frightened, terrified.

'If he's had an accident of some kind that's where they'd take him.'

'Come on.' Joe took her arm. They were doing no good here. If the O'Learys had roughed Toby up they weren't going to admit it. 'We'll go and see.'

'I'm coming with you. Wait a minute while I get changed.'

Teresa dashed out of the kitchen, deaf to her mother's protests. Bridget turned to her eldest son. 'You go with her.'

'Aw, Mam.'

'Don't "Aw, Mam" me. I'm not having our Teresa out in the dead of night without one of you with her. Go and get your clothes on and be quick about it, Patrick.'

Five minutes later the four of them were walking towards the Sunderland Royal Infirmary in Durham Road. The building was a grand one and had been extended several times, its spires reaching up into the black sky. Josie had never had occasion to enter its intimidating confines and her heart was thudding fit to burst as they walked up to the porter's lodge. He turned out to be a middle-aged man with a fatherly air about him, his face sympathetic as he listened to Joe. He checked his paper-work and then shook his head. 'No one by the name of Gray's been brought in the day, lad, and no unidentified patients either. Best thing you can all do is to go home and wait till morning and then check with the police if he's still not home, but ten to one he'll be back by then.'

'The police?' Patrick O'Leary looked alarmed; no one willingly spoke to the law.

Josie didn't know if she was relieved or more frightened. She didn't want Toby to have had an accident but if he wasn't in the Infirmary, where was he?

Toby's battered body was found at first light by two men on their way to work. Identification could be made only by his clothes. Maggie collapsed on the floor of the mortuary and two kindly constables had to carry her into the adjoining room, and even Ralph Gray was white and shaken.

The police agreed it was the worst beating they'd encountered for a long time and on talking to the family questioned the O'Learys at length but to no avail. Silas and his sons stuck to their story that Toby had been alive and well when he had left their house and that was all they knew on the matter. Teresa was inconsolable, the more so when Maggie said she didn't want her at the funeral. As far as she was concerned her son would be alive if he hadn't taken up with an O'Leary, and she would blame the family for her son's death however much they protested their innocence.

The day of the funeral dawned bright but bitterly cold, and the snow was packed solid on the pavements. The proceedings were a blur to Josie. She had hardly slept or eaten since the morning they had found Toby and felt sick and ill, but it was her mother she was really worried about. Since Maggie's breakdown in the mortuary she'd barely spoken and she hadn't cried again; in fact she went about her duties in the house like a clockwork toy, a glazed expression on her face and a dead look in her eyes.

It was as they were leaving the churchyard that Josie noticed the tall, dark figure standing on the outskirts of the throng of friends and neighbours who had come to pay their respects. She stared across the crowd at Adam, and when he raised his hand, his handsome face solemn, she couldn't respond. He was dressed in a black overcoat and hat, and looked as different from the working-class men that made up the throng as chalk from cheese.

She watched as he made his way towards her, and when he was standing in front of her, he said quietly, 'I am so very sorry about your brother, Josie. Is there anything I can do? Anything at all?'

The kindness, especially when she had thought she would never see him again, was almost too much. It took all her control to say softly, 'Thank you. It – it was a great shock.'

Her mother had appeared at her side, and as Josie put her arm round the frail frame, she said quickly, 'This is Mr McGuigan, Mam. Adam McGuigan. He – he comes to the Fiddler's Elbow now and again.'

Before Maggie could say anything, Adam took her hands in his fine leather gloves. His voice tender, he said softly, 'I can't imagine what you are going through, Mrs Gray, but you have my heartfelt condolences. I know the police haven't got anywhere with their investigation but I have taken the liberty of having your son's brutal death investigated privately, I hope you don't mind? My sole purpose is to bring the perpetrators to justice swiftly in the hope it will perhaps ease your mind a little. My family have some influence at the docks where your other son – Joe, isn't it? – is employed, and you have my assurance that he will be working full-time from now on and in an area which is less dangerous than most.'

Maggie's eyes had widened. She knew the McGuigans'

reputation but the initial fear she'd felt when Josie had introduced the handsome young man had faded as he had spoken. If anyone could lean on the O'Learys and force them to confess what they'd done it was the McGuigans, and what he had said about Joe was comforting. 'But why – why would you do that for us?'

Gently, Adam said, 'I have great admiration for your daughter, Mrs Gray.'

Maggie's eyes shot to Josie's face and what she read there could have worried her, but as Ralph joined them, Adam continued, 'We have only spoken a couple of times at the public house where she sings, but I was going to call round and ask your permission to take Josie to the theatre one evening and I thought perhaps you and your husband might like to accompany us? Of course, with the tragedy you have suffered, I didn't think it appropriate to disturb you for the time being, but I did want to show my support and that of all the McGuigan family on this sad day.'

Ralph stuck out his hand, his voice eager as he said, 'I'm Ralph Gray, Mr McGuigan, Josie's da.'

Adam looked at the undersized little man he'd heard about through Larry. He'd have no trouble with him; Josie's father clearly knew which side his bread was buttered. Gravely, he said, 'My condolences about your son, Mr Gray.'

Being addressed as *Mr* Gray by one of the McGuigans made Ralph's chest swell and he had a hard job to keep the elation out of his voice when he said, 'Aye, ta, thank you.' His words tumbling over themselves, he added, 'You'll come back to the house, Mr McGuigan? The wife's got a bit of a spread on for close friends and family.'

What an obnoxious little individual. Adam brought his gaze to rest on Josie and it was to her he said, 'Are you sure I wouldn't be intruding?'

She had had a few moments to pull herself together while Adam was talking to her parents and now she said formally, 'Of course not. You are very welcome.' Actually she was horrified at this god-like creature seeing where she lived and although she knew that was awful, she couldn't help it. At least she and her mam had cleaned the kitchen from top to bottom and washed and starched the nets at the window, but even so . . .

'That's settled then.' Ralph was beaming and he must have realized this as he hastily straightened his countenance into a more sober expression.

A couple of the other mourners had come up to speak to the bereaved parents, and Adam took the opportunity to gently move Josie to one side. 'Are you sure you don't mind me coming?' he said softly. 'I've been thinking about you all the time since I heard the dreadful news.'

'No, it's kind, very kind of you.'

'I meant what I said to your mother. We'll try and get to the bottom of who did this and I'll make sure Joe is well looked after at the docks. There might be a position in the office coming up in the near future which would pay very well.'

She didn't know if Joe could cope with that; he'd been

earning the odd penny or two here and there since he was in short trousers just to put food on the table and consequently had had little schooling, like Toby. The thought of Toby made her voice tremble as she said again, 'You're very kind.'

'I want to be kind to you, Josie. For the rest of my life I want to be kind.' He made a movement with his head. 'Oh, I shouldn't be saying this now, not here with what you're going through today, but can I just ask one thing? Do you like me, even a little?' With the brother dealt with he'd decided to play the humble game. He knew she wanted him. She was too inexperienced to hide how she felt. And he wanted her, how he wanted this girl.

Josie stared at him, so many different emotions tearing through her she felt she didn't know herself any more. Pain, grief, despair, and now relief that he was here. That he had come to pay his respects to Toby and to see her when she had thought she'd never see him again. Her voice barely audible, she whispered, 'Yes, I like you.'

'Then we can build on that. Look, people are beginning to go' – he tucked her arm through his as though it was the most natural thing in the world – 'so let me walk you home.'

Ralph came up behind them, practically dragging Maggie with him, followed by Joe and her sisters, and it was like that – as a family unit – that they left the grave-yard and the body of the young man in the cheap simple coffin that the gravediggers were now covering with clods of earth.

Chapter Five

The next weeks were painful. Josie cried herself to sleep most nights, missing Toby and thinking about what he must have suffered in those last minutes of his life. She was careful not to disturb her mother, who she knew was in agony about the manner of her son's violent death and tormented by it every waking moment.

Adam's investigations had yielded nothing so far but he'd told them that his brother had people keeping an eye on the O'Learys and if one of them slipped up and revealed something they'd know. With that they had to be content. Josie had moments of feeling guilty that Adam's presence in her life made so much difference at what was such a harrowing time, but comforted herself with the fact that Adam went out of his way to console her mother too. He was always bringing her mam gifts of chocolate or flowers and even hampers of food when he called at the house. He would sit at the kitchen table drinking tea as though he had always been a part of their lives, sympathizing with her mother like an old friend.

He had been true to his word regarding Joe's job at the docks too, and although Joe had said he couldn't cope with an office position, Adam had made sure he got full shifts and was regularly bringing home a healthy pay packet for the first time in his life. Adam had charmed Ellen, Kate and Nelly too, bringing them sweets and fancy hair ribbons and giving each of the girls a Saturday sixpence at the weekends.

He was perfect, Josie thought, as she left the Mullens' kitchen one night six weeks after the funeral. Adam was waiting to walk her home, something he had done each evening, which was another feather in his cap as far as her mother was concerned. There was just one thing she found confusing: he had never tried to kiss her. It might, though, be due to the fact that two of his oldest brother's employees followed them at a respectful distance. He'd said that there were lots of bad people about who had a grudge against the McGuigan name and that Bruce, who ran the family business, was nervous about him being in the East End every night at the same time. The men were there as protection, that's all.

She'd confided in her mother about Adam's conduct and could tell that he'd gone up even higher in her mother's estimation if that was possible. 'He's treating you like a lady, lass,' she'd said. 'Not rushing you.'

But, Josie thought now, she wouldn't mind being rushed – not by Adam. In truth she had been a bit nervous the first time he had walked her home from the pub; she'd never kissed a lad before and he was a grown man and she knew he must have had lots of lassies, looking like he did and being rich and all. But when night after night had passed and the most he had done was to put her arm in his while they walked and then hold her hands in his when he said goodnight on the doorstep, she had begun to wonder if he was regretting saying what he had. Yet he seemed to like her, and he showered gifts on her family; only the night before he had bought her father a couple of bottles of whisky and several packets of cigarettes.

She walked over to the Mullens' mirror and adjusted her hair. She had put it up for the first time tonight and hadn't let herself dwell on the fact that she was hoping it would make her look older and prompt Adam to kiss her. She would be sixteen in the spring after all, she wasn't a bairn.

He was standing by the door into the street when she left the Fiddler's Elbow and his eyes went immediately to her hair. 'You look beautiful,' he said softly. 'It suits you.'

She knew she was blushing and he laughed, taking her arm as he always did. Christmas was only two weeks away and the snow showers hadn't let up since November but tonight the sky was high and clear and its darkness was punctured by countless twinkling stars. They talked quietly as they walked and he made her laugh as he recounted his day; she didn't know if all the funny episodes that seemed to happen were real or made up but she didn't care. She didn't think about the two men some hundred yards behind him, she rarely did now.

There had been one or two folk about but as they reached Long Bank the street was deserted. The bitterly cold weather disguised the smells that were normally prevalent and the snow on the rooftops and pavements added its own charm to the scene.

When Adam stopped and turned her to face him her heart began to thud so hard she thought he would be able to sense it.

'You're so beautiful, Josie, and so young. Untouched.' He lifted her chin, his voice husky. 'I've been in love with you since the first moment I saw you. You know that, don't you?'

She didn't know how to answer, just staring at him as she began to tremble.

His eyes roamed over her face and then he said softly, 'May I kiss you?'

Still she couldn't speak but she leaned towards him, letting her body tell him. The next moment his lips were on hers, firm but gentle, and she shut her eyes as her heart soared. She had imagined this moment for so long and now it was happening, and he'd said he loved her.

The kiss only lasted a few moments and if Josie had but known it, it was the first time Adam had shown restraint with a girl. Normally it was the act itself that he was interested in and such niceties as paying court to a lass didn't come into it. But Josie was going to be the mother of his children, he had made up his mind about that and so it made her different.

When his mouth left hers she swayed slightly. She was

flooded with a feeling she couldn't put a name to but it was nice, wonderful.

He took her face in his hands. 'When are you sixteen?'

'What?' It wasn't what she'd expected him to say.

'When's your birthday?'

'In April, April the third.'

'Josie Gray, will you marry me on your sixteenth birthday and make me the happiest man in the world?'

Her eyes opened wide and such was her surprise she couldn't speak for a moment. Why, she hadn't even met his family, his mother, and he was asking her to marry him? He could have any lass he wanted. She took a step backwards in confusion, stammering as she said, 'But – but we've only just – I – I mean—'

'What's the matter?' His face had changed. It was subtle but she knew he didn't like her reaction.

'I've never even met your mam,' she said quickly, wanting to appease him, to take away the expression she had never seen before that had fleetingly turned him into someone she didn't know. 'She might not like me, especially me coming from round here and you – well, you know—'

'Is that all?' He was Adam again, smiling as he shook his head. 'Josie, no one matters but us and my mother will love you, everyone will.'

She looked at him, into the eyes that were dark and soft, and everything in her wanted to make him happy and say that of course she would marry him, but it was so soon. A lass and lad normally courted for years before they got wed, but of course he wasn't a lad, he was a man so perhaps that made it different? A thought occurred. 'She does know about me, doesn't she?'

'Of course she does,' he lied smoothly. 'Look, come and meet her, yes? Come for tea. I'll arrange it.' He was thinking quickly. He'd known he would have to tell his mother some time so it might as well be now. With her brother out of the picture, he'd got the rest of Josie's family in the palm of his hand so there'd be no difficulties there. His mother was the fly in the ointment but he'd make sure she behaved herself.

Now that Adam had invited her to meet his mother Josie was panicking, mainly because she had nothing to wear. Her coat was lovely thanks to Mrs Mullen, but her other clothes were worn and faded and her boots were serviceable enough but ugly. Even her Sunday dress had seen better days. She bit down hard on her lower lip before she said awkwardly, 'Please don't upset your mam, Adam. I mean, if she doesn't want me to come I'll understand.'

'Of course she will want you to come. She's been hinting for ages that I should settle down and find myself a wife.' That bit was true at least, he thought ruefully.

'Did she have anyone in particular in mind?'

He didn't answer this directly, smiling as he murmured, 'I have got a mind of my own, Josie.'

'Yes, yes, I know but—'

'You've never said it,' he said softly.

'Said what?'

'That you love me.' He brushed a wisp of hair from

her forehead with the tip of his finger. 'Do you? Do you love me, Josie?'

She gazed into the handsome face that featured so often in her dreams, her colour rising as she said, 'Yes, I love you.'

'And you'll marry me? You'll be my wife?'

'Yes, I'll marry you but—'

Her words were smothered as his mouth took hers once more but again he was careful not to let his passion run away with him. There were a couple of women he regularly visited for the needs of his body so it was no real effort to play the romantic suitor with Josie; in fact, he was enjoying the role. When he put her from him she was trembling and he smiled inwardly. 'Go on in now and I'll see you tomorrow.' He touched her face with his hand. 'And dream of me tonight.'

She waved to him before she entered the house and he blew her a kiss, but as he turned away and began walking towards the two bodyguards his face was thoughtful. He'd talk to his mother tomorrow morning over breakfast when it was just the two of them. If he was going to marry Josie in April – and he was – there were arrangements to make.

'I trust this is some kind of a bad joke?'

Adam stared steadily at his mother. She was plainly dressed but with a plainness that expressed exclusiveness, and even at breakfast her grey hair was immaculate. She was wearing a small round diamond brooch beneath the collar of her dark blue dress and there were more diamonds flashing on the third finger of her left hand where her engagement ring nestled next to her wedding band. His mother loved jewellery and his father had indulged her, but although her collection was large she was careful never to appear vulgar in her choice of adornment for different occasions. 'You know me better than that,' he said coolly. 'I rarely joke.'

'I *thought* I knew you,' she returned crisply, continuing in her task of buttering a slice of toast, 'but it appears not. How long has this' – she paused – 'dalliance been going on?'

'It is not a dalliance. It's a serious courtship and I have known Josie for some time.'

'Define some time.'

'A few months.' The exaggeration was necessary. If he admitted to a few weeks he knew his mother would say it wasn't long enough to know his own mind.

'And why didn't you tell me before this?'

'Because I knew you'd react exactly as you're doing now.'

Sadie ignored that. 'And you have asked this' – another pause; Sadie did pregnant pauses very well – 'this girl to marry you?'

'As I said. I've asked her and she's consented—'

'*Of course she's consented.*' Sadie put her linen napkin to her lips. She'd raised her voice and she considered that unbecoming. She had grown up in an Italian family and her parents had been fiery and loud, and she'd sworn to herself she would never follow their example. Quietly, she went on, 'Of course she's said yes, Adam. You've told me she is from Long Bank.'

'Meaning?'

'You are not a fool so don't act like one.'

'If you're insinuating she's a gold-digger you couldn't be further from the truth.'

'How old is she?'

'Nearly sixteen.'

Sadie raised her eyebrows. 'So you are telling me she is only fifteen at present?'

'Obviously.'

'I'll thank you not to take that tone with me, Adam. And what does this fifteen-year-old girl do for a living, may I ask? I presume she does work? So what does she do? Factory work? Shop or laundry assistant? Or is she in service?'

In view of the disdain his mother wasn't bothering to hide, Adam took a perverse pleasure in saying flatly, 'She sings in one of the East End public houses.'

Sadie had just taken a sip of tea and she choked, spluttering and gasping for some thirty seconds. Dabbing at her streaming eyes with the napkin, she croaked, 'She does *what*?'

'She has a beautiful voice, extraordinarily beautiful, and before you suggest anything else, that is all she does. Sing.'

'And how do you know that?'

'I know.'

'I can't believe you'd be such a fool as to be taken in like this, not you.'

'I love her and I intend to marry her, and if you met her you would understand why. She's not what you're thinking—'

'What about Bernice Chapman? The girl's madly in love with you and her father is a leading light in the town. What does this girl's father, if she's got one, do?'

Adam didn't like being interrupted and his voice reflected this. 'I wouldn't marry Bernice Chapman if she was the last woman alive, and her father is a buffoon as you well know. As for Josie's father, he is unemployed at present.' He stood up abruptly, sending his chair skidding backwards. Now his face was as cold as his voice when he said, 'I *will* marry her, with or without your consent. Let me make that perfectly clear. If you wish me to move out and stay at my club for the time being then I can do so today, it's up to you. All I wanted you to do was to meet Josie but if you are not prepared to do that . . .' He shrugged. 'So be it.'

Sadie was realizing she had handled this all wrong. More alarmed than she was revealing at the thought of Adam leaving home, leaving *her*, she said quietly, 'Of course I am prepared to meet her. I never said otherwise, did I? But you cannot expect me not to be upset when you drop a bombshell like this. I only want the best for you.'

'I know, I know, I'm sorry.' Now he'd got his own way Adam walked round the table and sat down beside her, taking her face between his hands. There was deep emphasis in his voice when he murmured, 'I don't want you to be upset, not you of all people, you know that. I couldn't bear it if we were at odds. You mean the world to me, you always have.'

Sadie stared into her son's beautiful face. And he was beautiful, she told herself. She had seen a number of pretty men in her time but Adam's looks went beyond that. From the first time the midwife had handed him to her and she had gazed down into his little face, her heart had melted. He had been a happy baby, always smiling, and the household had revolved around him, it still did, but the occasional rages that had taken him over even as a young child if he was refused anything had been frightening. And so she had made sure he *wasn't* refused anything and that wasn't wrong, was it? It was better to live in harmony after all. But just very occasionally, like now, she wondered how genuine his love for her was – how genuine his feelings were in general. But she was being silly. This talk about the girl had upset her, that was all.

She smiled at him. 'When do you want to bring the young lady to see me?'

She was rewarded for her concession in calling the girl a young lady by his brilliant smile. 'The day after tomorrow? Just for tea. Nothing formal.'

Sadie nodded. 'I'll tell Cook.' And in the meantime she would summon Bruce to the house and grill him about this chit from Long Bank who had got her claws into

Adam. She was in no doubt Bruce knew all about it and she'd have his guts for garters for keeping her in the dark about this. A baggage who sings in public houses of all things; she would have gambled every penny she had that her darling boy would have had more sense than to get himself entangled with such a type.

It was two days later and Sadie was having to revise her opinion of the lass Adam was smitten with. Instead of the brazen hussy she'd been expecting, the young girl – and she seemed a very young girl – was a shy, quiet little thing. She had presumed the wench would be tarted up to the nines but the girl was dressed very simply in a plain, somewhat faded dress with no combs or adornment in her hair, but it was her face which had startled Sadie the most. She was quite, quite beautiful with the purest deep green eyes and flawless skin. When Adam had brought her into the drawing room she could see at once what had captivated her son.

After the introductions had been completed she had rung for the tea trolley almost immediately, but now the maid had wheeled it away and she was sitting facing her son and the girl, who had barely said two words. Clearing her throat, she said quietly, 'I hear you have a lovely singing voice, Josie.'

The colour that had flooded the girl's face once or twice already rose again, and before she could speak Adam said heartily, 'Indeed she does.'

'Adam tells me you met at the public house where you

sing. The Fiddler's Elbow, isn't it, in the East End near the docks? This seems rather' – she paused – 'unusual employment for an innocent young girl. Aren't your parents worried for you?' She now knew all about Ralph Gray thanks to Bruce, but she wanted to hear what Josie would say about her father, who was clearly a ne'er-do-well.

Josie's chin rose a fraction. Her first impression of Adam's mother when she'd been ushered into the sumptuous drawing room where the elderly lady was waiting was that she looked pleasant and amiable. This had lasted as long as it had taken for Sadie to open her mouth, although it wasn't so much what she said as the way she said it.

She had sensed Adam was on edge earlier when he'd arrived to pick her up in a fine carriage, and during tea with his mother she'd understood why. Sadie McGuigan was dead against her marrying Adam. Nevertheless, she wasn't going to try and hide the circumstances at home and neither was she going to apologize for who she was or what she did. Quietly, she said, 'My mam would prefer me not to work there but my da arranged it some years ago.'

'I see.' Sadie nodded. 'Surely that makes you somewhat vulnerable?'

'Mr and Mrs Mullen, the landlord and his wife, are kind and have always made sure I'm all right so it's not so bad.'

'And how many of you are there at home?'

She was talking as though they bred like mice, Josie thought, and her voice stiff, she answered, 'My parents, three younger sisters and my brother, Joe, who's seventeen.' She had to swallow before she could add, 'My other brother died recently.'

'Yes, I heard about that. Most unfortunate.' Bruce had told her that the brother had been courting a Catholic girl and the menfolk of her family had objected to this. They were known to be violent individuals and the general consensus of opinion was that it was they who had beaten Toby Gray to death in a dark alley. 'My condolences.'

'Thank you.' Josie was finding that she didn't like Mrs McGuigan; she reminded her of Mrs Hardy, one of their neighbours, whom her mother always referred to as 'Poison Ivy'.

'I understand that as yet no one has been held to account for his murder.' Sadie shook her head. 'Your poor mother must be devastated. Does your family have any idea who may be responsible?'

'Not really.' She didn't want to discuss Toby's death with Adam's mother; it wasn't as if the woman was sympathetic, not really. In fact, there was an air about her that almost suggested it was Toby's fault he had got himself killed.

This last thought was borne out when Sadie said, 'Was your brother in the habit of mixing with unsavoury individuals?'

Josie's body straightened, her back rigid. How dare Adam's mother ask that, with the reputation the McGuigan family had got. Adam was different, she knew that, but the rest of them . . . Suddenly she appeared much older to Adam and his mother when she said coldly, 'I'm sorry, Mrs McGuigan. What are you suggesting?'

It was Adam who said hastily, 'I think Mother didn't put that as well as she might have done. We all know Toby was a good lad but working at the docks he must have come into contact with some rough types.'

He glared at Sadie who, like her son, had been surprised at the transformation of the shy, rather diffident girl. So the lass *had* got a bit about her, after all, Sadie thought to herself. Not quite as meek and mild as she appeared initially. It didn't make her like the fact that Adam had chosen someone from the very bottom of the ladder any better, but at least, given a bit of coaching from herself and dressed in the right clothes and so on, the girl might be able to hold her own in decent society.

Coolly, her tone unapologetic in spite of her words, she said, 'My son is right, my dear. I meant no offence.'

And pigs might fly. Just wanting to get out of this beautiful room that she was finding too warm and suffocating, Josie said in an equally cool voice, 'Thank you for a lovely tea, Mrs McGuigan, but I really have to be going,' adding, because she knew it would rankle, 'I have to be at the Fiddler's Elbow shortly.'

She stood up as she spoke, Adam with her, and now his mother became the gracious hostess as she smiled at them both. 'You must come again soon, Josie. Perhaps for Sunday lunch? We could invite your brothers and their wives, couldn't we, Adam, so Josie could meet everyone.'

'That would be great,' Adam said a little too heartily, taking Josie's arm as they made their goodbyes and walking her out into the enormous wood-panelled hall where the maid appeared as though by magic, helping Josie into her coat.

They didn't speak until they were outside in the cold clean air and as the McGuigan coachman – another tough-looking gorilla – brought the coach and horses round from the back of the house, Adam said quietly, 'She didn't mean anything about Toby, Josie. It's just her way.'

He got his second surprise in minutes as she looked straight at him and said flatly, 'Well, if that is so I'm sorry, Adam, but I don't like your mother's "way".'

For a moment he was nonplussed; this wasn't like the young, sweet girl he knew and although he might criticize his mother he didn't like anyone else doing so. His eyes narrowed but he bit back the sharp retort that had sprung to mind. 'She's an old lady, Josie. She isn't going to change the habits of a lifetime now.'

She made no answer to this and as he helped her into the coach he saw her face was set. The twilight was deepening as they drove across town in silence and now his anger was directed more at his mother. All he had asked her to do was to be pleasant and agreeable for a couple of hours but she just couldn't resist playing the grand lady, could she. As they reached the East End he put his hand on Josie's, and when she didn't withdraw hers he said softly, 'I'm sorry, really sorry if she upset you. I'll have a word with her when I get home, I promise, but she is rather irascible, I'm afraid.'

Josie didn't know what irascible meant but as he lifted her fingers to his lips and kissed them, she knew she didn't want to be at odds with him. It wasn't his fault what his mother had said, she told herself, and he had been so kind in trying to find out who was responsible for Toby's death and seeing to it that Joe was well set up at the docks. She lifted her face to his and when he kissed her, murmuring, 'I love you so much,' she could respond in like because it was true.

'I was going to take you out to dinner and give you this, go down on one knee and celebrate with champagne, but I can't wait.' He brought a small box out of his jacket pocket, opening it to reveal an exquisite diamond-and-emerald ring. 'Will you marry me on your sixteenth birthday, my love? You never really gave me an answer before and I don't want to wait. Do you?'

She knew that if she answered truthfully he wouldn't like it and she didn't want them to be at odds with each other again. As he took the ring out of the box and slipped it onto the ring finger of her left hand, she whispered, 'No, I don't want to wait but can all the arrangements be made so quickly?'

He kissed her again and this time it was different from all the times before. When his lips finally left hers she was trembling, her cheeks flushed and her eyes bright. Smiling, he traced the outline of her mouth with one finger. 'Leave it to me. I can do anything, anything at all . . .'

PART TWO

Adam

1891

Chapter Six

Did all girls feel so frightened on their wedding day? Josie stared at the ethereal reflection in the full-length mirror in one of the guest bedrooms of Bruce and Phyllis's house. She barely recognized herself and it was disconcerting, adding to the nerves that had gripped her all morning.

She wanted to be Adam's wife, she told herself, but the thought of walking down the aisle on her father's arm with all eyes trained on her was daunting. She knew lots of people would be wondering why Adam McGuigan, so handsome and wealthy, was marrying a nobody like her from Long Bank. Sadie had hinted at that very thing yesterday with a glance at her stomach, her meaning plain. It would have been funny if it wasn't so insulting because since their engagement she and Adam had barely had a few moments alone together. The wedding plans had taken him over completely and he was determined to have a wildly grand affair.

Josie sighed. He had insisted on planning every little thing and as he was paying for it all she had felt she couldn't object although she'd have preferred a simpler occasion. He would even have chosen her wedding dress, but here she'd put her foot down. After some discussion he'd reluctantly handed her over to Phyllis and told the two of them to go shopping in Newcastle with the wad of notes he'd pressed into her hand. She and Phyllis had bought the bridesmaids' dresses at the same time. Along with her three sisters there were Phyllis's two girls and another niece of Adam's, but apart from them the rest of his brothers' children were boys. Boys tended to predominate in the McGuigan family.

Everything would be different from now on, Josie told herself. No more singing in the Fiddler's Elbow for one thing and it had been emotional leaving there. Mrs Mullen had shed a tear as she'd hugged her. 'You can pop in any time and stop and have a cuppa with us, you know that, don't you?' Ada had said, wiping her eyes.

The Mullens were coming to the wedding, of course. She had explained to Adam that they were her dearest friends and she wanted them there, although she could tell he hadn't been keen on the idea. But at least she could see them in the future. When she had explained to Hans that she was getting married and her husband-to-be didn't want her singing at the Fiddler's Elbow once they were wed, they'd both known she was saying goodbye for good. 'So my little songbird is going to fly?' he'd said softly, smiling his warm smile. 'I will pray for your happiness, little one.' Jules had offered his congratulations too, and as she had watched them leave that night she'd had the desire to run after them and fling her arms round them. She hadn't, of course.

She had been so deep in thought that she hadn't noticed Phyllis come up behind her until Bruce's wife said, 'You are truly the most beautiful bride I have ever seen.'

'Thank you.'

'Or you would be if you smiled,' Phyllis chided gently. Josie dutifully smiled.

'That's better.' Phyllis grinned. The bridesmaids had been getting ready in another room and excited laughter and the odd shriek had filled the house for some time, but in the last minutes they had left for the church and now peace reigned.

Josie had spent the night before the wedding at Adam's eldest brother's house, and they had made her very welcome but she had missed her mother this morning. Adam had said staying there would be the best thing because Phyllis would be on hand to help her get ready and see to the bridesmaids too. She could see the sense of this, but she had wondered whether her being married from Long Bank would have been too much for Adam's mother to bear. She'd said as much to Phyllis, who hadn't disagreed.

The more she'd got to know Phyllis the more she liked her. Hilda, David's wife, was nice too but Audrey, the wife of the third-eldest McGuigan brother, seemed cold and standoffish. Phyllis said she thought Audrey was the way she was because she and Philip had been unable to fall for a bairn. Shirley and Laura, who were married to

Mick and Rory, Adam's twin brothers, were sisters and didn't talk much to anyone else but were civil enough. The one thing all the women had in common was that they didn't like their mother-in-law and Josie found this comforting. It was good to know that she wasn't the only one who found Sadie McGuigan difficult and unfriendly.

Josie looked at Phyllis now as she said jokingly, 'Do you think I'll pass with the dragon?' It was the secret nickname for Sadie that – with the exception of Audrey – the women all used.

Phyllis grinned. 'She won't be able to fault you, lass.'

Josie had to admit that the white satin dress with its full skirt and pearl bodice was exquisite. The minute she'd tried it on in the shop Phyllis had clapped her hands and said it was the one. 'You pay for class,' Phyllis had explained. 'It's all in the cut.'

Josie drew in a long deep breath, and as Phyllis adjusted the pearl combs in her upswept hair from which the veil flowed, she murmured, 'I'm frightened, Phyllis. I know it's silly but I can't help it.'

'Oh, don't be.' In the short time that they'd known each other they'd become close and now Phyllis took the slim figure of her future sister-in-law in her arms, whispering, 'I'll be there for you, lass.' She hugged Josie whilst being careful not to crease her dress. 'This is your day and you look beyond lovely. Adam won't be able to take his eyes off you, not that he ever can,' she added with a smile. And indeed Adam was absolutely besotted with her, she'd never seen a man so in love, Phyllis thought.

It bordered on obsession. She just hoped— And then she pushed away the concern that had been at the back of her mind ever since she had met Josie. Adam had always been a fickle character in her opinion – no sooner had he got something than he wanted something else – but that wouldn't apply to this beautiful child/woman he was marrying, she told herself. That would be too cruel, even for Adam.

The ceremony at St Michael's Church in Bishopwearmouth where the McGuigans attended went without a hitch. Although of Saxon origin, the church had undergone alterations and additions over the decades, being embellished with crenellations, large Gothic windows and a tower sporting a clock. It was very different to the little chapel that Josie had attended in the past and that added to her nervousness.

The April day was cold and it was raining heavily and blowing a gale; Josie felt chilled to the bone as she took her vows. When the minister pronounced them man and wife and Adam kissed her, even his lips were cold, but then they were walking back down the aisle and everyone was smiling and nodding and her mother was crying with happiness. That was one good thing, Josie told herself as she exited the church and Adam hurried her to the waiting carriage and horses, her mother just adored Adam. Even not being involved in anything to do with the wedding and her daughter sleeping elsewhere the night before the ceremony was all right if Adam decreed it.

Her father had given her away in an expensive suit bought by Adam and her mother's finery was down to him too, and although Josie knew it was kind of him and he had been anxious that they didn't feel the poor relations at their own daughter's wedding, she wished they'd been able to get married at the chapel where everything would have been much simpler.

The wedding breakfast was being held at the Queen's Hotel in Fawcett Street. The hotel had been established in the middle of the century and Josie had never stepped over its threshold before. It boasted a fine dining room with a capacity for over a hundred and ten guests and the cuisine was excellent, Adam had assured her. When they arrived they were escorted by the manager into a small room with a roaring fire where coffee and biscuits had been laid on for them. Once all their guests were seated in the dining room they would be announced, the manager told them, but for the moment they could relax a little.

Josie was glad of the fire first and foremost to thaw her frozen limbs, but also the chance to be alone with Adam for a few minutes. As soon as the manager left them he pulled her into his arms, his voice husky as he murmured, 'At last, at last you're mine. You don't know how I've ached for this day.' He kissed her long and hard and for the first time that day she felt reassured. This was Adam and he loved her. Everything would be all right. She didn't ask herself why she had to feel reassurance on this point.

When they were ushered through to the dining room by the manager, who announced them in great style, everyone rose to their feet and clapped. As she sat at Adam's side she realized she didn't know most of their guests.

The meal consisted of several courses, most of which she pecked at, but with Adam's encouragement she did sip at her glass of wine. She had never tasted alcohol before and she wasn't sure if she liked it or not. Adam drank a whole bottle to himself and then ordered another when they were only halfway through the meal.

When the speeches began they seemed to go on for ever. Adam insisted everyone sing 'Happy Birthday' to her when he spoke and presented her with a diamond pendant on a gold chain. It took him several attempts to fasten the clasp round her neck and it was then that she realized he was drunk. She had never seen him intoxicated before and when he related several stories about his late father with tears rolling down his cheeks she felt embarrassed for him, but everyone else just smiled and clapped. He finished with a toast to his mother amid cheers, and then sat down heavily in his seat, clicking his fingers at the waiter and asking for more wine.

By the time the guests began to disperse several had to be helped out of their seats and assisted to waiting horse-drawn cabs by the hotel staff, her own father among them, who was, as her mother whispered to Josie as they left, pie-eyed. *Everyone seemed to have had a good time so why did she feel so disappointed?* Josie asked herself. Ridiculous, but she had imagined her wedding day to be a more personal, warm affair; she on Adam's arm as they chatted and laughed with folk and circulated among their guests. As it was, Adam was sitting slumped in his seat talking to Bruce on the other side of him and had been for the last hour or more.

For an insane moment she wondered what he would do if she suddenly jumped up and ran out of the hotel all the way back to Long Bank; would he even notice? And then she felt his arm round her and his wine-laden breath in her ear as he murmured, 'I've arranged for us to have the bridal suite tonight. A surprise for my beautiful wife. Our bags are already in there.'

Josie smiled, pleased and touched but most of all relieved. The house that Adam had bought in the next street to his mother's was in the process of being redecorated from top to bottom and wouldn't be ready for them until they returned from their honeymoon in France. The plan had been for their wedding night to be spent in Adam's room at Sadie's house and she hadn't liked the idea of their married life beginning under his mother's roof, especially with the intimacy involved in them sleeping together for the first time. 'Thank you,' she said softly. 'That will be lovely.'

Adam's face was flushed and his eyes were somewhat glazed when they were shown to the bridal suite a couple of hours later. Although the other guests had left earlier, the McGuigans had stayed on. Adam and Bruce had sat themselves at a table with the other men and they'd all got louder and more rowdy as time had gone on.

Phyllis and Hilda had come to sit with Josie and she was glad of this. It made her feel less of an outsider, especially as she was aware of Sadie's gaze on her every so often and not in a friendly way. Phyllis must have noticed this too because she whispered, 'Don't take any notice of the old bat, Josie. She's had her nose put out of joint good and proper today. Adam didn't tell her till this morning that he'd booked the bridal suite and she didn't like it, not that it's anything to do with her.'

On entering the room, Josie realized just how tired she was. Downstairs and with Sadie's gimlet eyes trained on her, she had forced herself to play a part but now she wanted nothing more than to sleep. But sleep, she knew, wasn't an option, not before this thing happened which she knew so little about. She had tried to ask her mother what went on between a man and a woman in the bedroom, but her mam had got flustered and said she'd find out soon enough. And now it *was* soon enough . . .

Adam walked across to a table holding an ice bucket and two glasses. There was the clink of ice as he removed a bottle of champagne and opened it, the cork popping as he said, 'A toast to our new life together,' slurring his words as he spoke.

She took her glass with a smile but when he downed his in two gulps and promptly poured himself another, she put hers down without tasting it. Her feet were aching in her satin shoes and she slipped them off, wiggling her toes. She would have liked to take her dress off too – the waist had been pulled in so tightly it had become increasingly uncomfortable throughout the day – but the thought of beginning to undress in front of him was discomfiting.

She glanced round the room. It was decorated mainly in cream and various shades of pink and the walls, she noticed, were not painted or papered but were made up of silk panels to match the rose-pink quilted bedspread and the velvet drapes at the window. A patterned carpet covered the entire floor and an ornate chaise longue stood at the foot of the bed. The head of it had yards of flowing cream lace which reminded her of a miniature waterfall. It was all somewhat overwhelming but had no doubt cost a fortune.

Adam had thrown himself down in one of the two armchairs standing in the bay of the window, a glass in one hand and the bottle of champagne in the other. His face held an expression that she hadn't seen before and it was unnerving, but his words were more so when he muttered, 'Well, take your clothes off then. I want to see you.'

She stared at him, shocked at the crudeness and total lack of tenderness. This wasn't how she had imagined it would be – Adam fully clothed and sitting watching her. He dropped the empty glass on the carpet and took a few swigs from the bottle, and when she hadn't moved he raised his eyebrows. 'Well? What are you waiting for?'

Through the panic and bewilderment, she stammered, 'My – my dress is fastened at the back with little buttons. I – I can't manage them myself.'

'Come here.' He stood up as she approached and he

almost went headlong, staggering forwards before righting himself and putting the bottle down. Turning her around, he began to fumble with the tiny pearl buttons before cursing irritably. What happened next caused her to cry out in protest as he tore the dress from the neck downwards, causing the buttons to pop right off. Alarmed, she tried to extricate herself but he ripped the material again so that the bodice became loose and then, swinging her round to face him, he pulled the bodice down to her waist, pushing the frill of lace on her corsets away to expose her small firm breasts.

'Nice,' he mumbled thickly, his mouth clamping onto one nipple as he arched her body backwards and carried her over to the big four-poster bed. Hoisting her full skirt up, his hand clawed at her lace knickers, tearing them, but when he pushed her legs apart with his knee and immediately forced himself into her, her shrill cry of pain caused him to put his hand over her mouth.

A few thrusts of his body and it was over. He gave a shuddering groan and then rolled off her, still fully clothed but unbuttoned with his genitals exposed. He was asleep in the next breath.

Josie lay frozen, terrified that if she moved he would grab her again, and then she slowly inched herself away from the proximity of his body, trembling violently. She swung her legs over the side of the bed, the enormity of what had just happened too much to take in. She sat for some moments gathering herself and then walked to the bathroom, shutting the door behind her.

She spent a long time in there. Even with the door shut she could hear him snoring as she washed the smell and feel of him off her skin. She didn't cry, in fact she felt numb.

The bedroom was still dimly lit by the tulip-shaped gas wall lights when she quietly opened the bathroom door, a towel wrapped round her. She found her case and pulled on one of the fine lawn nightdresses she had bought for their honeymoon. All her clothes were new – Adam had insisted that she shop for everything she would need in her role as Mrs McGuigan.

He was still lying sprawled on top of the bedspread exactly as she had left him and she averted her eyes from the sight. Going to the big mahogany wardrobe she found extra blankets and pillows and made a bed for herself on the chaise longue. Frozen to the bone, she curled into a small ball, trying to ignore the throbbing ache between her legs.

She didn't know what she was going to do; she couldn't think, which was strange because up to this point in time she had always known her own mind. Her eyes were dry, her whole body felt dry as though she had shrivelled up and become very small, and exhaustion was sweeping over her in great waves. She gave in to it in spite of her fear that he would wake up and come at her again, her last thought not of what had happened or what the future held but of Toby, who hadn't wanted her to have anything to do with Adam McGuigan.

Chapter Seven

She was brought from a deep sleep by someone stroking her face. As she opened her eyes she saw it was Adam and the events of the previous night caused her to shrink from him. He was on his knees by the side of the couch and when he saw the look in her eyes, he murmured, 'I'm sorry, I'm sorry, don't be frightened. I – I can't remember much about last night but I know I behaved badly. It was the drink, I had too much.'

She pulled the blanket more tightly round her and seeing that the look was still on her face, he stood up, saying again, 'I'm sorry, truly sorry. I'd planned to make last night special and I spoiled it, didn't I.'

She stared at him. He said he couldn't remember much of the night before and she believed him; her own father was the same when he was drunk. Her voice very small, she said, 'Why did you drink so much?'

'It's a weakness of mine. When I start I find it hard to stop and I was so happy yesterday, but of course that is no excuse. Did I hurt you?'

Bluntly she said, 'Yes.'

'Oh, my darling, forgive me. Can you? Can you put this behind us?' As soon as he had awoken with a killer of a hangover and seen her asleep on the chaise longue, snippets of the night before had come back to him. He'd treated her roughly, he'd realized, like one of his whores, not as the future mother of his children. It was a bad start, he acknowledged, but not the end of the world and he hadn't meant to be brutal. He'd be penitent and tender and she'd soon come round. Women endured much worse, after all. He kneeled down beside the couch again, taking one of her hands in his and pressing it against his cheek. 'I love you so much, you know that, don't you?'

She had thought she did. Josie knew how he wanted her to respond; it was clear he thought saying sorry was enough and that she should fall into his arms, but it was beyond her. The Adam of last night had taken her without love and the one this morning – the Adam she had fallen in love with – was a different being and that frightened her. She pulled herself upright, extricating her hand from his under the pretext of adjusting the blanket. 'I need to go to the bathroom.'

'Of course.' He drew her to her feet and when she was standing in front of him, pressed his lips to her hair. 'I adore you,' he said softly, using all his charm. 'Just remember that, and I wouldn't hurt you for the world.'

But he had, and a few words didn't make that better. She found herself tensing as he raised her chin with one finger and lightly kissed her forehead. She looked into the beautiful face that had mesmerized her from the first moment she had laid eyes on him, and with a little shock of self-awareness she realized it no longer had the power to captivate her. She had seen what was beneath. But she was married, she was his wife.

'Hurry up in the bathroom and then we'll go down to breakfast. I don't know about you but I'm starving.' His tone was jocular, almost playful.

He had already washed and shaved and got dressed, and as she walked into the bathroom and shut the door it came to her that if he had been really remorseful he would have awoken her immediately, full of guilt and self-reproach. That would have been the natural thing to do, wouldn't it?

She stared at her reflection in the bathroom mirror. She half-expected that she would look different but actually she looked the same, if a little pale. But she wasn't the same, not inside. She felt aeons older than her sixteen years this morning. She'd been stupid, so stupid to allow herself to be rushed into this marriage, she thought wretchedly, fighting back the tears that had been hovering since she had opened her eyes. But with Toby gone, there had been no one to urge caution and her mam and da had been all for it. Adam could do no wrong in their eyes. And then she shook her head. No, she couldn't blame them. She couldn't blame anyone but herself and now all she could do was to make the best of things.

* * *

After they left the hotel later that morning, a cab took them to Adam's mother's house. They had a light lunch with Sadie before their luggage was loaded into the carriage and they were driven to the station where they caught the train to London. They spent three days in the capital before crossing over to France, and Adam only had a glass or two of wine with his evening meal during that time.

He took her to see Buckingham Palace and the Zoological Gardens, and on the second evening, just before they left for her first visit to a theatre, he presented her with a pair of diamond earrings to match the pendant he had given her on their wedding day. He had been careful to be very gentle with her each night when he had made love to her and gradually she had relaxed as his charm and devotion had won her over. She felt a huge sense of relief, as though she had been standing on the edge of an abyss which had disappeared, and once in France she had begun to respond to his lovemaking and enjoy it.

The weather was cold but bright during the week they spent there and he made sure they saw all the sights, including Versailles, which she found enchanting, the Conciergerie and Notre-Dame. On their last evening, after he'd made love to her in their big soft bed, he got dressed again.

She had just come out of the bathroom and she stared at him in surprise.

'I'm just going to the restaurant for a snack,' he said quickly. 'I won't be long.'

'But there's room service.' They had already used this

facility a few times in the last days, besides which they'd enjoyed a wonderful meal just a couple of hours ago. He couldn't be hungry again surely?

He cupped her face in his hands, kissing the tip of her nose. 'I won't be long,' he said again.

He left the room before she could protest further and she stood staring after him for a few moments before climbing into bed. She wasn't sure how long she lay awake waiting for him but when he entered the room again he roused her from a deep sleep as he stumbled about, swearing softly as he attempted to undress.

She lay quite still, every muscle in her body tense. He was drunk, she realized, as there was a thud followed by more cursing. Pickled, as her mam would have said. Hardly daring to breathe, she waited for him to climb into bed, making up her mind that if he attempted to use her as he had on their wedding night she would fight him tooth and nail.

The smell of spirits wafted over her as he fell heavily onto his side of the bed, bouncing the mattress, but still she remained as stiff as a board, waiting for his hands to reach for her. They didn't. Within a minute or so he was snoring fit to wake the dead.

Josie was wide awake, and as the fear that he was going to try to touch her diminished, anger took its place. He had gone downstairs with the sole purpose of pouring whisky down his throat and he had lied to her. *Why did he feel the necessity to do that?* she asked herself. He'd had his usual couple of glasses of wine at dinner – three, actually, if she remembered correctly. The drunks she had grown up around in the East End had at least had reasons for their drinking – grinding poverty, bitterness at their lot in life, chronic ill health or grief and sorrow – but Adam was young and healthy and rich. In fact he'd never wanted for anything in his life.

How was she going to handle this in the morning? Although she felt tired, she didn't expect to be able to sleep again because her mind was presenting her with various scenarios. One thing was for sure, whatever she said he wouldn't take kindly to her challenging him in any way. When they had been courting she had only seen him for an hour or two normally, but being in his company constantly since the wedding had shown her that although he was charm personified when everything was going his way, he could change with the wind. Having to wait for a cab, a waiter taking too long with their meals or, in Adam's opinion, not being deferential enough, would turn him into a different person. It was as though she had married two men, she thought miserably. The one she loved, but the other . . .

She bit down hard on her lower lip, alarmed at the path her mind had taken. As their honeymoon had progressed she had made the decision to put their disastrous wedding night behind her. It had been a one-off, she'd reassured herself, when he hadn't been in his right mind. He might be prone to having a quick temper if thwarted but lots of folk were like that, her own da for one. And Adam loved her, he was always telling her so, besides which she was a married woman now so she had no option but to make the best of things. Most people would be of the opinion that she was incredibly fortunate to be whisked out of Long Bank and into a life of luxury and she was. *She was*, she emphasized now. Nevertheless, when she drifted into an uneasy sleep just before dawn, the feeling that she was teetering at the edge of an abyss was back.

As she had expected, Adam became cool and curt when she broached the matter of his drinking as they were dressing for breakfast, virtually refusing to discuss it. They went down to the dining room in silence and when she attempted conversation he answered in monosyllables. It distressed her – the last thing she wanted was for them to be at odds with each other – and she could barely eat anything. Adam, on the other hand, had a hearty break- fast and joked and laughed with the young waitress who served them. Josie had seen the girl ogling him several times before but it hadn't bothered her then, she'd just felt proud that Adam was hers.

By the time they returned to their room and waited for the bell boy to collect their bags she was close to tears but determined to hide it. It was when they were in the cab on the way to the port that he said coldly, 'I think I need to make one thing perfectly clear, Josie. When I married you I wanted a wife, not a mother who fusses over what I do or don't drink. And that applies in other areas of my life too. I can't feel constrained, I'm not made that way. Now if you remember that we'll be happy together, which is all I want because I love you. Do you understand what I'm saying?'

She stared at the individual who was Adam and yet not Adam. How could he say he loved her and flirt as he had with the waitress and then talk to her like this? Who was he really? Her voice didn't convey her turmoil when she said quietly, 'And I love you, Adam. That is why I am concerned when you drink to excess.'

'Don't be.' His tone was a little warmer. 'I can handle my drink, I've always been able to.'

It was clear what he termed handling his drink was quite different to her definition. It was on the tip of her tongue to mention the disaster that had been their wedding night but she bit the words back. She had promised herself that she wouldn't bring it up again when she had decided to forgive him. Instead she said, 'But it can't be good for you and as your wife surely I am allowed to worry about you?'

He reached out and pulled her closer to him, lifting her chin and kissing her full on the lips for some moments. 'Don't let's argue,' he said softly, his voice velvety now. 'It upsets me. So, are you excited to see our home with everything finished? It's all for you, my darling, I want you to be happy.'

All for her? The old Josie would have accepted his words at face value but as he spoke she realized the last couple of weeks had changed her more than she had been aware of. Adam hadn't really encouraged her to have much of a say in the decoration and furnishings, in fact he had dismissed several of the suggestions she had put forward and made her feel quite gauche in the process. He had intimated that he was more familiar with what was needed for such a large and grand house. People expected a certain opulence in his level of society, he had told her, and it was necessary for the house to reflect this. It was better that she left everything to him.

She hadn't argued about it at the time, she thought now – she'd felt he was probably right – but in hindsight she wished she'd been more forceful. She might have come from Long Bank but she still had a mind of her own and knew what she liked and what she didn't. His mother's house for example was definitely not to her taste. It was far too fussy.

Adam didn't wait for her reply. Instead he began chatting about the items of furniture he'd acquired and the way he wanted the grounds of the house landscaped. As the cab trundled through the cobbled Paris streets his previous ill temper seemed to have melted away. He held her hand, caressing it as he talked and dropping kisses on her nose and forehead now and again.

Josie tried to relax. When he was like this, the old Adam, she could almost convince herself that she imagined the darker side to his personality. She wanted things to return to the way they had been when they'd been courting, she acknowledged pensively, but perhaps that would never happen? Maybe marriage was all about tolerating each other's shortcomings? She was far from perfect, she knew that, and Adam had been so good to her family, after all. Was she expecting too much?

Nevertheless, she couldn't capture the way she had felt the previous day before Adam had gone downstairs to the bar. A faint sense of foreboding had settled on her and even though she responded to his conversation in the manner she knew he wanted her to, her heart wasn't in it.

The long journey by boat, train, and then a horse-drawn cab from the station had been tiring. As the vehicle passed between two open wooden gates and onto the drive of their new home, Josie looked wearily at the house where she would properly begin married life.

In appearance it was similar to Bruce and Phyllis's, being built of natural stone with a dark slate roof. It had the same three tall windows on either side of the front door with replicas above them but on a smaller scale, and above these were the attic windows. It was gone ten at night and dark, and lights seemed to be blazing from all the windows on the ground floor. For a brief moment Josie thought about what her mother would say about such extravagance, but then the front door was being opened by a uniformed maid. Adam and his mother had interviewed potential staff in the weeks before the wedding, and now, as the girl curtsied and welcomed them in, Josie felt like a guest rather than the mistress of the house. This feeling intensified as Adam led the way into the drawing room.

The last time she had seen it before the redecorating had begun she had thought it was a lovely room, but now she had to admit it was far grander. Adam's choice of furnishings and decoration were clearly expensive but not so fussy as his mother's, which was a relief. Several couches and chairs were positioned about the room along with occasional tables and other furniture, and a wall-to-wall carpet covered the floor in various shades of red, blue and cream. Heavy blue drapes hung at the windows and the walls were covered in a pale blue flock wallpaper.

The fireplace was enormous and ornate, and in spite of the vastness of the room the blazing coal and logs had made it as warm as toast. The maid had followed them and once they were divested of their outdoor clothes she told them that Cook had refreshments prepared for their arrival.

Adam nodded. 'In fifteen minutes or so. And see to it we have coffee and brandy.' Once the girl had scurried off with their coats and hats, he took Josie in his arms. 'Well, my darling? Do you like it?'

She could say truthfully that she did and he grinned at her, looking almost boyish. 'We'll explore properly tomorrow but come and see our rooms upstairs. We can change out of these clothes. I feel as though I've brought half the dust from Paris back with me.'

He took her hand in his as he rushed her up the wide curving staircase in a manner that was again boyish, and once they reached the master suite she gazed about her wide-eyed. Along with a lovely bathroom complete with lavatory, on the right-hand side of the bedroom was a large dressing room for Adam and what he called a boudoir for her on the left. Leading off full-length windows in the bedroom was a balcony edged with intricate wrought-iron railings. 'We can have breakfast here in the summer,' he said enthusiastically, flinging the doors wide so the cold night air flooded in. 'And the view over the grounds is marvellous and completely private. One could imagine we're deep in the country rather than the town.'

'It's wonderful.' And it was, it was wonderful, she told herself; so why did she feel so alienated from her surroundings? Perhaps because she hadn't had a hand in choosing anything but that would quickly pass and it would soon feel like home. Coming from where she had to this was bound to feel strange at first, but she would do her best not to let him down. She just wished she was older, more poised and self-possessed, but people didn't need to know what she was feeling like inside. She could put on a show like she had in the high-class, fashionable hotels they'd stayed in on honeymoon. Phyllis had confided that it had taken her a while to assume the role of Mrs Bruce McGuigan but if you watched plenty and said little, you soon cottoned on. 'And let's face it, lass,' Phyllis had murmured, 'the McGuigans come from working-class roots and not so far back either. They might like to act as lords of the manor but they still get their hands dirty, if you know what I mean.' She hadn't admitted that she didn't really know what Phyllis meant but had assumed, rightly, that it was all to do with the crime empire Bruce ran. But Adam wasn't involved in that.

'You're so beautiful,' he said as he turned from the

windows. 'You turn heads wherever you go and every man alive is jealous of me.'

She smiled. He said such nice things when he was happy.

'I want to dress you up and show you off so they can all see what they're missing, Chapman and the rest of his type who think they're somebody.'

She stared at him, her smile dimming. He'd made her sound like a doll, and who was Chapman anyway?

He had turned away and was beginning to undress as he continued, 'Bruce can't see it but even when they're toadying to us they think they're better.'

'Who – who is Chapman?'

'A councillor Bruce has got in his pocket, one of many such men, I might add,' he said over his shoulder as he walked into his dressing room. He looked back at her as he added, 'Hurry up and get changed, I need a stiff drink after that journey.'

He had bought her so many clothes she doubted if she would ever have the opportunity to wear them all, but she walked into her boudoir and quickly selected a dress from the extensive wardrobe. It was made of silk in a deep emerald-green colour with a row of tiny buttons on the bodice, and for a moment she thought back to her wedding dress and the way Adam had fumbled with those buttons before ripping the dress off her. Perhaps that was why the sense of foreboding was stronger than ever when she joined him to go downstairs, and try as she might she couldn't shake it off.

Chapter Eight

Over the next weeks Josie became acquainted with what was required of her in running a large house and instructing staff, and here Phyllis had been invaluable, proving herself to be a real friend. On the first morning after they'd returned from France, Phyllis had arrived at the house after Adam had left for work with a basket of flowers to welcome Josie home, and also a large black leather ledger.

'For your household accounts and notes,' Phyllis had stated matter-of-factly, ignoring Josie's look of alarm. 'You'll have to get used to ordering what's necessary and paying bills and the like. Adam's mam did all that and he'll expect it of you.'

After that Phyllis came every morning for an hour or two, always ready to answer Josie's numerous questions. Edith Bell, the cook, also played a part in guiding the young mistress, suggesting appropriate menus and giving Josie detailed lists of what food was required and the best places to order what was needed. Now the butcher, grocer, baker and fishmonger made regular deliveries, and the massive coal bunker in the kitchen yard was well stocked, with a good supply of logs and kindling nestled next to it under a lean-to.

All this had been achieved without Josie having to ask Adam's advice, for which she was grateful. Since their marriage, she'd recognized something which hadn't been apparent before – he could be condescending towards her at times and even a little scornful. She knew she'd got a lot to learn – even Ida, the maid, who was Mrs Bell's niece, knew how to set a table with the correct knives and forks and glasses and so on – but she also was aware that she learned quickly and had a good memory. On the whole though, Adam was attentive and pleasant and as he was out for a large part of each day she was pleased to see him when he returned home in the evening. She missed her singing and time hung heavy now and again.

There had been several occasions when he had stayed downstairs after dinner once she had gone to bed, and she had known it was with the intention of drinking, but although he had been drunk when he had come upstairs he hadn't been what Josie termed pickled. Neither had he made any demands on her when he was intoxicated.

She had confided in Phyllis that Adam sometimes drank too much but her sister-in-law had just smiled, saying, 'Oh, lass, the McGuigans have always been the same. Bruce likes a few whiskies or a brandy or two after dinner and I know the others do too, but it's not a problem. Don't worry about it.'

She hadn't liked to say that with Adam it wasn't a few whiskies or a brandy or two when he had a drinking bout. She knew he could get through a whole bottle in one sitting because part of her housewifely duties was keeping the spirit cabinet stocked along with the wine supply. It had seemed disloyal to go into details though, even with Phyllis, and the subject hadn't been mentioned again.

A week after they'd returned home they'd had a house-warming party with the McGuigans and her family which had gone very well, although she had been embarrassed at the way her father had ingratiated himself with Adam's family, practically tugging his forelock when Bruce spoke to him. The next week they had gone to dinner at Bruce and Phyllis's with the rest of the McGuigans, and the week after that a dinner had been held at David and Hilda's house. On neither occasion had her parents been invited. Phyllis had explained that the McGuigans got together regularly and rarely invited anyone else.

Josie would have enjoyed the gatherings more if Sadie hadn't been present, but she had noticed that when his mother was around Adam curbed his alcohol to some extent, which wasn't a bad thing. The evenings always ended in the same way. Once the dinner was over, the men stayed in the dining room drinking and laughing and getting louder and louder, and the women retired to the drawing room for coffee and sweetmeats where they made conversation until the men were ready to leave. Josie found it prudent to say little but she began to understand the dynamics of the family she'd married into better.

Sadie was very much queen bee among the women and her sons gave their mother a great deal of respect, but Josie suspected Bruce humoured her rather than took notice of her like the others. There was no doubt he was the head of the family and his brothers were deferential to him. She found David, Philip, Mick and Rory much of a muchness on the whole, but not so their wives. Phyllis was the nicest of the women by a long chalk. Hilda was all right but Josie didn't know if she would altogether trust her, and she definitely wouldn't have any confidence in Audrey, who seemed as thick as thieves with Sadie. Shirley and Laura were observers, but Josie got the impression that there was plenty going on behind the sisters' blank facades.

It was towards the end of May, when Josie had been married for just over seven weeks, that Phyllis had a quiet word in her ear. Josie had been feeling off colour for the last few days, especially in the mornings, and when she'd had to excuse herself on two consecutive days during morning coffee with her sister-in-law and hurry to the downstairs cloakroom where she was sick, Phyllis was waiting with a strange expression on her face when she returned, a little white-faced.

'All right, lass?' Phyllis said quietly.

Josie nodded, embarrassed. 'I think it must be something I've eaten that's upset my stomach.' Thankfully, she always improved during the day and by the time Adam came home felt well enough to enjoy the evening meal with him. He didn't like illness in any shape or form and had little patience with those unfortunate enough to experience ill health. This was another thing she had found out about him since they'd been married.

'Can I ask you a personal question?'

Phyllis had leaned forward, her voice even lower, and although it was only the two of them in the drawing room, Josie found herself answering in like tone. 'Yes, of course. What is it?'

'Your monthlies? When was your last one?'

It was the last thing Josie had been expecting and she blushed furiously. From the first day she had started her periods and gone to her mother in tears, alarmed at the strange thing that was happening to her, the matter had never been discussed again. Her mother had said it was something that happened to every girl when she reached a certain age and that was all. She had given her a wad of old rags to use in her knickers; told her she had to wash and dry them herself without her father or the lads noticing, and that had been that. It was as though it was shameful and Josie had accepted it as such.

Her cheeks burning, she stammered, 'I – I don't know.'

'Have you had one since you got wed?'

Mortified, Josie thought for a moment before shaking her head.

'And were you regular before?' Phyllis persisted.

Josie took a gulp of hot coffee – which hadn't tasted quite right for the last few days – before she could say, 'Aye, aye, I think so.'

'Lass, I think you'd better make an appointment and see the doctor,' Phyllis said gently.

Totally bewildered, Josie stared at her.

Seeing her confusion, Phyllis sighed. 'Didn't your mam tell you about what happens before you have a baby?'

'A baby?'

'Lass, I think you might be expecting.' Phyllis took a sip of her own coffee, feeling she needed it. 'Look, I'm going to go through it all with you because even if you're not pregnant you ought to know a few things.' She had realized Josie was an innocent the first time she had met her but not the extent of it. *Fancy her mam not telling her about the birds and the bees*, she thought indignantly; but you'd have thought where Josie came from she'd have heard and seen things which would have made her catch on. Obviously not.

At the end of the conversation and the facts that Phyllis had related practically in a down-to-earth manner, Josie was far better informed. 'And you think I ought to go and see a doctor?' she said nervously.

'I'll come with you. We'll go and see Dr Preston. He's the one all the McGuigans use but he's lovely,' Phyllis said bracingly. 'I'll pop in the surgery on my way home and we'll go tomorrow morning, but perhaps better not to mention anything to Adam till you're sure.' She smiled and gave Josie's hand a pat, thinking how vulnerable and young she seemed. 'All right, lass?'

Josie nodded. Actually she felt far from all right. A baby was lovely and she wanted bairns, of course she did, but she'd imagined a family somewhere in the future, not now. She still felt overwhelmed with how much her life had changed in such a short time. She had been to see her mother a few times since she had been home and the stark difference between Long Bank and where she lived now had been disturbing, not least because she felt she didn't belong in either place, not really. Her mother was so thrilled that she had married well and went on and on about how lucky she was and how wonderful Adam was, and she didn't feel she could really talk to her mam any more except on a superficial level. And her da . . . Her nose flared in distaste as she thought about her father. He was all over her now, treating her like a queen. He'd even gone so far as to get out his handkerchief and wipe the seat for her when she had sat down in their kitchen the other day. She always took a basket of groceries with her when she visited and gave her mother a pound or two and her father some money for his beer and baccy, but she had to admit that if he was present she couldn't wait to get away. Even her sisters seemed different, shy somehow as though they were in awe of her.

Once Phyllis had left she sat for some time in the drawing room, deep in thought. A baby. She touched her flat stomach. A little life. Part of Adam and part of her. A small smile touched her lips and she stroked her stomach again. Suddenly she knew she would be bitterly disappointed now if Dr Preston didn't think she was expecting.

'Well?' Phyllis took her arm as they left Dr Preston's surgery the next morning. The practice was a grand affair, all leather seats and fine landscapes on the wall in the waiting room, but once she had entered Dr Preston's office Josie had relaxed a little. He was a middle-aged man and although he spoke in what Josie would have termed a la-di-da way, kindness and warmth shone out of his face. His examination had been thorough but even though he was a doctor Josie had found it embarrassing. At the end of it and once she was sitting in the chair in front of his desk once more, he smiled. 'Well, I'm pleased to tell you that you are expecting a baby, Mrs McGuigan. When was your last period?'

'The third week of March.'

'Yes, that would be about right. So, a December delivery, m'dear, probably around Christmas, though these things are not always precise. Rest assured you will be well looked after.' His voice was hearty but in truth he was slightly concerned. She was very slight in body. Still, he told himself, with the McGuigan money behind her she would have the best care in the event of complications and hopefully all would go well. The young were resilient.

Josie had thanked him and left, and now she smiled at Phyllis as they walked arm in arm along the wide, tree-lined street near Barnes Park. It was a beautiful day, but although the sun was shining in a cloudless blue sky it was still a little nippy. 'You were right,' she said softly. 'I'm expecting.'

'Aw, lass, that's wonderful.' Phyllis grinned at her. 'Adam's going to be cock-a-hoop.'

'I'll probably tell him when we get home tonight before

bed so don't say anything to Bruce yet, will you.' She and Adam and the rest of the brothers and their wives were meeting up at a fancy restaurant in town that evening to celebrate Sadie's seventieth birthday. There had been a lot of fuss about presents and flowers and so on, and if she told Adam before the event he'd be full of it. She doubted her mother-in-law would appreciate the limelight being taken away from her and that was fair enough, after all. The old lady might be a tartar and nasty with it, but reaching seventy wasn't to be sneezed at.

'I won't let on, it's not my news to tell, is it. When I hear I'll make out it's a big surprise,' Phyllis promised. 'Adam will want to think that he's the first one to know anyway so don't let on I came with you to the doctor's.'

Josie nodded, grateful Phyllis understood. She didn't know what she'd have done over the last weeks without her. She had never really had a close friend before, unless you could count Toby, but he'd been her brother and that was different. After school her father had always carted her round the pubs and made her sing and 'earn her keep' as he'd put it. She hadn't played out like other bairns.

Voicing her thoughts, she said, 'Thank you so much, Phyllis. Not just for this but for all you've done over the last weeks. I'd have been lost without your help and advice.'

'That's all right, lass.' Phyllis squeezed her arm. 'Us women have to stick together, don't we.'

Whether she meant they had to stick together against their mother-in-law or their menfolk or life in general,

Josie didn't know and she didn't ask. She had noticed how Phyllis and Bruce were with each other. Their relationship certainly wasn't like Hilda and David's very close one, but then Audrey and Philip barely spoke two words to each other if they could help it, and Shirley and Laura seemed quite distant from their husbands. 'I've taken up so much of your time,' she said apologetically.

'Nonsense, I've enjoyed it. With all the bairns at school I feel at a loose end most days to tell you the truth. I'd love to do my own baking and that but' – she shrugged – 'you know.'

Josie did know. Adam had made it clear he didn't expect her to set foot in the kitchen unless it was to give instructions to Mrs Bell. He'd told her she had to remember her position as mistress of the house at all times, and Phyllis had said Bruce was the same.

'Now the weather's getting better we can have lunch in town sometimes or go to the Winter Garden, things like that. I used to take the bairns there all the time when they were little to see the tropical plants and flowers, and the aviary and goldfish pond. Your little one'll love that.' Phyllis smiled. 'There's lovely days ahead, lass.'

Josie stopped suddenly. 'A baby, Phyllis. I can't take it in.'

'I was like that with my first. You'll believe it better when you start to feel it move but that's not for ages yet. First you've got the morning sickness to get through.'

*   *   *

Josie was thinking of Phyllis's words when she got ready to go out later that evening. Today the morning sickness had lasted well into the afternoon and she was still feeling a little queasy. She had pinched her cheeks to put some colour in them before she had joined Adam, who was waiting downstairs.

'Ready at last?' he asked a trifle irritably. 'I don't want to be late. You know what Mother's like about punctuality.'

She didn't point out that they were in plenty of time although she knew what the real reason was for his demeanour. He didn't like to be kept waiting for a minute and the fact that he'd been ready early wouldn't be an excuse. Just a few days ago she might have apologized even though she wasn't at fault, but tonight the desire to appease him was absent and she merely inclined her head as she said, 'Shall we go then?'

He stared at her for a moment before saying curtly, 'Of course. The carriage is waiting.' In the last week he had bought a carriage similar to Bruce's and a fine horse, and engaged a man who was to be both coachman and gardener, as well as seeing to any jobs that needed doing. The man in question had been recommended by Bruce and lived in the East End at present, but the loft above the stables was being converted into living accommodation for him. On meeting Shelton, Josie had thought he looked the same as most of the individuals who worked for her brother-in-law, being big and muscled with a boxer's battered face and crooked nose.

As the carriage trundled through the streets, she found

herself wishing the evening was over before it had begun. The nausea that had lingered all day wasn't conducive to eating a big meal with numerous courses. She would have preferred something light at home and an early night.

They were the first ones to arrive at the restaurant. The manager ushered them to a long table bedecked with flowers and pink ribbons with some ceremony, a fact that improved Adam's mood. He ordered several bottles of champagne to be put on ice for when the rest of the party made an appearance and a double brandy for himself. Josie refused a glass of wine and asked for water instead. She was well acquainted by now with how much wine and spirits would flow at a meal with the McGuigans and wanted to keep a clear head. As the others began to arrive, she stitched a smile on her face and prepared herself for a long night.

It could be said that the evening was a pleasant one.

The conversation at the dinner table was mostly centred around Sadie, and therefore she was gracious and affable as the belle of the ball. The food was excellent, the champagne flowed, and when Sadie was presented with a wildly expensive diamond-and-ruby necklace and matching earrings by her offspring, she became almost girlish.

Phyllis caught Josie's eye at this point and made a face. She'd been given the job by Bruce of finding the present for his mother and had told Josie she'd just bought the most pretentious item in the shop.

It was just before eleven o'clock when the first of the

carriages arrived to take them home. The time had been prearranged, and Josie had been counting the minutes. When Sadie announced she was ready to leave Josie hoped that would be the end of the evening. Bruce and Phyllis had brought Sadie to the restaurant but Audrey immediately offered to take her mother-in-law home, leaving Philip with no choice but to agree although he clearly didn't want to go. Josie sighed. She was exhausted but there was no point in asking Adam if they could leave when he was drinking with his brothers.

Midnight came and went, and now the curtains at the restaurant windows were closed and the other tables had been cleared and re-set for the morning. It would have been obvious to a blind man that the manager and the one remaining waiter were anxious to go home. Hilda had even pointed this out to David but he'd just shrugged helplessly and carried on talking and making merry with the other men. Josie and her sisters-in-law had long since kicked off their shoes and Phyllis had even loosened her corsets. It was just gone one o'clock when Adam called to the manager for another bottle of brandy for the table.

The man came hurrying to them, his manner apologetic when he said, 'I'm very sorry, Mr McGuigan, but I really do need to close up now.'

'What did you say?' Adam's voice was thick and slurred.

'It's very late, sir.'

'I'm aware what time it is. Just get the damn brandy and be quick about it.'

'Yes, sir.'

Clearly the manager wasn't going to argue with the McGuigans, Josie thought, feeling sorry for him.

Moments later, the waiter came scurrying over but as he turned to leave, Adam said belligerently, 'Your boss thinks we've outstayed our welcome, lad. What do you think?'

'I'm sorry, sir?' The waiter couldn't have been more than eighteen or nineteen and was clearly scared to death.

'Your boss, Mr Ferry.' Adam pronounced it Fairy as the other men sniggered. 'Fairy by name and fairy by nature, is he?'

'Mr Ferry is a family man, sir.'

Josie looked at Phyllis, who raised her eyebrows, and then back at her husband. This was horrible, baiting the poor waiter, who hadn't done anything. Without giving herself time to think, she said, 'Adam, I'm tired. Could we go now?'

Not just Adam but all the men stared at her and she saw Adam's eyes narrow as his jaw tightened. She had an odd feeling inside her, a racing, sick, odd feeling, and she was aware of Phyllis standing up and saying directly to Bruce, 'Cissy won't be able to go to bed until we're home as she's keeping an ear out for the children,' and then Hilda rising to her feet too.

There was silence for a moment and then Bruce nodded. 'The ladies have spoken,' he said expressionlessly as he too stood up. All his brothers apart from Adam followed suit and as the waiter hurried off to get their coats and hats goodbyes were said, but the atmosphere was uncomfortable.

Adam took his time finishing his glass of brandy and all the others had left when he eventually stood up. Without speaking he pulled on his coat and hat. Bruce had paid for the evening and had told Adam to bring the last bottle of brandy with him, and now he picked it up and, still not saying a word, walked out of the restaurant without offering her his arm as he normally would have done. She followed in his wake, thanking the manager as she left, who bowed and said the right things, but she could tell he couldn't wait to see the back of them and she didn't blame him.

Theirs was the only carriage in the street now and as she stepped onto the pavement she saw that Adam was already inside. Shelton's face and demeanour were impassive as he helped her up into the carriage, and once she was seated he shut the door. She shivered – the night air was cold after the warmth of the restaurant. As the carriage jolted and began to move, she forced herself to look at Adam and his eyes were waiting for her. 'What the hell do you think you're playing at?' he said through gritted teeth.

'Playing at?'

'Talking to me like that in front of everyone.'

'I merely asked if we could go home.'

'Don't play games with me, I'm not in the mood.' He stared at her while waiting for a response, and when none was forthcoming, snarled, 'You made me look a fool in front of my family.'

'I did nothing of the kind.' Part of her knew this was

the wrong tack to take – he was drunk and attempting to pacify him would be the sensible thing to do – but he had been a bully back there, she told herself, and she had always loathed bullies.

'Don't play the innocent.' The words were deep and guttural.

'I am not, as you say, playing the innocent. If you feel you looked a fool it was your own doing, not mine. That waiter was just a young lad trying to earn a living and there was no need to treat him the way you did.'

His look of amazement would have been funny in any other circumstances. For a moment he was speechless, and then he said through gritted teeth, '*You*, to tell *me* how to behave. I picked you up out of the gutter and don't you forget it. Singing for a few pennies a night in a pub that's little more than a brothel and being ogled at by every Tom, Dick and Harry. You need to learn a little gratefulness, damn you.'

Josie didn't reply to this. She raised her chin, staring at him in a manner that maddened him still further by its silent accusation.

He made a low growling sound in his throat that could have come from a dog as he raised his hand to slap her, and it was then she said, 'I'm expecting a baby, Adam.'

The words hung in the air between them and it occurred to her that she had never imagined having to break the news to him to avoid being assaulted. She sat still and tense as he slumped back in the seat. 'What did you say?'

'I went to see Dr Preston today. I'm pregnant.'

In one of the mercurial changes of mood she had come to associate with him since they had been married, she found herself gathered into his arms. 'A baby? Already?'

She remained stiff and unyielding in his embrace but she doubted he even noticed in his drunken state.

'And there's Philip and Audrey been trying for years.' He laughed, his voice exultant. 'Audrey won't like this.'

Phyllis had been right, she thought. He was cock-a-hoop but not in a nice way. What had Philip and Audrey's misfortune to do with it?

He laughed again and his voice was high and excited when he said, 'Why didn't you tell me before?'

'It's your mother's birthday.'

He must have understood what she left unsaid because he nodded, saying, 'Ah, yes. But tomorrow we'll shout it from the rooftops. When's it due?'

'Towards the end of December, probably around Christmas time,' she said flatly. Telling your husband that you were expecting his first child should be a joyous, wonderful moment, shouldn't it? she asked herself. But instead this was all wrong.

He was speaking above her head now, his voice happy and exuberant. They would invite everyone round for dinner and make an announcement, do it in style, he enthused. And one of the bedrooms at the back of the house would be ideal for a nursery. And their child would only have the best of everything. There was a grand shop in Newcastle they could visit; it was pricey but they didn't let riff-raff through the doors.

He dropped little kisses on her hair as he talked and gradually she allowed herself to relax against him. She was tired, tired in mind and body, and she had no fight left in her. He had said some horrible things tonight but he seemed unaware of it now, and not for the first time she wondered about the nature of the man she had married. She knew she had practically worshipped him before they had got wed but that had finished on their wedding night. Nevertheless, she was his wife and he was her husband and now there was a baby on the way.

'For better, for worse, for richer, for poorer, in sickness and health, until death do us part . . .' She'd made her bed and she had to lie on it, she knew that, but she'd give the world to be able to confide in someone exactly how she felt. No, not someone. Toby. She missed him so much . . .

Chapter Nine

It soon became clear that the pregnancy was not going to be an easy one. The customary morning sickness lasted all day and well into the evening, and the only real respite Josie got from the constant nausea was when she was sleeping. She felt deathly tired too with a muzzy head and bouts of giddiness. On one of her weekly visits to the house Dr Preston's midwife, a friendly, motherly soul, told Josie that she had known a few other women who'd been just as poorly and that it would pass. She was young and healthy, Mrs Fletcher assured her patient, and the baby was growing as it should, but she did need to try and eat more if she could. Josie couldn't. She knew she'd become skin and bone but no food would stay down for more than a few minutes.

Adam had been sympathetic initially, still elated he was going to be a father, but as the first flush of euphoria had worn off Josie knew her indisposition irritated and repelled him. He was rarely at home now in the evenings, leaving the house immediately after his evening meal and not returning until she had retired for the night. It was clear he was drinking heavily and once or twice she'd smelled stale perfume on his clothes, but she simply didn't feel well enough to challenge him as to whether he was seeing another woman.

She spoke to both her mother and Phyllis about the situation and received differing advice. Her mother kept her rose-coloured glasses on about Adam and said she was *sure* he wouldn't be unfaithful and least said soonest mended, whereas Phyllis's reaction had been more down to earth. 'Selfish beggar,' her friend had said hotly. 'He wants a good kick up the bum, lass. His mam spoiled him from when he drew breath and he thinks the world revolves around him. That's the trouble. Tell him you want him home in the evenings – you're the one feeling bad, not him. It's the least he can do. And if you're really worried he's messing about, ask him about it. You'd know if he lied, wouldn't you?'

Josie had stared at her sister-in-law. *Would* she know? She was a married woman and carrying her husband's child but since their wedding it seemed as if the ardent beau who had courted her so tenderly had gone. In his place was a man who seemed little more than a stranger at times. Adam hadn't made love to her since she had told him about the baby, not that she had particularly wanted him to when she was feeling so ill, but a gesture of affection now and again – a kiss, a hug – would have been comforting.

When Phyllis had left that day, Josie had sat for a long

time just thinking. She had come to the conclusion that she wouldn't ask Adam to stay with her in the evenings, nor would she question him about what he was doing, for the simple reason that to do so would be pointless. He would do exactly as he pleased and she would humiliate herself for no purpose. All that mattered now was getting through the pregnancy as best she could and having a healthy child at the end of it. Their marital issues could wait. She needed all her strength to survive at the moment.

Bruce looked at his youngest brother with a mixture of sympathy and irritation. He couldn't for the life of him understand how Adam's marriage had gone wrong so quickly, especially with Josie being pregnant and all. Adam had been like a dog with two tails at first but in the last couple of months he'd rarely been at home in the evenings from what Phyllis had told him. He'd had Larry look into it after that, and it appeared that if Adam wasn't drinking at their club he was visiting a certain house of ill repute.

He had come to the club himself tonight with the express purpose of finding out what was what, but Adam was in one of his difficult moods. Drawing on his limited patience, Bruce said, 'I'm going to ask you again, what the hell is the matter, man? We all thought you were over the moon about Josie being in the family way.'

Adam knocked back his glass of whisky and then poured himself another from the bottle at his side. 'You know I am.'

'Well, if that's the case why are you out every night?'

Adam shrugged. 'Josie's not well, you know that, and I'm better out of the way.'

'Is that her opinion or yours?'

Adam shrugged again and his tone turned surly when he said, 'I'm not cut out to be a nursemaid.'

'Does Josie know you frequent Ma Peabody's establishment?'

'Leave it, Bruce. It's up to me where I go and don't go.'

'I don't understand you, I don't straight. Why pay for it with one of Ma's girls when you've got a looker like Josie at home?'

'I told you, she's not well.'

Bruce shook his head. They stared at each other for a moment and then Adam pushed the bottle of whisky towards his brother. 'Sit down and have a drink. I could do with the company.'

'Look, man, it's you I'm concerned about in all of this,' Bruce said quietly as he seated himself. 'You've got a baby on the way and the first one is never easy sailing. Women can be up and down when they're expecting, I know Phyllis was, but it doesn't mean Josie doesn't want you with her even if she's a bit difficult at times.'

'She's not, it isn't that.'

'What is it then?'

Adam waved his hand irritably. 'Can we change the subject? Things'll work out, let's leave it at that.'

'Aye, all right.' It was like getting blood out of a stone

at times with Adam, Bruce thought. He knew his brother had an aversion to illness in all its forms but pregnancy wasn't an illness, not in his book at least, though maybe Adam saw it that way? Whatever, he'd said as much as he could, which would get Phyllis off his back. She'd been nagging him to speak to Adam for days now. Changing the subject as requested, he said, 'I hear you had a spot of bother with one of the families in Silver Street, the Rileys, isn't it?'

Adam nodded, taking a slug of whisky before he said, 'It's being dealt with.'

'Oh aye?'

'I'm sending the bums in tomorrow and they'll find themselves out on the street. They gave my rent man some story about being behind with the rent because they're on their uppers but I know for a fact Riley's in work at Doxford's. They need to be taught some respect.'

Bruce nodded. When Adam had first taken over the property side of things he'd wondered if his brother would get a handle on the business and more importantly the low life they rented to, but he needn't have worried. Adam had surprised him with just how ruthless he could be.

By unspoken mutual consent the subject of Josie wasn't mentioned again, but once his brother had left, Adam sat brooding. He couldn't help how he felt since she'd become pregnant. Her present state repelled him, and he felt cheated that the lovely child-woman he had married had lost her beauty. She'd become pale and drawn and as thin as a lath. The thought of intimacy was distasteful, and why should he force himself when Ma Peabody's girls were happy to oblige? One of them had told him that they all fought over who was to service him because it wasn't often that they got young, handsome customers. He had liked that.

The leather chair was comfortable – the club provided only the best of everything for their illustrious clientele – and he shut his eyes, allowing his thoughts to wander. As though in protest to an accusing voice, he said to himself, *Josie can't complain at her lot. I took her from Long Bank, didn't I, and she's living in clover now. It takes money to dress like she does and I don't keep her short of cash. No, she can't complain.*

He opened his eyes, glancing round the elegant, wood-panelled room and the men seated at various tables and chairs. They were all from the upper echelons of society. Eustace Chapman had been in the night before and as usual the man had made a beeline for him, buying him a couple of drinks and being his obsequious self. Eustace hadn't mentioned Bernice from the day his engagement to Josie had become public knowledge, Adam thought now, and although the girl had been invited to the wedding with her parents, only Eustace and his wife had attended. No doubt the empty-headed girl imagined she was nursing a broken heart. Adam's lip curled. Women were a stupid species on the whole, intellectually and physically inferior to men and as gullible as children, which made them boring on further acquaintance. For a brief time he had imagined Josie was different.

He straightened and rose to his feet, signalling for one of the smartly uniformed staff to come and remove the partly consumed bottle of whisky and place it behind the bar under his name. He tipped the man and in spite of the amount of alcohol he'd drunk he walked steadily out of the room.

He knew which of Ma's girls he would ask for tonight, a young brunette who had recently arrived at the brothel from the country. Flora was fresh and pert and voluptuous, and not yet jaded by the life she had chosen. He had slept with her a few days ago and apart from knowing numerous tricks to make a man happy, she had made him laugh with her cheeky repartee. And he needed someone to laugh with tonight.

The summer proved to be a hot one. This didn't help Josie's condition, but by the beginning of September when the nights became cooler she began to feel more like her old self. Although the nausea reared its head now and again it wasn't so bad, and as autumn turned the trees in the garden to a vision of copper and bronze and yellow, she found the nip in the air made taking walks with Phyllis pleasurable once more.

It had become clear that Adam found the whole aspect of her condition distasteful. Even though she was feeling better he made no effort to touch her and it seemed to her that he had removed himself physically and emotionally, which she found hurtful.

Phyllis had tried to reassure her that some men were

like this and it was nothing to do with her as a person. 'They're afraid that if they – you know what – it might affect the baby,' her friend had said earnestly. 'It's daft, I know, but I bet Adam's like that. He still loves and wants you, lass.'

Josie had nodded and changed the subject, but deep inside she didn't think it was like that with Adam. To him her pregnancy presented itself as a sickness and as such he found it repellent. It had distressed her at first and as time had gone on and there had been no change in Adam she'd cried herself to sleep more than once, but of late that had changed. *She* had changed.

She was sitting in the drawing room and now she stood up and walked over to the window, looking out over the garden. It was the middle of November and as the last glories of autumn had faded the view had become bleaker as all the leaves had dropped and been cleared away. This morning, though, a heavy frost during the night had brought a glinting sparkle to the garden. She watched a fat little robin pecking at the cake crumbs that Ida had put on the bird table before it flew away into the cold blue sky.

She wished she could do that, she thought pensively. Fly far away. And then she shook her head at herself. She wouldn't want to leave her mam and her sisters. Just him. Adam.

Turning abruptly she walked back to the sofa and sat down. Phyllis was coming for coffee in a few minutes and she would be glad of the company as a distraction to her thoughts.

Staring into the dancing flames of the fire she sighed heavily. If she dwelt on it, she was actually frightened by how much her feelings had changed in the last months – but just as love begets love, maybe indifference could do the same? She had long since come to terms with the fact that Adam had hidden his heavy drinking from her before they were married, and that in itself wouldn't have been such a problem if everything else between them was all right.

She thought back to the service at St Michael's they'd attended the week before. Sadie insisted each of her sons and their families were churchgoers and as usual the McGuigans had sat together at the front of the building in the pews that were unofficially theirs. The minister had been preaching from St Matthew about the scribes and the Pharisees and she hadn't really been concentrating until something he said made her sit up and take notice. Jesus had been telling the Jewish leaders of the day what He thought of them in no uncertain terms: '"Woe unto you, scribes and Pharisees, hypocrites! for ye are like unto whited sepulchres, which indeed appear beautiful outward, but within are full of dead men's bones and of all uncleanness."'

She had glanced at Adam beside her, who had been half-asleep. That was him. He was beautiful on the outside but inside he was cruel and cold and uncaring. And then she had felt terrible for thinking such a thing in the house of God and had spent the rest of the service asking the Almighty to forgive her.

But it was true, she thought now. And this was the father of the little person inside her. She leaned back against the couch, her hand on her stomach. How could she have been so foolish as to rush into marriage like she had? She didn't know what time Adam had come up to the bedroom the night before but he'd dropped his clothes where he had stood before climbing into bed and snoring loudly within moments. This morning she had been able to smell a cheap, sickly scent emanating from the heap. It was at times like that she had to quell the urge to fly at him and rake her nails down the beautiful face.

She was brought out of her dark reflection by Ida announcing Phyllis, and once they were enjoying their coffee and a plate of Mrs Bell's shortcake she felt better. Her mam had labelled Phyllis a card and she was right, and today her sister-in-law was on top form, making her laugh until she had to beg her to stop. 'Any more and I'll be having this baby right now,' she protested, as Phyllis finished a very good impression of their mother-in-law telling the butcher boy he'd brought the wrong order. 'Although perhaps that wouldn't be a bad thing. I'm the size of a house.' Dr Preston had suspected at one point that she might be having twins but now he seemed certain there was just one baby. Sadie had taken great delight in telling her that all her boys had been whoppers, which hadn't exactly been comforting.

'You'll be fine.' Phyllis leaned forward, her face solemn now. 'I was as big as you with my first but it was all water.'

Josie nodded. Although she was apprehensive about

giving birth she was longing to meet her baby. Already she loved it beyond words. And once she'd had the child she was determined to seize the reins of her life again. She felt she'd been in limbo the past months. She knew there would be difficult decisions ahead, the main one being how she and Adam moved on in the future, but things couldn't remain as they were. Some wives might be able to turn a blind eye to their husband's infidelities but she wasn't one of them. It was at times like this that she missed Toby more than ever; she loved her mother but it was Toby who had been her rock since she was a little girl. It pained her that the police were still no nearer to bringing anyone to account for his murder, and Adam had told her that although Bruce was sure the O'Learys were behind it, there was no proof.

Once Phyllis took her leave the rest of the day passed slowly. Dinner with Adam was its normal sombre affair; he spoke little and with the memory of the smell of the sickly sweet scent still at the forefront of her mind, she spoke even less. As soon as Ida served coffee he drank his down scalding hot before standing up and saying, 'I've got business to attend to in town and no doubt you'll be asleep by the time I get back so I'll say goodnight now.'

This was the same routine as every other night but instead of replying as she usually did with a cool 'Goodnight,' she surprised him as well as herself when she said, 'The same business that left that trashy perfume on your clothes last night, I presume?'

'What?'

'You heard what I said.'

He'd gone slightly pink but his voice was cold when he growled, 'I've no idea what you are talking about. I spent the evening with Bruce at the club.'

'Then your brother's choice of scent leaves a lot to be desired.'

His eyes widened for a moment; whether at the words themselves or the quiet, contained tone in which they were spoken she didn't know. She watched his face darken and his jaw clench before he said, 'What are you suggesting?'

She actually gave a 'Huh' full of scorn which preceded her saying, 'I'm not *suggesting* anything, Adam. The time for suggestions has long since gone and we both know that. But I've had all I'm about to take. I think it would be best if you moved into one of the spare rooms and then you can come and go as you please.'

He gazed at her, utterly taken aback. He could not link the figure staring at him with such cold disdain with his pliable young wife who had chosen not to challenge him before as to his whereabouts in the evenings. And then the astonishment was replaced with fury. 'I don't answer to you or anyone else,' he bit out angrily, 'and I won't be spoken to in this way.'

Part of her was railing against herself that she had brought this out into the open before the child was born and she was fit and well again, but it had been the perfume that had done it. His clothes had stunk with it; whoever the woman was she must have been all over him, added to which she had reached the end of her tether. She hadn't planned to speak out tonight and yet when she had done so she had realized it was inevitable. She couldn't have gone on another day without doing so.

He whirled round now, marching to the door and yanking it open before banging it violently behind him. She heard him shouting something to someone in the hall and then the sound of the front door also being banged shut. A minute or two later the carriage came round from the back of the house and horses' hooves disappeared down the drive and out of earshot.

Josie felt a sickness riving her chest. She sat quite still, her coffee cup untouched. After the initial shock of the confrontation – a confrontation she knew she had brought about – she realized she didn't regret bringing things out into the open. She had told him she'd had all she was about to take and she had meant it. She had done nothing to deserve the way he was behaving. She had thought Adam was the best of the McGuigans, that he wasn't like his brothers. How could she have got it so wrong? He was worse. She couldn't imagine Bruce or David or the others treating their wives as he treated her.

She shut her eyes tightly for some moments and when she opened them she saw Ida had come quietly into the dining room and was looking at her in concern. 'Are you unwell, ma'am?'

'No, I'm quite well, thank you.' Josie took a deep breath. 'But I need your help, Ida. Leave clearing away for now and come with me.' She stood up slowly – her distended stomach prevented doing anything quickly – and led the way upstairs to the master bedroom. She had to stop at the top of the stairs and draw a deep breath before she continued along the landing. Once she had opened the door she stood for a moment, her heart thudding. What she was about to do would send Adam into the mother and father of all rages.

Was she frightened of him? The answer to this brought her soft mouth into a grim line. She would not give in to that fear.

Turning to Ida, she said, 'I'd like you to move Mr McGuigan's clothes and other personal possessions into the blue room, Ida.'

This room was almost as large as the master bedroom and had its own bathroom and dressing room. It was situated at the far end of the landing with three other smaller bedrooms between it and the master, which made it ideal.

Ida stared at her, wide-eyed. 'Everything, ma'am?'

'Yes, please, Ida. Everything.'

It took a while but eventually it was done. After the maid had disappeared to attend to her duties downstairs Josie took a leisurely bath and got ready for bed. The bulk of her stomach made sleeping difficult and for the last few weeks she'd had disturbed nights which meant she was tired from the moment she awoke in the mornings.

The last thing she did before climbing into bed was

walk across to the door and turn the key in the lock. It was strange, but all the fear had gone from her. She felt an empty coldness which bordered on numbness. She could imagine the consternation in the kitchen because Ida would have related the happenings to Mrs Bell, but it didn't bother her that they both knew although she realized it would infuriate Adam. She had been brought up in a neighbourhood where someone only had to sneeze and everyone knew about it. There had been no secrets in Long Bank and despite the grinding poverty she would give everything she possessed to turn back the clock; to be sleeping with her sisters on the mattress in the front room and know that Toby and Joe were in the kitchen. She had been happy then.

She stopped her mind from continuing down this path – it was weakening and she couldn't afford to be weak. There was a battle ahead and it would begin when Adam returned home. She didn't fool herself that by her taking this stand he would be brought up short and would see the error of his ways – he was too arrogant and self-obsessed for that. No, she had made a declaration of war with her actions tonight and he would be incandescent with rage.

In spite of being exhausted she lay wide awake once she was in bed, but rather than fretting or going over her decision she found her mind had fallen into a kind of vacuum. She waited for what was to come.

* * *

It was hours before she heard him walk up the stairs and come along the landing. She lay quite still, her hands bunched into fists by her sides, but as he tried the door handle her head lifted sharply from the pillow. He rattled it again, in frustration rather than anger, clearly thinking the door had caught for some reason. She sat up, one hand going to her throat. There was a moment's silence and then his voice came low and thick and befuddled, 'Josie? What the hell's going on? Let me in.'

Heaving herself up, she threw back the covers and padded over to the door. 'Your things are in the blue room.'

'What?'

She cleared her throat, and now her voice came stronger when she repeated, 'Your things are in the blue bedroom.'

'What are you talking about?'

'I don't want you sleeping in here.'

When he banged his fists against the door she jumped in shock, taking a step backwards. A spate of obscenities followed as he pounded once more on the wood and, terrified that the door wouldn't hold against the onslaught, she retreated further.

It was a full minute before the noise stopped abruptly and then the reason became clear when she heard him say, 'Get back downstairs, the pair of you. This is nothing to do with you.'

Ida and Mrs Bell must have come to see what was going on, she thought through the panic and fear. A woman's voice said something – she thought it was Mrs

Bell's – and then Adam bellowed, 'She's perfectly all right, damn her, and I'm not telling you again, this is none of your business.'

It was a minute or two before his voice came again and now it was low but none the less menacing as he hissed, 'You dare to treat me like this, *you*. I took you out of the gutter and gave you everything. You're nothing without me, less than nothing, just you remember that. Now open this door.'

She sank down onto the floor, her legs unable to hold her, and after a few moments there followed a mouthful of abuse, some of which she hadn't heard before, some of which she had. She felt dirty at the sound of it, dirty and ashamed, and her remaining strength leaving her she collapsed full length and lay there shivering.

When silence fell she continued to lie where she was for a little while until she realized she was frozen to the marrow and her teeth were chattering. She pulled herself up and walked over to the bed like an old woman, slipping under the covers where her feet found the stoneware hot-water bottle that Ida placed in the bed each night. Slowly the warmth permeated her flesh and she stopped shaking. She didn't try to think or reason – her mind was as exhausted and spent as her body – but as her physical comfort increased a blanket of sleep enfolded her and she went into it gratefully.

Chapter Ten

'You can't altogether blame her,' Bruce said mildly.

He had just spent the best part of ten minutes listening to his youngest brother rant and rave about his wife. Adam had arrived at the house before Phyllis and the children were even up. Bruce always rose early, winter and summer. He had never been able to sleep past six o'clock in the morning.

'*I damn well do blame her.*'

'If your clothes reeked of another woman like she said and you're out every night, she's got a point, Adam.'

'I don't believe this. So you're saying it's all right for her to lock me out of our bedroom?'

'Of course I'm not saying that. I can just see that she might have been provoked, especially in her condition.'

'*For crying out loud!*' Adam raked his hand through his hair. 'She's landed in clover, hasn't she? After the hovel she was born in she's living in a beautiful house with servants and everything a woman could want, the ungrateful slut. She ought to be down on bended knee thanking me for how different her life is. Has Phyllis ever treated you like that?' He didn't wait for an answer – the question had been rhetorical. 'No, she damn well hasn't.'

Bruce didn't point out here that any sexual diversions he indulged in were conducted discreetly without Phyllis being aware of them. Instead he took a sip of the coffee he'd got Cissy to bring through to his study when Adam had arrived, breathing fire and damnation. 'What are you going to do?'

Adam gulped at his own coffee before he said, 'If she wasn't in the family way I'd teach her a lesson she'd never forget but that'll have to wait. As it is, I'll see to it that Ida gets everything put back where it was and I'll take charge of the damn key. For two pins I'd wring her scrawny neck, I would straight.'

Bruce drained his cup and leaned back in his big leather chair, surveying his brother through narrowed eyes. He was aware of Adam's volatile temper, which had got worse in the last months, whether because of the problems in his marriage or the amount of alcohol he drank, he wasn't sure. It could be a mixture of both. Whatever, only a couple of weeks before when they'd been drinking in a pub with David and Philip, Adam had gone for a barman he imagined had slighted him. He'd smashed a bottle and driven it into the young man's face before they'd dragged him away. That little episode had cost him a pretty penny to pacify the youth in question and his father, who had wanted to get the police involved. In view of the number of witnesses at the scene it had been easier to pay the young man off rather than send in his heavies to shut their mouths. The whole incident had been in danger of getting out of hand and the last thing he wanted was the law sniffing about. Now, to Adam's surprise, he said quietly, 'Don't talk like that. She's your wife, not one of the floozies at Ma Peabody's, and she's going to have your child. Treat her with some respect.'

Adam spluttered into his coffee before snarling, 'Treat her with respect? Like she did me last night?'

'Stop and take stock and you'll see you brought that on yourself.'

'*I've had enough of this*!'

Adam leaped out of his seat but stopped in his tracks when Bruce said with deadly intent, 'Sit down.'

He hadn't raised his voice, he hadn't needed to. There were times when Bruce's cold menace was frightening and this was one of them. Sullenly Adam dropped back into his chair. 'I can't see why you are taking her side.'

Silently Bruce prayed for patience. 'Adam, you're my brother and you'll always come first with me, you know that, which is why I'm going to say this. It's to your advantage if your home is a happy one. Every man needs an oasis he can call his own, a place where he can shut the front door and expect calm and peace. Phyllis knows that's what I expect and that it is her job to provide it, and in return I treat her with courtesy and due regard.'

'And you're saying I don't do the same with Josie?'

'Do you?'

Adam shrugged sulkily.

'In a few weeks you are going to be a father and that brings different responsibilities. Perhaps now is a time to reflect on that and get your marriage on track again?'

'I won't be told what to do or where to sleep in my own house.'

'Meet her halfway, that's my advice.'

'*She locked me out of our bedroom!*' His voice was a bawl.

'So you've said, but forget that for a moment. You've told me that you've not been intimate for months. Why not let her sleep alone until after the bairn's born? It's no skin off your nose, not really. You could put it to her that because of her condition you're allowing her some privacy for the time being at the same time as reassuring her there's not another woman. Lie through your back teeth. Act the misunderstood husband.'

Adam ground his teeth. 'That's your advice, is it?'

'It's more than advice. I expect you to do as I say.'

'Now look—'

'*No,* you *look, damn you*!' Bruce's voice was like the crack of a whip and it caused Adam to visibly jump. 'I had a man murdered to clear the way for you to marry her because nothing else would do, so that gives me the right to say what I please, understand? I got stick from Mam about you taking up with Josie and it upset the apple cart in more ways than one, but you wanted her and so I got her for you. I'm blowed if all that was for nothing. You'll do as you are told now and that's my final word. Sweet-talk her – you've had plenty of practice along that line with women after all.'

Adam stared at his brother. From a child he'd rarely got on the wrong side of Bruce. But that didn't mean that deep down in his psyche he was unaware that when Bruce talked in a certain way you didn't argue. Quietly now, he muttered, 'Aye, all right.'

'Now drink your coffee.' Bruce's voice had mellowed. 'It'll all work out for the best. Trust me.'

In the hall, Phyllis straightened. She had been standing with her ear pressed to the door. On hearing voices downstairs so early in the morning she had come to see what was occurring, and recognizing one of them as Adam's, and thinking that he'd come to tell them Josie had started labour, she'd been about to knock and enter the study when she had realized an argument was going on. Curious, she'd eavesdropped, but now she wished with all her heart that she hadn't.

Trembling, she made her way upstairs again and once in her bedroom sank down on the edge of the bed, Bruce's words burning in her mind. Bruce had had Josie's brother murdered because Adam had asked him to. There was no other way she could take the conversation she had overheard. It hadn't been the O'Learys after all.

She felt ill, physically ill, and as nausea rose in her chest she swallowed hard a few times before rising and walking over to the window where she opened it and breathed in the cold frosty air. *Now that she knew, what was she going to do with the knowledge?* she asked herself. *Should she tell Josie? But how could she when Josie was so near her time? And it would be the finish of her friend's marriage for sure.*

Leaving the window open, she sank down into one of the small velvet armchairs either side of the bay, her head spinning. Adam didn't love Josie, he couldn't or he wouldn't have instigated such a terrible thing. He must have known how much Josie thought about her brother; even now her eyes filled with tears whenever she mentioned him.

She shivered violently, although the chill was less to do with the icy air flooding the room and more because of her thoughts.

It was a full ten minutes before she shut the window and by then she was frozen to the marrow, her teeth chattering. She had known what Bruce was when she had married him, but suddenly the dark, frightening side of her husband had come to the fore like never before.

She couldn't tell Josie what she knew before the bairn was born; if it caused a miscarriage she would never forgive herself. And should she tell her at all? She didn't know. She put her cold hands over her face, moaning softly. Would she want to know in similar circumstances? The deed was done, there was no going back, and very soon there would be a bairn in the equation. But how could she *not* tell her?

By the time Phyllis had washed her face and tidied herself she'd come to a decision of sorts. She could do nothing until the safe arrival of Josie's baby and so that gave her time to think. Perhaps the way ahead would become obvious then. But one thing had become crystal clear; knowing or not knowing, her friend was going to need her in the days and weeks and months ahead. Bad as Bruce undoubtedly was, he wasn't a patch on Adam.

When Josie awoke she lay quietly for some time with her eyes closed, her mind blank with tiredness. She could tell it was still early – it was dark outside – and at some point she must have dozed off again because when a knock sounded at the bedroom door she came to with a start. As the events of the night before flooded in, it was a relief when she heard Ida's voice saying, 'Ma'am? I've brought you a cup of tea.'

Josie swung her legs out of bed and after putting on her dressing gown she padded over to the door and unlocked it.

'Are you all right, ma'am?' Ida said solicitously, her pleasant round face anxious.

Josie didn't answer this directly. What she did say was, 'What time is it?'

'Past ten o'clock, ma'am. I was going to wake you earlier but Cook said you might need the rest what with the baby and all.' Ida hesitated and then added, 'The master left hours ago, ma'am.'

Josie nodded and as her body seemed to deflate she realized she'd been holding herself rigid. 'Thank you, Ida.'

'Cook says would you like a tray up here, ma'am?'

'No, I'll come downstairs shortly but just tea and toast today.'

'Yes, ma'am.'

Once Ida had left she walked across to the window and drank the tea looking out over the grounds. The weather had changed and the sky was heavy and overcast with a few snowflakes drifting in the wind. It was going to be a long hard winter.

The thought brought her chin up and her back straightened. 'One day at a time,' she murmured to herself. 'You will get through this one day at a time.'

She spent most of the morning in the room they'd designated as the nursery. She'd had it decorated in a pale yellow and cream with a children's wallpaper on the walls and bright lemon curtains. The crib was already made up for its occupant and the chest of drawers was full of baby clothes. She sat in the nursing chair for some time looking about her. It was a beautiful room for her son or daughter, she thought sadly, but the delight it had once caused had faded over the last weeks and months. She would have been satisfied living in a little two-up two-down terrace if she was bringing her child into a home where love reigned. She had made such a mess of things.

Phyllis called by for tea and cake in the afternoon but she mentioned nothing of what had occurred the night before. It was still too raw to discuss, besides which Phyllis hadn't seemed herself; she'd been preoccupied and quiet and had only stayed an hour.

It began to snow in earnest towards evening and she was seated in front of a roaring fire in the drawing room when she heard Adam's voice in the hall. She stiffened, her heart racing and her throat dry as she waited for the door to open.

He entered the room quietly and as she raised her head and looked at him they stared at each other for a long moment. He was the first to speak. 'How have you been today?' he asked softly.

She blinked. He didn't normally enquire after her well-being. 'Fine, thank you.'

'Good, good.' Her voice had been cool and immediately his temper flared but he warned himself to go steady. He'd mulled over the conversation with Bruce all day and had come to the conclusion he would do as his brother had ordered. Certainly until the child was born. 'I think we need to have a talk,' he said gently as he sat down opposite her, holding out his hands to the fire.

When she made no comment he sighed, before saying, 'You seem to be under the misapprehension that I have been unfaithful to you.'

'*Don't.*' He actually jumped, so sharp was her voice. 'Don't lie to me on top of everything else, Adam. You've barely been here for months and you come home in the early hours stinking of drink and' – her breath caught in her throat – 'another woman.'

'You've got this all wrong.' He had rehearsed what he was going to say all afternoon and now the words came pat as he stared earnestly into her face. 'Yes, I've behaved badly, I know that, with the drinking and leaving you every evening, but to be truthful I've been scared what will happen when you have the baby. You hear such things about childbirth and I don't want to lose you. Every time I've looked at you your changing shape reminds me of what could happen and so I've tried to block it out and the best way to do that was to absent myself. Foolish, I know.'

He paused, but when her expression didn't change and she made no move towards him, he continued, 'But I swear to you on our baby's life I haven't been with another woman. I can understand your suspicions—'

'Adam—'

'No, listen to me, my darling.' He had become the young ardent suitor of their courting days, his voice soft and husky with emotion and his dark eyes like melted chocolate. 'I admit I've frequented public houses most nights when I wasn't at the club and some of them have women who ply their trade there. You know what it's like at the Fiddler's Elbow – these women will come and drape themselves over you and even try and sit on your lap. The dockside dollies have no shame. But I promise you they hold no interest for me.' He forced an expression of distaste onto his face. 'How could they when at home I have you, pure and good and sweet? Why would I endanger everything we have by going with such scum? Part of my drinking was to quell my natural desires until we could come together again as man and wife.'

'I – I wouldn't have refused you.'

Lowering his head, he said on a groan, 'Oh, my love, don't you understand? I couldn't. I've been in hell, a hell of my own making, I know that, but until the child is born and I know you are all right . . .' Gauging the time was right, he rose from his chair and dropped down by the side of hers, taking her hands in his as he pleaded, 'You're all I ever wanted, Josie. You must believe me. I know I'm far from perfect and the biggest fool in God's kingdom but one thing I would never do is to betray our marriage vows. You must believe me,' he added, forcing a sob into his voice.

Josie's lips were trembling. Part of her wanted to believe him but the other, the newborn part that had emerged over the last months, was more wary.

'I was angry last night,' he said after a moment, 'but now I'm glad you did what you did. It forced me to take stock and realize I had to speak to you, to explain. I don't expect to come back into our bedroom, in fact I think I should stay where I am until the child's born – you'll sleep better – but I need things to be right between us. Are they?'

Withdrawing her hands from his, she eased herself out of the chair. Once she was standing he also rose to his feet and said quietly, 'Well?' He was amazed at her response; he'd expected to have her eating out of his hand by now.

There was a long pause before she spoke and when she did her voice was low and level. 'I can't turn my feelings on and off, Adam, and I've been very hurt by the way you've been. But you know that. You'll have to give me time to – to believe you again.'

'How much time?'

'I don't know but I agree it's better if you continue to sleep in the blue room.'

He gazed at her, his lips slightly apart and his handsome face expressionless.

It was at that moment that Ida knocked on the door and put her head round it to say, 'Dinner's ready, sir, ma'am,' before scuttling ahead to the dining room. As she said to her aunt later that evening, 'They might not be shouting and carrying on again but whatever's happened, it's not over.'

Chapter Eleven

For the last weeks of her pregnancy, Josie felt slightly unwell. Whether this was because the baby had caused her stomach to become as tight as a drum and was taking all the room inside her causing her to lose her appetite and making sleep nigh on impossible, or more because of her uncertain frame of mind regarding Adam, she didn't know. It was probably a combination of all those things. Adam now stayed in each night and they sat together in the drawing room after dinner until Josie retired, whereupon she knew he remained downstairs drinking for some time before going to bed himself. He was attentive and charming and solicitous of her welfare and sometimes she almost believed everything he had said that night. Almost.

Her mother and Phyllis were regular visitors to the house and sometimes her sisters came for a while but other than them she saw no one apart from the midwife and doctor. The month of December was one of thick snow and bitter winds and she had no desire to even take a ride in the carriage, which she'd been in the habit of doing. She'd called to see the Mullens several mornings since her pregnancy even though she knew Adam didn't like it, but through December she became like a dormouse in its nest.

It was three days before Christmas when the backache she had been experiencing all night and into the morning moved to her stomach and she had her first definite pains. She had been sitting in front of the fire in the drawing room dozing on and off after another sleepless night, but as she awoke she gasped for air as her stomach cramped.

During the next hour she had several more contractions, and when she rang the bell and told Ida the midwife needed to be sent for and to let her mother and Phyllis know the baby was on the way, the maid's composure deserted her. Mrs Bell came scurrying from the kitchen to sit with Josie, but it was only after Ida had left that Josie realized she had said nothing about notifying Adam. However Mrs Fletcher, the midwife, had warned her several times that first labours were usually long affairs and so she decided there was no need to bother him anyway.

The midwife, along with Josie's mother and Phyllis, were with her when Adam walked into the house later that evening. He immediately became the epitome of loving concern, and when Mrs Fletcher suggested Josie might be more comfortable in bed, he insisted on gathering his wife into his arms and carrying her upstairs despite her protests that she could walk. After that Mrs Fletcher shooed him away, saying this was women's work and men only got in the way.

Dr Preston called at the house after evening surgery. He had confided in the past to Mrs Fletcher that he was anxious about the size of the baby with the patient being so young and slender, but after examining Josie he declared himself satisfied that things were progressing as they should. 'Mrs Fletcher will look after you, m'dear,' he smiled, patting Josie's hand, 'and should I be needed she will let me know.'

Josie nodded. The sickness she had experienced in the first months had returned with a vengeance and she didn't feel much like talking.

The night proved to be a long one and at daybreak Josie sent her mother home to see to the girls. Maggie protested at first, but when Mrs Fletcher told her it could be another few hours she reluctantly left the house saying she'd be back shortly. Adam had spent the evening working through a bottle of whisky and then snoring his head off in the blue bedroom. He came to see her briefly on his way down to breakfast but couldn't get out of the room quick enough when Josie experienced a contraction.

By mid-morning when Maggie returned, the pains were coming thick and fast. Mrs Fletcher was confident the birth was imminent. Josie hoped so. The pain was excruciating and she was exhausted.

At one o'clock in the afternoon Dr Preston was summoned. After examining the patient he announced that something needed to be done immediately if they weren't going to lose both mother and child. Josie couldn't be moved, but a Caesarean section was the only viable answer. To that end, the doctor, Adam and Shelton carried the kitchen table into the bedroom. Ida brought dishes of hot water and towels and Adam took Maggie, who was in a state of collapse, downstairs with him. Mrs Fletcher and Phyllis prepared to assist Dr Preston.

The good doctor was just about to administer the chloroform to his patient when Josie gave a mighty groan and a strong-limbed and -lunged male child shot out from between her legs. 'Like a cork out of a bottle,' Phyllis told Bruce later.

The next minutes were ones of controlled panic, but by the time Phyllis went downstairs to fetch Adam, Josie was in a clean bed and nightdress holding her son, who was – as Sadie would have said – a whopper.

Adam entered the room apprehensively. He'd spent the morning drinking coffee heavily laced with brandy in an attempt to block out what was happening upstairs. The two or three minutes he had spent in the bedroom with Josie that morning had been enough to horrify him. He wasn't sure what he expected to see when he looked towards the bed. The Josie of that morning had been a writhing sweating figure with a red face and damp hair which had repelled him. Now she was attired in a lacy lawn nightdress, her hair brushed and tied loosely with a ribbon and a radiant smile on her face. She was holding what he could only describe as a miniature version of himself. Bruce had warned him that all babies were red and ugly when they were born – like skinned rabbits, his brother had said – but the child in Josie's arms was beautiful.

His eyes fixed on the baby, he approached the bed virtually on tiptoe, captivated by his son, and it was Dr Preston who said what everyone was thinking, 'Like father, like son. He's the very image of you, lad,' as he clapped the new father on his back and offered his congratulations.

The doctor and midwife, along with Phyllis, left the room, Phyllis saying over her shoulder, 'Your mam'll want to come up in a few minutes, lass.'

Adam didn't even hear her or realize they'd gone. His whole being was wrapped up in the infant, and when Josie said, 'Do you want to hold him?' he couldn't speak, merely nodding as the tears poured down his face. He took the baby reverently, staring down into the small face topped with a mass of curly black hair as he sat beside Josie.

His obvious wonderment melted Josie's heart. She had hoped he would be pleased they had a healthy strong child but she hadn't expected anything like this. Softly, she murmured, 'Isn't he beautiful?'

He had to swallow hard before he could say, 'The most beautiful sight I've ever seen.' He tore his eyes away from the little face, smiling at her as he said, 'Thank you, my darling, thank you for giving me my son. I love you so much.'

And Josie found herself saying words she'd never imagined she would say again: 'I love you too.'

'We'll call him Luke, after my father. Luke Adam.' He cradled the baby in his arms, who was now fast asleep, exhausted by his fight into the world.

For a moment Josie's smile dimmed. She'd been going to suggest they name him Toby, if not for the first name then the second, but she brushed the thought aside for now. They could discuss names later. Their baby was here, safe and healthy, and she and Adam were all right again. A child's birth was always a miracle but she felt as though more than one miracle had taken place today and she thanked God for it.

Relaxing against Adam she put her head on his shoulder as they gazed down at their son, and they were still like that some minutes later when Maggie came to see her first grandchild.

For the next little while Adam was everything Josie could have wished for. That Luke was the joy of his father's heart was plain for everyone to see and Adam made no apology for being completely besotted with his son. He moved back into the master bedroom even though she had Luke's crib at the side of the bed so she could feed him easily in the night, and consequently woke Adam three or four times. Probably due to his size the baby was constantly hungry and only slept a couple of hours between feeds, but rather than objecting to their broken nights Adam would bill and coo over his son while she fed him. The whole atmosphere of the house was different and as far as she was aware Adam had remained sober since the child's birth.

One fly in the ointment was that Sadie was constantly on the doorstep these days and as time went on it tested

Josie's patience. Her mother-in-law had no compunction about interfering in the baby's care and was full of 'good' suggestions, and when Josie raised the matter with Adam she was upset at his response. He was of the opinion that it was perfectly natural for his mother to take such an interest in his first child and furthermore, he told Josie, she ought to be grateful for Sadie's help and advice. It didn't help that she'd overheard Adam and his mother discussing possible schools for Luke too, something he hadn't mentioned to her, and already Adam and Bruce were talking about where the child would fit into the family empire. Part of her felt it was ridiculous to think about such matters when the baby was only weeks old, but it began to cause a growing apprehension about the future. It seemed as if the McGuigans were claiming Luke in body, soul and spirit.

Today, though, it had been Luke's christening service at St Michael's and she had tried to put any fears to the back of her mind. It was the second Sunday in March but the harsh northern winter showed no signs of loosening its grip. Sleet and snow blown into a mad frenzy by the bitterly cold wind had made the journey to and from the church into something of an ordeal, but now inside the house it was as warm as toast.

Plenty of Adam's friends and business associates had come back to the house along with family for the reception, and Mrs Bell had been baking for days. The table in the dining room was positively groaning under the weight of food and the drink was flowing freely.

Josie had insisted on inviting the Mullens even though Adam had protested, but as he'd got his way over having Bruce and Phyllis as godparents she didn't feel he had cause for complaint.

Josie looked across the drawing room to where Phyllis was chatting with Ada Mullen and her daughters. She couldn't rid herself of the feeling that there was something wrong with her friend, although when she'd broached the subject several times Phyllis had said all was well. Her gaze travelled round the other guests and as she watched she saw Sadie sail up to her mother, who was holding Luke, and whisk the baby out of Maggie's arms.

Suddenly she felt so angry she fairly flew across the room. Her mother-in-law had monopolized the baby all afternoon. Past niceties of thought or action, Josie in her turn snatched the child out of Sadie's arms, glaring at her as she said, 'He's due for a feed.' Turning to her mother, she added, 'Come on, Mam, come up to the nursery with me.' Luke was now sleeping in his own room as he'd been going through the night for a week or two. 'You'll be able to have a proper cuddle with him up there.'

Once upstairs Josie shut the door to the nursery and let a long-drawn breath out before she said, 'I'm sorry, Mam, but that woman is driving me round the bend. Here' – she handed her the baby, who had slept through the whole incident – 'sit down and hold him for a while. I saw her take him from you.'

Maggie did as she was bid but her voice was hesitant when she said, 'She won't like what you did down there.'

'No, I don't suppose she will.'

'Sadie McGuigan is not someone to cross, lass.'

'Mam, I'm fed up with her and the lot of them, truth be told, apart from Phyllis of course. They think they have the right to tell me what to do and dictate—' She stopped abruptly. 'I'm Luke's mam,' she said flatly, stating the obvious.

Maggie rocked the sleeping baby as she stared into her daughter's face. 'What's the matter, lass?'

Josie shrugged. Her mother wouldn't understand, she thought miserably. She was always full of how wonderful it was that she'd married into wealth and had such a lovely house and so on, and according to her Adam was the bee's knees. 'I just want a say in how my son is brought up,' she said after a long moment. 'That's all.'

'He's a McGuigan,' Maggie said softly.

'Meaning what?'

'Lass, you knew what the family were like when you married Adam, didn't you?'

'Not really, not properly, and I thought Adam was different.' She pressed her lips together, closed her eyes and shook her head for a moment before she said, 'And he can be, he can be lovely, but—'

'But what?'

'He – he was seeing someone else, perhaps more than one woman, when I was pregnant, Mam, I know he was. He denies it but—'

'You don't believe him?'

'No, I don't. I've tried to make myself but at bottom,

no, I don't. And then when Luke was born he was the old Adam again, like when we were courting, and he still is for most of the time.' She took a deep breath. 'But more and more I can see that as far as he's concerned Luke is his son, not mine. He's planning out Luke's future with his mother and Bruce and the rest of them and I don't want—' She paused again. 'I don't want Luke to be like them.'

'Oh, lass.'

The two words were full of fear for her, and Josie's instinct was to reassure her mother by saying everything would be all right, but she couldn't. Something had happened in her when she had seen Sadie snatch Luke. It had been like she'd had a glimpse of the future and she couldn't shut her eyes to the way things would be if she didn't do something about it now. The McGuigan menfolk were violent and ruthless – gangsters by any other name – and Adam was no different to his brothers.

Maggie stared at her daughter. She had known Josie was unhappy long before the baby was born but she had hoped whatever was wrong would blow over. Men, especially those with money like the McGuigans, often had a bit on the side at various times in their lives but if you were in clover like Josie you could afford to turn a blind eye to any dalliances, couldn't you? It was a woman's lot to swallow your pride. And all this about the McGuigans controlling what would happen with Luke in the future, well, it was always going to be that way. The McGuigans were the McGuigans. Josie would have to accept the inevitable and the sooner she realized that the better. Quietly, she said, 'Listen to me, hinny. You've just had a babby and you aren't thinking straight. You're Adam's wife and Luke is his son and he's got every right to do what he thinks is best for the boy, any court in the land would say so. And the McGuigans are dangerous, don't forget that. They have money and influence and power. Maybe Adam is different to the rest of them like we thought and maybe he isn't, but what's done is done. You have to make the best of it.'

'And what if I can't?'

Maggie looked down at the sleeping baby. 'Do you want to lose him? Because if it came to it and you went up against his father you wouldn't win, lass. Not in a month of Sundays.'

Josie's voice expressed a wealth of hurt when she said, 'You still think Adam is wonderful, don't you.'

'Truthfully? No, lass, I don't, but there's a lot worse than him too. I thought he was going to make you happy and I'm sorry you're not, to the heart of me I am, but he's your husband and your place is here, in your home, making it as nice for him and any bairns you have as you can. If you're canny you'll manage him and his mam and the rest of them, find a way to steer through. He loves you, lass. You know that.'

She had known her mam wouldn't understand.

Their glances held for some moments before Maggie said softly, 'It's you I'm thinking of, hinny, not Adam or his mam and not even my grandson. You could wind

Adam round your little finger if you tried. You're young and beautiful and as bright as a button up top. Luke and any other bairns you have will have the best of everything, not like the majority round here, and if he steps into a ready-made future where everything's handed to him on a plate, is that really so bad? Toby and Joe were out working when they were knee high to a grasshopper with no schooling to speak of and your da taking every penny they earned, and there was you singing in the pubs from a little bairn.'

'I know, Mam, I know.'

'Just count your blessings, that's what I'm saying. You are still at the beginning of your life really and there will be other trials ahead of you no doubt, but learn which battles to fight and which to ignore.'

Josie kneeled down by the chair and put her arms round her mother, the baby snuggled between them. Her mam had struggled with poverty all her life and on top of that she'd had her da to contend with, she thought remorsefully. She shouldn't have worried her with how she was feeling. Like her mam had suggested, she had to find her own way to negotiate the months and years ahead. And she would.

'I love you, Mam,' she said quietly.

'And I love you, me bairn.'

Chapter Twelve

Which battles to fight and which to ignore. Josie thought about her mother's advice more than once over the following weeks and accepted the wisdom behind it. She had a firm but courteous chat with Sadie, designating certain afternoons each week when Adam's mother would be welcome to call. It was still too often if she was being honest, as she remarked to Phyllis, but she felt it was a compromise. They saw Adam's family every Saturday evening for dinner at one or another of their houses, and after church each Sunday everyone congregated at Sadie's for Sunday lunch and tea, so she didn't feel her mother-in-law was hard done by. Adam didn't mention the new arrangement so whether Sadie had brought it up with him she didn't know, but as a cold March gave way to the inconsistent weather of April Josie had other things to think about. Adam had begun to drink again.

Now that Luke was sleeping in the nursery their intimacy had once again become a regular occurrence and she had thought that it satisfied him. She enjoyed their lovemaking and never refused him, but once or twice when he had been out late, allegedly with his brothers, he had come home in the early hours drunk and she was sure she could smell that same cheap scent on his clothes. She didn't want to accuse him of seeing someone else again – she had hoped that period of their married life was behind them even though she had never got to the bottom of what he was doing – but then one night in the third week of April Adam didn't get in till gone four in the morning. He was swearing and falling over as he undressed before flinging himself on the bed and snoring fit to wake the dead, and again the faint perfume she could detect emanating from his clothes and person wasn't hers. Suddenly she felt as though she was right back to those awful days before Luke had been born.

She lay awake for the rest of the night trying to convince herself that she was imagining she could smell something. She didn't want to be the sort of jealous wife who drove her husband into the arms of other women, after all. Eventually she decided to say nothing, but two weeks later the same thing happened and this time she was sure. In the row that followed Adam hotly denied any wrong-doing and assumed the role of the injured party so convincingly she began to doubt herself. He came home the next evening with a huge bouquet of flowers, full of apologies for getting drunk, but again assured her that he had been with his brothers the whole time. He promised her he would stop drinking, told her that she and Luke were the only things in the world that really mattered to him, and that night made love to her in their big bed so tenderly she felt guilty for her distrust. The promise to curb his drinking lasted a week.

It was towards the end of June, when the meadows were thickly adorned with the white flowerheads of clover and forget-me-nots, and wild flowers covered the banks beneath lush hedgerows, that things came to a head. Luke was now six months old and although normally a happy and contented baby had been fractious all day. He was teething, and when Adam arrived home didn't want to go to his father, which was unusual. It was clear to Josie that Adam was irritated with the incessant grizzling by the time she took the baby upstairs for his last feed, and when at last Luke was asleep and she came down again, Adam scowled at her as she walked into the drawing room where he was sitting drinking brandy. 'What the hell is the matter with him?' he asked aggressively.

'I told you, he's teething. It's completely natural.'

'He was up countless times last night.'

Josie didn't point out that it was she who'd gone into the nursery each time while Adam had turned over in bed and gone straight back to sleep. 'Some children teeth hard.'

'He seems to settle all right when *you* have him.'

There had been a peevish note in his voice and suddenly she understood why he was disgruntled. He was jealous; jealous that Luke instinctively wanted her when he was in pain. Keeping her voice expressionless, she said coolly, 'Not really. He has been difficult all day and the hot weather doesn't help.'

'He's relying on you too much, it's not healthy. You need to take him round to my mother's more often and leave him with her. She'll know how to handle him.'

Over her dead body. 'I'll think about it.'

'Do it, Josie. Don't think about it,' he said tightly.

Any reply she might have made was prevented by Ida putting her head round the door to say dinner was ready. The meal was conducted in silence; she tried to make conversation a few times and then gave up. He was clearly in a foul mood.

Once they had eaten and before Ida brought coffee, he stood up. 'I'm going into town.'

Josie nodded. It was useless to protest and when he was like this she didn't want his company anyway.

He glared at her and his tone was confrontational when he growled, 'There's going to be some changes made here.'

'Oh, yes?' She raised her eyebrows.

'I'm not having my son grow into a milksop.'

She stared at him, taken aback. 'What on earth are you talking about, Adam? He's six months old. He's a baby.'

'I know how old he is, dammit.'

'Then you must realize you're being ridiculous.'

'Don't you dare take that tone with me. I'm your husband and don't you forget it.'

Josie was about to fire back at him when she wondered how many glasses of brandy he'd consumed while she had been upstairs putting Luke to bed. He had finished the decanter of wine during their evening meal too. Aiming to pour oil on troubled waters, she said quietly, 'Don't let's argue, Adam. Do you have to leave immediately? Can't we have coffee and talk this over?'

'There's nothing to talk over. I'm master in my own home and my son will be raised as I see fit. Do you understand that?' He took a step towards her, his manner threatening. 'Do you understand?'

She didn't reply, standing straight and stiff as she rose to her feet and faced him although her stomach was churning.

It was a full ten seconds before he made a sound deep in his throat and swung on his heel, leaving the room and banging the door behind him. She stood exactly where she was until she heard the carriage outside and then the sound of it disappearing down the drive. A moment later Ida came in with the tray of coffee.

At eleven o'clock she told Ida and Mrs Bell to go to bed. She always did this when Adam was out in the evening; she didn't see why they should have to wait up until he was back.

After a day of grizzling and crying Luke now seemed to be sleeping soundly when she looked in on him. She stood by the side of the ornate and beautifully carved wooden cot that Sadie had bought when Luke was born looking down at the baby. His little face was flushed and one small fist was tucked under his chin, his black curls falling across the downy forehead. She loved him so much it was a physical pain, and again fear for his future rose up, causing tears to prick at the backs of her eyes.

She stood for nearly an hour watching him sleep, her thoughts tossed in a sea of uncertainty and anxiety. She wanted to protect him from anything that might harm him or mar his mind in the years ahead, but how could she when the threat was within his own family? She'd been so gullible, so stupid, so beguiled by Adam Mc-Guigan. Even after Luke was born and he had seemed to revert to the old Adam once more she had wanted to believe him and trust it was genuine, that their marriage could flourish. But the real Adam, the Adam she had seen again tonight, was a McGuigan through and through.

At midnight she slowly got ready for bed but sat in a chair in the bay of the window looking out over the sleeping garden. Apart from the occasional hoot of an owl all was quiet and peaceful, the antithesis of how she was feeling inside.

After a while her tired mind sought refuge in a kind of numbness but she felt no inclination to go to bed. One o'clock, then two o'clock and three o'clock came and went, and it was getting on for four in the morning when she heard Adam come home. She sat quite still in the darkness and as he opened the bedroom door and stumbled into the room he brought a strong smell of alcohol and a sickly sweet perfume with him.

He began to divest himself of his clothes where he stood in the middle of the room, and when she spoke he visibly jumped. 'I'm surprised you bothered to come home at all. Another two or three hours and you could have gone straight to the office.'

He peered at the outline of her silhouetted against the dim light coming from the window and his voice was thick and slurred when he mumbled, 'Mind your tongue.'

'Mind my tongue?' She stood up, drawing her dressing gown more tightly round her. 'You come back stinking, yes, *stinking* of some floozy and you tell me to mind my tongue? You're disgusting, do you know that? I thought you were different to your brothers and you are – you're a hundred times worse than them. Not one of your brothers would treat their wives the way you treat me.'

'The way I treat you?' He gave a hic of a laugh. 'You've never had it so good.'

'You've been with a woman tonight and not for the first time since we've been married. I've had enough of your lies.'

'So what if I have? That's my business.'

'Your business?' she said incredulously.

'When I bought the marriage certificate I bought you, get that into your stupid little head. I own you. I took you out of the sewer you were living in and gave you everything so don't come whining to me about what I do.' His voice was rising. 'You ought to be down on your knees thanking me for what I've given you.'

'You didn't buy me, Adam, whatever you think.' He had made her angry before but never like this. 'And you don't own me. You will never own me. I am going to leave you and whatever you and the rest of your family do, I won't come back.'

'The hell you won't.' His voice was a snarl. 'You're nothing without me.'

'And what are you? A drunkard and a womanizer and more besides. This is the real you tonight, isn't it. The drink strips away the mask you wear when it suits you, that of the charming, handsome Adam McGuigan. I see that now. And you're right, I have been stupid – about you. But no more. My eyes are well and truly open and I'm not having my son brought up in the shadow of your family. Luke will come with me.'

He moved with a swiftness that belied his drunken state, slapping her across the face with such force her head jerked like a puppet's. For a moment she was too stunned with shock to respond, but then she fought back, tearing at his face with her nails as she tried to free herself from his grasp.

Swearing and cursing, he doubled his fist and levelled it at her and but for her jerking her head it would have smashed her nose for sure. As it was, the blow caught the side of her head, sending her off balance. As she fell, Adam went down with her, landing on top of her and knocking the wind out of her chest. Then he was tearing at her nightclothes like a madman, his drunken breath in her face as he hissed, 'You need to be taught a lesson, damn you, a lesson in respect.'

Dazed and struggling to breathe, she was aware of him forcing her legs apart but his closeness brought the smell of the woman he'd been with to the fore. He was preparing to thrust himself into her and had raised himself slightly, but the surge of strength the odour had brought enabled her to push him as hard as she could, at the same time as twisting away beneath him. Taken off guard he fell backwards and she clambered away on all fours before scrambling to her feet. As she reached the bedroom door and flung it open he came at her again and they both stumbled, fighting, onto the landing.

She was never very sure what happened next. One moment they were grappling with each other and he had hold of her upper arms and the next Adam was teetering at the top of the steep stairs. Panic flashed across his face and then he fell backwards with a high-pitched scream, his arms and legs flailing as he thudded over and over to land in a sprawled heap in the hall.

Josie stood poised to take flight if he got to his feet but when he remained still and silent she moved cautiously down the stairs, ready to fly back up if it was a trick. She reached the hall as first Mrs Bell and then Ida came running from their quarters. As they joined her, Mrs Bell looked in horror at the figure at the bottom of the stairs. 'Oh, ma'am, what on earth's happened?' And then she took in Josie's torn nightdress gaping open and showing bloodied scratches on her breasts.

'He – he attacked me.' Josie was holding on to the wooden banister for support. 'He – he's drunk.'

Mrs Bell kneeled down and felt for a pulse and as she looked up and said, 'He's alive, ma'am,' Adam groaned.

Unable to think, Josie stared helplessly at the cook and Edith realized she was in shock. Standing up, she turned to Ida, who was standing white-faced beside her with her hand over her mouth. 'Go and get dressed and fetch Mr Bruce. Tell 'em Mr McGuigan's fallen down the stairs and we need help.' Slipping off her dressing gown to reveal her pink flannelette nightdress, she slipped the robe around her young mistress. 'Here, lass,' she murmured, formality going out of the window, 'come and sit down a minute.'

'I – he—' Josie was shaking from head to foot, staring at Adam. 'He fell . . .'

'Come on, hinny.' Edith helped her put her arms through the dressing gown and then fastened the cord round her waist, leading her into the drawing room as she said, 'You sit down a minute and I'll get a blanket to put over the master, all right? Ida'll go for Mr Bruce. He'll know what to do.'

Josie sat in numb disbelief at what had happened until Mrs Bell returned with a coat over her nightdress and holding a glass of brandy. 'Get this down you, ma'am,' she said. 'You're in shock and no wonder. What a to-do. I've covered the master up and he's unconscious but breathing. I'm sure he'll be all right,' she added somewhat lamely.

Josie took the brandy but the first sip made her cough and splutter. Her eyes streaming, she tried to hand it back to the cook.

'Drink it, ma'am, all of it,' Mrs Bell insisted. 'It'll clear your head and you need to think about what you're going to say to the master's brother. And ma'am' – Mrs Bell's voice dropped to a whisper although it was only the two of them in the room – 'if anyone asks, I shall say I saw it all and it was an accident. The master had been drinking and causing a carry-on and I came to see what was what and I saw him fall.'

The cook's meaning was clear and as Josie stared into the concerned eyes, it dawned on her that if Adam died the McGuigans would hold her to blame. 'I didn't push him, Mrs Bell,' she whispered back. 'He – he attacked me and I was trying to get away and he fell. I don't know how.'

Edith nodded. The master was a devil, that was the truth of it, she thought vehemently. Carrying on like he had when the mistress was expecting the babby; hardly ever here and drinking himself senseless, and then starting his old games again the last few weeks. She'd thought having a son and the master being fair barmy over the lad would put things to rights but there, a dog always returns to its vomit, as her old mam used to say. 'I believe you, ma'am,' she said gently, 'but it won't do no harm to have someone back you up, it being the McGuigans, if you get my meaning?'

Oh, yes, Josie thought. *She got Mrs Bell's meaning.* She thought of Luke fast asleep upstairs and a shiver snaked down her spine. Finishing the brandy in a couple of gulps, she rose to her feet and walked through to the hall. The neat alcohol had stopped the shaking and now she kneeled down by Adam's head. As she did so his eyes flickered but he didn't open them, merely emitting a gurgling groan before becoming silent again. She drew down the blanket Mrs Bell had covered him with to see if there was any blood visible but it appeared not. He had clearly banged his head and his legs were at an unnatural angle but she didn't dare to try and straighten them in case it was the wrong thing to do. Pulling the blanket up again she found that tears were trickling down her face, but whether they were for Adam or the situation or even herself she didn't know.

Chapter Thirteen

It was two days before Adam regained consciousness. He had been taken to the Sunderland Hospital and his mother had insisted on sitting by his bedside night and day in spite of the matron attempting to insist Sadie kept to visiting hours. When Josie had gone in her mother-in-law had made it very clear she was tolerating her under sufferance and had barely spoken a word.

Once Adam was awake he was still far from being compos mentis. He didn't seem to be aware of where he was but accepted his mother's ministrations without protest. Sadie would arrive at the hospital early in the morning to feed him his breakfast and wouldn't leave until late at night, refusing to let the nurses give him his meals or wash him down, doing this herself. She upset all the staff but she didn't care.

The doctors had ascertained that he had damaged his spine in the fall, how badly they weren't sure but they kept him lying flat. Bruce had arranged for an eminent consultant from London to come and see him once it became clear Adam couldn't move his legs. He had no feeling from the waist down.

It was a week after he was admitted and on the same day that the London consultant confirmed Adam's back was broken that he became more alert and responsive. Josie hadn't been to the hospital that day – Luke had diarrhoea and sickness and the medical staff had told her they didn't want her carrying infection to the patient. It was early the following morning that Phyllis came knocking at the front door.

Josie was just carrying Luke downstairs when Ida opened the front door, and the moment she saw her sister-in-law's face her stomach turned over. 'What is it? What's happened? Is he worse?' she said, as Phyllis followed her into the dining room where Ida had laid the breakfast table and positioned Luke's highchair ready for him to eat.

Phyllis didn't reply to this, gesturing at Luke as she said, 'How is he? Any better?'

'Much, thank goodness. He slept all night and seems hungry this morning.' Josie settled the baby in his highchair with a hard rusk to gnaw on, and then poured a cup of tea for herself and Phyllis before she sat down. 'Well?' she said apprehensively. 'What is it?'

'Adam's properly back in the land of the living.' Phyllis looked Josie straight in the eye. 'He said you were fighting when he fell down the stairs.' She paused. 'Actually, he said you pushed him, lass.' Josie had told the family that she and Adam had been having an argument about his drinking and coming home at all hours, but nothing else.

'I didn't push him, Phyllis,' she said, shocked. 'He attacked me in our bedroom when he lost his temper and I managed to get onto the landing when he came at me again. He was drunk and unsteady on his feet and he fell down the stairs, that's the truth.' She took a deep breath. 'He'd been with another woman, that's what we were fighting about. It – it wasn't the first time.'

'Oh, lass.'

The sympathy in her sister-in-law's voice was nearly Josie's undoing, making her want to howl her distress. 'He – he got into a rage when I confronted him about it.' She had to wet her lips before she said, 'He tried to force himself on me.'

Again Phyllis murmured, 'Oh, lass.'

'So he's told the family that I pushed him? On purpose?'

Phyllis nodded. 'And he was in his right mind when he said it, Bruce told me. You can imagine Sadie's reaction. There's something else too. He – he won't walk again. He was demented when they broke the news to him.'

Josie was as white as a sheet. 'I didn't push him,' she said again. 'Mrs Bell will verify that.'

'Did she see it happen?'

'She'll say she did.'

Phyllis understood immediately. She took a sip of her tea. 'Look, lass, I'm on your side in this. You know that, don't you? But we've got to face facts here. The McGuigans are a law unto themselves and Sadie's a nasty piece of work. She'll want her pound of flesh whatever you and Mrs Bell say and if it's your word against Adam's' – she shrugged – 'no contest.'

'They can't prove anything.'

'They don't have to,' Phyllis said grimly.

'But I'm his wife.'

'Lass, they make people disappear. You know that as well as I do. Now I married Bruce knowing what he was so in that respect I made my bed and I've got to lie on it. But you were duped into marrying Adam, I've always thought that. I hoped because he seemed to love you so much it would work out but I should have known a leopard doesn't change its spots. He's a McGuigan through and through.'

Luke was slurping at his rusk, the dining-room windows were open to the warm morning air scented with climbing roses that covered the wall outside and she could hear birds chirping in the trees. It was a beautiful morning and yet Josie felt as cold as ice. She was shaking. 'They – they wouldn't hurt me? I'm Luke's mother.'

Phyllis stared at her and her silence was telling even before she said, 'This is Adam, the golden boy.'

'If they go to the police Mrs Bell will stick to her story.'

'It's the McGuigans, lass,' Phyllis said flatly. 'They won't go to the police. They sort any problems themselves. Look, there's something you should know. I only found out about it recently myself and I've been wondering whether I should tell you because I knew what it would mean. But now . . .'

Josie felt herself go even colder. 'Tell me.'

'It's about your Toby.'

'Toby?'

'It's awful, lass. Wicked. But – I – I heard Adam and Bruce talking one morning when he came round ours and I wish to heaven I hadn't.' Phyllis took a deep breath. 'It was clear Adam asked Bruce to have Toby done away with so it made the way possible for him to marry you.'

The words hung in the air in a terrible silence. The ice inside her seemed to have frozen her lips because she could barely open them when she whispered, 'No, Phyllis, no. He wouldn't have. He couldn't. Not Toby. It was the O'Leary menfolk.'

'That's what they wanted us all to think but it was Adam. Not the actual deed, of course, Bruce sent in his heavies for that, but Adam asked him to. I'm sorry, lass, I didn't want to add to your trouble but you need to understand what they're capable of. They're dangerous, and anyone who gets in their way or upsets them . . .'

Luke banged his rusk on the tray of his highchair, slipping sideways as he did so and beginning to grizzle. Josie straightened the baby automatically and placed the rusk which he'd dropped back in his little chubby fingers, and as she did so she knew without a shadow of a doubt that it was true. It explained so many things. She looked at her son again, at the little face that was so like Adam's. A fear greater than anything she had experienced thus far swept over her. She had to get Luke away from here. He couldn't be allowed to turn into his father and already the McGuigans were claiming him.

Toby, oh, Toby. Her heart was breaking all over again. *They killed you, battered you to death, my darling brother.* She felt Phyllis's arms go round her but she couldn't respond.

They sat like that for some moments and then Josie whispered, 'I can't stay in Sunderland, can I. I have to get right away.'

It wasn't really a question but Phyllis answered it anyway. 'Yes, you do, but where would you go, lass? Their arm is long. Look, I'll help you—'

'No.' Josie straightened. 'You can't put yourself in danger, you've got your bairns to consider. And Bruce mustn't know you've been here today and warned me.'

'I've got some money hidden away that Bruce doesn't know about. I've saved a bit here and there through the years; a sort of insurance for the future, you know? You can have it, lass, 'cause you're going to need every penny you can lay your hands on.'

'I couldn't, Phyllis.'

'You could and you're going to. Does Adam keep a safe in his study like Bruce?'

Josie nodded – she was finding it hard to think.

'Can you get in it? Do you know the combination?'

'I think so.'

'Open it and take everything you can, and all your jewellery. Adam's bought you some pieces that should fetch a good price. And don't go to your mam's, not with your da being the way he is with the McGuigans.'

'The Mullens. They'd help me. They can't stand the

McGuigans. I'll go there and then think how to get right away without them finding me. Phyllis? Do you think they'd take Luke from me if I stayed?'

Phyllis's eyelids blinked. 'Truthfully? That's the least they'd do. Sadie's already saying she wants Adam home with her and you know how obsessive she is with Luke.'

That woman wasn't going to get her hands on him. Josie nodded. 'I'll go today once it's dark. You don't think they'll try anything before then?'

'I doubt it. Bruce likes to plan these sorts of things thoroughly, that's why nothing's been traced back to him through the years. But you'll need someone to help you—'

'Mrs Bell will help me. Like I said, you can't be seen to get involved. You need to stay with the family tonight.'

They sat together for some minutes more, discussing this and that, before Phyllis took her leave. She stood on the doorstep looking at Josie with Luke in her arms. 'I'll go round and see your mam once you've gone, lass, and explain everything. Shall I say you'll write when you can?'

'Aye, yes. Tell her I didn't come because of Da and that I'll send any letters to Flo, her next-door neighbour, for the same reason. They've been friends since schooldays and always helped each other out. Mam can trust Flo.'

'You're sure? I'd say send them to me but with Bruce . . .'

'I'm sure. They're like sisters.'

'All right.'

The two women stared at each other, realizing that this was probably goodbye. When Josie held out her free arm and pulled Phyllis to her they hugged, both in tears. 'You're a good friend,' Josie said softly. 'I don't know what I'd have done without you.'

'Did I do the right thing in telling you? About Toby? I would have done so before but I thought you and Adam were getting along all right and that it would ruin everything for you.'

'I don't think we've been all right since our wedding night.' Josie didn't elaborate on this. 'I've excused a lot by telling myself the drink was to blame and that it turns him into a different person, but I was a blind fool. I see that now. Toby was right all along. He knew Adam was bad.'

She stood watching Phyllis walk down the drive and when her friend turned and waved before disappearing, the lump in her throat threatened to choke her. They'd arranged that Josie would ask Ida to pop to Phyllis's later on the pretext of fetching a bag of baby toys that her children had outgrown but in which the money would be concealed. Josie didn't want to risk Phyllis coming again. Bruce was well aware of their deep friendship and that was already problem enough for Phyllis. When Ida was out she would take Mrs Bell fully into her confidence and ask for her help later that night under cover of darkness.

Walking into the hall she stood for a moment looking about her in something of a daze. The shock and fear of hearing that Adam was accusing her of pushing him down the stairs and causing his injuries, and the connotations that threw up, had paled into insignificance beside learning about his part in Toby's death. To think that she had been in love with this man, sharing his bed and bearing his child, brought such self-loathing and shame and guilt that she didn't know how she would go on. And then Luke gurgled in her arms and there was her answer.

She spent the rest of the day trying to think clearly and prepare for her departure. Once Ida had trotted off to Phyllis's house, she explained everything to Mrs Bell, including the part Adam had played in Toby's murder. The cook had been horrified, promising she would help in any way she could. 'An' you can rest assured me lips are sealed,' she'd added vehemently, 'even on pain of death.'

'Let's hope it doesn't come to that, Mrs Bell.'

When Luke was having his morning nap she had gone into Adam's study. She'd watched him open the safe to give her the housekeeping money many times and was fairly sure she knew the combination and so it proved. She found various legal-looking papers and documents which she didn't bother with, along with a thick wad of banknotes, two of Adam's watches and several items of jewellery which belonged to her and which Adam had deemed expensive enough to keep in the safe. The rest of her jewellery was in a velvet-lined box on her dressing table.

Her hands were trembling as she counted the money and she was amazed to find it added up to over eighty pounds; well over a year's wages for a miner. Sitting back on her heels, she stared at it. All this wealth and money. Had it been worth the price of the McGuigans selling their souls to the Devil?

Carrying the money and jewellery upstairs to her bedroom she fetched one of the leather suitcases from the attics and proceeded to pack some of her clothes and Luke's things in it. The money, along with Phyllis's which had amounted to thirty pounds, and all the jewellery, she placed in a small portmanteau which would be easy to carry even with Luke in her arms. She needed to keep hold of that at all times, she told herself.

During the afternoon she had to resist the longing to go round and see her mother one last time, knowing that her father would probably be there. He could sniff out that something was amiss better than anyone she knew, and she couldn't risk her escape being foiled. She just hoped her mam would understand once Phyllis had talked to her. Where she was going to go and what she was going to do once she left the Mullens she didn't know. She was just praying they could help in some way. One thing was for sure, she couldn't afford to stay more than a day or two with them even though she felt sure they would hide her away in their own quarters. In the East End the walls themselves had ears.

She had half-expected a visit from either Bruce or his mother breathing fire and damnation all day, but it didn't happen. After putting Luke to bed she forced herself to eat the meal Mrs Bell had cooked and settled down to wait for the cover of darkness. The sun had set, the long twilight had begun. In the town and in the East End in particular she knew it would be a hive of activity. The gin shops and pubs would be doing a roaring trade; bairns would be playing their games in the streets and in the gutters; housewives would be sitting on their front doorsteps with their skirts hitched up to their knees watching the world go by and chatting to neighbours or gossiping in the back yards over the walls; sailors would be coming off the boats ready for a drink and a bit of attention from the dockside dollies – she had seen it all since a bairn, and she had never longed for that life more. In the quiet secluded grounds of Adam's house – and she thought of it as his, not theirs – she could have been a hundred miles away from the rest of humanity and whilst that had been a novelty in the early days, she hated it now.

She glanced round the drawing room where she was sitting with the French doors open to the warm scented evening. It was a beautiful room of course but of late the whole house had started to feel like a gilded cage. She was under no illusion that in leaving Adam her life would be hard but she would survive and make a future for herself and her child. Her small chin rose with the thought as her green eyes narrowed. Adam had called her stupid but she wasn't, she knew that. Furthermore, she was tougher than she looked; under the fine clothes and carefully coiffured hair she was a product of her upbringing, a bairn from the East End who had worked for her living since she could toddle in the roughest pubs of the town. She wouldn't let the McGuigans win and she wouldn't let them take Luke, not while she had breath in her body.

Adam lay immobile in the narrow hospital bed but his mind was active. His eyes were shut but he could still picture his mother sitting at the side of him; her stiff black dress crackled when she moved and the combined scent of lavender from the sachets she placed among her clothes and antiseptic from the ward itself impregnated his nostrils. He had told her to go home several times but she insisted on staying and her continual presence was driving him mad.

For the first time in his life he was experiencing a deep, dark desolation which was making him feel as if he was hollow right through. He would never walk again. The fancy London doctor had looked him straight in the eyes when he had delivered his verdict, adding that he was fortunate that he still had the use of his arms and upper body and his intellect was as sharp as ever. If he'd had a gun in his hands he would have used it, firing straight into the smug, patronizing face. As it was, he had screamed at him to get out and he had continued to scream until the sister on the ward had given him something, after which he had gone into a deep dreamless sleep. But when he had awoken this morning he had still been lying in this bed surrounded by sickness and disease and his mother – damn her – had still been here. He had wanted to kill someone. No, not someone. Her, Josie.

It was an effort to pretend that he was asleep but he couldn't stand his mother's fussing. It hadn't been so bad when he'd thought he was going to get better but now . . .

He could smell himself and he knew his bowels had evacuated again. This repeated indignity, along with others, made him feel as though he was losing his mind and that frightened him. He was in hell, a clinical, sterile, regimented hell, and he couldn't do a thing about it.

'Mrs McGuigan? I really think you should go home and get some rest now. He's fast asleep and probably won't wake until morning.'

It was the sister's voice and he could detect the intense irritation she was trying to hide. *Could his mother?* he wondered. It wouldn't make any difference if she could, she would do what she wanted to do.

There was a moment of silence and then he heard his mother say, 'I *am* rather tired.' This was followed by a rustling and movement of her chair. The next moment a featherlight kiss touched his forehead. When he was sure she had gone he opened his eyes. The ward was bathed in semi-darkness; a couple of the patients were snoring, another was gently moaning in pain. The next moment the sister was peering down at him. 'I'll come and get you comfortable in a moment, Mr McGuigan,' she said briskly.

He knew what that meant. Another humiliating episode when she and one of the young nurses washed him and changed the soiled material caking his backside. He ground his teeth together but said nothing and after a moment she bustled off.

Sister Lee was of the same mould as that damn London consultant, he thought viciously. She had already told him he should count his blessings. He had called her every name under the sun on that occasion.

He looked at his hands clenched into fists on the white cotton counterpane and imagined them smashing into the sister's face. There was a wild anger in him, a desire to hurt and destroy. He had told Bruce that he wanted Josie dead and he felt no remorse for accusing her of pushing him down the stairs; she might as well have, he thought bitterly, because the end result was the same. It was down to her he was lying in this hospital bed with the life of a cripple to look forward to. He wouldn't be able to stand it. He'd do away with himself once he was out of here but only when he knew Josie had got what was coming to her. Only then would he be able to rest in peace.

He saw the sister and a pretty young nurse approaching and his stomach curdled in protest; again he cursed Josie to hell and back.

Chapter Fourteen

Josie left the house at two in the morning. She was carrying Luke with the portmanteau over her arm and Mrs Bell trotted along at the side of her, holding the suitcase. Luke had thrown one of his screaming tantrums when she'd woken him, kicking and crying until she had calmed him down.

The night was pitch black with just a thin crescent moon peeping out now and again behind scudding clouds but that suited her purposes. It was a couple of miles to the Fiddler's Elbow and the streets were silent and mostly deserted apart from the odd cat or two. Luke had fallen asleep in her arms as soon as she had begun walking and she and Mrs Bell spoke little as they made their way towards the East End. As they neared their destination Josie's heart beat faster. She was terrified of being seen and having her whereabouts reported back to the McGuigans. Bruce had his spies everywhere and there was little that went on that he didn't know about.

The Fiddler's Elbow was in darkness when they arrived. She led Mrs Bell through the pub's courtyard and round to the back where empty beer barrels and crates and other paraphernalia were stored. She knew the heavy studded oak door would be bolted but Mr and Mrs Mullen's bedroom was above it, and she was banking on their window being open on such a warm summer's night. To her overwhelming relief it was.

Bracing herself, she called as softly as she could but it still sounded terribly loud in the still night. When, after a minute or two, there was no response she raised her voice slightly.

It was just as Mrs Bell murmured, 'Shall I throw a pebble at the window, ma'am?' that George Mullen's head poked out and his disgruntled voice bellowed, 'What the dickens is going on?'

'It's me, Mr Mullen. Josie.'

Mrs Mullen's head appeared beside that of her husband. 'Josie, lass? What on earth are you doing out there? Hang on a minute and we'll be straight down, hinny.'

When the door opened the Mullens ushered them in, their faces full of concern which deepened as they took in the suitcase that Mrs Bell was holding. Once upstairs in the sitting room, Josie told them the full story, leaving nothing out. When she reached the part about Adam's role in her brother's murder, Ada dug her husband in the ribs, making him jump. 'There, didn't I tell you? There was something that didn't add up in all that. Everyone was pointing the finger at the O'Learys but didn't I say that although they might be handy with their fists, what happened to young Toby was something else.'

George ignored his wife. As he stared at Josie, he thought, *The lass is scared to death and no wonder. This is a right beggar's muddle.* 'Are the doctors sure Adam won't walk again? Is that definite? It's early days, after all.'

Josie nodded. 'They got a London doctor up to see him, a top specialist. He said Adam's back's broken.'

'Dear, oh, dear.' It was a crying shame that she'd ever set eyes on the man. George sighed. The McGuigans would want their pound of flesh over this. 'And you say you didn't push him?'

'It would be self-defence if she had,' Ada cut in indignantly. 'A big man like him attacking a slip of a thing like Josie. They're vicious, the lot of them, scum of the earth.'

Josie looked at the publican. 'It happened so fast but I'm sure I didn't push him. He overbalanced and fell. But – but he's saying I did and his family will believe him.'

It was at this point that Edith finished the last of the tea Ada had given her and straightened her hat and coat, standing to her feet. 'I'd best get back before it's light, ma'am, and I'll wait for Mr Bruce or one of them to come knocking rather than let them know you've gone.'

'Thank you for all you've done, Mrs Bell.' Josie stood up and hugged her. 'You've gone above and beyond.'

When they drew apart Mrs Bell sniffed and wiped her eyes. 'I wish you well, ma'am, and the littl'un.' Luke had gone to sleep on Ada's lap. 'You're doing the best for him an' all.'

When it was just the Mullens and herself again, Josie said softly, 'I'm sorry to involve you in this but I didn't know where else to go. I'll leave tomorrow once I've arranged transport and—'

'Listen, lass, you can stay as long as you like. You'll be safe here, all right? No one'll know. There's a spare room next to ours that me old mam uses when she comes on a visit from Newcastle and I keep the bed aired. We'll put our heads together tomorrow an' decide what to do.'

'Today.'

'What?' Ada stared at George.

'It's getting on for daybreak, tomorrow's here.'

Ada gave her husband a look that would have quelled a lesser man before saying, 'Come on, lass, and I'll show you where it is. You bring the suitcase, George.'

The room was comfortable but on the small side. All the furniture it possessed was the bed standing against one wall, a chest of drawers and narrow wardrobe and a little table with a jug and basin on it. Overcome with gratitude at their ready acceptance of her, Josie said huskily, 'It's lovely, Mrs Mullen. I can't thank you enough. You've always been such good friends to me and so kind.'

'Don't be daft, no need to thank me, lass.' Ada handed over Luke and watched as Josie placed him in the bed and tucked him securely against the wall. He didn't stir. George Mullen deposited her suitcase in the room and then took his leave but Ada lingered. 'I've an idea come to me you might like to consider, hinny. When you say you want to get right away, how far exactly?'

'I don't know. As far as I can, I suppose.'

'Well, Hans was in tonight. His boat's just docked and he was asking after you, he always does. Anyway, as I understand it he's bound for America in a day or two. I reckon he might be up for taking you an' the bairn with him when he knows about what's happened.'

'America?' Josie stared at her in shock.

'It's just a thought. Mull it over. There'd be no chance of the McGuigans tracing you there, that's for sure.'

America? That was the other side of the world. She'd heard of it of course, but to think of going there . . . 'I couldn't do that, Mrs Mullen.' It would mean leaving everything she had ever known, *everyone*, her mam. Another town would be hard enough but another country . . .

'No? Well, like I said, think about it.'

She did think about it. Through what was left of the night and the day that followed, incarcerated in the small room on the upper floor of the public house where she tried to stop Luke from grizzling for fear of someone hearing him. The enormity of what she had done – leaving Adam and the weight of the McGuigan empire – had swept over her at regular intervals. And she had taken Luke. She had taken his son. There was no coming back from this. She had nailed her colours to the mast. Which brought her back to Hans and his ship.

By the time he came up to her room later that evening

she knew what she wanted to do. He hadn't changed a jot except that his ready smile wasn't evident. Instead his weather-beaten face was solemn and his blue eyes had lost their twinkle. 'My little songbird,' he said as he took her into his arms in a fatherly hug. 'I am heart sorry to hear of your trouble.'

'Thank you.' She found she was fighting back tears, as much with seeing him again as with his words. She hadn't realized she had missed him.

'This man, your husband, he is bad.'

'Yes, he is bad, and his family too. They – they're very powerful, Hans,' she said as she drew away and he came fully into the room, shutting the door behind him. 'I have to get away, far away.'

He nodded, his broad-shouldered body seeming to fill the space. He glanced at the bed where Luke was fast asleep, his black curls framing his baby face. 'Ada has told me,' he said softly. 'And this is your son?'

'Yes, this is Luke.'

He continued to look at the baby for some moments before he sighed. 'It will be a hard road you travel, my little songbird. You understand this? The world is no place for a woman on her own with a child.'

'If I stay I'll be in fear of my life every single day, Hans. I can't live like that. And – and there's Luke too. I don't want him growing up like the rest of them. I should never have married Adam, I know that now. If I hadn't met him Toby would still be alive and—'

'That was not your fault, *min skjoun*. You know this?'

After staring at her intently for a moment, he repeated, 'What happened to your brother was not your fault.'

She was different, he thought sadly. Of course she had married and had a child, but it wasn't that. She was still beautiful but now those great green eyes held an emotion that pained him. From what Ada Mullen had confided to him Josie was right, though; she did need to get away from her husband and his brothers, who were all bad. 'I can take you and the child with me to America.' The words were quiet, flat. 'I have a friend there, Jack Kane, a good friend. He will help you.'

'Oh, Hans, thank you. I—'

He stopped her words by shaking his head. 'It won't be easy, Joo-see. Forgive me but I need to ask, do you have money? America is seen as a land of dreams by many but dreams can turn into nightmares very easily.'

'I have money, Hans, yes, and my jewellery too. It will be enough at first. If I can leave England I know I will be all right.'

'You have heard of Ellis Island, yes?'

'I don't think so.'

'Ellis Island is the principal federal immigration station since the beginning of this year. Men and women, whole families, have to pass medical and legal inspections and have the right papers. Those who do not pass are returned to their country of origin. You understand what that would mean for you, *min skjoun*? And single women are not allowed in unless they can prove family are waiting for them. Hundreds of souls arrive every day on packed ships, I have seen this. My friend's family went there from Ireland before he was born, and the stories he can tell of how they were treated . . . All bad, Joo-see. All bad.'

She stared at him. 'I have to go.'

'Then it will not be through' – he hesitated – 'the conventional route. You have no papers, no certification. Now, my friend will be able to help with these things later for a price. By the – how do you English say it – through the back door, yes?'

So his friend was a criminal? She was escaping one lot for another? She nodded.

'When we dock you will be travelling as my wife and child if any officials ask. The authorities in the wharf where we unload know me and my boat. They have no trouble with my men. On some vessels the crew drink when they go into town and end up in gaol, but not my men. I will go and see my friend and explain.'

'But what if he won't help?'

'He is my friend,' Hans said as though that settled the matter. 'We are sailing the day after tomorrow. I will come here tomorrow night. It is best you board under cover of darkness, yes?'

'You – you won't get into trouble for taking me?'

'If anyone found out I was smuggling you into America? Yes, big trouble so we won't shout about it.' He grinned at her.

'But your men? They'll know.'

'They have all sailed with me for years. I will explain. They might be seafarers but they would not treat a woman as your husband has treated you, my songbird.' His face had darkened and for a moment he didn't look like her Hans.

'I will never be able to thank you enough for helping me,' she murmured with a lump in her throat. 'I must pay you and—'

'No, no, no.' Like someone chastising a child, he wagged his finger at her. 'I will have no talk of payment. Now you must rest and prepare yourself for the days ahead. You and the little one will have my cabin and I will sleep with my men but it will be cramped, Joo-see. No luxuries.'

'I've lived without luxuries most of my life, Hans.'

'Ah, yes, but the sea, she goes up and down.' He shook his head. 'This is not always easy until you get your sea legs.'

'I'll be fine,' she said, with more confidence than she was feeling.

He put out a large hand and patted her shoulder. 'There are many men – runners, pseudo-lawyers, tricksters of all kinds – who prey on immigrants coming off the ships, but you will be safe with my friend. I know this. I will come after midnight tomorrow and now you must sleep, yes?'

She nodded. *America.* She was going to a country of which she knew next to nothing. Furthermore, as Hans had put it, she was being smuggled in and would be totally at the mercy of a stranger when she got there. But what was the alternative?

They talked a little more and when Hans left she got ready for bed. Luke had cut his two bottom front teeth in the last few days and was sleeping through the night again for which she was thankful. After she had extinguished the oil lamp and the room was in darkness she lay awake for a long time, her mind in turmoil, and by the time she drifted off into a troubled sleep populated with nightmarish images the sun was beginning to rise.

PART THREE

Jack

1892

Chapter Fifteen

As Hans helped Josie down the gangway and onto the dock in New York she told herself that she would never, *ever* again board any kind of ship. The journey across the Atlantic had been a nightmare of constant retching and sleeplessness. The only comfort in it all was that Luke had been totally unaffected by seasickness, although having to tend to him had taken all her remaining strength. Hans and Jules and the rest of the crew had been kindness itself, but at times she had even wondered if she was going to die, here in this ship in the middle of the ocean, she had felt so desperately ill.

But now all that was over. Hans's ship had been docked at a quay in Manhattan for some hours. She had stayed in the cabin while Hans had dealt with the dockside official, who had come on board in order for the crew to unload their cargo. The man was well known to Hans and after certain papers had been signed he'd disappeared, unaware of her presence. She had been so anxious that this part of the proceedings would go wrong and she would be taken into custody and shipped off to Ellis Island that even the sight of the Statue of Liberty, magnificent though it was, had failed to move her.

Hans had been aware of her nerves and now he said quietly, 'You see, Joo-see. All is well.' It was past midnight and the day had been a sizzling-hot one; even now the air was sticky and sultry. She had Luke in her arms and Hans was holding her suitcase and portmanteau; he wanted to take her to his friend's house under the cover of darkness but there were still people about and she was frightened. More than frightened – terrified, she confessed to herself silently. And not just for herself. Hans was risking so much to help her.

'Stop trembling.' Hans put the suitcase down and gave her a brief hug. 'No one is going to take any notice of a family finding their lodgings.'

Nevertheless, until the dockside was behind them and they had ventured into the city Josie was on tenterhooks. As they walked she became aware of tall dark buildings looming high above them either side of the roadway and a plethora of noise and people even though it was so late. As Hans led her into what quickly became a warren of streets she was aware of something else too – even though America was on the other side of the ocean the smells of poverty were recognizable. The pavements were caked with mud and there were piles of manure now and again in the roads; dirt and debris hung in the sticky air and they passed beer saloons and rum shops where men were hanging about. Somehow she hadn't expected this – it could have been the East End in Sunderland but magnified a hundred times.

Whether Hans was aware of her thoughts she didn't know, but he said softly, 'There is a huge divide between rich and poor here, Joo-see, even more than you have been used to at home. This is an area of – how do you say – tenements? Yes? Five Points and the East Side hold much misery and yet in Fifth Avenue and 44th Street the wealthy dine out and have private balls that are magnificent affairs. The way of the world, yes?'

She nodded. She was too exhausted to speak. The voyage had taken all her reserves and now she walked in a daze, Luke fast asleep, his little head tucked under her chin.

They walked between incredibly tall reeking houses and in the dim light their laden fire escapes, useless for their appointed purpose, bulged with household goods and rubbish; drying clothes hanging like ghosts from metal railings. The smells of cooking, some spicy and exotic, vied with less savoury odours and in places it was slimy underfoot.

How long they trudged along she didn't know – it was all she could do to put one foot in front of the other – but she became aware the streets were a little cleaner as Hans continued to tell her about Manhattan, as much to keep her going as anything, she suspected. It appeared the immigrants had settled into separate ethnic groups in their own enclaves by and large in the Lower East Side – the Jewish Quarter, Little Italy, Chinatown, Little

Hungary – the list was endless. Five Points, where they were passing through, was a densely packed area full of dark airless buildings and Hans warned her it wasn't a place to walk alone after dark. She didn't reply, she needed all her breath to keep walking.

Just when she knew she was unable to walk any further, Hans led her through a tenement hallway, across a court and up into a rear building. The stairs were narrow and steep and dungeon darkness reigned. Josie was too bone-tired to feel anything but a numbness of mind. She just wanted to lie down, she no longer cared where.

'A lot of Irish have moved to this area,' Hans said softly, 'Hell's Kitchen. Like the Germans, they've moved uptown a little.'

Hell's Kitchen? It didn't sound any more upmarket than the snaking alleys and tangle of streets they'd passed through, she thought. She'd entered hell. For a moment she felt a kind of hysterical laughter bubbling up inside her before she took a hold of herself. She couldn't go to pieces, she had Luke to care for.

Hans had paused on a landing to let Josie get her breath before knocking on the door in front of them. 'My friend has the attic apartment,' he said, waiting for some moments before knocking more loudly. He hadn't been able to notify his friend that they were arriving and the last time he'd seen Jack had been three months ago. He was hoping he was in and that he was still living at the same address. On the third knock the door opened.

Josie was leaning against the wall and she registered

that the man standing in the doorway was tall, very tall, and that he was holding an oil lamp, but little else before her legs finally gave way. She found herself sliding slowly down the wall, still clutching Luke to her, in a half-faint that had her ears ringing.

Jack Kane was not a man who was easily surprised, being tough and streetwise and more than a little cynical. His parents had come to America decades before at the crest of the Potato Famine in Ireland, and although life there had been cruel, emigrating had not been a joyful event. Jack had been raised on stories of the battle for survival his parents had endured; forced to live in dank cellars and shanties, partly because of their poverty but also because Americans had considered the Irish detrimental to the neighbourhood. These living conditions had bred sickness and early death; nine of his eleven siblings had died before the age of three. The Irish brogue and dress had provoked ridicule, their poverty and illiteracy scorn which had affected his mother deeply and even now she rarely spoke outside her home. Nevertheless, his parents had come to love America but had never given up their allegiance to Ireland or their hatred of the English.

Jack was twenty-seven years old and his earliest memories were ones of violence and discrimination. The days of 'No Irish Need Apply' might have passed, but they'd formed a culture in which the Irish tenaciously clung to each other but Jack, unlike some, did have friends outside the community. Now as he gazed at one of them and the young girl at Hans's feet, for once in his life he was lost for words.

'Help me with her. Here, take the child.' Hans plucked Luke from Josie's arms and handed the still-sleeping baby to Jack as he hauled Josie to her feet, keeping his arm round her as they stepped into the room. Although some tenement apartments were wretched and dirty, others were clean and cared for and Jack's was one of these. He had enough memories of some of the filthy lodgings his parents had been forced to live in before his father, following the Civil War and the need for enormous expansion in a rapidly industrializing America, managed to acquire a job in a boatbuilder's and work himself up to a position of responsibility. By the time Jack and his two sisters had left home, the girls both marrying men from the Irish-American community, his mother was in a nice apartment enjoying a standard of living that was luxurious by comparison to the life they'd known in Ireland or in the first couple of decades in America. He respected his father but had had no wish to follow him into the boatbuilding trade, which had caused tension between them; and when he'd begun work as a bartender after a succession of other jobs which had only lasted for a few months at a time, he deemed at the age of twenty-one it was time to get his own place and for the last six years had enjoyed his independence.

As Hans half-carried Josie to a couch he noticed the young woman emerging from the bedroom still buttoning her dress and heard Jack say, 'I'm sorry, Rose. I'll see you tomorrow, all right?'

The woman nodded, smiling at Hans, and left without speaking, Jack shutting the door behind her after giving her a kiss. 'That was Rose,' he said ruefully. 'Now, what's all this?'

'I'm sorry, my friend.' Hans straightened. 'There was no way to let you know but I need your help.'

Jack looked down at the infant in the crook of his arm. 'Yours?'

'No, no.' Hans looked suitably horrified. 'Joo-see is a respectable married woman but there are the problems too great. She has been ill on the voyage and needs to rest. Is there anywhere . . .'

The apartment consisted of a bedroom and the living space in which they were standing, and now Jack inclined his head towards the former. Josie had fallen into a deep sleep as soon as Hans had laid her on the couch and barely stirred as he picked her up and carried her into the room, Jack following with the child. The bedroom, like the other room, was clean and fresh, but small, holding a three-quarter-size bed and a single wardrobe. The windows of both rooms opened onto an alley far below. The other floors had a shared water closet at each level but Jack preferred to be in the attic; the air shaft was too narrow to convey much light to the lower floors whereas up in the sky where he was both ventilation and noise quality were better. It was a small sacrifice to walk down a few stairs and use the water closet on the floor below. In some tenements, where interior room windows faced dark, putrid air shafts, the residents chose to keep them closed for fear of poisonous gases.

Hans laid Josie on the bed and Jack tucked Luke in beside her; neither woke. Once in the living room, Jack said quietly, 'Tell me.'

As Hans explained Josie's story, keeping nothing back, Jack listened without interrupting after pouring them both a glass of whisky. The beauty of the girl – for in spite of being a married woman with a baby she was little more than a girl – had taken him aback, he had to admit, and she was dressed very well; she was as unlike the average immigrant as it was possible to be. But then she wasn't the average immigrant, from what Hans was saying. There was nothing average about Josie McGuigan at all. 'And this husband and his family, you say they are criminals? You know this for sure?'

Hans nodded. 'They are feared and they are dangerous.'

'So why did she marry him, knowing this?'

'It was, how you say, a lamb to the slaughter? She was innocent, trusting, and he charmed her. She believed him to be different to the rest of the family. Alas, not so.'

'And do you believe her when she says she didn't push him down the stairs?'

'Implicitly.'

Jack stretched out his long legs and threw back the last of the whisky in his glass in one gulp. At six foot four inches he towered over most men and this, combined with his rugged good looks and silver tongue courtesy of his heritage, had caused him to lead something of a charmed life thus far. Women tended to adore him and men wanted him as a friend. He was intelligent and charismatic and could have risen in the world like his father but was devoid of ambition, content to breeze through life on his own terms. In the last year he'd been promoted to manager of the bar and restaurant where he worked, but this was less to do with drive or motivation on his part and more that the owner of the establishment liked him. Everyone liked Jack Kane.

'She has money to get started,' Hans continued, 'and I understand she has brought her jewellery with her. She is not destitute. Not yet.'

'Money has a way of slipping through the fingers in this city, my friend, and she has a baby to care for. Even if she is prepared to work a child will complicate things. This jewellery you spoke of? She has receipts to prove it is hers?'

'I doubt it.' Hans smiled. 'That's where you come in.'

Jack grinned. He had many contacts in the city and not all were the type of individual he could introduce to his mother. He had dabbled in the occasional spot of illegal activity in between jobs in the past but since working at the bar had kept on the right side of the law. 'She won't get as much for it as she could if she sold it to a reputable shop but I daresay I know a few guys who could help,' he drawled easily. 'Do I take it you want me to give her a bed – *my* bed,' he added sardonically, 'for the time being until she finds a place of her own?'

'Would you?'

'You wouldn't have brought her here if you didn't know the answer to that.'

Hans smiled again. 'Thank you, my friend. You are a good man.'

'There's those who would disagree with that.' Jack poured them another glass of whisky. 'So, she and the child will need certain papers. That can be achieved but it won't be cheap. She understands this?'

'She is young but she is not foolish, except, perhaps, in the matter of the husband.'

'And he and his family have no idea where she is?'

'None, and Joo-see wants to keep it that way. She is terrified of them, Jack.'

They talked some more until Hans took his leave, promising to return before he sailed again. Jack shut the door behind his friend and stood for a moment leaning against it, looking across to the closed door of the bedroom as he shook his head. His mother had a saying – one of many – that you never knew what the good Lord would provide but he could well have done without this particular provision. A young mother, very young, and a child, and English to boot. He had been brought up to hate the English but once he had been old enough to form his own opinions he'd come across a few who were all right, but he found them to be on the whole a cold race. You never really knew what they were thinking and you could never get under an Englishman's skin, which made them good at poker.

He smiled wryly to himself. He'd lost a pretty dollar

or two gambling in the past before he'd made up his mind it was a mug's game and he was no mug.

So, it looked as though it was going to be the couch for him for a few days. Hans had told him her money was English currency so he would have to get that changed, again with someone who wouldn't ask any awkward questions. Mind, even if she had entered the country through the legal route she would have had to use Ellis Island's Money Exchange and some of the money changers weren't averse to cheating the immigrants. He'd do his best for her for Hans's sake but as with the jewellery his contacts would demand a price and she would have to pay it.

Walking across to the couch, he poured himself another glass of whisky and sat down, cradling it in his big hands. He couldn't have refused Hans but the last thing he wanted was the responsibility of another human being. A human being and a half, he thought with wry amusement. His sisters had four children between them and he didn't mind playing genial Uncle Jack who arrived with bags of candy and took them for outings to Central Park now and again, but that was entirely different to being confronted by a baby in his own home. It would also mean Rose couldn't drop by.

He frowned. The amount of money the girl had brought with her and what he could get for the jewellery would dictate the kind of apartment she could afford. What was she expecting? He paid ten dollars a month for this attic but the three-room apartments on the floors below were fifteen, more if they came furnished. Of course, apartments were cheaper south of Five Points where decrepit wooden houses and slums allowed criminals and the gangs to lie low, but he couldn't see this girl being content to take her child there? Had Hans explained how tough life would be for her here? He doubted it. Hans visited a few times a year when his boat docked and unless you lived in New York you couldn't fully understand the dynamics. The different communities were as tight as a drum and she wouldn't get a welcome in the Syrian Quarter or Chinatown or the rest of the strongholds stretching from the Battery.

He swallowed his whisky and poured another. Those tenements had turned into death houses too. In his mind's eye he pictured Roberto, an Italian pal of his who'd lived in the Mulberry Bend area. He'd emigrated from Italy's poorer, largely agricultural south with his family, and had worked peddling fruit in a pushcart. He'd been trapped when his five-storey tenement had crumbled over him. Before the accident he knew Roberto and other tenants had notified the landlord about dangerous cracks in the wall and even filed a complaint with the Bureau of Inspection of Buildings but they'd just been immigrants, worthless, and Roberto and his family had died.

Hans had told him Josie came from a poor family originally but there were degrees of poor. If she had rose-coloured glasses about life here she was going to have to take them off pretty sharpish. The privileged few in their apartments in Fifth Avenue or 72nd Street lived the life of old Riley with their bathrooms and servants' quarters, but the rest of Manhattan's inhabitants were lucky to scrape a living. He'd made up his mind he would never marry; looking after himself was fine but the responsibility of providing for a wife and children wasn't for him.

He finished the whisky and stretched out on the couch, which was too small for his long frame. Anyway, this girl wasn't his problem, he told himself as he shut his eyes. He'd do what he could with regard to selling the jewellery and getting her the necessary papers, but once she was renting somewhere she'd be out of his hair for good. He was sure Hans had meant well in bringing her across the ocean in view of this gangster family she'd married into, but it could well be she'd find herself out of the frying pan and into the fire.

He shut his eyes, and in spite of the fact that his legs were dangling over the edge of the couch he was asleep within moments.

Chapter Sixteen

When Josie felt herself being shaken by the shoulder and emerged from a deep, all-consuming slumber, the first thing that registered was that the awful rolling and heaving of the ship had stopped. She opened eyes dazed with sleep to see a tall stranger stand back from the bed she was lying on. He smiled, saying, 'There's a cup of coffee ready for you.'

And then it all came flooding back. She wasn't on the ship any more. She was in America. And this must be Hans's friend. She remembered walking through endless streets for what had seemed like an eternity and then arriving somewhere, but after that, nothing. She struggled up, aware of Luke fast asleep at the side of her. The man was staring at her and she lowered her lids, suddenly shy. 'Thank you,' she said uncomfortably, aware she must be in his bed.

'Always a good way to start the day, a cup of coffee,' he said cheerfully. 'Leave the boy sleeping – Hans *did* say it's a boy?' – Josie nodded – 'and come through. We need to talk before I leave for work.'

After straightening her clothes and smoothing into place tendrils of hair that had escaped the chignon at the back of her head, she joined him, glancing around her. This room was much larger than the bedroom and it too was clean and tidy. It housed a sofa and two chairs, a small wooden table and four hardbacked chairs and a dresser holding various items of crockery. There was a small fireplace and a little kitchen area with a cooking stove and shelves stacked with a number of items.

The aroma of coffee and fresh bread made her mouth water. She had been quite unable to keep a morsel down throughout the sea voyage but now for the first time she felt hungry, she realized.

The man gestured towards the food. 'Fresh from the bakery in the next street this morning,' he said easily. 'Come and eat.' Along with the rolls she saw a jar of preserve and a pat of butter and some kind of meat in a large sausage shape off which the man had already cut himself a chunk.

In spite of her hunger she didn't move. 'Thank you so much, Mr . . .'

'Jack will do. Jack Kane.'

'Thank you so much for allowing us to stay here last night but I won't impose on you further, I promise. I'll find somewhere today, a lodging house—'

In spite of his earlier thoughts, Jack found himself saying, 'Hey, hey, slow down, there's no rush. After such a journey you need to rest up for a bit and get your bearings and then I'll help you find something, all right?'

She liked the way he talked. She had heard an American accent once before in Sunderland in one of the public houses she had sung in before the Fiddler's Elbow, but it hadn't been as mellow and languid as his.

'How do you like your coffee?'

She walked hesitantly across to the table and sat down. 'With milk if you have any?'

'Sure thing.' He indicated the stone jar on the table. 'Got that this morning too. Nothing lasts more than a day in this heat.'

'I'm sorry for just turning up on your doorstep, Mr Kane, but—'

'Jack,' he drawled. 'And you're Josie, right?'

'Yes.'

'So, Josie, eat and drink and then we'll have a chat about a few things, OK?' Now he was seeing her properly he was amazed that this thin young girl with the beautiful sad face and remarkable green eyes was old enough to have been married and furthermore be a mother. She looked fourteen, at the most fifteen. No more. And vulnerable, very vulnerable. She'd be eaten alive on the streets of New York. He sighed inwardly. What the hell had Hans landed him with? His face betrayed none of this, however, as he ate his breakfast and indicated for her to do the same.

After a moment she sat down and helped herself to a roll, spreading it with butter and preserve but refusing the sausage meat he offered her. He found he was fascinated by the fragility and beauty of her and had to remind himself she was a grown woman who, according to Hans, had been married to a prominent crime lord in the town she'd lived in, who was now seeking vengeance for leaving him paralysed. Not your average young girl then.

They ate in silence, and once she had finished he leaned back in his chair. 'You spoke of finding somewhere, a lodging house, but you have to understand that there are a lot of folk out there who would cheat you out of every penny you've got without a second thought. I don't know what you've been used to back home but I can assure you it'll be nothing like what you can expect here.'

Josie stared back into the piercingly blue eyes. There had been something in his tone that had her hackles rising. 'I'm well acquainted with ne'er-do-wells, Mr Kane,' she said flatly.

'Jack,' he said for the third time. 'And that's as may be. Hans told me something of your situation, but here you won't have the protection, however dubious, of your husband and his family. You're in another city, another country, and the rules are different, OK? How do you think you're going to change your money into American currency for a start?'

'Hans – Hans said you would help me.'

'And I will, but it will need to be done carefully with the right people, along with the disposal of your jewellery and obtaining the necessary papers and so on. These things are a mite sensitive and can't be rushed.'

'I didn't want to impose on you any further.'

'Lady, I'm not suggesting you live here indefinitely,

believe me, but getting to America with the kid was the least of your problems. You need to understand that.'

She didn't think she liked Hans's friend. He was good to have taken her in but she got the impression he didn't approve of her and thought she was reckless and stupid.

'Now, I normally work afternoons and evenings but there's a delivery due shortly that I need to supervise.' He didn't explain that if he wasn't around, bottles of brandy and whisky might disappear. A spot of petty pilfering was common with both the delivery drivers and bartenders. 'Once I'm finished, I'll make a few enquiries and we'll see about getting your money changed. It'll cost, of course.'

'I'll pay you whatever you want.'

'Not me,' he said easily, although she felt she'd annoyed him. 'The guys I'll have to deal with. It'll be the same with any jewellery and so on. Nothing comes cheap in New York.'

She nodded stiffly. 'I understand.'

'So, what's going to be your story?'

'My story?' She stared at him blankly.

'Well, I'm assuming you won't want the truth known far and wide?'

She flushed. He was making her feel stupid, gullible. 'I – I'll say I'm a widow. My maiden name was Gray, I'll use that. I don't want my son brought up as a McGuigan.'

'Fine. Just get your story straight and stick to it. Is that what you'll tell the kid too? That his old man's dead?'

His voice had been expressionless but she felt he didn't approve. Coldly now, her words weighted with bitterness, she said, 'My husband is a violent, wicked man. He had my brother murdered to suit his own purposes, something I was unaware of, and he started being unfaithful shortly after our marriage when I was expecting his child. I will be doing my son a favour if he thinks his father is dead.'

His eyes had narrowed. 'Did he beat you up?' he asked softly.

'That last time, when I confronted him about his other women, yes. That's when – when he fell down the stairs and was injured.'

'Sounds like it couldn't have happened to a nicer guy.' There was a gentleness to his voice now that was harder to take than the condescension because it was weakening. Horrified that she might break down, she stood up, her throat tight. 'I need to see to Luke.'

'Sure.' He rose to his feet. 'No one'll bother you here. Help yourself to what you want and rest up. Hans said you're done in.'

Praying he hadn't seen the tears pricking the backs of her eyes she turned swiftly, walking into the bedroom. Luke was beginning to stir and as she picked him up, rosy-cheeked and tousled from sleep, she breathed in his baby smell. He was what mattered, nothing else, and she would make a good life for him here in America whatever Jack Kane thought.

It was three weeks before all her jewellery was sold. Josie had no idea if she'd received a reasonable price, but she had come to realize that although Jack Kane had a habit of rubbing her up the wrong way he'd have done his best for her.

He had converted her cash into American dollars and they were waiting for the papers to prove that she was a Mrs Josie Gray, a widow from England with a dependant who had emigrated to America where she had relatives. The forging of the health certificate from Ellis Island was particularly expensive. Due to the great flow of immigration at a time when diseases – especially trachoma, which often resulted in blindness – could be brought into the country, the authorities were understandably nervous.

Along with the important medical card, they were buying birth certificates for herself and Luke and a marriage and death certificate for her 'dead' husband. Jack had assured her that the forger was an expert and the papers would stand the closest scrutiny.

He'd given her a lesson in American money – dollars, quarters, dimes and nickels – and told her that five dollars was equal to one English pound so she could begin to understand how much things cost in her new country, and explained the difference in meaning of some words too. But perhaps the greatest help was walking her round different areas to familiarize her with the city, along with train rides from Lower Manhattan up to Harlem, and across the Brooklyn Bridge which connected the two cities.

'You need to get a feel for where you are,' he told her on their morning excursions before he went to work. 'For the different communities. There are two New Yorks in essence: one that is borne down by disease and grinding poverty with families crowded into tenements, and the other where wealthy citizens like the Vanderbilts and Astors live in virtual palaces and have extravagant balls at the drop of a hat.'

Josie enjoyed the rides on the elevated railways once she had got used to the disturbing sensation of being up in the air looking down at the city below, and she often thought they must look like a married couple – Jack inevitably holding Luke and she trotting along at his side. She found such thoughts discomfiting, the main reason being that the more she had got to know Jack the more she'd realized her first impressions of him had been misleading. True, he could be sarcastic and cynical and was somewhat disenchanted with his fellow men, but he was also, as Hans had told her, a good friend and further-more had a certain magnetism that had made her wary at first until she had realized it wasn't like the charm that Adam had been able to turn off and on like a tap. With Jack what you saw was what you got, for good or bad.

He had made no bones about telling her that finding work with a young baby would be difficult, but if she paid for someone to take care of Luke during the day it would cost more dollars than she could afford. Furthermore, some of the women who were child-carers lived in insanitary conditions and often had a fondness for drink. One way to supplement her rent was to take in work, he stated. Garment contractors and manufac-turers used homeworkers as cheap labour but the pay was poor and most women who undertook the job did it to supplement their husband's income out of dire necessity. It was the same with any factory homeworkers. She would work fourteen hours or more a day and earn two or three dollars a week.

She had stared at him with a mixture of frustration and annoyance. 'So you are telling me that whatever I do, I can't win?'

'Hey, hey.' He'd raised his hands in protest, grinning. 'I'm saying it's gonna be tough, that's all.'

She'd worked that out herself but she couldn't continue staying with Jack. He wouldn't accept any payment despite the fact that they continued to sleep in his bed and eat his food; neither would he let her pay for the train rides or contribute to buying food. She knew he had a girlfriend called Rose although she hadn't met her, and she couldn't imagine that the lady in question was happy about another woman living in the apartment.

The proceeds from the sale of her jewellery along with her other cash had amounted to just over seven hundred dollars after she'd given Jack money to pay for her papers. She knew that would seem like a fortune to the immigrants south of Five Points, but she would need to provide a roof over Luke's head and feed and clothe him in the months and years ahead. Until he was old enough to go to school, she intended to look after him herself. This would mean only home work would be possible, even though it paid a pittance, but as far as she could see she had no choice in the matter. She wouldn't entrust him to strangers.

The morning after she had received the payment for her jewellery she awoke in the early hours. It was still dark outside. She had been dreaming that she was back in the Fiddler's Elbow singing to a packed pub. Heaps of sovereigns had been piled up on the floor, more money than she had seen in her life, and Hans had been there. His voice was still ringing in her ears even though she was awake. 'You see?' he'd cried. 'You see, my little songbird? You cannot escape your destiny, did I not tell you this? You were born to sing and sing you must.' And then she'd realized she wasn't in the Fiddler's Elbow at all, it was a different establishment, and Hans had changed into Jack.

Josie sat bolt upright in bed, her heart racing as Hans's voice rang in her mind. Could she do it? Could she sing here in this other country and earn money like she had in Sunderland? Everyone had liked her voice back home but this was a foreign city and she was English, not American. Nevertheless, she felt the dream had been telling her something and she had to take notice.

She sat mulling things over for the next hour or two, aware that she had to think carefully about the pros and cons. There was Luke to consider, which was the most important thing, and she wasn't going to leave him with a childminder; also, she hadn't sung for a long time – what if her voice wasn't the same? And who would give an English girl a job in this city, especially with a young baby in tow? She needed to be independent somehow, but how? Answers came into her mind, some feasible and some not so feasible, but by the time it was light she knew what she intended to do.

She got dressed quietly and, leaving Luke fast asleep, she went through to the sitting room. She would need Jack's assistance if her plans were going to come to fruition but she had no idea what his reaction would be when she talked to him.

He was sitting at the table drinking coffee when she made an appearance and he looked up from his paper and smiled at her. She could see he'd already been out for rolls and croissants. She knew he was no cook; he'd bought the ingredients and she'd made the dinners since she'd been staying with him, something she gathered his girlfriend had usually been in the habit of doing. That had made her feel doubly guilty about Rose; not only was she preventing the other woman from coming here but she'd spoiled their cosy dinners together too.

As she joined him at the table she thought that although he wasn't handsome his rugged attractiveness had a drawing power all of its own. She had noticed how many women turned their heads for a second glance at him on their excursions, and the fact that he seemed oblivious to their interest only added to his appeal.

'I've had an idea,' she said, sitting down at the table.

He raised quizzical eyebrows. She'd noticed in the last weeks he could express a lot with them.

'I'm going to see how much that run-down bar near here is to rent and sing there in the evenings.'

He choked on his coffee, coughing and spluttering before he managed to say, 'You're going to do *what?*'

'Before I got married I used to earn my living singing in a bar in Sunderland.' She helped herself to a croissant with an air of serenity she was far from feeling. 'I know I can make more money singing than I could ever earn taking in work at home.'

'Are you crazy?'

'Far from it. Actually, suddenly everything is very straightforward.'

Jack stared at her. The last three or four weeks had been baking hot. He wondered if the heat had affected her brain. 'What do you know about running a bar?'

'Not as much as I'd like, but I thought you could fill me in on stuff. I could sell food too. Have tables where folk could eat and drink while I sing.'

'And you'll be running around in an apron seeing to them while you serenade them? Is that it?'

Josie tried hard not to react. 'Of course not. I'd employ a cook and a waiter.'

'So you're intending to be an employer too? Well, I hate to point out the obvious but you happen to be a woman and that could be one hell of a problem. Beer saloons and bars are mostly male territory.'

'Like I said, this wouldn't just be your average kind of bar but somewhere to eat too and where a man could take his wife or sweetheart and listen to music and—'

'You singing,' he finished for her.

'Yes, me singing.' She was angry now, her green eyes shooting sparks and her mouth tight.

'All right, I'm a customer. Sing for me.' He leaned back in his chair, his blue gaze challenging as though he expected her to refuse.

Josie picked up the gauntlet. Rising to her feet she moved a few feet away, glaring at him before she took some deep breaths and attempted to compose herself. She hadn't sung in public since her marriage and she had hoped to be able to practise before she did anything like this. *Typical Jack*, she thought furiously, although she couldn't have explained what she meant by that.

After a few moments she shut her eyes and then tried to imagine herself back in the Fiddler's Elbow. She began to sing 'I'll Take You Home Again, Kathleen', partly because of Jack's genealogy but also because she found it easier to sing than some other songs. She knew she wasn't doing well at first but then as the joy of singing took over she let her voice have free rein.

Jack found he was holding his breath and had to remind himself to exhale. He hadn't dreamed that the girl who had lived with him for over three weeks, who had accompanied him on their trips here and there and who appeared so artless and defenceless, had a talent like this, a gift. As he'd got to know her he'd found it hard to reconcile the fact that she had married what he would term a gangster because in spite of her past she seemed an innocent, but here was yet another facet of her that was even more unbelievable. He'd always prided himself on being a good judge of his fellow man and liked to think that nothing surprised him, but with Josie he was constantly on the back foot and he didn't like that. He didn't like it at all. Several times over the last days he had cursed Hans for bringing her here but that didn't stop him being glad either. Damn it, she'd drive him round the bend before she was finished and now there was this too, her voice.

When the last note died away Josie opened her eyes. Jack was staring at her and though she couldn't put a name to the look on his face it made her stiffen.

It was a moment or two before he said, 'Why didn't you tell me you could sing? That you'd sung in England?'

'That was part of my old life.'

'But now you want to bring it into the new?'

'Aye, yes, I do.'

He nodded. 'I might be able to ask a few people if they want a singer, there's lots of bars and clubs in this city and—'

'No.' Now it was she who interrupted him. 'I've told you what I want to do and it's not singing for someone else. That bar for sale has accommodation above, that's what the notice said, and I could make it into my home. Luke could be asleep upstairs while I sing and I could pop up and keep an eye on him now and again when I take a break. If it goes well I might even be able to buy the premises or somewhere else, another bar. I – I would be in charge of my own life.'

'This is pie in the sky.' He shook his head. 'You've got no experience in running a place, woman.'

She wanted to tell him not to 'woman' her. Instead she said quietly, 'You have.'

He stared at her. 'Oh, no. No, no, no.' He shook his head. 'I have a good job already and I'm not leaving it for something that spells disaster.'

'I wasn't asking you to, just to give me some advice and help me find a suitable person to run the place, and a waitress.' It wasn't quite the truth, she admitted silently, because she'd harboured just the slightest hope that Jack might join her in this venture, but she couldn't blame him for not wanting to take what would be a huge risk. And perhaps she was crazy as he'd suggested, but if she could pull this off it would mean a home and job in one. Somewhere where she could live and care for Luke but work too. She had to try. Now she had thought of it, she *had* to.

'Josie, I wasn't kidding when I said disaster. I don't know what things are like back in England but here there's all sorts of complications you haven't taken into account. It's dog eat dog on the streets and to build up a business takes a hell of a lot of hard work and luck to make it a success. You're just a young woman—'

'*Don't.*' She glared at him. 'Don't say that because I'm not "just" anything. My husband called me stupid and thought I wouldn't be able to exist without him telling me what to do, and I'm not letting anyone treat me like that again or talk to me as if I'm not worth anything.'

Jack made a sound of exasperation. 'I didn't mean it like that. Hell, I was just trying to say how it is out there.

You're casting me as the bad guy when all I'm trying to do is stop you from making a big mistake. Your money will go and you'll be left with nothing. How will you take care of Luke then?'

'Luke will always come first with me.'

'Then prove it. If you are really determined to try your hand at singing here – and I have to say you've got a fine voice, by the way – I dare say I can twist the arms of a couple of people I know to give you a trial.'

He hadn't listened to a word she'd said. 'I don't want you to twist anyone's arm. I will do this and I'll succeed, with or without your help, Jack Kane, and frankly I'd prefer it to be without, all right? I can take care of myself.'

He raised disbelieving eyebrows.

'And don't look at me like that. You might think you're God's gift to the whole of mankind but I don't. You're self-opinionated and rude and bigoted.'

To her fury he had the gall to smile, but the movement of his features altered his whole face, the arrogant look going and making his Irish charm very evident as he said, 'Guilty as charged but if we're being honest you're wilful and unreasonable and a pain in the butt.' His head was back and he was laughing as he added, 'And all that in a little package that appears so delicate and fragile.' He brought his head forward and held her gaze for a moment as he added, soberly now, 'But you're not delicate and fragile, are you, Josie? Not inside. Who are you really? Because I'm damned if I know.'

Her lips were tight-pressed for a moment – his tone

hadn't been complimentary – and then she said, 'You know who I am. I haven't kept any secrets from you.'

'Except that you could sing.'

'That wasn't a secret,' she protested, annoyed that colour was suffusing her face. 'There was just no occasion to mention it. It wasn't important.'

'It's important enough for you to gamble your whole future on it,' he pointed out, one corner of his mouth lifted in an ironic smile.

He had an answer for everything, she thought with intense irritation, turning with a flounce and saying over her shoulder, 'I need to see to Luke.'

Once in the bedroom she plumped down on the bed and looked at her son, who was still fast asleep, his thumb in his mouth and his dark curls tousled. Was she being ridiculous in thinking she could run her own bar and make a success of it? She knew she had drawn the customers in at the Fiddler's Elbow; the Mullens had told her their takings had dropped once she had stopped working there, but they might have just been kind in saying that. And she was a stranger here, they weren't her people. They might even be hostile to a foreigner, a woman, thinking she could run her own undertaking. As Jack had just pointed out so condescendingly, she could lose all her money and then what would she and Luke do? She had brought him away from the McGuigans to give him a better start in life free of their criminal influence, not to starve on the streets of New York.

The bedroom was stuffy, the humidity was high, and

outside she knew the air would be like a suffocating blanket as the high-rise buildings trapped the heat. Suddenly she felt an intense homesickness for the sights and smells of the East End docks, for the keen north-east wind that was still cool on the hottest of summer days, and for her mother. She missed her mam, she thought, close to tears; she missed her so much. And Phyllis, she had been a good friend and here she had no one. She had promised herself that as soon as she had a permanent address she'd write to her mother care of the next-door neighbour, Flo. She needed that link with home, a tangible link with her mam. She sniffed, wiping her eyes.

After a while Luke began to stir. Forcing herself out of her melancholy thoughts, she fed and changed him. She was in the process of weaning him and now only breastfed him once in the morning and at bedtime. He was just over seven months and had taken like a duck to water to mushed-up rusks and vegetables reduced to a pulp. He was bonny and healthy and that was the main thing, she told herself as he smiled and gurgled at her. He slept well and was happy most of the time.

Once he was in his day clothes she picked him up and carried him through to the other room, preparing herself to face Jack again. The room was empty – he must have gone out, which was a relief because she was beginning to feel guilty about the way she had gone for him now she'd had time to think about it.

They had landed unannounced into his life, disrupting his relationship with Rose, his girlfriend, and invading his home, she told herself as she lay Luke on a blanket on the floor and gave the baby one of his rattles. And she had told him he was self-opinionated and rude and bigoted. And he *was*, she thought ruefully, but that wasn't the point.

She cleared away the breakfast things and put the flat to rights, which took all of ten minutes, and then sat down, the day seeming to stretch out endlessly in front of her as she watched Luke banging his rattle for all he was worth. She would go along and have a proper look at the bar, she decided, because it was clear Jack didn't intend to take them on one of their jaunts around the city before he went in to work at midday. Had she offended him? Probably. Which was another reason for her to move out as soon as she could.

She and Luke were on the verge of leaving when the door opened and Jack strode in. He eyed her coat and bonnet. 'Going somewhere?'

'For a walk.' She thought it prudent not to say where.

'Good. Then you can walk in the direction of that bar you were speaking about. You've got an appointment to look round it this morning. OK?'

'*What?*'

'That's what you wanted, isn't it? To see what it's like? The shop-owner next door has the keys and I know him.'

This didn't surprise her. Jack knew everybody. Whenever she was out with him she was amazed at the number of people who spoke to him. She stared in astonishment. 'But you said you thought it was a disastrous idea.'

'I still do.' And he was hoping when she saw the work involved to get the place up and going, let alone making the two floors above habitable, that she'd come to her senses.

'Then why . . .'

'You won't be satisfied until you've seen it,' he said shortly, 'and it doesn't hurt to let the people concerned know you're a friend of mine.'

A frisson of excitement swept through her.

Seeing her face, Jack groaned inwardly but his voice was expressionless when he said, 'I understand from Seamus, the guy next door, that the previous inhabitants ran the place down and then did a runner owing umpteen weeks of rent. The owner's had a couple of such instances and he's sick and tired of the aggravation and was looking to sell but has had no takers, hence the "For Rent" sign. Hell's Kitchen is not as bad an area as down in Lower East Side south of Five Points but you still need to keep your wits about you. The competition will be fierce if you open the bar and the clientele will be a mixed bunch.'

Josie nodded. She realized what he was doing. His offer to take her there was to show her he was right and this was a mad idea. But she wasn't going to engage in another argument. 'Shall we go then?' she said brightly.

Jack took Luke from her without further words and they made their way downstairs and out onto the street. The heat hit her like a brick wall and already it was busy but then the city never seemed to sleep. In some ways it was like Sunderland – you had the poor immigrants, who were less educated and from the peasant classes, living in tenements where there were no inside bathrooms and kerosene was the only source of lighting; but then there were the richer areas too where electric street lights lit the night and the middle-class families and the wealthy lived in their beautiful apartments. But in most respects New York was a different world from the one she had left behind.

The tenement line did divide rich from poor, she thought as they walked along dusty pavements, but also those who had access to all the new products and technology Jack had told her about from those who did not.

The city, with its horse-cars with coloured lights and jingling bells, and the rapidly rushing elevated trains overhead, gave an air of briskness to the streets that Sunderland had never had. Money had been important back home, of course, but here it seemed to be the god that governed everything, a calling card that enabled progress to be purchased. And there was such a diverse mix of cultures and people everywhere and so far she liked that. It seemed like a big melting pot. Street music, whether played by black folk, Jews, Italians or Irish, was everywhere and it was a common sight to see hats on the pavements for offerings from the wealthier citizens.

She was well aware that she had been under the protection of Jack thus far though; how she'd fare when she was on her own she didn't know. Nevertheless, she intended not only to survive but to carve out a future for herself and her son in this vibrant city of stark contrasts that was both cruel and benevolent.

The thought brought her head up and her eyes narrowing with determination. She could do it. Given a chance she could make something of herself here. There would be those who disapproved, of course. Even here on the other side of the world women were expected to make the sphere of home and family life their primary focus. If they had to work, then it should be as a shop girl or domestic or in a clothing factory, or for those with a young family taking in homework. But not as a bar owner, she thought wryly. Never that.

It seemed as though Jack had read her mind because he stopped suddenly. Looking down at her, he said quietly, 'You do understand that if you take this on it will alienate you from respectable society?'

Perversely now, in view of her earlier thoughts, Josie said, 'I don't see why. Women should be able to go into business if they choose to do so and be independent.'

He raised his eyebrows in the superior way that always hit her on the raw. 'I see I've got a Victoria Woodhull on my hands.'

She looked at him warily. 'Who is she?'

'A passionate supporter of suffrage and the first female presidential candidate who worked as a stockbroker and founded a weekly newspaper.'

'Well, good for her.'

'Not really. Her opponents made sure her reputation was destroyed and she was left bankrupt and ostracized.'

'Because she dared to challenge this male-dominated society?' Josie asked indignantly.

'That, and her advocacy of more radical ideas such as socialism and in particular free love,' Jack said drily.

In spite of herself, Josie blushed. 'She was entitled to her own opinions surely, whatever they were?'

'Of course she was. I'm just pointing out that if you continue with this ridiculous notion you'll be misunderstood by certain people, that's all.'

'Well, maybe Miss Woodhull thought standing up for what she believed in was worth the cost.'

He stared at her. 'Maybe she did at that,' he said after a moment or two. He began walking again and after looking at him for some seconds she hurried to catch up. 'People are welcome to think what they like about me,' she said defiantly. 'I'm not a stranger to gossip and tittle-tattle.'

That might be true, Jack thought, but he found he didn't like the notion of Josie being the subject of speculation and that in itself bothered him. He kept telling himself that she was a married woman with a kid, the last sort of female he wanted to get mixed up with, but somehow she'd got under his skin. He hadn't been aware of her existence a month ago, so how come he was now thinking about her all the time whatever he was doing? It was crazy; everything about the current situation was crazy. He knew his mother would be horrified if she found out he had a woman living at the apartment; she was very strait-laced. And Josie was English, that would put the cat among the pigeons. There was Rose too. She was getting increasingly unhappy about the situation and he couldn't blame her.

His voice flat, he said shortly, 'Just don't say that I didn't warn you.'

'I wouldn't dream of it,' she said primly.

Annoyed and irritated though he was, Jack wanted to smile. *She was one on her own. She really was.*

The bar was situated in Horatio Street not far from the piers where the big liners like Cunard and White Star docked. As they reached it, Josie found her heart was racing. While Jack popped next door to get the key from Seamus she looked up at the building, which was sandwiched between Seamus's grocery shop on one side and a laundry on the other. It was less than imposing. The ground-floor windows had been boarded up and a couple in the two floors above were cracked and broken. An old sign hung lopsidedly on a rusty chain above the flaking front door but the lettering was so faded she couldn't read what it said.

Jack appeared with the key and she noticed that a man, Seamus she presumed, had followed him to the door of the shop and was standing looking at her. She raised her hand and waved, and he called, 'Top of the morning to you, m'dear,' in a broad Irish accent.

Jack didn't turn to look at him, adjusting Luke in the crook of his arm as he inserted the large key in the lock. As the door swung open and they stepped into the interior of the building the smell of stale beer and cigarette smoke greeted them. It was dark and dingy with no light coming from the boarded windows but she could see Jack hadn't exaggerated when he'd said that the previous tenants had run the place down.

They were standing in a large room divided into two areas. To the left the bar had a number of stools – some of which were lying on their sides – and a few small tables. To the right were larger tables and chairs. Everything reeked of neglect.

Josie said nothing, walking across to a door which led into an internal passageway. Halfway along this they found a good-sized kitchen. It possessed two stone sinks with taps so there was clearly piped water into the property; a beast of a range which reminded Josie of the one at the Fiddler's Elbow; and a battered old table and chairs. Apart from a few shelves on one wall there was nothing else – no cupboards and no cooking utensils. 'I understand from Silas that the family who rented it took all the pots and pans and glasses and what-have-you when they did their moonlight flit,' Jack said expressionlessly.

Josie just nodded in reply. His tone had made it quite clear what he thought of the property.

The back door of the kitchen led into a small private yard containing a brick-built lavatory and an enormous coal bunker. The lavatory was filthy – the family clearly hadn't been too particular in their habits, she thought grimly – but the state of it was practically pristine compared to the two in another much larger yard at the far end of the passageway, which had obviously been for the customers' use. A padlocked and bolted door led into the street through which she assumed deliveries could be made.

Retracing their footsteps, they entered the building and

walked to the opposite end of the passageway where a
staircase led to the first floor. The stairs were steep and
narrow and Josie was thankful of the handrail. There
were two rooms on this level, one a large sitting room
with a fireplace and another which was considerably
smaller, possibly used for storage. The top landing led on
to two bedrooms of equal size which had a distinct odour
of stale urine. One held a big iron bedstead with no
mattress and the other was empty.

Once they were standing in the bar area again, Josie
turned to Jack. He hadn't said a word throughout the
inspection except at one point to console Luke, who had
begun to grizzle. 'If I wanted to buy this, how much
would it cost?' she said without any preamble.

'*Buy it?*'

'If I'm going to spend money and time doing the place
up and getting it nice, I don't want to line someone else's
pocket. That doesn't make sense.'

'And buying this' – he paused, seemingly lost for words
for a moment – 'this heap of garbage does?'

'I can see beyond what it looks like now.'

'I don't believe this,' he said ominously.

'It's not in the really bad part of the city and in a fairly
respectable street. That's a start.' She had been reading
the papers over the last weeks and had taken note of the
property prices, along with absorbing the feel of the
different districts that Jack had taken her to on their
excursions.

'A start?'

'Aye, a start,' she said sharply, nettled by his tone. 'I'm hardly going to get somewhere in Fifth Avenue or overlooking Central Park. Once I start eating into my money to live it will dwindle away – this is my only chance to make it work for me. I'm fully aware I can't compete with fancy restaurants and the clubs uptown, and actually I wouldn't want to. This'll be for ordinary men and women to come for a simple meal or just a drink while they listen to me sing for them now and again.'

'This is sheer madness.'

Neither his vehement disapproval nor his somewhat incredulous attitude swayed her, not after what she had escaped from across the ocean. 'Well?' she said in a clear, unswerving tone that told the man in front of her she meant business. 'Do you know how much this place is?'

'More than you can afford.'

'Then perhaps I can come to some arrangement with the owner. Pay him by instalments, something like that. I'll get the details from Seamus and go and see him.'

For once in his life Jack was at a loss as to what to say and when she turned and walked out of the front door, leaving it open for him to follow, he did just that, feeling as though he had just been run over by a steamroller.

Chapter Seventeen

'It's been over two months since she vanished into thin air, taking my son with her.'

'I know, man, I know.' Bruce's tone was consoling. 'I'm doing all I can.'

Adam had raised his upper body on his elbows when his brother had first come into the bedroom, but now he sank back against the pile of pillows propped behind his back. The room was dark although the sun was bright outside – he kept the curtains closed day and night – and it smelled strongly of antiseptic with an underlying, more unpleasant smell of stale air and faeces. His tone aggressive, he said, 'Well, whatever you're doing it's not enough. Someone has to know where she is. How much have you offered for information?'

'Plenty, you know I have.'

'I don't believe that Bell woman doesn't know anything. Thick as thieves they were.'

Bruce harboured his own suspicions about the part Adam's cook had played in Josie's departure, but after speaking to her he knew he wasn't going to get anything out of her and it was easier to deny it to his brother. 'If she knew owt she'd say, with the amount of money I waved in front of her nose. Don't forget she and the maid are out of a job now and they'll be lucky to get something that pays as well.'

When it had become clear that Adam was destined for the life of an invalid, their mother had insisted her youngest son, her baby, came to live with her. At the time he and Phyllis had thought it was a bad decision but Adam hadn't cared one way or the other and so his mother had got what she wanted. Adam's house had been put on the market and the staff had been dismissed. Adam was already regretting it as Bruce had known he would. Their mother fussed about everything and was constantly in his room, arguing with the nurse he had employed to take care of his brother and causing one upset after another.

'I want her to pay for what she's done and I want Luke back under my roof, damn it,' Adam growled.

Bruce didn't point out that it wasn't Adam's roof he was living under. Instead he said gently, 'So do we all.' Every time he visited his brother he wanted to wring Josie's neck and he wouldn't rest until she was six foot under. It was eating his mother up too; all she spoke about was revenge. As for Adam, he believed the only thing keeping his brother alive was the thought of his wife getting her just deserts. Even having his son back paled into insignificance beside that. His hate was consuming him. They'd had several leads in the last weeks which had proved false and sent his men scurrying here, there and everywhere, but as Adam had said, it really was as if she and Luke had vanished into thin air.

Now Bruce broached the topic his mother had urged him to raise with Adam. 'Look, lad,' he said softly, 'you've got to eat something now and again.' He didn't add, 'Especially with what you're drinking,' because Adam was getting through a bottle of whisky a day or more, and raised merry hell if their mother or the nurse tried to limit him. He'd told her she had to be firm – it wasn't as if Adam could fetch the bottles himself, was it – but she had just burst into tears and said that he didn't know how bad things were. 'It's all he's got,' she'd sobbed, 'and if I try to restrict it he goes berserk and talks about killing himself. The nurse found a pile of tablets he'd hidden when she'd thought he'd swallowed them just the other day. He rants and raves and throws things, and sometimes when Nurse Potts has to change him he' – she put her hands over her eyes – 'he cries. What are we going to do?'

Adam was glaring at him and his voice was quivering with the temper that flared umpteen times a day as he said, 'She put you up to this, didn't she. Our dear mother?'

It would be useless to deny it. 'She's worried to death about you, we all are.'

'Would you want to eat if you were like this?' Adam said savagely. 'A cripple, wallowing in your own filth? Well, would you? Looking at four walls and wishing you could just die?'

'It doesn't have to be this way. The doctor said if you eat and drink properly and get into a routine your bowels would become more regular. You could get used to that wheelchair I got. Come downstairs for meals and meet people. Even go into the office if you wanted to.'

'And risk soiling myself in company?' Adam ground out bitterly. 'I prefer people to remember me as I was.'

'The doctor said—'

'*Don't talk to me about him.*' For a second or two there was silence as Bruce watched Adam trying to control himself. Then he repeated, 'Don't talk to me about him,' in a quieter tone that nevertheless vibrated with rage. 'He congratulated me on the fact that I still had use of my arms and head. Do you know that? I could have killed him there and then.'

Bruce stood up from where he'd been sitting in an armchair pulled close to the bed. His voice grim, he said, 'Well, you do, don't you.'

Adam swore, a foul profanity. 'Get out.'

'I'm going, but think on this. If you continue to lie here rotting away she's won. In every way she's won. Now I'll find her, I promise you that, and before I'm done with her she'll be begging for me to put her out of her misery, but I'm not bringing Luke home to a father who's six foot under because he hadn't got the guts to fight.'

Adam's voice was a scream when again he cried, '*Get out!*'

'You can still live a life. All right, not the one you would have chosen but it doesn't have to be in this lair shut away from the light like some injured animal. The exercises you were told about to strengthen your arms and chest would be a start. And you don't have to live here with Mam. I could see to it you get somewhere else when you're ready, even build you a place that's adapted to your needs.'

When Adam threw the bottle of whisky that had been on his bedside table it missed Bruce by a whisker, smashing into the empty fireplace on the other side of the room.

Bruce didn't react, merely walking slowly towards the door with his eyes on his enraged brother. 'You see?' he said quietly as he opened it. 'You've got more strength than you think in spite of trying to starve yourself.'

He shut the door just before there was another crash inside the room and stood on the landing with his hand over his eyes. He hadn't cried since he was a bairn but now he was near to doing so. When the nurse came running from her room next door to Adam's, he stopped her going in to his brother. 'Leave him,' he said flatly. Repeating this in the next moment when his mother came flying up the stairs, he added, 'I mean it.'

As the nurse walked hesitantly back into her room, Bruce took Sadie by the arm, almost dragging her down the stairs and into the drawing room. Once in there he pushed her down none too gently onto the couch. 'You give him an hour or two to think about what I've said before you start on the mollycoddling,' he said grimly.

'*Mollycoddling?*'

'Aye, mollycoddling.'

'How can you say that? Because of that woman he's a cripple, barely able to move an—'

'He can move, Mam, as I've just told him. All right, not his legs but the rest of him.'

'*You didn't say that!*'

'Yes, I did and you shouting at me isn't going to help things. Now listen to me. I understand he needed indulging and looking after when he came out of hospital but that was some weeks ago. It was you who insisted he came out and that you'd have a nurse to tend to him when the doctors wanted him to stay in a bit longer and I went along with it, hoping it'd snap him out of how he was feeling. Instead he's ten times worse. All this pampering and cosseting isn't doing him any good, and neither is the whisky he's pouring down his throat and the raging tantrums he's throwing at the drop of a hat.'

'I can't believe you're talking to me like this,' Sadie said furiously.

'Someone has to and as usual in this family it's me who carries the can. You told me yourself he hid some tablets and that can't happen again, neither can him not eating and making that room of his into what's virtually a hiding place from the world.'

'You're cruel. To talk about him like this when he's so ill. Cruel and unfeeling.'

'Do you want to lose him, Mam? Well, do you? Because if you don't join with me in this and try to help you're going to walk into that room one day and find him dead, the way he's going on.'

For a moment Bruce thought she was going to fly at him, such was the look on her face, but then it crumpled and she burst into tears. He sat down beside her, putting his arm round her as he said, 'I love him, Mam, same as you, which is why I'm saying all this. Now you might not believe that—'

'I do, I do.' Her hand moved and rested on top of his.

This has almost destroyed her, Bruce thought, more moved at the gesture than he would have been able to express. His mother was fire and brimstone normally, fashioned in iron with no weaknesses, but then Adam had always been her Achilles heel. 'Well, then,' he said softly, 'we have to all pull together in getting him as well as he can be. There's no reason why he can't use that wheelchair in time and even learn to manoeuvre himself in and out of bed and so on. Wash himself, things like that. A man needs such independence. You understand that, don't you?'

Her head nodded.

'But with his horror of illness and distaste of all things medical, he won't try unless he's pushed. Depending on how he manages he might even be able to return to work and get involved in the business again. It'll give him a focus, a reason to live.'

'She took away his reason to live when she took his son,' Sadie said bitterly.

'I'm working on that. I won't stop until I find them both. I promised him that and I'm promising you. I'll bring Luke home where he belongs.'

'And her?'

'She'll be disposed of,' Bruce said grimly.

'I want her to suffer like he's suffering—'

'Mam, stop.' Bruce squeezed her hand. 'Let's concentrate on Adam, all right? Now, I've been thinking about this for a few days so hear me out before you speak. I know someone, a man who's been looking after an invalid in a similar position to Adam for years.'

She stared at him. 'What do you mean?'

'Larry, who works for me, it's his eldest brother. He used to be a footman at a big house Durham way but when the owner of the estate was injured in a hunting accident apparently he couldn't stand having nurses attend to him. To cut a long story short, Arthur eventually took over his care and he'd been seeing to the man for nigh on twenty years until he died a few weeks ago. He'd got close to the old man in a master-and-servant way, a sight too close as far as some of the family were concerned, and when the master popped his clogs Arthur found himself out on his ear without so much as a by-your-leave. Now, he used to see to all the old man's needs and he'd even been trained regarding his medication and things like that. More of a male nurse than anything, Larry says, and nothing throws him. He's as strong as a bull and used to taking some stick – the old man could be a right so-an'-so when the mood took him like all the gentry.'

Sadie removed her hand from that of her son and wiped her eyes with a handkerchief before saying, 'You think he'd come and work here?'

'I don't know but I could ask. It's not working with the nurse, is it? Adam doesn't like her and she's certainly not equipped to do what Arthur could, like heaving him about, taking him to the bathroom and assisting him with bathing, getting him in the wheelchair and so on. It's not good for him to be confined to bed all the time, Mam. You must see that? Bed baths are all right for those who need them—'

'Adam needs them.'

'No, he doesn't, Mam. Not any more. He's got to get back to some sort of normality and Arthur could help with that. He'd be employed as a manservant and that's the way we'd put it to Adam.'

Sadie stared at her son. She could see the sense of what he was saying and the tablet thing had frightened her more than a little. 'You're a good lad, Bruce,' she said quietly. And so were the others. So why was the feeling she had for her other offspring lukewarm compared to how she felt about Adam? And now that chit had ruined his life. She hadn't known what real hate was until she had stood by Adam's bedside in the hospital and looked down at his broken body.

She stood up, walking over to the ornate fireplace and standing looking down at the flower display in the grate before she turned, saying, 'All right. See if this Arthur wants the job and if he does I'll get rid of Nurse Potts. As you say, it's not working with her. I'll tell Adam what we've decided when it's settled but you know he'll play up, don't you? It won't be easy.'

'Nothing ever is,' Bruce said a little wearily. And if Adam *did* improve and wanted his own place, there'd be hell to pay with his mother, but he'd cross that bridge when he came to it. They were a long way from that at present. 'I'd better be away but I'll call in later and let you know what Arthur says. He's staying with Larry and his wife for the time being until something turns up.'

Sadie nodded. She'd thought that when she brought Adam home everything would be as it had been before he'd got married, which in hindsight had been silly. Nevertheless, she hadn't bargained for what would virtually be a male nurse if this Arthur came to stay, and in truth she wasn't enamoured of the idea. But as Bruce had said, they had to try something else. She didn't want to lose him.

It was six-thirty the same evening and Adam was filled with a cold black fury that had been building all day since his brother's earlier visit. He ground his teeth, the pain in his body nothing compared to the torment his mind inflicted every waking moment.

He had just caused Nurse Potts to flee out of the room in tears after he'd sworn and thrown a glass of water in her face, spitting out the pills she'd been attempting to give him. If he could have got his hands round her throat he would have, he told himself. He was sick of being talked to as though he was a toddler, with her 'Now, now' this and 'Be a good boy' that. The woman was driving him mad and she had a face like a battered pluck to boot.

He looked up as the door opened, ready to shout at her to get out, but it was his mother not the nurse, and he could see from the look on her face that she wasn't happy. Well, neither was he, he thought bitterly.

'You've done it this time,' his mother said expression-lessly. 'Nurse Potts is leaving.'

'Good riddance.' His voice was petulant, like a child's, and he scowled at her.

'She's a very experienced nurse, Adam, and she's done her best for you. I understand you threw water in her face when she refused to bring you another bottle of whisky?'

He glared at her. 'Damn right.'

'She was only following my orders. When you eat something you can have a glass or two now and again, but no more bottles in your room.'

His eyes narrowed. 'Oh, I get it. You've been talking to Bruce.'

'Your brother is worried about you. We all are. You need to eat properly if you are going to get well.'

'But I'm not going to get well, am I, Mother dear?' he said with deep sarcasm. 'It may have slipped your mind but I am paralysed.'

'No, it hasn't slipped my mind. I think of little else.' She surprised him by walking across the room and opening the curtains before flinging the windows wide. The late-evening sunshine and the sweet perfume of climbing roses spilled into the room. Paying no attention to his curses, she said, 'It's a beautiful evening.'

'The hell it is.'

'As you have successfully got rid of Nurse Potts you'll need someone in her place, someone who won't be affected by your bullying.'

He was astounded. 'By my what?' he snarled.

'Fortunately for you, Bruce had already had someone in mind and the person concerned can start tomorrow.'

'I don't want another damn nurse.'

'Good, because you won't be getting one.' Sadie didn't know where the strength was coming from to talk to her beloved son like this. 'Arthur is Larry's brother and he'll be engaged as your manservant. He has experience of caring for an' – she had been going to say invalid, but altered it to – 'a person with your particular needs.'

Adam stared at his mother. 'Over my dead body.'

'Well, the way you're going on, that will be soon, won't it,' Sadie said without a trace of humour. 'Anyway, you've complained incessantly about Nurse Potts so I would have thought you'd be pleased. Arthur will be able to take you to the bathroom and assist you with dressing, attending to your needs twenty-four hours a day if necessary, and once you're getting about in the wheelchair he can drive you wherever you wish to go.'

The sunlight after weeks of shadowed gloom was hurting his eyes and outside he could hear the grass being mown. He didn't want to be reminded that there was a world beyond the four walls of his bedroom that he could no longer function in, and now, his voice rising, he shouted, 'Shut up and get out. Whatever you and Bruce have hatched up between you, you can forget it.' His breathing was becoming rapid, his heart racing inside his chest, and not for the first time he wondered why everything worked from the waist up when his legs were dead. If only his heart had stopped in the fall he'd be out of this hell now. 'And bring me a bottle of whisky, damn you.'

In the light from the window Sadie could see just how white and skeletal he'd become, the sunshine accentuating his sick pallor and lacklustre hair. It frightened her, in fact it terrified her, and it was this fear rather than everything Bruce had said that prompted her next words. 'I told you, Adam,' she said tightly through the churning in her stomach, 'until you eat, no more whisky. Your supper will be arriving shortly. If you eat it, I'll bring you a glass of whisky myself.'

'Mam, I need it.' His voice had become pleading. 'It's all I've got. Please, Mam.'

For a moment she almost weakened, her heart breaking. Her lips moved one over the other. It had been like an appeal from a child, like the boy he'd once been. Drawing on every scrap of strength she had, she walked to the door. 'It's a light meal, an omelette followed by one of Cook's lemon soufflés,' she said flatly, before she opened the door and walked out, closing it quietly behind her.

Chapter Eighteen

Flo McHaffie had been waiting most of the morning for Ralph Gray to leave the house. Maggie had told her that Josie would be writing at some point and Flo didn't need to be told why the letters couldn't be delivered directly next door. Why Maggie had ever married the man, she didn't know, Flo told herself for the umpteenth time. Her friend had been pretty once, before life and grinding poverty had made her prematurely old. And him. Ralph Gray. Flo's lips curled. Her Hector had his faults, but he was a saint compared to that swine.

Peering out from behind the faded kitchen curtains, her patience was finally rewarded when she saw the small, skinny shape of Maggie's husband leave the house through the back yard and walk into the lane beyond. She finished the last of her tea in the enamel mug, took off her apron, hitched up her ample breasts with her forearms and left the house by the back door, walking through her yard and into the one next door, the letter from America safely hidden in the pocket of her serge skirt.

She saw Maggie through the kitchen window and tapped on the glass before entering the house. Her voice low, although they were alone, she said, 'It's come, lass.'

'Praise God.' Maggie made the sign of the cross. 'I was beginning to think . . .'

She didn't say what she had been thinking but Flo knew anyway. She drew the letter out of her pocket as she said, 'I told you she'd be all right, didn't I? She might be young but your Josie's bright up top.' *Except in her choice of a husband*, she qualified in her head. *If ever there was a family not to get mixed up with, it was the McGuigans.*

Maggie took the envelope, the sight of Josie's familiar handwriting bringing tears to her eyes. She'd been worried to death as the weeks had crawled by. Ralph had told her that the McGuigans had offered a hefty reward to anyone with information as to Josie's whereabouts, and she didn't doubt that if Bruce got his hands on her it'd be the last anyone heard of her lass. Ralph had been in a foul mood too. For one thing, he could no longer bask in the dubious glow of having a daughter who'd married into the family that controlled most of the crime in the East End, and he was desperate to get back into the McGuigans' good graces again. He refused to believe that she didn't know where the lass and bairn were, losing his temper with her a few times but careful to hit her where it didn't show.

'Sit down and I'll put the kettle on,' she said to Flo, although she would much rather have been alone to read the letter in peace and quiet.

'Thanks, lass. I could do with a cuppa,' Flo said as though she hadn't had several during the morning. She sat down at the kitchen table, which although battered was scrubbed and clean. More than once when Josie had been married to Adam McGuigan there had been a vase of flowers in the middle of it and bowls of hyacinths in the spring. Scented the room, they had, she thought wistfully, but there'd be no more such gifts now, nor any of the groceries Josie had brought her mam each week along with money slipped Maggie's way. She'd been good to her mam, had Josie, she'd give the lass that, even though she had brought all this trouble on the family. No one in their right mind would want to be on the wrong side of Bruce McGuigan and his brothers.

Once the tea had mashed and Maggie joined her at the table, Flo said eagerly, 'You gonna open the letter then?'

Suppressing a sigh, Maggie took it out of the deep pocket of her apron. She'd been hoping Flo would take the hint that she'd put it away to read later.

She'd had little schooling and she read slowly and laboriously, savouring each word from her lass.

'She all right?' Flo asked after a minute or two.

'Aye.' Maggie had to wipe her eyes. 'She's got somewhere for herself and the bairn to live, and a pal of the sea captain who took her to America on his boat is helping her to settle in. She said not to worry and the bairn's well and happy.'

'Aw, that's grand, lass. I told you she'd be all right,

didn't I? Your Josie's got her head screwed on the right way and she's as bonny as a summer's day; she'll always come out on top.'

Maggie nodded. Aye, she was as bonny as a summer's day all right but that had been the trouble in the first place with Adam McGuigan. And now Josie was in a foreign country with no family or friends, apart from this man she'd mentioned. And who knew what his intentions were?

'Do you want me to take the letter back and hide it at mine?'

It would be the sensible thing to do but she desperately wanted to keep it here where she could read and re-read it when she was alone. Maggie shook her head. 'I'll hide it here, I've got a place where I keep anything I don't want Ralph to get his hands on. There's a loose brick at the side of the range.'

Flo understood this. She had her own secret place under one of the floorboards in the bedroom. It didn't do for your man to know if you managed to save a penny or two out of the housekeeping for a rainy day, especially if the thirst was on them. Not that her Hector drank as such, but nevertheless. Smiling at her friend, she said warmly, 'Well, now that you can write to her and she can write to you, you'll feel better, lass.'

Maggie gave a flicker of a smile back but didn't comment. She knew Flo didn't understand how she felt about Josie, how she had always felt. There were some who said you loved all your bairns the same but she didn't believe that. How could you when they were all different people with their own ways and natures? She had loved Toby and she loved Joe, the three girls too, but there had always been a special bond with Josie from when the lass was a toddler and it was a heart thing that you couldn't put into words. The knowledge that she might never see her again was a physical pain in her chest. But the lass had had to go, she knew that.

When Phyllis had come round that morning and explained how Adam had been left after the accident and that he was blaming Josie, she'd understood why the lass had had to flee during the night. Of course, it didn't help with the McGuigans that she'd taken Luke with her, but what mother worth her salt would leave her babby behind? But they wouldn't accept that; it had been clear from day one that Sadie in particular looked on Luke as solely a McGuigan and Josie had told her that Bruce and Adam had already been making plans for the little lad's future.

Maggie shifted in her chair. Phyllis had told her how Adam had attacked her lass that night and about his carrying-on with other women, and it had forced her to open her eyes to what she'd been trying to ignore ever since the marriage. Her lass had been unhappy, desperately unhappy. But for it to end the way it had . . . And Phyllis had confided that the McGuigans had had a hand in Toby's death too, which had made her sick to her stomach. When Bruce's wife had left that day, she had given in to a storm of weeping and raging against the McGuigans until she'd exhausted herself, the intensity of her hate and bitterness at what they'd done to her lad actually frightening her in the end. She prayed every night they'd burn in hell for all eternity and she wasn't going to apologize for it either, whatever the good Lord said about forgiveness.

She and Flo talked a little more before her friend left, promising she'd bring any further letters round when she was sure that Ralph was out of the way. 'My Hector's always left for the docks when the postie comes,' Flo said, 'not that he'd say anything to Ralph if he did know. But better to keep it atween us, lass, eh?'

Once she was alone, Maggie made another pot of tea and then re-read the letter through several times, her finger tracing the words her lass had written and pressing the envelope to her heart before she tucked it away in her hidey-hole. The relief of knowing that Josie and Luke were safe had taken a great weight off her mind, but she knew she'd have to be careful not to give anything away to Ralph. He had a way of picking up on things that was uncanny at times and he'd have no compunction about going to the McGuigans with a reward in the offing.

She'd have to let Phyllis know about Josie, of course, she told herself as she began her baking, but here again she'd need to be canny. Phyllis had come to see her a couple of times since Josie had gone, but the lass had warned her not to come to her own house in case Bruce was around or he found out from one of the servants that she'd called. She'd wait till Phyllis paid her another visit here, that was safest.

Whatever happened, Bruce McGuigan mustn't find out where Josie and the babby were – her lass was safe across the ocean and Flo was right; Josie would make a new life for herself. She was courageous and strong and intelligent but all that would count for nothing if the McGuigans got their hands on her. Look what they'd done to her boy; devils they were, devils.

Wiping away the tears that always came when she thought of Toby, she put the bread tins on their shelf to prove and then poured a cup of tea. Many a time she and Josie had enjoyed a quiet sup together, she thought, and she missed her more than words could say, her lad too. She'd lost them both in different ways, but at least her lass was still in the land of the living and she thanked the Lord for preserving her and the bairn. She'd pay a visit to Toby's grave tomorrow and tell him his sister was safe; he'd be glad about that, bless him.

Chapter Nineteen

'The sign's been put up,' said Josie, grinning from ear to ear as she opened the door of the building to Jack.

'So I noticed. It looks great.' So did everything else. The broken windows had new glass and had been painted, along with the front door, and the white sign hanging on a gleaming chain simply read *Gray's*.

Josie had been working on the place for two months and living there for six weeks once she'd got the two bedrooms clean and furnished. A carpenter Jack knew had built cupboards in the kitchen and a plumber, who was the carpenter's brother, had added washbasins in the two customer's lavatories and the one off the kitchen which Josie and her staff would use. He'd also installed a boiler in the kitchen to provide hot water. Where possible, Josie had done all the work herself to keep costs down and if she never saw another paintbrush in her life she would be happy, she thought now as she ushered Jack in.

They had gone to see the owner of the building – a

Mr Allen – together. He had initially been reluctant about Josie's idea of paying by instalments, but after some persuasion had agreed that she could put a down payment on the premises with the rest of the money to be paid off within five years. A contract to that effect had been drawn up by a reputable solicitor who'd warned Josie that if she didn't keep to her side of the agreement, Mr Allen would be perfectly within his rights to claim the building back lock, stock and barrel. Jack had baulked at this but Mr Allen had made it clear it was a 'take it or leave it' deal. Josie had taken it.

'This room looks welcoming,' Jack said now. She had paint in her hair and smudges on her face but she looked adorable. She always did as far as he was concerned, he admitted to himself ruefully. Which was becoming more of a problem lately. He knew Josie regarded him simply as a friend and after the abuse she'd suffered at the hands of her husband she wasn't looking for a romantic rela-tionship, but unfortunately what his brain told him and how he felt were at loggerheads. For the first time in his life he wanted a woman who didn't want him and it was unsettling.

'It does, doesn't it,' said Josie, gazing around with immense satisfaction. She had been working whenever she could in the day but once Luke was in bed she'd beavered away till dawn. She had invested in a peram-bulator for the baby and when she surrounded him with his toys he played happily most of the time, watching her while she worked, but still needed feeding and changing at regular intervals. She had survived on catnaps now for weeks but the excitement and vision for what she had wanted to accomplish had kept her going.

Jack had come along and lent a hand for a couple of hours before he had to go to the bar where he worked, but overall she had achieved most of the renovation herself. And she was thrilled with the results. Exhausted but thrilled. All right, it wasn't a grand place like some of the establishments New York's rich and elite patronized, but then she hadn't been aiming for that. She knew she couldn't compete with the din and dazzle of Broadway, where on warm nights the theatregoing crowds kept cool on lovely roof gardens which featured musical comedies and other shows along with a refreshing breeze, and where the bars and cafés did a roaring trade, but Gray's wasn't a shoddy place either.

She'd decided at the beginning that she would focus on cleanliness and inviting surroundings, along with low prices for the folk who came to eat and drink at Gray's. The kitchen would provide fast, inexpensive meals served by the waitress she'd employ and made by a female cook. There were a good number of women who needed employment in the male-dominated workplaces where male chefs and waiters were the norm. She was interviewing several women who had replied to the advertisement she'd put in the large front window that very afternoon, and had been anxious to get everything finished before then. And she had, she congratulated herself, as she walked into the bar-cum-restaurant with Jack at her heels.

It was a very different environment to the dismal room she'd encountered on her first visit. The bar gleamed and the long mirror behind it made the area seem bigger than it was. New red stools and some easy chairs sat in the area, and beyond them in the restaurant the white-painted tables and chairs were bright and welcoming with their crisp linen tablecloths and thick cushioned seats on the chairs. The pale-lemon painted walls reflected any sunshine and the new blinds at the windows and polished wood floor gave the welcoming ambience she'd been aiming for. She had got the carpenter to build a narrow, eighteen-inches-high platform in one of the alcoves which was where she intended to sing, perhaps for twenty minutes or so at hourly intervals. There was no room for a piano, which was a shame, she thought, but she would make do.

Jack gazed round him. The early-morning sunlight was streaming in the large main window and everything looked fresh and sparkling clean. He knew the kitchen was the same and now stocked with plenty of pots and pans and crockery and other necessary equipment. The sitting room and the smaller room next to it on the first floor had been the last things on Josie's list, and looking at her this morning he assumed she had been up all night again finishing those. 'I take my hat off to you,' he said softly. 'If sheer determination brings success then you'll go far.'

Their glances held for a second before Josie said, 'But you have your doubts.'

He was saved a reply by the sound of Luke shouting,

'Mama!' as he woke up in his bedroom. The first thing he did every morning was to bellow for his mother. He was a happy child on the whole but Jack had noticed he was given to furious tantrums if he didn't get his own way – though that didn't happen very often. Josie spoiled him, but then that was probably a mixture of regrets and guilt about the past, Jack thought. She had been the means of removing the child from all the family he had, from his father and grandparents and aunts and uncles. He understood why, of course; even without the incident which had caused her to leave England the boy would have been brought up under the influence of his father's family, which inevitably would have led to him becoming embroiled in their criminal pursuits, but still it must have been one hell of a decision to make.

Josie had sped off as soon as the child had called and now Jack walked through and climbed the stairs to the sitting room. It smelled strongly of fresh paint and like the room below had been transformed into a bright, clean and comfortable place to sit and relax. The second-hand three-piece suite and rug in the centre of the wooden floor were all of reasonable quality and the fireplace contained a small vase of dried flowers. A box of Luke's toys stood in an alcove and above this were several shelves, as yet devoid of objects. The curtains at the window were thick and a deep scarlet colour, and Jack could imagine the room would be cosy in the winter months with a fire and the drapes closed to shut out the weather. Everything she did displayed good taste, he told himself, but would that be enough for her to make a go of the bar and restaurant downstairs? He hoped so. She'd put her heart and soul into the place.

Josie came into the room carrying Luke. The baby was all smiles and held out his chubby arms to Jack. As he took the child and sat down on the floor with him, extracting a top from the toybox and twirling it so it spun, causing Luke to squeal in excitement, Josie said, 'Have you had any luck in finding a suitable manager yet?' Jack had told her to leave the appointment of a barman-cum-manager to him and concentrate on the waitress and cook.

'Uh-huh.' Jack put out a hand and ruffled Luke's dark curls. 'You're looking at him.'

'*What?*'

'It's going to be enough to do getting this place up and running without worrying if some smart alec is creaming off some of your profits,' Jack said expressionlessly, concentrating his gaze on Luke.

'But— You said—' Josie was struggling and took a deep breath. 'You think this might fail, don't you – and if that happened you'd be out of a job.'

'We'll have to make sure it doesn't fail then, won't we.'

'I can't let you do that—'

'I've already done it. I gave in my notice a month ago and left last night when the new guy started.'

'Jack, you shouldn't have.'

'Why not? Don't you want me?'

Oh, she wanted him all right, Josie thought wretchedly,

and not just as her manager for the bar and restaurant. She had fought the attraction which had grown the more she got to know him – she was a married woman after all and in spite of how Adam had behaved she wouldn't break her wedding vows, but fighting it wasn't the same as conquering it. Jack Kane had a charisma, an animal maleness, which was quite unlike Adam's charming manner and smooth handsomeness, but its very rawness was beguiling. Of course she knew he'd helped her because he was Hans's friend, and furthermore under the tough exterior he had a kind heart, but that didn't mean he liked her in *that* way. And even if he did, which she knew he didn't, she still had a husband who was Luke's father, and Jack had Rose, who appeared to be devoted to him in spite of the fact that, as Jack said, he wasn't the marrying kind.

Finding her voice, she said lamely, 'It's not that I don't want you – I know you'd do the job perfectly – but I feel awful that you've left a well-paid position to start here with the risk that involves.'

'You've been telling me for weeks that this is a sure-fire bet.' Jack looked up, his eyes crinkling at the corners as he smiled. 'I'm not a gambling man so odds like that appeal.' As Luke began to grizzle, he added, 'Now, I think this little guy wants his breakfast so why don't I go downstairs and start making a list of what we need to stock the bar and kitchen? A meal at one of the fancy eateries could cost up to three dollars per person, so I take it we'd be looking at something like thirty or forty cents? The Chinese and Russian and Spanish places down on East side do their own cuisine pretty good so we don't want to compete with those either. We're aiming for good food for working- and middle-class families, right? Somewhere couples or families can eat and listen to the best vocalist this side of the Brooklyn Bridge.'

He was waiting for an answer and she nodded dazedly.

'Well, time's money.' He whisked up Luke and stood, handing the baby to her before leaving the room.

Josie stood staring after him for some moments and for the life of her she couldn't have said whether she was pleased or dismayed by the sudden turn of events. It would be wonderful to have someone she knew and trusted to help her run things and guide her through the many pitfalls of having a business in a foreign country but that in itself would involve working closely with the person concerned, and if that person was Jack Kane . . . Why couldn't Hans's friend have been old and bald and ugly? she asked herself ruefully, before Luke – annoyed that his demands for food were being ignored – upped his grizzling to a wail and pulled at her hair. Adjusting the baby on her hip she prepared to go downstairs, hoping the day wouldn't provide any more surprises.

That afternoon Josie interviewed four young women who had applied for the job of waitress and one older woman for the position of cook. She had asked Jack if he wanted to sit in with her but he'd declined, saying it needed to be her choice, besides which he would keep Luke occupied and out of the way upstairs.

The older woman arrived at two o'clock and fortunately, as she was the only applicant for the post as cook, Josie liked her immediately. Carmella Covello had arrived in America forty years before with her parents and two older brothers, worlds away from her native Italy. Within two months her mother had died and so ten-year-old Carmella had taken on the job as housewife to the menfolk. 'My brothers married and left home and I remained,' she said quietly. 'My father wished it to be so. He died a few weeks ago. My eldest brother said I could live with his family but I do not want this. I want—'

She paused, and Josie said encouragingly, 'Yes?'

'I want something different. My brother' – again she hesitated – 'he is like my father.'

Reading between the lines, Josie said softly, 'You want a little independence?' A thought struck her. 'Are you saying you will need to live in, Carmella?' She hadn't bargained for that but neither would she be able to pay a high wage to the cook and waitress. The manager's wage would take most of the money she'd allotted for employees. Thinking quickly, she said, 'I do have a spare room but it's very small, just large enough for a single bed, I'm afraid. It's next to my sitting room.' She had earmarked it in her mind for storage like the previous occupants.

'This would be fine,' Carmella said, her Italian accent, which was still strong despite her having lived in New York most of her life, giving the words a lilting edge.

When they discussed what dishes Carmella was familiar with, Josie learned more about her. It appeared that as well as caring for her father she had been at the beck and call of her brothers' families, often cooking and cleaning for them on a regular basis. Her eldest brother had risen in the world and was something in the city, regularly holding dinner parties for business associates when Carmella would be the unpaid cook. The upside of this, as far as Josie was concerned, was that the Italian woman didn't just know about Italian cuisine but had a vast experience of cooking all kinds of different foods from simple dishes to elaborate ones.

The more Carmella spoke, the more Josie wondered what kind of a life she had led, chained to a family who had treated her as little more than an unpaid servant and drudge. There was a timidity about her, a humbleness that went beyond a natural diffidence. It was clear her father's opinions and attitudes had been sacrosanct and from what the Italian woman let slip she had only ever left his apartment to shop or go round to her brothers' homes. She was dowdy, her black hair already streaked with grey pulled back into a tight bun and her dress and coat worn and faded.

After some twenty minutes or so, Josie said softly, 'Would you like to come and see the room which would be yours? It's very small as I said but if you are happy with it the job is yours, Carmella.'

'It is?'

There was a note in her voice that brought a lump to

Josie's throat. 'Come along,' she said warmly, 'and you can meet Jack Kane – he's the manager and barman – and also my son, Luke. You don't mind baby noise and paraphernalia? He sleeps well except when he's teething and then you might hear him.'

Carmella's face lit up. 'I love bambinos.'

By the time the first of the girls for the waitress job arrived, Carmella had left. They'd arranged Jack would call round the following day to the apartment her father had rented as the landlord had served her notice to leave within the week. Josie had made a mental note to put up some shelves in the little room for Carmella's possessions and buy a single bed with enough room for a trunk to slip under it. It was the best she could do in the circumstances. She hadn't reckoned on having another person in the house with herself and Luke but now it had happened she felt quite happy about the prospect. Carmella seemed so sweet and she was sure they would be friends. Once Jack helped her bring her things here hopefully Carmella would settle in just fine.

It was different with the girls for the waitress job. After the third one had left Josie was somewhat in despair. One had smelled strongly of alcohol, another had told her that for the money Josie was offering she'd rather carry on working where she was, and the third had been wearing a blouse that showed her full breasts to indecent proportions, leaving nothing to the imagination, with her face caked in make-up.

When the fourth applicant knocked on the door, Josie

opened it resignedly, wondering if she was being too pernickety. A bright rosy face under a straw hat smiled back at her. 'It's Eliza O'Neill,' the young woman said, her American twang giving the merest hint of her Irish heritage. 'I've come about the job, but I'd better tell you straight off I've not done any waitressing before.'

It transpired that Eliza had been working as a receptionist at one of the theatres in the Bowery, but having recently got engaged to be married her fiancé had objected to some of the more risqué shows featured. 'He thinks the customers look on the receptionists the same as the chorus girls,' Eliza said with a little giggle.

Jack had told Josie a little about the third-class theatres situated principally in the Bowery, where working-class New Yorkers relied on the price of admission being low with performances suited to the tastes of the audience. He'd told her they were a mite on the tawdry side and some had a sexual, suggestive edge, but a good time was always guaranteed. Clearly Eliza's fiancé was worried about what this 'good time' could mean for his future bride.

'I've told him I wouldn't put up with any guy trying it on,' Eliza went on, her big blue eyes wide, 'but, bless him, he's got a real bee in his bonnet about it and after all, he's more important than a job.' And then she blushed hotly. 'I don't mean a job, this job, isn't important,' she said hastily, 'just that I want Clarence's mind to be at rest.'

'I know exactly what you mean, Eliza,' Josie reassured

her. 'But do you think you would like waitressing? It's very different from sitting in a box office.'

'I know I'd love it. You're with people, aren't you, and that's what I like. Clarence understands that. He works in the kitchen at Delmonico's at 26th Street and Fifth Avenue, and they're training him to be a chef,' she said proudly. 'They print their menus in French as well as English – for the upper-crust customers, you know? – and he's taught me some French words.' She then reeled off a few, giggling again as she added, 'My dad says they're having Clarence on at Delmonico's and teaching him swear words in French. He doesn't really mean it but he thinks Clarence is a bit stuffy and likes to tease him.'

Josie smiled back. There was something about Eliza that reminded her of Phyllis and there and then she decided to offer her the job, which Eliza accepted with alacrity.

When Eliza left, Josie stood for some moments looking around the bar and small restaurant before she went upstairs to relieve Jack of Luke. In a few days they would open for business, the thought of which was both exhilarating and terrifying. If she didn't make a success of this she would lose everything, and the future she had promised herself she would provide for Luke would be in ashes. She'd been practising singing every day, sometimes for hours at a time while she worked. Luke seemed to like it – the baby would often jog and wave his arms and shriek with excitement and more than once she'd stopped whatever she was doing and picked him up and danced about until she was breathless. It was at those times she felt at peace with the world and about what she had done in bringing her son halfway across the world.

She still couldn't look back on the events of the last months in England without bitterness and pain, she reflected, and horror at how they had ended. Manipulative and cruel as Adam had been to her, finding out that he had orchestrated Toby's death was the worst thing. It had confirmed that he was a McGuigan through and through and she wished from the bottom of her heart that his blood didn't flow in Luke's veins; but she would do everything within her power to bring her precious boy up in the right way, free of the McGuigan curse.

She made a small motion with her head in acquiescence to the thought and then squared her slim shoulders. It was up to her now and failure wasn't an option.

Chapter Twenty

Rose Flannagan stared at the man she loved with all her heart but who she knew didn't love her. At least, not in the same way.

From the day she'd met Jack Kane he'd never pretended to be the marrying kind, she had to give him that. No, he had laid his cards out on the table from the word go, but it hadn't made any difference. She'd fallen into his lap like a ripe plum, she told herself ruefully.

Jack hadn't been her first lover. She had been engaged to be married when she'd first come across him, and it had been Sean who'd taken her virginity on the evening they'd become betrothed. He'd felt that in giving her a ring he'd had the right and in truth she hadn't protested too much. She'd liked him and they'd known each other since they were children, their families being great friends in the Irish community. But then one cold rainy evening she'd been walking home from work with a bag of shopping her mother had asked her to buy and the handle had torn off, strewing the groceries across the wet pavement. Jack had been passing and had stopped to help. She had looked into his laughing blue eyes and it had been as quick as that for her.

But tonight his eyes weren't laughing. She had just told him that she thought he was crazy giving up a well-paid job for something that might last barely a few months and it hadn't gone down too well. 'Why didn't you discuss it with me a month ago before you gave in your notice?' she said now, ignoring his tight face, 'or at least tell me what you'd done?'

'Because it was my decision and it doesn't affect us.'

He surely wasn't so dim that he believed that? she asked herself angrily. She had put up with this other woman and her child living with him for weeks knowing that he was doing it as a favour to his friend, but that didn't mean she'd liked it. And he knew she didn't. That was the real reason he hadn't told her he'd thrown in the towel at his old job. And as for this woman taking on a bar and intending to sing there at nights – well, she was hardly the respectable widow Jack had made her out to be. She probably had never even been married to the father of her child. But it seemed she'd spun Jack a story and he'd swallowed it.

The feelings of jealousy and being hard done by rose up in a flood and she battled to hold her tongue. She had thought things between them would get back to normal once Josie and the child left over a month ago, but although she and Jack had taken up where they'd left off, with her often cooking dinner and staying the night, things weren't the same. Her mother thought she was mad to put up with the situation and it caused a lot of rows at home, with the fact that Sean still liked her and hadn't had a steady girlfriend since she had left him being brought up constantly. 'You don't think Jack Kane is ever going to marry you, do you?' her mother had said just the evening before. 'His reputation speaks for itself.'

She had answered that no, she didn't think Jack would offer marriage, and had lied that anyway she didn't want to get wed, she was perfectly happy as she was. Marriage wasn't for everyone and she had never particularly wanted children; she liked her job working in a clothing factory where she had progressed to forewoman and now earned a good wage – that was enough for her.

Her mother had looked at her with disbelieving eyes and had turned away, mumbling something about there's none so blind as them that refuse to see and not to come crying to her when it all went belly up, while her father had sat sorrowfully shaking his head.

Remembering the look on her father's face, Rose bit down on her bottom lip. She knew she'd disappointed everyone when she had taken up with Jack but just the thought of not being part of his life was unbearable.

She'd been a month off twenty when she had met him and she was twenty-three now and well aware she wasn't getting any younger, even without her mother reminding her every opportunity she could. At first she'd hoped she would be able to change Jack's mind about settling down and that if she made him happy he'd realize he couldn't do without her just as she couldn't do without him. She no longer thought that way.

Sean had adored her, she'd been his sun, moon and stars. She'd known her feeling for him wasn't so intense, but she hadn't known what love was until Jack Kane had come into her life. It had shown her that you couldn't choose where you loved, not the kind of love Sean had had for her and which she had for Jack. More's the pity.

He was sitting with his lips pressed together and a mutinous expression darkening his rugged countenance, for all the world like a child who knew he was in the wrong but wasn't going to admit it. If it hadn't been for the nagging fear that there was more to Jack and Josie's friendship than he was letting on, she could have smiled.

But Jack Kane wasn't a child. He was an attractive and captivating man, who drew women to him like moths to a flame. This woman had lived in his apartment for weeks and she didn't believe for one moment that Josie wouldn't find him beguiling; it was how much Jack was drawn to her that Rose wasn't sure of. She didn't think for one moment that he had been physically unfaithful – he had surprisingly conservative views about a couple being loyal to each other while they were in a relationship – but to her mind there were more ways of being unfaithful than just the physical one.

'So,' she said now, walking across the room and sitting down beside him, 'you've promised that you'll be her barman-cum-manager more to pick up the pieces when she fails than anything else? Isn't that taking your promise to Hans that you'll look out for her a bit far?'

Jack said nothing. There was nothing he *could* say, he admitted to himself. Rose was right, it'd been a crazy thing to do but he'd just known he couldn't have lived with himself if Josie had struggled and floundered and he hadn't tried to help. There were all sorts of ways she could be cheated, not only by suppliers but by the person she employed to oversee the bar and restaurant. He'd lived in New York all his life and he had a handle on most things but she was such an innocent. And she might just succeed. She certainly had more guts and determination than any other woman he'd met.

Rose put her hand on one of his. She knew she ought to ask if there was anything between him and Josie and what he really felt about the girl but she was too frightened of the answer. And she hated her fear, hated that it made her into someone she didn't want to be, but nevertheless . . . She couldn't do without him. It was as simple and humiliating as that. And *she* was the one who slept in his bed at night, who shared the whispered endearments that lovers murmur, who felt his hard strong body and knew every inch of his muscled frame intimately.

Until Josie had come on the horizon it had been enough, but was it now? She looked at him, her heart aching. She wasn't sure and it came back to the fact that she had to know what was going on between them. She couldn't ask him, she just couldn't, and so she would have to go and see Josie. That was the only answer, humiliating though it would be.

When the knock came at the front door at five o'clock in the morning it took Josie a few seconds to emerge from sleep. She had been working into the early hours putting up some shelves in the room that was to be Carmella's, and had gone to sleep with her mind full of the bed and bedding and other bits and pieces she needed to buy for her new cook.

Once she was awake though, she pulled on her dressing gown and sped downstairs, anxious that Luke wouldn't be disturbed as the knocking came again. Flinging open the front door, she stared in surprise at the tall young woman standing on the doorstep. Strangely, although she had never met her, she sensed instantly who she was, even before the woman said, 'I'm Rose, Jack's girlfriend.'

She was pretty, Josie thought, her heart thudding harder in her chest as she tried to compose herself. In spite of her disquiet she managed to say calmly, 'Come in.'

Rose hesitated. She was taken aback by just how beautiful her rival was and was wishing she had left well alone. She looked very young too, barely old enough to have a child. As Josie stood aside for her to enter the building, Rose straightened her back. Jack would raise the roof if he knew she had come here but she had every right to do so, she told herself as she marched past Josie.

Josie shut the front door and then walked ahead through

to the kitchen, Rose following as she glanced about her. She was impressed with what she saw but would rather have been hung, drawn and quartered than say so.

Josie turned and waved her hand for Rose to sit down. 'Would you like a cup of tea or coffee?'

'I don't want a thing from you,' Rose snapped with uncharacteristic rudeness, 'except to know what's going on with Jack. He tells me he's going to work for you, is that right?'

Josie nodded. She could see the other woman was spoiling for a fight but in all honesty she couldn't really blame her. In Rose's place she would have been none too pleased either.

'How did you manage to persuade him to do that, or do I really need to ask?'

It was deliberately insulting. Josie stiffened and her voice was cool when she said, 'I didn't persuade him. I had asked him if he knew anyone who could take on the role of barman and manager here when I open and he told me yesterday that he'd left his previous employment to do the job himself.'

Rose gave a 'huh' of disbelief. 'Do you expect me to believe that?'

'I don't care what you believe but it's the truth.'

Rose arched her eyebrows. 'And I suppose it's the truth that you were married and widowed?' she said scornfully. 'Do you even know who the father of your kid is?'

Josie's cheeks were burning and her stomach was churning but her voice was still controlled when she said,

'Oh aye, I know. My husband wasn't a nice man and I'm not sorry he's gone but my son is not illegitimate.'

'Well, of course you'd say that, it's all part of this act you put on, isn't it. The poor little misunderstood woman trying to make her way in this big bad world. You might have fooled Jack but you don't fool me. I've known plenty of your kind, believe me.'

Josie had had enough. Her voice was scathing when she said, 'I don't doubt your knowledge of certain types is extensive but just because you mix with women of loose morals don't tar everyone with the same brush.'

So the cat had claws. Rose flicked back her long dark hair as her eyes narrowed. 'You won't interest him for long, not a man like Jack, you know that, don't you?'

'You seem to be under the misapprehension that I *want* to interest him.'

'Oh, come on, don't play the innocent.'

'I'm not interested in a relationship with Jack or anyone else. My son and this business I intend to make a success of are my only concern.'

'So you're telling me you haven't started something with him?'

'Jack took me and my son in as a favour for a friend of his and we were literally dumped on him out of the blue. I count him as a friend now and I think he feels the same about me but that's all, all right? I had no idea he was going to give up his job and come to work here and if I'd known before he did it I'd have tried to stop him.'

'So why did he do it?'

'Ask him.'

'I have. He says he's worried you'll be taken for a mug with you not knowing anyone and he feels responsible for you on Hans's behalf.'

'But you don't believe him?'

'Jack's spent all his life making sure he isn't responsible for anyone.' There was a bitter note to the words.

'I don't know about that. All I do know is that I have no intention of "starting something" with him or anyone else, as I've already said.'

There was the ring of truth to the words. It didn't lessen the jealousy Rose was feeling one iota, however. Josie might not be interested in Jack as anything other than a friend, Rose thought, but there was more to it on Jack's side. She'd bet her bottom dollar on it. He'd been different since this woman had come into their lives and she hated her. She should never have come here today, though. It hadn't accomplished anything and it had given Josie the upper hand.

Gathering what little dignity she had left, Rose said stiffly, 'I'd prefer Jack not to know I've been here today.'

'All right.' Josie felt she owed her that. 'That's fine.'

'I have your word?'

'He won't hear anything from me. It's up to you if you tell him or not.'

Rose inclined her head and spun round, walking out without another word. Josie followed her and shut the front door after Rose had stepped down into the street. She watched Jack's girlfriend march off, her back straight.

It must have taken a lot for Rose to come here today, she thought pensively, and she had certainly been spoiling for a fight in the first few minutes.

Retracing her steps to the kitchen she put the kettle on and made herself a pot of tea, sitting down at the table and drinking it slowly. She could understand Rose – hadn't she felt beside herself when she'd suspected Adam was messing around with other women? – but the fact of the matter was that Jack hadn't done anything. *Did Rose believe that?* she asked herself as she finished her first cup of tea. Perhaps, perhaps not, but she couldn't dwell on that now. She had too much to do. She would just have to make sure in the future that she kept a tight control regarding her feelings for Jack Kane but then she'd already decided that before Rose had come to see her. She sighed, reaching for the teapot. Why was life always so complicated?

It was a few more days before Gray's opened. The bar was stocked, menus had been printed, and Eliza's crisp black dress and little apron and white cap looked just right. Josie didn't sleep a wink the night before, tossing and turning as the hours crept by and imagining one disastrous scenario after another.

Carmella had settled in as though she'd always been there. Luke had immediately taken to her, beaming whenever he caught sight of her and demanding to be picked up whereupon he would gabble away in baby talk. Carmella would pretend to hold a conversation with him, which delighted the child, and the two had formed a close bond. It both pleased and saddened Josie. Carmella would have made a wonderful mother, and the fact that her father had selfishly deprived his daughter of having a husband and children was so wrong.

The bar was going to open from lunchtime, but the little restaurant wouldn't begin serving meals until four o'clock. Josie had decided she would begin singing once Luke was asleep and settled in bed, which was normally by seven, and for twenty-minute sessions every hour. This would mean she could help Carmella in the kitchen when required, whilst keeping an ear cocked for Luke in case he woke up and called for her. Fortunately, though, he always slept like a log.

One unexpected bonus had come in the form of a friend of Jack's from the Irish community. Septimus played the accordion, and the man had jumped at the chance of accompanying her and also playing in between times for the customers. She was paying him a small fee along with free beer and a meal at the end of the night. He had turned out to be a nice old boy, and he reminded Josie of pictures of Irish leprechauns, his cheery red face being topped by a mass of wiry grey hair and his beard so long she wondered how it didn't get caught in the accordion. Jack had told her that years before he had lost his wife to consumption along with two of their six children and had never married again, but the surviving children had all married and lived within a stone's throw of their father.

They had been practising together a few times over the

last days and Josie had to admit that having Septimus playing gave her much-needed confidence. Nevertheless, on the morning they were opening she came downstairs to the kitchen feeling sick with nerves. Even the smell of Carmella's delicious home-made rolls couldn't tempt her to eat, and she was glad when Luke woke up to take her mind off things.

Jack arrived just after ten o'clock. He took one look at her and then said, 'Have you had anything to eat this morning?'

'I – I'm not hungry.'

'Hungry or not, you're going to eat something. You look like death warmed up.'

She bristled. 'Thanks a lot.'

They walked through to the kitchen where Luke was sitting in his highchair gnawing on a hard crust Carmella had given him, between banging a spoon on his little wooden table and shrieking with delight at the noise.

'I've been told I look awful and need to eat something,' Josie said flatly, still piqued at Jack's frankness.

'I didn't say you looked awful.' He smiled at her irritation. 'You could never look awful.'

Their eyes held for a moment too long and it was Jack who turned away, putting an arm round Carmella as he said, 'I could do with a couple of your delicious pastries myself if there's any going?'

Carmella laughed. 'Sit down and I will see what I can find. I think you have the bottomless stomach, yes?'

'It's your fault, you shouldn't be such a good cook.'

'But then I would not be here.'

'That's true, but I'm in danger of getting fat and I shall blame you.'

They continued to banter and Josie sat down at the kitchen table wondering why she couldn't have such an easy rapport with him as Carmella. He teased Carmella constantly, making her laugh, and she treated him as if he was a schoolboy, but it was clear that in the short time they'd known each other they had become friends. And of course she and Jack were friends but not in the same way. She didn't want to travel down that path in her mind and now she took the cup of coffee and pastry Carmella handed her with a smile of thanks before saying, 'Right, I think we're on schedule with everything and Eliza will be arriving at two o'clock.' As Eliza would need to stay late into the evening Josie had given her the mornings off. 'Once she's here we'll—'

'Eat,' Jack interrupted her, lifting the plate with the pastry she'd put down on the table and making her take it. 'And drink. You'll feel better with something in your stomach.'

She wanted to say she felt fine but from the way they were both staring at her she knew she probably looked as ropey as she felt, and she had to admit that once she'd eaten it helped the collywobbles somewhat. What would be, would be, she told herself as she sipped her coffee. She was committed. And she had done all she could, putting flyers advertising the bar's reopening and empha-sizing the restaurant in any shop windows that would take them as far as Five Points, as well as talking to folk in the local community. She knew Jack had done his bit in this regard too, and Eliza had told her that it was her mother's birthday in a day or two and her father had promised to bring her for a meal to celebrate. That was at least two customers for the restaurant in the foreseeable future, she thought wryly.

Luke had finished his crust and tired of his game, beginning to wriggle and snivel in his highchair. She could pop him in his pram standing in a corner of the kitchen with some toys, or take him up to the sitting room where his wooden playpen confined him to a certain area. He was beginning to hitch himself about on his bottom and no doubt would soon be crawling. Or, she told herself, she could take him for a walk, perhaps to Central Park? She had been there a couple of times and Luke had liked the menagerie with its bears, monkeys, polar bears and other animals, the elephant being his favourite. For the impoverished citizens of Lower Manhattan it took at least two nickels to ride the elevated train or horse-car to the park and back, which made it a rare event for some, but Horatio Street was within walking distance and she liked pushing the pram through the busy streets. It took a while but a few hours away from the bar would do her the world of good, she decided, and the fresh air would be beneficial for Luke.

She finished her coffee and stood up, announcing her plans. Jack nodded approvingly. 'It'll do you good. It's sunny but cold outside so wrap up warm.' It was the middle of October and an autumn chill had made itself felt for the last couple of weeks. She had bought paraffin heaters for the bar and restaurant and had lit a fire in the sitting room the last few evenings.

Once she was ready she manoeuvred what Jack called the baby carriage out into the street and set off. Luke was sitting up, bright-eyed and bushy-tailed, and he looked adorable in a little thick blue coat and matching hat with a pom-pom, his dark curls cascading over his forehead. He was all smiles and looked so like Adam it made her breath catch in her throat. There wasn't a day that went by that she didn't wonder how Adam was and what was happening back home, but at the same time she had come to terms with the fact that she couldn't have stayed in England and had had no choice but to escape across the Atlantic. It had been a matter of survival, but in taking Adam's son she knew she had put the final nail in her coffin as far as he and his family were concerned.

Central Park was known by New Yorkers as the lungs of the city and every day the bridle paths were filled with private barouches, cabs and coupés – the full oceanic tide of New York's wealth and gentility, along with poorer citizens enjoying the beautiful surroundings and free menagerie on foot. Jack had told her that four decades before, the area had been nothing but a rocky, swampy mass between 59th and 106th Streets, but the city had paid off and kicked out the hundreds of immigrant German and Irish as well as African Americans who had lived there, eking out a living raising hogs and rag-picking.

Extending the area to 110th Street, thousands of engineers, labourers, stonecutters and other workers had dredged swamps, laid underground pipes for the new man-made lakes and pond, and set off gunpowder to blast rocky outcroppings and create a mostly pastoral, romantic-style setting.

'My father knows men in our community who were paid a dollar a day to risk life and limb working in the very area where they'd lost their homes,' Jack had said a trifle bitterly. 'But the rich and powerful wanted their promenades and carriage parades which would give them a new place to show off their wealth.'

'Surely the park is for everyone?' she'd protested at the time. 'And actually the poor can enjoy it even more than the rich, who can go where they like and purchase what the park gives free? The lawns and shady groves and lakes and wooded dells? How would the poor have fountains and bridges and statues all around them and be able to have a ride on the boats on the lake or skate on it in the winter?'

He had grinned at her. 'OK, OK, I get your point but I'm just saying what it was like in the beginning. Until Boss Tweed and his cronies took control of the city charter nearly thirty years ago the lower classes felt unwelcome there, but they relaxed some of the rules and regulations that cut out the poor and added things like pony rides and free concerts and the menagerie and boat rides on the lake. It wasn't always like it is now, that's for sure, and it was built on the blood, sweat and tears of immigrant labour. I reckon it didn't do New York any harm in the eyes of visitors from Europe either, which those in power would have been well aware of.'

'You're just a cynic,' she'd teased him, and he'd nodded and agreed with her while adding that he wasn't usually wrong either.

Josie was thinking about that conversation when she eventually reached Central Park. The grounds were beautiful at any time but with the trees arrayed in colours of gold and bronze and copper and orange it was quite breathtaking. Shallow sparkles of sunshine flickered through the leaves as she strolled along, Luke pointing at things that caught his eye and gabbling away in baby talk. As the wide-open spaces and captivating environment worked its magic, she felt her nerves, which had been stretched as tight as piano wire, begin to relax. If she could earn a living from the bar and restaurant as well as having times like this with her son she would be content, she prayed silently. She didn't want to be rich and God knew that. She just wanted enough money to provide for Luke in this new land she'd brought him to.

When they reached the menagerie Luke squealed and bounced up and down with excitement. They spent a long time watching the monkeys, which all the children loved, and after feeding Luke his lunch which she'd brought with her the baby eventually dozed off for a while. Josie sat on a bench in the sunshine watching the world go by and thinking of nothing in particular, just focusing on what was around her.

Jack had told her that in the winter a red ball or flag would be hoisted on top of Belvedere Castle signalling that the ice on the lake was thick enough to skate on, and although there were other lakes the one just beyond Bethesda Fountain was his favourite. To boost the odds that it would freeze over it would be drained of most of its water every winter. The ice-skating was clearly a popular draw and one of the few activities men and women in polite society could enjoy together, and she found herself wondering how often he'd come with Rose in the past. This thought punctured her tranquillity and once gone she couldn't recapture it, worries that no one would come to her bar and restaurant resurfacing.

She got back to Horatio Street just before four o'clock and after the bright sunshine earlier it had turned colder, the chill of autumn definitely making itself felt. As she approached Gray's her stomach was full of butterflies, even as she told herself she was being ridiculous because it was the first day they'd been open, after all, and she couldn't expect much.

As she opened the door of the building several things registered at the same time. She was aware of Jack looking up from behind the bar and immediately making his way over to her; that there were a good number of people sitting or standing drinking; and that over in the res-taurant part of the room two tables were already occupied and Eliza was standing talking to a party of four at one of them. Septimus must have come early because they'd agreed he wouldn't start work each day until five o'clock but he was sitting playing a popular song on the little stage she'd had constructed, looking more like a smiling leprechaun than ever.

As Jack reached her, he said, 'Here, let me help you take the baby carriage through,' and manoeuvred it up the step.

'There – there's so many people here,' she whispered as she relinquished the handle.

'It was fairly quiet till two-ish but it's certainly picked up,' he said cheerfully as she followed him across the room and out into the passageway, and as they entered the kitchen she found Carmella ladling soup into several small individual bowls standing on a tray on the table. The next moment Eliza came in, notebook and pen in hand as she said, 'The other table want to start with your vegetable soup too, Carmella, and they'll have the steak pie and stuffed cod, two of each, for after.' Smiling at Josie, she added, 'We've already got a table for two for six o'clock and have had a number of enquiries.'

As Jack disappeared back to the bar, Josie smiled at the two women, who were clearly pleased at the way things were going. She had to admit it was better than she had dared to hope for on the first day of opening. Although it might be curiosity and sheer old-fashioned nosiness that had brought people in, it didn't matter. She would make sure that everyone was treated well and got value for money so that they would spread the word to family and friends. Jack had said word of mouth was the best advertisement you could have when she'd put the notices in shop windows and he was right, but she'd felt she had to start the ball rolling too, so to speak.

But this was a good start. She hadn't been faced with an empty room and long faces and her staff twiddling their thumbs. Mighty oaks from little acorns grow, as her mam would have said.

There was nothing she could do in the kitchen although if they got busier in time, that would change, and so she lifted Luke out of the pram and carried him upstairs, settling him in the playpen with some toys. She wanted to practise some of the songs she intended to sing later. Whether they had one customer or whether each table was full, she had made up her mind that she would sing nevertheless. It wasn't just that she hoped it would draw folk in, it was something she needed to do for herself. She had missed it. She went to a different realm when she sang, somewhere where any cares or sorrows took second place and furthermore it was an integral part of her, what made her *her*. Adam had never understood that. He hadn't wanted to.

He had been an incredibly selfish man, she thought sadly. Perhaps his mother was to blame for spoiling him: the youngest of the family, Sadie had almost treated him like an only child. But Bruce and the others had played their part too; he'd been brought up to think that what-ever he wanted should be his. Like her. He had wanted her and so Bruce had cleared the way by having Toby murdered. She would always hate him for that, hate all of them.

Agitated, she began to pace the room before stopping and shaking her head at herself. She was doing it again, dwelling on the past when she knew the only way forward was to concentrate on the future. Composing herself, she breathed in and out a few times and then began to quietly sing.

Luke was ready for bed early, tired out by his day in the fresh air, and after she had settled him in his cot she went into her bedroom and changed into the dress she'd chosen, a simple affair in blue satin which she'd brought with her from England. Although simple, the cut of the dress spoke exclusivity and it had been ridiculously expensive. Adam had arrived home with it one day when they'd been going to a dinner party at Bruce's, saying he wanted her to outshine every other woman who'd be there.

Fixing her long thick hair into curls and waves on top of her head took a while; normally she wore it in a chignon at the back of her neck, but the end result was worth it. It made her look chic and elegant, she thought, staring at herself in the spotted full-length mirror she'd bought for her bedroom from a second-hand shop in Five Points. And she needed the lift it gave to her confidence.

She hadn't checked how many people were in the restaurant for the simple reason she didn't want to know – if it was empty it would be crushing and if it was full it would be terrifying. As it was, when she walked into the room just before seven o'clock to the strains of Septimus playing what sounded like an Irish lament, it was half full and the bar on the other side of the room was busy.

She was aware of many pairs of eyes as she walked across to Septimus, who grinned and nodded at her approach, showing several missing teeth. They'd practised some songs that Josie had sung at the Fiddler's Elbow, family favourites that were on the whole sentimental about true love and mother love, but also some that were a comment on social conditions such as 'If it Wasn't for the Houses in Between' which was about the overcrowded living conditions in London's East End, and Marie Lloyd's 'My Old Man Said Follow the Van and Don't Dilly-Dally on the Way' about a family doing a moonlight flit to avoid paying the rent. Josie felt she'd chosen songs that would be as relevant across the Atlantic as they would in England, like 'The Sea Hath its Pearls', but she wasn't sure. 'Silver Threads Among the Gold' was a relatively safe bet and so she began with that one, hoping it would go down well.

The room became absolutely silent as she sang; even the customers in the bar stopped their chattering. Unable to gauge if this was a good or a bad thing, she attempted to lose herself in the song as she usually did, but her nerves made it difficult. She glanced across at Jack at one point and he had stopped polishing a glass in mid-act and was just standing staring at her, which didn't help.

When she finished, the silence continued for a split-second more and then along with everyone clapping there were shouts of 'More, more!' from the bar. Flushed and pleased she began 'Goodnight, Goodnight, Beloved' and again the room fell quiet.

She sang for over twenty minutes and for most of the time people seemed to be listening and any conversation was muted. When she finished and thanked the room there was more applause and by the time she entered the kitchen she knew her cheeks were rosy red. But it had gone well, she told herself as she sat down at the kitchen table and accepted a cup of coffee Carmella had waiting for her. She just hoped it wasn't a flash in the pan because it was a novelty being opening night, and that customer numbers would increase.

By the end of the week she felt more secure. Jack had told her that all the comments he overheard while serving drinks at the bar were good and on Saturday night the restaurant was full. They already had some reservations for the following week too. Carmella was proving to be a wonderful cook and Eliza was a little ball of energy for whom nothing was too much.

As Josie lay in bed on the Saturday night she relived all the events of the week, sleep a million miles away. It could work – the bar, the restaurant and everything – it could work. She had to hand it to Jack that he was brilliant as a barman-cum-manager, keeping up a banter with the customers and exchanging jokes but able to close in on anyone who drank too much or might be trouble and nip any unpleasantness in the bud. She heard Carmella singing to herself every night as the Italian woman got ready for bed and there was no doubt she was happy, and Eliza had reported that when her parents had dined in the restaurant they'd enjoyed not just the food but the whole experience, saying it was the best time they'd had in their lives. Josie thought that might be a bit of an exaggeration but she appreciated the sentiment nonetheless.

She had written to her mam and posted the letter that very morning, a long one this time telling her how well things were going but ending with another warning for her mother to keep the letters hidden where her father was unable to find them. Always, at the back of her mind, was the fear that somehow the McGuigans would trace her here. It seemed foolish – she was on the other side of the world after all – but deep down she wouldn't put anything past them, Bruce in particular. She had Adam's son and they'd want the child back as well as needing to mete out their kind of justice for what they imagined she'd done. Adam had signed her death warrant as far as his family was concerned when he'd accused her of pushing him down the stairs.

It was a long time before sleep came, and probably because of her earlier thoughts her dreams were populated by dark threatening figures who wished her ill. When she tried to escape from them it was as though her feet were bogged down in thick mud and she could only stumble when she needed to run, feeling they were right behind her and any minute they'd catch her.

In spite of the chilly night she awoke at one point bathed in sweat. After changing her nightdress and putting on her dressing gown she padded down to the kitchen, hearing Carmella's raspy snores as she passed her room, which actually was comforting. It was nice to know that there was another adult in the house.

After making herself a hot mug of cocoa and eating several of Carmella's delicious shortbread biscuits she felt a lot better, and when she climbed into bed again she fell into a dreamless sleep that lasted till morning, though when she awoke there were still those dark shadows at the back of her mind. Shadows, she realized, she'd have to learn to live with but which she prayed one day would fade away altogether.

Chapter Twenty-One

It was a number of weeks later in December, two days before Christmas on Luke's first birthday, that the incident happened that set the course for the next decade.

They had all sung 'Happy Birthday' to him at lunchtime just before the bar opened at twelve and had a slice of the delicious cake Carmella had baked for the occasion before the working day had begun in earnest.

It was a day of mixed emotions for Josie. She remembered how thrilled Adam had been to have a son and how she'd hoped that being parents would heal the rifts that had already appeared in their marriage. She had been happy for the first time in months but her happiness, everything, had been built on a series of lies, the worst one being that it hadn't been the O'Learys who had murdered Toby but her own husband. But out of all the heartache and devastation she had Luke, she told herself, as she watched the child cram cake into his mouth, getting most of it on his face and bib.

With business picking up rapidly she had been helping

out in the kitchen most days. She had bought another playpen, which was standing in a corner of the kitchen well away from the range and table; Luke played happily in there a lot of the time and she was always on hand to pick him up and give him a cuddle if he became fractious. Today, though, she intended to devote the whole day to Luke and Eliza had come in early to help Carmella.

It was bitterly cold outside and had been snowing on and off for the last two weeks, and although the pavements and roads were relatively clear, in Central Park children were apparently sailing down the snow-covered hills on toy sleighs and the ice on the lake had been thick enough to host skaters for some days. She knew Luke would enjoy all the activity as well as visiting the menagerie, and she had decided to get a horse-cab to the park and back. Luke had taken his first steps a couple of weeks ago and she had bought him a pair of little sturdy boots to keep his feet warm and dry outside. He loved tottering along holding her hand.

Once they were ready Jack hailed a cab for her and then helped them into the vehicle, holding Luke while she climbed up and then passing the baby to her. They could have been a married couple, the husband assisting his wife and child to go out and enjoy themselves. It wasn't a new thought – there had been several little instances lately when she'd thought the same – and now Jack added to her uncomfortableness when he said, 'Be careful at the park. A little snow tends to send the young ones wild and I don't want you both knocked over by a sleigh.'

She forced a smile. 'We'll be fine.'

As the cab driver clicked his tongue to the horse and they began to move, Luke squealed with excitement, bouncing up and down on the seat beside her. She had her hand on him to make sure he didn't fall and as he pushed at it to remove the restriction, she said, 'No, Luke. Mam needs to keep you safe.'

For a moment his face darkened and she thought they were going to have one of the tantrums that occurred if he was thwarted in any way, but then his expression cleared as his attention was caught by the moving scene outside and he was all smiles again.

They had a lovely time at Central Park and arrived home as the sun was setting in a mother-of-pearl sky. Luke was ready for bed at six o'clock and asleep as soon as his little head touched the pillow. Josie had just come down to the sitting room and begun to tidy Luke's toys away when Jack popped his head round the door. 'Where's the birthday boy?'

'Already asleep. He insisted on walking whenever he could today and he's tired himself out.'

Jack smiled, coming fully into the room. He was holding a painted pull-along wooden dog and a big bunch of flowers. 'The dog is for Luke and the flowers are for you,' he said softly, putting the toy down and handing her the bouquet.

Their fingers touched, and Josie felt the slight contact in every nerve and sinew. It made her voice stiff when she said, 'Flowers for me? Why?'

He shrugged. 'I thought that today might have been a difficult one in some respects, that's all.'

Josie stared at him. If he'd thought that, the day had just got a whole lot more difficult, she thought with a smidge of hysteria. She had been trying to fight the attraction she felt for this man for months, especially after Rose's visit, and now Jack had to go and buy her flowers. And that wasn't fair because it highlighted something she had been trying to ignore for some time and that was that Jack was attracted to her too.

She had tried to disregard what her senses had been screaming at her but there had just been too many times when their eyes had locked for some moments, when Jack had avoided touching her in even the most casual way, and – oh, a hundred and one things. He wanted her. Physically. He'd had his fair share of women, no doubt, and his affair with Rose had been going on for ages. Another such liaison would mean little to him. Whereas – *she loved him.*

The self-knowledge hit her like a blow to the solar plexus. She tensed, feeling as though the ground had been taken away under her feet. She turned, terrified of revealing anything to those piercing blue eyes. 'The day has been fine,' she said coolly. 'Why shouldn't it have been?'

'You know why.'

She had gained her composure and now she looked at him again. 'You mean because of Luke's father?'

His eyes had narrowed as if he was trying to work out

how she was really feeling and there was silence between them for a moment, and then, his voice low, he said, 'Exactly that.'

'Every day I live with the fact that I chose to leave my husband and take our child away from any family he has.'

'I didn't mean it like that. You had no choice.'

'No, I didn't. If I had stayed then Luke wouldn't have had a mother. In going, he hasn't got a father, but at least my boy is free of the influence of the McGuigans.'

'I know, I know that. You did what you had to do.'

She stared straight into his face now as she said quietly, 'And I shall go on doing what I have to do. Luke will grow up believing his father is dead and I am a widow, but the truth is I am a married woman. In leaving Adam I've placed myself in a position where my life will remain devoid of love, at least the love between a man and a woman, but that doesn't matter. I have Luke and I'll bring him up the best I can, knowing right from wrong.'

Jack's gaze was tight on her face. He knew what she was saying but he found he had to ask the question anyway. 'You mean you intend to remain on your own for the rest of your life? Isn't that a little unnecessary?'

'I said Luke will be brought up knowing right from wrong. Adam is alive. Adultery is wrong.'

'He doesn't deserve your faithfulness.'

'I'm not doing it for Adam. I'm doing it for Luke. If he ever discovers his father is still alive, at least he'll know that one of his parents respected their marriage vows.'

'And you mean to say you'll continue like this for what – a decade? Two decades? A lifetime? It's madness, Josie. What if you care for someone and they care for you? Are you going to deny yourself happiness for ever because Adam fooled you into marrying him?' He raised his eyebrows at her and when she said nothing he shook his head, making a sound in his throat that spoke of deep frustration. Then, his face changing and his voice coming deep and low, he murmured, 'Josie, oh, Josie.'

'Don't.'

'I need to tell you how I feel.'

'No. I can't, Jack. I can't. It's the way I'm made. I let Luke down by giving him a father like Adam McGuigan—'

'And so you intend to punish yourself for ever more?'

'I don't expect you to understand.'

'Good, because I don't.'

She watched him now turn to the side and rub his hand tightly across his mouth. He would be angry and resentful because that was the way *he* was made. She swallowed deeply. To Jack this was so simple. He didn't believe in marriage – he'd told her that in the first few days she was ensconced in his apartment – and so she would be the perfect relationship in his eyes. A woman who was married and couldn't ask for a divorce from her husband because that would mean revealing where she was. No commitment needed on his part.

And then she caught at the thought. No, that was unfair. She was assuming too much here but it didn't make any difference anyway. However much he liked her, even if he loved her, she couldn't be what he wanted her to be. She wasn't like Rose with no dependants, fancy-free and answerable to no one.

It was some moments before he looked at her again and she saw his expression had changed; he'd schooled his features into a wry smile but although he was smiling she felt it wasn't genuine. Nevertheless, she was thankful he wasn't pursuing the conversation further. 'I think we will have to agree to disagree,' he said easily. 'Don't you?'

She nodded.

'Ironic really,' he said quietly, half to himself. 'I've told many women I don't believe in love in the past. Attraction between the sexes, lust, desire – I could buy all that, but love, the for ever kind that poets prattle on about, was just a fleeting deception, a ploy mostly used by a woman to trick a man into agreeing to be her meal ticket for life. Cynical, eh?'

She nodded again.

He shook his head slowly as he said, 'Well, we'll have to see, won't we.' And then, his voice becoming brisk, even businesslike, he added, 'Friends?'

She had the urge to let the tears flow but found the strength to smile a little shakily. 'Of course.'

'I'd better get back to the bar; I've left Eliza looking after things for a minute or two and adding up isn't her strong point.' He held her gaze for a moment before turning abruptly and marching from the room, shutting the door behind him.

She stared for some seconds towards the door and then

sank down onto the sofa beside the flowers she had dropped there as they'd talked. Her gaze went to the wooden dog and the lump in her throat threatened to choke her.

Somehow she got through the evening but she was vitally aware of Jack every single minute she was singing. She felt bereft, which was ridiculous really, she told herself, because nothing had changed from what it had been before they'd talked. But it had. He had said he didn't understand the stance she was taking and she couldn't have expected he would, not being the sort of individual he was. But now this thing that had never properly been discussed, this feeling that was between them, had been dealt the death blow. She had Luke and the business and he had his Rose, and that was the way it had to be, but knowing that didn't make it any easier to bear.

She was jealous of Rose, she admitted painfully, even though she had absolutely no right to be. The thought of them together – laughing, talking, eating together and sharing a bed – made her feel sick inside, which again was stupid because she could have changed all that earlier this evening if she'd agreed to what she knew he wanted.

Once she was in bed she tossed and turned for a couple of hours, sleep a million miles away and her mind so confused and agitated she felt she was going mad. At three o'clock when she still hadn't closed her eyes, she got up, pulling her thick dressing gown over her nightdress and slipping her feet into her slippers. She needed to break the cycle of her thoughts; she'd make a hot drink and have something to eat because she hadn't been able to face the thought of food after the conversation with Jack.

When she entered the kitchen still deep in thought she jumped a mile. Carmella was sitting at the table with a mug of cocoa in front of her. Jerked out of her own problems, she said, 'Carmella, is something wrong?'

'No. Yes. Not really.' Shaking her head at herself, Carmella said, 'It's silly because everything is good. For me, it is good.'

'But?'

'My brothers, they are angry with me for finding a job and refusing to live with one of them.'

I bet they are, Josie thought. *They lost their free cook and dogsbody.*

'They say, they say that family is everything and my first duty is to them.'

Josie felt anger rising up but tried to keep her voice calm when she said, 'Family is important, of course it is, but as for your first duty being to them that's just plain selfishness, Carmella. If anyone has given their all to their family it's you, but now your father has died it's time for you to choose what you want to do with your life from this point on.'

'They say I am trying to become someone I'm not.' Carmella touched her hair.

The unconscious action gave Josie a clue to what had been said. She and Eliza had persuaded Carmella to visit a hairdresser for the first time in her life a few days before, to have her long thick hair cut and styled. Previously, Carmella had always trimmed it herself. She had come back looking ten years younger, soft waves framing her face and a new spring in her step. Quietly, Josie said, 'No, you are becoming the person you want to be and that's entirely different. Your brothers and their families have their own lives, Carmella, and I'm sure they do exactly as they please?'

The Italian woman nodded.

'They have no right to dictate to you, you must see that? You cared for your father for years so that they didn't have to; they ought to be thanking you for all your sacrifices and encouraging you to do what you please now you are free. You have to be strong and follow your own heart and do what is right for you, and no one should tell you what that is. It's up to you.'

As she said the words, they registered deep within. That was what she was doing, Josie told herself silently. She was a mother first and foremost and she had to do what she believed was good for her son. Jack didn't understand, he would never understand, how could he? He wasn't a parent. He lived his life on his own terms, but she had to think what was the best for Luke and it wasn't sleeping with another man when his father, her husband, was alive. In marrying Adam and then leaving him and taking their son, she had made decisions that would reverberate down the years. She had made her bed and she had to lie on it – alone.

Carmella reached forward and took her hands. 'Thank you,' she said simply. 'I am very happy here and I wish to stay.'

'Good.' Josie smiled. 'Apart from being a wonderful cook I count you as my friend and I would hate to lose you.'

Carmella made more cocoa and they talked for some time, and when eventually they went to their rooms Josie climbed into her bed in a more peaceful frame of mind. Not happy – she doubted if she would ever be truly happy again – she thought in the moments before she fell asleep, but she had a lot to be thankful for in this new life and she would count her blessings when the longing for what could never be became too painful.

PART FOUR

Luke

1904

Chapter Twenty-Two

Luke Gray sat in the warm classroom longing for the day to finish. Although it was October and there was a chill in the air outside, the sun coming through the windows was making him drowsy. He was bored, they all were, apart from those swots Gregory and Morris, he thought scornfully, his lip curling as he looked at the two boys in the front row, who were busily writing.

He had no time for either of them and last week he and his pals had debagged Morris outside the school just as a group of girls were passing, holding him down and laughing as he desperately tried to cover his genitalia with his hands. He'd half-expected Morris would report them and they'd get hauled over the coals by old Gould, the headmaster, but Morris was too frightened of them to do that, he thought with some satisfaction.

Luke glanced at his best friend, Irwin Wallace, who was sitting at the desk next to him yawning at regular intervals, his eyes half-closed. The other boys in their gang – Addison, Theodore and Art – were sitting behind them and Luke knew they'd be doing the minimum of work. The five of them were bright and always got good marks, even though they made a practice of coasting through lessons when they could. This one, a history lesson about the two battles of Charleston fought in South Carolina in 1776 and 1780, was particularly tedious in Luke's opinion. Who cared if the Americans won the first battle and delayed the invasion of the South by the British for four years? In the second they'd had to surrender after a forty-five-day siege anyway so it all seemed pretty pointless, added to which he was more interested in the present day than events that happened over a hundred years ago.

He shifted in his chair, causing it to creak loudly, and the teacher, a young slim man in his late twenties, glanced up and met his gaze. Insolently Luke stared him out and when the teacher dropped his eyes, Luke smiled to himself. Irwin had caught the exchange and smirked at him. The teacher was new to the school and nervous and they had already tried it on once or twice.

The bell eventually rang to signal the end of the day and as Luke gathered his things together he saw Gregory and Morris shoot out of the classroom as they'd done each day since the incident last week, making sure they were long gone before he and his friends emerged. He liked that. Liked the feeling of power it gave him.

The small select private day school for boys in East 127th Street, situated in what once had been a family house, was for middle-income parents and Luke had attended it for the last five years. Before that he had been at a local one close to where he'd once lived in Horatio Street, but when they'd moved to an elegant apartment on the Upper East Side his mother had decided to pay for his education, something she reminded him about if his monthly reports weren't up to scratch. He accepted she was in her rights to do that, along with her encouragement to work hard and obtain good results. After all, she had risen from obscurity to be a fairly wealthy woman since he'd been born by a mixture of hard work and business acumen.

When he and his pals emerged into bright sunlight they went to a small local park close by and played ball for an hour or so before going their separate ways. As he walked home he was aware of glances in his direction from girls he passed but he was used to that. He knew he was handsome – his nickname among his pals was Don for Don Juan but he didn't mind that. It was better than Irwin's Beaky because of his big nose, or Art's Dodger because his family had moved from Brooklyn where folk were nicknamed Trolley Dodgers on account of the city's tangled web of streetcar lines.

He had found he had a way with girls. He'd been invited to Irwin's sister's birthday party a few weeks ago, and during a game of hide-and-seek when he and one of Irwin's sister's friends had squeezed into a wardrobe together, he'd put his hand up the girl's dress and pulled her knickers down, thrusting two fingers inside her. She had resisted at first, but when he'd said he liked her and wanted her to be his girlfriend, she'd let him have his way.

He didn't like her. She had buck teeth and frizzy hair and he wouldn't be seen dead with her, he thought scornfully, but that hadn't mattered in the dark. He'd imagined she was Irwin's sister, who was a cracker. Afterwards he'd had to go and clean himself up in the lavatory.

He whistled to himself as he walked along, his book bag slung over one shoulder and his long legs making short work of the walk home. He hoped Carmella had had time to make one of her fruit cakes; he always had a snack when he got in and he was famished. He knew he shouldn't be but he was irritated with how much time Carmella was spending at one of her brother's houses these days, since June when the family had been involved in an accident on a paddle steamer. It had been an annual event for St Mark's German Lutheran Church but one of Carmella's sister-in-law's friends had invited her and the children to go along; Carmella's brother and his two oldest boys had stayed at home. Apparently the boat was only an hour into the trip and the band was playing when a fire struck with terrifying suddenness. The steamer was opposite 135th Street in the East River and the New York shoreline was no more than three hundred feet away, but the captain chose to steer for North Brother Island and the vessel burned to the waterline. The smoke and screams brought New Yorkers to the riverside, Carmella's brother and his sons included, but there was nothing anyone could do. Trapped women were throwing their babies overboard and Carmella's brother had collapsed shouting for his wife and their five younger children, all of whom had perished.

It was sad, Luke thought, but he didn't see why Carmella had to be at her brother's house most days, cooking and cleaning and what-have-you, when he could perfectly well afford to employ someone to do it. He'd said the same to his mother and she had replied that Carmella felt she had to do it, and that had been that. 'Over a thousand people have died, mostly women and children,' she'd said quietly, 'and that is a terrible catastrophe, Luke, and for Carmella's brother to see it and be unable to do anything must have been horrendous. Carmella said he wants family around him, not a stranger in his home.'

Luke compressed his lips as he remembered his mother's words. From what he knew of Carmella's relations, the brother wanted an unpaid skivvy, that was the truth of it.

As he entered the apartment his mother called to him from the sitting room. He normally headed straight for the kitchen to see what Carmella had left for him, and as soon as he entered the sitting room he knew he was in trouble about something or other. His mother had *that* face on.

Ignoring the cool atmosphere, he walked across and kissed her, employing his natural charm and smiling.

'Sit down please, Luke.' She made no effort to return his embrace. 'I had a visitor today.'

'Oh, yes?'

'The mother of one of your schoolfriends, Morris Henderson. She told me that her son returned home one day last week very upset but wouldn't say why, but last night she got to know what had happened to put him in such a state after he had woken up crying after a nightmare.'

Luke sat back on the sofa, the picture of innocence. 'What has that got to do with me?'

'Did you and your friends attack him and pull his trousers down in the street? And I want the truth, Luke.'

'Oh, that.' He feigned nonchalance. 'It was just a joke. It didn't mean anything.'

'It meant a great deal to the boy concerned.'

She was angry, he could see that, really angry, but he still thought he could win her over. His mother always wanted to believe the best of him, he had worked that out long ago and often used it to his advantage. 'Well, I'm sorry if Morris was upset but he was laughing at the time,' he lied smoothly. 'Like I said, it was just a joke. We often rib each other, all of us do.'

'It was cruel, Luke, and you know it. What's more, apparently this boy is so scared of you he begged his mother not to say anything.'

His temper was rising but he tried to control it. 'Morris is a milksop. He's scared of his own shadow.'

'And so it wasn't a joke then? You and your friends picked on someone you knew wouldn't retaliate?'

'It wasn't like that,' he said sullenly.

'I think it was exactly like that.'

'You weren't there.'

'So there is no remorse over your actions?'

'I didn't do anything wrong,' he bit out, his voice rising. 'We were all just fooling around. It could have been me or Irwin that it happened to but it was Morris and of course he has to go crying to Mummy.'

'I don't think for a moment it would happen to you, Luke, or any of what Mrs Henderson called your gang. You're nothing but bullies, the lowest form of life. You will write a letter of apology to both the boy and his mother, and you will not persecute him again or anyone else for that matter. Until I am sure you understand the seriousness of your actions you will receive no pocket money and you will not leave this house except to go to school, when you will immediately return home. Do I make myself clear?'

He was scarlet now and as he jumped to his feet his hands were clenched into fists at his sides. 'You can't do that.'

'Oh, but I can.'

'You don't believe me then? You're taking the word of Morris and his stupid mother over mine?'

'That's exactly what I am doing. Don't you realize how grave this is? If Mrs Henderson had gone to the school you and your friends could well have found yourselves expelled for bringing the school name into disrepute. You were wearing your uniforms, everyone would have known where you were from. But worse, much worse than that, it was cruel and callous to subject someone to such indignity and I am bitterly disappointed in you.'

He stared at her. He'd always known he could twist his mother round his little finger but today was different. She had never spoken to him like this before. But he'd gone too far to back down now. 'It was just a joke,' he said for the third time, 'and stuff like that happens all the time to everyone. Trust Morris to go and make a big deal of it. Anyway, *I'm* disappointed in *you*. Any other mother would believe me.'

As the key turned in the front door and they heard Carmella come in, Josie said, 'Go to your room.'

'Don't worry, I'm going. I don't want to stay with you.'

He brushed past Carmella, who had come to the open sitting-room door, saying as he passed, 'I hate it here. I get blamed for everything.'

Carmella came fully into the room. She looked tired and drained. Her brother had come home from work early and sat and cried for over an hour. 'Trouble?' she said softly.

'It doesn't matter. You've got enough on your plate.'

'Tell me.'

Josie told her, finishing with, 'Mrs Henderson believes Luke was the ringleader. The other boys follow him and do what he says. How could he humiliate someone like that?'

'He's not a bad boy—'

'It was cruel, Carmella. That poor boy . . .'

They stared at each other for a moment. Carmella put

a comforting arm round her before she said, 'I'll make some coffee.'

'No, you look exhausted. Sit down and I'll make some.'

Once in the kitchen, Josie put the kettle on and then leaned against the work surface as she shut her eyes. Mrs Henderson had been a nice woman, almost apologetic, but she'd been in tears as she related the effect the attack had had on her son. She knew Luke had a temper and liked his own way, but this was something else. Something nasty. He was clearly a popular boy – he was always receiving invitations to his friends' homes and some weekends she hardly saw him – but she'd imagined his pals were nice boys. But this – to find out he was the leader of a group who weren't averse to terrorizing those individuals weaker than themselves – brought all her deep-seated fears about Luke's ancestry to the fore.

She hugged herself, feeling physically sick. She'd attempted to instil good values and morals in him as well as giving him a happy and privileged life. Where had she gone wrong?

In the twelve years that had passed since she'd become the owner of Gray's, their lives had changed considerably. That first bar and restaurant had been a great success, and after she had bought it she had gone on to buy other premises. Now she owned a string of such establishments dotted about the city. She had kept to the formula which had served her well – that of smallish, clean and bright premises serving tasty, inexpensive food with entertainment in the evenings. She still made guest appearances three or four times a week in one or another of them, but at each restaurant had employed a resident singer, often young and relatively inexperienced girls who needed a break.

Now, at the age of twenty-nine, she was a comparatively wealthy woman, but it would all be for nothing if Luke went astray. Everything she had fought for had been with him in mind, even moving to this elegant apartment. She'd been determined to send him to a good private school as soon as she could and had known he would need a middle-class address so that he wouldn't feel at a disadvantage with the friends he made.

Carmella had moved to the apartment with them, and at the Italian woman's insistence had taken on the role of cook and housekeeper. Josie had been hesitant about this, remembering how dismal Carmella's life had been before her father died. She hadn't wanted to take advantage of her friend's sweet and giving nature as her family had done. She had soon realized, however, that Carmella really wanted to do it and was happy to give up her job as cook at Gray's and look after herself and Luke. They had become as close as sisters whilst living in the flat over the bar and restaurant, and Carmella's friendship and affection had met a deep need in Josie. She pined for her mother and sisters and even Phyllis but with Carmella around things never seemed so bad. They laughed together and on occasion had cried together too, and Carmella looked on Luke as the son she'd never had.

This had its drawbacks, Josie thought now, as she made

the coffee. Carmella only saw the best in the people she loved and she knew her friend would be sitting making excuses in her mind for what Luke had done right now. Many a time in the last months she had wished she could talk to Jack about Luke and even ask him to have a word with her son, but strangely Luke had never liked Jack. Or perhaps it wasn't so strange. Maybe Luke sensed how she really felt about the man who was her manager and resented it? Certainly there was nothing concrete for her son to object to; she and Jack had kept their relationship purely platonic both in word and deed. Her heart was a different matter.

She had often wondered if she had done the right thing in refusing Jack's advances all those years ago and she supposed she would never know. He had carried on seeing Rose for some years, but when Rose had reached the age of thirty she had given him an ultimatum. She wanted to have a family of her own before it was too late. Jack had wished her well and said goodbye, and two months later Rose had married her ex-fiancé with his blessing. Jack had had other girlfriends since then but none of them had lasted long.

She carried the tray of coffee into the sitting room where Carmella was sitting with her head back and her eyes shut. 'How was Alberto today?' she said softly as her friend opened her eyes.

'Not good.' Carmella took her coffee with a smile of thanks. 'But he will get better. I know this. His two boys need him and he is a good father.'

Josie nodded. 'Perhaps I'm not a good mother.' She met Carmella's gaze. 'You think I was too hard on Luke, don't you.'

Carmella hesitated. Then speaking softly, she murmured, 'I think that perhaps you are over-sensitive because of how his father was, that is all.'

It was a valid point but not the whole truth. But close as she was to Carmella, she knew her friend wouldn't understand about this. It wasn't because of how Adam had been that this episode had disturbed her so profoundly, but of how Luke *was*. For years, ever since he was no more than a toddler, she had tried to dismiss the characteristics in her son that were pure McGuigan, she told herself painfully. Many a night she had lain awake tossing and turning after some incident or other. Little things on the whole but nevertheless disquieting.

They drank their coffee silently, each lost in their own thoughts, and then as Carmella rose, saying she wanted to freshen up before dinner, she added, 'It is a storm in a teacup, Josie, do not worry. He is a good boy, I know this. Just a little exuberant at times, yes?'

Josie smiled but didn't reply. She could have coped with exuberance, even downright naughtiness, but this other side of Luke, the dark side, unnerved her, along with the beguiling charm which he could turn on and off like a tap. The screaming tantrums of childhood had stopped; now he used manipulation to get what he wanted.

She shook her head, telling herself she was the worst

mother in the world to think like this, and took another sip of coffee. He was just a boy after all and lots of lads went through horrible phases – pulling the wings off butterflies, badgering those smaller and weaker than themselves, and throwing their weight about with their friends. It didn't mean they'd all grow up to be violent individuals or criminals for goodness' sake. Perhaps Carmella was right, perhaps she was over-sensitive? It had been a hateful thing for Luke and his friends to do, but perhaps it *had* been a bit of fun that had gone too far? But try as she might she didn't believe that.

She glanced round the sitting room, at the beautiful furnishings, the tasteful wallpaper, the thick curtains and the glittering chandelier overhead. They all told her that she had done what she'd set out to do twelve years ago and given her son a secure future with a ready-made business that he would take over one day. A legitimate business, not one built on extortion and crime. He would be able to hold his head high and be proud of his name, and men would regard him with respect and not fear.

She drew in a deep, shuddering breath. She had worked all hours of the day and night, made sacrifices, especially in the early days, worried herself silly that it would all collapse like a pack of cards if she didn't make the right business decisions, but it had been worth it because she was doing it for Luke. Some folk – like her son's best friend's family – she knew regarded her with some condescension. She was 'new money', after all. Nevertheless, they were still accepted in their social circle, which was all that mattered because it was part of building a foundation for Luke's adult life.

She finished the coffee and walked to the window, looking down at the pleasant tree-lined avenue below. She didn't allow herself to think about what she had given up with regard to Jack Kane, not when she was trying to be strong. She had learned from bitter experience that it could crush her.

By the time the three of them sat in the small dining room eating dinner, the matter – at least outwardly – had been resolved. Luke had written the two letters of apology she had requested, and although he was still sticking to his story that a group of them had been horsing around and it was sheer chance that it was Morris who'd been debagged, he had said he was sorry to her and that he'd make sure nothing similar ever happened again. He had put his arms round her and kissed her, saying she was the best mother in the world and he was sorry for what he'd said to her, and Carmella had looked on smiling and clearly believing every word.

She just wished she could, Josie thought, as she took a forkful of the delicious spiced cod on a bed of chorizo-infused beans Carmella had made. She wished she could believe that Luke's penitence was genuine and not because he wanted his pocket money and freedom to go where he pleased restored as soon as possible. She glanced at her son as he sat chatting to Carmella and thought how beautiful he was with his black wavy hair and heavily lashed eyes; he was the image of his handsome father, but the genes that had given him his outstanding looks had passed on other less desirable things too. And there was nothing she could do about that.

She put down her knife and fork, leaving most of her meal untouched as a flood of fear and worry swept over her. Pray God He would give her the insight and strength to steer her precious boy in the right paths, because she had never felt so apprehensive about his future. She would give her life in an instant to protect him from harm, but how could she protect him against himself?

Chapter Twenty-Three

Ralph Gray stood perfectly still, peering out of the crack in the privy door, which was slightly ajar. He had left the house earlier to meet a couple of pals of his but had only got as far as the end of the back lane before he'd had to retrace his steps at a trot. Something he'd eaten had disagreed with him and he had barely had time to pull his trousers down when he'd reached the lavatory. He'd sat there for some time before he could get off the wooden plank seat with a hole cut in it, and he'd been just about to open the privy door when the gate into the yard had creaked.

It came naturally to him to snoop and spy on folk so rather than open the door and announce his presence, he eased it undone just a smidgen to see who was there. Flo, their next-door neighbour, sidled past, and something about her manner interested him. It was furtive and she was carrying an envelope in her hand.

He watched her open the kitchen door and step inside and only then did he leave the privy, bending almost double and making his way to the side of the window.

Carefully he raised himself enough to peer over the sill, making sure he wasn't seen. His wife and Flo were sitting at the kitchen table and Maggie was opening the envelope.

His mean little eyes narrowed. What was all this about? Something was going on. Why would Flo bring a letter round to show Maggie, and who the hell would be writing to Flo anyway? He had no time for his wife's pal and he knew Flo couldn't stand him but Maggie and her were as thick as thieves.

He watched Maggie read the contents of the envelope and she was smiling and talking animatedly to Flo although he couldn't hear what was being said. And then, to his great surprise, after a minute or so his wife tucked the letter back in the envelope but instead of giving it to Flo, Maggie walked across to the range and fiddled with a brick at the side of it. She had her back to him and he couldn't make out what she was doing but when she rejoined her friend the envelope was gone.

What the dickens? And then it came to him. There was no one on earth who would be writing to Maggie except for her, Josie, the little scut who had dropped him right in the mire with the McGuigans when she'd taken off with that brat of hers. From basking in the glow of having a daughter who was married to Adam McGuigan, overnight he'd become like a leper. No one had wanted to be seen with the father of the girl who'd done the dirty on the McGuigans.

When had Josie contacted her mam? How long had these letters been going on? Clearly Flo was in on it and had agreed for any communication to come through her. By, he'd like to wring that scrawny old neck of hers. He could just imagine the pleasure she'd took in getting one over on him.

He stood for a few moments more and then crouched down again, his head almost touching his knees as he walked across the yard and out into the back lane. Moving swiftly now, he made his way to the end of the lane where he stood, thinking hard. Maggie would go out shopping in a while and the coast would be clear for him to investigate. If he found she had been corresponding with Josie he'd take it out of her hide, damn her. She knew the McGuigans had offered a reward for Josie's whereabouts.

He had to wait for an hour or more before his patience was rewarded, but eventually he saw the back gate open and his wife emerge with her shopping bag over her arm. He waited until she was out of sight and then walked quickly from the opposite end of the lane, excitement filling him.

Once in the kitchen, he went straight over to the range and it took just a few moments to find Maggie's hidey-hole. He drew out the bundle of letters, reading the top one swiftly. Then he stuffed them all in his jacket pocket. He knew exactly what he was going to do with these.

Bruce McGuigan stared at the undersized little man standing in front of him. He'd never had much time for Ralph Gray and when Josie had skedaddled, he'd told her father to keep out of his way if he knew what was good for him. He'd wisely heeded the warning.

Bruce settled back in his leather chair in the office near the docks where he conducted most of his business. 'Well?' he said softly. 'You want to see me?'

'Aye, Mr McGuigan.' Ralph's eyes darted from Bruce to the huge hulk of a man standing to one side of the desk. He knew there were more of McGuigan's heavies in the vicinity and the man who had shown him into the office was positioned behind him. Nervously he cleared his throat. 'I've news at last – about me daughter, Josie.'

Bruce didn't speak but the sudden coiled stillness in his body was chilling.

'She's – she's over the water,' Ralph stammered.

'Over the water? Ireland, you mean?'

'No, sir. Further than that. America.'

'*America?*' Bruce sat up straight. 'And you know this how?'

'I found some letters, Mr McGuigan, from our Josie that me wife had hidden. They've been writing to each other but the wife never let on to me.'

'Your wife's been receiving letters all this time and you didn't know?'

'No, sir, I swear. The next-door neighbour's took 'em in. It's her address on the envelopes. Here.' Ralph dug the bundle out of his jacket pocket. 'I only found 'em by chance today.' He placed the stack on Bruce's desk and then stepped back a pace. 'The wife don't know I've clocked her. I waited till she'd gone shopping to get 'em and then I come straight to you here.'

Bruce reached forward, examining the top envelope before he opened it. He extracted the contents and read it before selecting another envelope. When Ralph went to speak he held up his hand whereupon Ralph immediately became silent.

There were over fifty envelopes in all, and after Bruce had read a few of the letters he looked at Ralph again. 'Seems your daughter's done well for herself.'

A shiver snaked down Ralph's spine. It hadn't been a compliment. 'I didn't know, Mr McGuigan, sir,' he whined. 'The wife never let on.'

'So you're not master in your own home?' Bruce said softly. 'Is that what you're saying?'

Ralph stared at the hard, thickset face and for the life of him he didn't know how to answer. He licked his dry lips, stammering again as he said, 'I – I didn't kn-know.'

'Aye, so you've said.' Bruce turned to the man standing by the desk, his voice expressionless as he murmured, 'There was a reward offered for information as to my brother's wife and child's whereabouts if I remember rightly?'

The man stared back at his boss, his tough face impassive. He knew better than to answer what was a rhetorical question.

Ralph swallowed hard. This wasn't going as he'd have liked. He was sweating profusely, and he rubbed his damp palms on his trousers. 'I didn't come for no reward,' he lied. 'I just thought you ought to know, Mr McGuigan, sir.'

'You are right. I should. I should have known twelve years ago when your daughter did the dirty on my brother. If he had been able to deal with her and get his son back, it would have meant the last years wouldn't have been so painful. But your missus was able to pull the wool over your eyes, wasn't she, eh? Now, I don't blame her. Mother love is the most powerful emotion there is, stronger than fear and hate, and I respect that.'

'I – I'll take it out of her hide.'

'You'll do no such thing. She's gone shopping you say? How long is she usually away?'

'An hour or so, Mr McGuigan, or more. She – she looks for bargains an' that.'

'And you came straight here when she'd left after you found the letters?'

'Aye.'

'Well, if you nip home sharpish and put them back where you found 'em she'll be none the wiser, right?'

Ralph nodded nervously. 'What – what if she's there when I get back?'

'Then you wait for a suitable opportunity and replace them. No mistakes. I don't want her knowing we're on to her.' Bruce had been making a note of the address while he spoke, and now he stood up and walked over to a big safe in the corner of the room. After punching in some numbers and opening the heavy door, he returned to his desk, a thick wad of banknotes in his hand. He dropped the bundle in front of Ralph, who had gone goggle-eyed at the amount of money. 'As soon as the job's done, you come back here and this'll be yours,' Bruce said quietly, 'and you don't say a word to her, all right?'

'Aye, yes, Mr McGuigan. I'll go now, shall I?'

'You do that, and straight back here when you've done the necessary so I know.'

'Yes, Mr McGuigan.' Ralph picked up the envelopes, stuffing them in his pocket.

The big man with a bull neck and shaven head who'd been standing in front of the door opened it after a nod from Bruce, and Ralph emerged on to the mezzanine floor above the clothes factory the McGuigans owned. It was one of their legitimate enterprises in the day but used as a gambling den after dark. He scurried down the metal steps and through the lines of women working at tables, who didn't lift their heads as he passed.

Once in the street, Ralph hightailed it home as fast as he could, the image of the wad of cash at the forefront of his mind. Since Joe and Ellen and Kate had married and left home, there was only Nelly's wage and what Maggie earned taking in washing for some of the big houses coming into the house. More than once he'd been reduced to picking up cigarette stubs in the street and scrounging drinks from some of his pals, although most of them were wise to him now. The beer and baccy money Maggie doled out each week was soon gone, and she'd taken to keeping the rent money in a cloth bag she wore tied under her clothes next to her skin, damn her. She even slept with it under her nightdress. He'd swing for her one day, so help him. Shrivelled-up old crone. But with the reward money he'd be sitting pretty.

He entered the house quietly but could see straight away no one was home. The pot roast for their dinner was cooking in the range, made with scrag ends as usual. He'd be able to treat himself to some slap-up meals in town with Bruce's cash, but he'd be careful so Maggie didn't get a whiff of it. Two could play at hiding stuff, he thought viciously. She wouldn't see a penny of it.

Once he had replaced the bundle of letters where he'd found them he breathed easier, although he hadn't really expected that Maggie would be back. She always did her shopping in the evening and hung about the Old Market waiting for the stallholders to reduce their goods at the end of the day. She was forever bringing home bags of spotted vegetables and bits of meat you wouldn't feed to a dog, he thought derisively, giving his wife no credit for her thriftiness at making a penny stretch to two.

It was already dark outside when he left the house through the back yard. It was the middle of November and the evening was dry after two weeks of constant rain and sleet and howling winds. The air was sharp and clean, the black sky high and star-filled.

Ralph felt cock-a-hoop as he hurried back to the clothes factory. He'd got one over on Maggie, he told himself gleefully. How dare she keep Josie's whereabouts from him? He had a right to know, damn her. When he thought about the trouble his daughter had caused he'd have wrung her neck himself if he could have got hold of her. She'd left a devil of a hoo-ha behind her when she'd put Adam McGuigan in a wheelchair and then disappeared with the bairn. She hadn't thought about anyone but herself. He'd been terrified to leave the house for weeks because of what Bruce McGuigan might have in store for him being Josie's da, and all the time Maggie had known where Josie was. They could have been in clover for years on that reward money.

When he reached the factory something made him hesitate for a few moments. He went over exactly what Bruce McGuigan had said and his unease grew. It was almost as though Bruce had been blaming him rather than Maggie when he'd said that bit about mother love and the rest of it. But the lure of the money was too strong to resist. Telling himself he was imagining things, he made up his mind to go in. It was knocking-off time at the factory, and as he still stood nerving himself to enter, a stream of chattering women began to emerge.

Once the last woman had disappeared the door banged shut, and suddenly Ralph felt panicky. He didn't want McGuigan to change his mind about the reward if he had longer to think about it, he told himself. Best to get in there now.

When he knocked on the door and tried the handle he found it was locked or bolted from the inside, but within moments it was opened by a pockmarked youth with a foxy look about him. He was half the size of the bruisers who'd been in the office. Grinning, he said cheerily, 'You Ralph Gray? I'm Terry, I man the door for McGuigan.'

Feeling reassured by the youth's demeanour, Ralph nodded. 'Aye, that's me.'

'The boss said you might be back the night. Follow me.'

They walked through the deserted factory to the steep steel staircase, and once at the top on the narrow plat-form, Ralph's guide knocked on the door. The office had a large window so that the inhabitants could survey the factory below if they so chose, and Ralph had seen Bruce McGuigan still seated at his desk looking at some papers. There was no sign of his henchmen, which further encour-aged him.

After a second knock, a voice within said, 'Come in,' and the youth opened the door, stepping aside to let Ralph pass him. He remained outside when he shut the door.

Bruce's eyes narrowed as he looked up. 'Did you get them back without her knowing?'

'Aye, yes, Mr McGuigan,' Ralph said eagerly. 'She'll be none the wiser, you can rest easy about that. As far as she knows her secret's safe.'

'And you will keep it that way?'

'Of course, Mr McGuigan, if that's what you want. I won't say a word.'

'What about if you have a row or get drunk? You like a drink, don't you? You won't be tempted to blab?'

'No, no.'

Bruce leaned back in his chair, his smart leather-fronted waistcoat straining against his belly. He was the picture of a wealthy businessman, his suit, made of some kind of tweed, clearly expensive and his face clean-shaven. 'It's a lot of money I'm giving you. Won't your missus wonder where it's come from?'

'I won't let on I've got it.' Ralph was feeling nervous again. Something wasn't right. 'I can be as crafty as she's been.'

'I'm sure you can.' His voice conversational, Bruce continued, 'What if your conscience troubles you, especially after we've . . . dealt with your daughter? You do realize she's now living on borrowed time?'

The door behind Ralph opened and as he turned he saw the two heavies enter. For such big men they were surprisingly light on their feet. They said nothing, neither did they glance at him, but stood impassively to his right and left. The same sickly feeling he had experienced the first time he had come into the office returned, but stronger. His voice almost a whimper, he said, 'Me conscience is clear about our Josie, Mr McGuigan. She deserves everything she gets for what she's done to your brother.'

'You're right, she does.' Bruce nodded. He reached into his desk drawer and took out the bundle of notes, placing them in front of him. 'You see, I was so sure you'd come back I didn't even bother to return it to the safe. It's not quite thirty pieces of silver but near enough, eh?' He smiled, glancing at his lackeys, who sniggered obediently. And it was to them that he said, 'The thing is, I've got something of a dilemma. Can you trust the word of a man who would sell his daughter, his own flesh and blood, for a few pounds?'

The two men said nothing; they could have been made in stone so still did they stand. Looking again at Ralph, Bruce raised his eyebrows. 'You see my predicament?'

Ralph's stomach was turning over and he had the desire to empty his bowels. 'I promise you, Mr McGuigan, I'll say nowt to no one.' He licked his dry lips. 'As soon as I saw them letters me one thought was to get 'em to you.'

'Very commendable.' Bruce gestured to the money. 'Well, what are you waiting for? It's yours, take it.'

Ralph's hand went out and then stopped before, tentatively now, he picked up the wad of notes, stuffing them into the pocket of his frayed jacket. 'Thank you, Mr McGuigan. I – I swear I won't—'

'Get out of my sight.'

'Yes, Mr McGuigan.'

He turned but the two men didn't move, blocking his exit, their eyes on their boss. 'Escort our friend here out, would you,' Bruce said quietly, 'and the back way, all right?'

They nodded, positioning themselves one to the front and one to the rear of Ralph, and it was like that the three of them descended the stairs to the factory floor. The youth who had let him in was sitting on one of the work tables eating a meat sandwich, his eyes bright as he said, 'The back way?'

'Aye.'

'This way.' The youth led them over to a door at the far end of the workplace, opening it to reveal a stone-slabbed yard holding a brick-built privy and a number of wooden packing cases piled against one wall along with other bits and pieces. There was a door into the street outside with three heavy bolts, and again it was the young man who said, 'Go on then, that's your way out.'

Ralph moved forward, his skin prickling with fear, and he was fumbling with the first bolt when the knife entered his body with some force between his shoulder blades. He was aware of the youth beginning to laugh as he turned, his fingers still grappling with the bolt, and then the knife came again, piercing his heart. He didn't have time to cry out before he fell to the ground; he was dead before he hit the slabs.

The henchman with the knife bent down and retrieved the notes from Ralph's jacket, handing them to the youth, who was still laughing as he said, 'Take it up to Mr McGuigan and tell him we'll dump the body in the river,' as the other man slid the bolts and opened the door into a dark side street. After wiping the blood from the knife on the body, he hoisted it up across his shoulder as though he was carrying a sack of potatoes and then the two of them stepped into the back alley. They walked swiftly away as the younger man bolted the door behind them and went back into the building to deliver the money before retracing his steps and washing the stone slabs clean. It wasn't the first time they'd been scrubbed to rid them of blood and it wouldn't be the last.

*   *   *

Adam stared at his brother, barely able to comprehend what he was hearing. He had to gulp in his throat a number of times before he could say, 'You're sure?' Bruce had just told him Josie and his son were living in America.

'Quite sure. Seems she's been writing to her mam for umpteen years but having the letters delivered to the next-door neighbour so Ralph wouldn't cotton on. I've seen them.' He quickly explained all that had happened over the last hours, finishing with, 'He's been disposed of so there's no loose ends.'

'And she owns some bars? She's a businesswoman of sorts?'

'So it appears,' Bruce said grimly.

'And Luke? He's alive and well?'

Bruce nodded. 'I only read a few of the letters, I was anxious her father got them back before her mam discovered they were gone – the last thing we want is Josie being forewarned. But yes, Luke's thrived apparently, but then he's your son.'

Adam shook his head. 'I can't believe it. I'd given up ever knowing.'

So had Bruce, but now he said, 'I told you I'd find them, didn't I?' He put an arm round the thin shoulders and gave his brother a brief hug before sitting down in a chair opposite Adam's wheelchair.

Arthur, who had been standing behind Adam, cleared his throat. 'A brandy, sir?'

'I think we could all do with a drink,' Adam said, looking up at the big bulky figure as Arthur nodded and walked across the room to the drinks cabinet. Although Arthur was technically an employee the two men had become firm friends over the years and Adam was well aware he owed his life to the gentle giant who looked after him. In the early days when he had still been living at his mother's house he had treated Arthur abominably, swearing and cursing and throwing things at him, but Arthur had taken it all in his stride whilst not letting up on his encouragement to get Adam to do more and push himself. And it had worked. Arthur had insisted on a certain amount of exercise along with a period of fresh air outside – whatever the weather – every day.

He had taken charge of his patient's diet along with his medication, enforcing a strict regime which had gradually meant Adam had been able to control his bodily functions better. This had been a huge step forward as far as Adam was concerned. He was no longer confined to the house and garden for fear of soiling himself unexpectedly. He'd finally gone back to the office two or three days a week with Arthur at his side, and once Bruce had fulfilled his promise to build him his own, specially adapted house, he had engaged a maid, housekeeper and cook and even started entertaining occasionally. He tired easily; the accident that had robbed him of the use of his legs had also caused problems with his heart, but overall his life had become tolerable.

Once the three men were seated with their brandies, Bruce said quietly, 'What do you want me to do?'

Adam swallowed half his brandy. The news had shaken

him and he was having a few palpitations. He took several deep breaths as Arthur had taught him before he said, 'I want them brought back here.'

'Both of them? Not just the boy? Wouldn't it be better if she disappears abroad?'

'I want her to see what she's done to me before she's done away with.'

'All right, but it would be easier for her to have an accident where she is so we just have the boy to deal with.'

Adam shook his head. 'I want to see her.' He turned to Arthur. 'What do you think?'

Arthur didn't think it strange that his master was asking for his opinion about such a personal matter; they had no secrets and he knew Adam trusted him implicitly. Apart from the six McGuigan brothers themselves, he probably knew more about the workings of their crime empire than anyone as Adam had kept nothing back over the years. He was a non-violent man himself, even passive, but the fact that he had been drawn into the grim McGuigan fold didn't bother him. He was paid exceptionally well, far in excess of anything he could have once imagined, and he considered himself a fortunate man. He thought for a moment before he said, 'I can understand Mr McGuigan's reasoning but it might be the case that it's actually easier to persuade the boy to come if his mother's with him. If she was . . . disposed of, it wouldn't be the ideal way for him to meet you.'

It was Bruce who said, 'Aye, that's a good point, Arthur. All right, we'll get them both back here.'

Adam leaned back in his chair. He felt exhausted but excited. The years of pain had grooved deep lines in his face but they'd been unable to erase his good looks completely, although he looked at least twenty years older than he was. The streaks of silver at his temples gave his lean appearance a distinguished look and added to his inherent charm, but it was his eyes that betrayed the inner man. They held a bitter hardness that was chilling. Looking at his brother, he said simply, 'When?'

'Give me a day or two to pull things together and then I'll leave. I'll take a couple of men with me.'

'How will you make her come back?'

'That's my problem but I can assure you it'll happen,' Bruce said grimly, 'even if I have to drug her and put her in a box.' He was only half-joking. Whatever it took, he'd get her and the boy home. It was never discussed, but he was aware that Adam's heart had grown considerably weaker in the last twelve months. The slightest thing tired him now, and whereas once he'd been able to manoeuvre himself from the bed into his wheelchair and even bathe in his specially adapted bathroom, he now relied on Arthur to lift him and do what was necessary.

In fact, Bruce thought, glancing at Arthur, he doubted whether his brother would be here now if it wasn't for this man. And not just because Arthur took care of the physical side of things with a matter-of-factness that made Adam feel at ease, but because he was intuitive, knowing when to cajole, when to talk straight, and perhaps most of all how to elicit laughter when Adam was particularly down. Larry, his brother, had the same sixth sense with people, which was why he'd always been useful in finding out information and twisting folk round his little finger. Thinking about it, he'd take Larry with him to America too. He might prove helpful with the lad.

'Don't say anything to Mam for the time being. I can't stand her round here fussing and getting worked up.' Adam drained the last of his brandy. 'Arthur has to fend her off at the door most days and then she gives him an earful.'

Arthur grinned. 'I don't blame her, she's your mam and she worries about you. I'm big enough and ugly enough to take some stick. Water off a duck's back.'

Aye, he was a good man, was Arthur, Bruce thought as he grinned back at Larry's brother. He'd see him all right when— He stopped his mind from going down that path. He didn't dare imagine how his mother would be when the inevitable happened. Shaking off the darkness that was apt to swamp him when he allowed himself to think about his brother's demise, he swigged back the last of his brandy and stood up. 'I'll get on to it then. I'll pop round again before I go, all right?'

Adam nodded, and then, as his brother turned away, he said, 'Bruce?'

'Aye?'

'Thanks, man. Not just for this latest but for – well, everything.'

Bruce looked down into the gaunt face of this brother he loved. Forcing a smile, he said, 'Go on with you,' and then walked quickly out of the room. Once in the hall, he bowed his head and stood for some moments gaining control of himself.

How he was going to keep from strangling the life out of that little she-devil when he came face to face with her, he didn't know. He drew in a great breath of air. But sooner or later he'd see to it she got her just deserts. 'I'm coming for you, Josie McGuigan,' he whispered to himself softly, 'and believe me, before I'm done you'll wish you'd never been born.'

Chapter Twenty-Four

Luke stood scowling at his mother. He'd brought home his report card and she had just opened the envelope and read the contents, and told him she wasn't happy.

'Why? I did all right, I know I did.'

'But you could have done much better. Listen to what Mr Gould has written. "Luke is an able student and a natural-born leader among his peers. He has obtained good marks throughout all subjects but every one of his teachers assures me he could have achieved far higher if he had applied himself more. Luke needs to understand that if he wishes to succeed and go to the university of his choice in the years to come, he needs to work *now*."'

Josie paused, looking at her son as she said, 'The now is underlined. Three times.'

'Huh.'

Ignoring his sullen expression, she continued reading: '"I would be failing in my duty as Luke's headmaster if I didn't add that Luke and his group of friends do not bring out the best in each other, quite the contrary in fact. According to some of my staff, when the boys are together they can become disruptive at best and insolent at worst. In view of this, starting from next term, the boys will be split up where possible so that they can concentrate more on their education and less on behaving in a manner that does not become young gentlemen."'

'That's so unfair! They can't do that.'

Taking no notice of Luke's explosion, Josie read on: "'I trust the school will have your cooperation and support regarding these new measures. I'm sure we all want the very best for Luke and to see him reach his full potential in the future."'

Josie raised her gaze to her son's furious face. 'Do you and your friends play some of the teachers up, Luke?'

He glared at her. 'No more than anyone else does. Some of them are drips.'

'So I take it by that that you do then?'

He shrugged, his whole attitude mutinous.

As she watched him, Josie found irritation and disappointment rising in equal measure. She wanted to shake him, much as she loved him. Opportunities lost were rarely recovered and he needed to make the most of his schooldays. The school offered a first-class education if only he would take full advantage of it.

She glanced across the room to where Carmella was sitting by the beautifully bedecked Christmas tree. It was two weeks before Christmas and Luke's school was closing for the winter break soon, hence the report from his teachers.

She had planned lots of outings for him in the run-up to Christmas. A trip to the theatre for a pantomime via the New York underground station, which had only opened a couple of months earlier and was still a huge novelty; a slap-up meal at Delmonico's on Fifth Avenue, and of course a big party for all of his friends on Luke's birthday. She was going to take them to Coney Island, a ribbon of land jutting off the southern end of Brooklyn into the Atlantic Ocean. The big resort area had to be experienced to be believed. She and Carmella had taken Luke there a couple of years ago and it had been amazing.

They had been totally in awe of the spectacular amusement parks and expensive hotels, one of which – the Elephant Hotel – was built in the shape of a multi-storey pachyderm, but it had been the rides Luke liked best. The Sea Lion Park featuring the Flip Flap railroad, an upside-down roller coaster, had been one of his favourites although it had reduced Carmella to a nervous wreck, and the Shoot-the-Chutes water flume had splattered them from top to toe. Steeplechase Park had had scale models of world landmarks such as the Eiffel Tower, and the Trip to the Moon attraction – an imagined rocket ride. From the moment they'd arrived the sense of carnival and frivolity had been infectious with all the minstrel shows, merry-go-rounds, Punch and Judy enterprises, fat women, big snakes, giant, dwarf and midget exhibitions, circuses and menageries, flying horses, fortune-telling booths and more.

Since then Luke had heard that Dreamland had been

built and he'd been on at her for months to go back for a day. According to the advertising, one million electric lights lit up the miniature railroad, fake Venetian canals and Swiss Alpine peaks. Three hundred dwarfs lived in its Lilliputian Village and a one-armed lion tamer commanded the big cat enclosure. There was now Luna Park too, which had taken over Sea Lion Park since they'd been there – a city within the park lit up by even more electricity than Dreamland, with spires, domes, minarets and other fairytale-like architecture. Elephants and camels apparently strolled round the grounds and there were wild animal shows, along with disaster spectacles which allowed visitors to get a feel of what it was like to experience a flood, a volcano eruption or an earthquake.

It was an expensive day out and taking Luke's friends would increase the cost considerably but she had thought it would be a lovely treat for his thirteenth birthday. Since the incident involving Morris Henderson, Luke had been on his best behaviour as far as she was aware. Now she wasn't so sure. He seemed to have little respect for his teachers at the school anyway.

Carmella returned her gaze, her round face troubled, and for once she didn't try to pour oil on troubled waters as she said quietly, 'Luke, you must understand that doing the best you can is important? You want to succeed in life, yes?'

Luke scowled at her. 'I did all right,' he said again, turning to Josie as he added, 'Better than most, in fact.' He didn't see why he had to work any harder, he thought irritably, and he certainly wasn't going to turn into a swot like Gregory or Morris and have the mickey taken out of him. And as for old Gould splitting him up from his friends, why wasn't his mother up in arms about it like any normal mother would be? She was never on his side.

For the first time since she had opened the envelope after he'd come home, Josie lost her temper with him; and she almost barked at him now, 'Don't you see that better than most isn't the point if it's not the best you can achieve? This is a country of great opportunity but everything won't just fall into your lap, Luke. You have to work to get to where you want to be in life like anyone else.'

'I do work, and so do Irwin and the others – it's just that some of the teachers have got it in for us, that's all.'

'Oh, for goodness' sake!' Excuses, excuses, excuses. He could never admit to being in the wrong. She was just about to say more when there was a knock on the front door. Apart from Jack it was rare that anyone called and he had been that morning with a list of the costs for refurbishment of the original Gray's in Horatio Street which needed some attention.

Her mind full of Luke's report she walked to the door and for once didn't look through the small round spyhole as she usually did, opening it almost without thinking.

As she took in the big burly man in front of her and the two equally brawny individuals standing behind him with the smaller diminutive figure of the man she recognized as Larry making up the rear, she tried to slam the door. But Bruce already had his foot in the way, his voice soft as he said, 'Hello, Josie. I've come a long way to see you. Aren't you going to invite us in?'

She tried to speak but had to clear her throat, her heartbeat pounding in her ears. 'What do you want?'

'Now, that's not very friendly, is it.' He smiled a smile that didn't reach the bullet-hard eyes. 'Where are your manners?'

'I said, what do you want?' She had thought she was going to faint when she'd first seen him but her voice was stronger now. 'You can't come in, it's not convenient.'

'Is that so? Well, let me tell you—' His voice was cut off, his eyes widening as his gaze fastened on the young lad who had come into the hallway.

For a moment Josie saw Luke as Bruce must be seeing him – a younger replica of Adam. She tried to shut the door again but to no avail as she said, 'Go away or I'll call the police.'

'I don't think so.' Bruce didn't take his eyes off Luke as he murmured, 'It's Adam as a lad.' He took a deep breath. 'And you've kept him from his da all these years, you she-devil.' He swore harshly and for a moment she thought he was going to hit her but he merely pushed her aside and came into the hall, the others right behind him.

Luke backed away, and it was the fear in her son's face that caused Josie to spring forward, throwing herself between them as she cried, 'Go into the sitting room, Luke, and shut the door. Stay with Carmella.'

Bruce had seen the fear too and now he said, moderating his voice, 'Don't be frightened, lad. I'm your uncle and I wouldn't harm a hair of your head. I've come to take you to your da.'

One of the heavies grabbed Josie, jerking her out of the way and twisting her arms behind her back. She gave a cry of pain and Bruce turned, saying, 'Leave her,' as he gestured for Larry to come forward. 'Take the boy into the sitting room.'

Larry took Luke's arm but the boy stood his ground, staring at Bruce with an expression Josie couldn't describe. It wasn't fear now but a mixture of incredulity and confusion and something else. 'Who did you say you are?' he whispered.

'I'm your uncle Bruce, lad, from England. Your mam told you about your family there? No? I'm not surprised. Well, I'm taking you to your da, your father, all right? He's been waiting a long time to see you.'

'My father's dead.'

'No, lad, your father's not dead. Your mam tell you what she did to him?'

'I didn't do anything, it wasn't like that.' Josie looked at Carmella, who was standing in the doorway of the sitting room. 'Carmella, take him in and shut the door.'

'You said my father's dead.' Luke stared at Josie, his face white with shock. 'That's what you've always said, that he's dead and we've got no family, that you were left a widow with me.'

'She's no widow, lad.' Bruce's voice was quiet but it

had the ring of truth. 'And there's plenty of family, on her side as well as your da's.'

'Is it true?'

The expression on his face was causing a physical pain in her chest. 'I can explain—'

'I said, is it true? Yes or no.'

He hadn't raised his voice but the tone cut Josie to the quick. She nodded, beyond words.

'I have a father who's still alive?'

'Not just a father.' Bruce glanced at Josie's desperate face, relishing the moment. 'There's aunts and uncles, cousins, grandmas, the whole caboodle. And your da thinks the world of you, lad. Always has, from the moment you were born. He's never given up hope of finding you.'

Larry was the same height as Luke, who was tall for his age. Now he employed the gift of persuasion and charm that made him so useful in wheedling out things for Bruce. He put a comforting arm round Luke's thin shoulders like an older brother as he said, 'I tell you what, let's go and sit down, eh? Then we can talk this all out properly.'

Luke looked into the friendly, open face and allowed himself to be led into the sitting room, the rest of them following.

Josie was feeling sick with dread. The thing she'd always feared – which had come to the fore in countless nightmares since she had left England – had happened. Bruce had found them. And the reality was so much worse than any dream. She had to make Luke understand that she'd had no choice but to escape and take him with her, and explain what kind of man his father was and what the McGuigan crime empire was built on.

Once in the sitting room Larry sat beside Luke on one sofa, and Carmella was on another, but the rest of them stood. 'Please listen to me, darling,' Josie said, tears choking her voice. 'I did what I thought was best for you.'

'By lying to him and taking him away from his father?'

'*Shut up.*' She rounded on Bruce with such ferocity she made them all jump. 'Just shut up. You've had your say—'

'Oh, I haven't even started, lass, believe me.'

Ignoring him, Josie went on, 'Your father's name is Adam McGuigan and he's a criminal. I didn't realize he was like the rest of his family when I met him and we got married soon after – in fact, he had sworn to me that he wasn't and I believed him – but within months I knew he'd lied. He drank and – and had other women but by then you were on the way and I wanted to make the marriage work. After you were born it was all right for a while but then he went back to his old ways—'

'You don't think he's going to believe this picture of you as whiter than white?' The words held a deep ring of bitterness as Bruce glared at the woman he hated. 'Your mother was a street urchin singing in pubs for a few pennies when your da saw her and fell in love,' he said to Luke, 'and he took her out of the hovel she was living in and gave her everything a woman could want, including marriage. She jumped at it, lad, I'm telling you, and I don't blame her for that. What woman wouldn't? Now, I'm not saying your da didn't have his faults – we all do, don't we, no one's perfect – but he didn't deserve what she did to him, that's for sure.'

Luke's gaze travelled from Bruce to his mother. 'What did you do?' he asked bewilderedly, his face white.

'There was an argument one night when your father was drunk and—'

'She pushed him down the stairs and put him in a wheelchair for life, lad.' Bruce's eyes were black slits, seemingly lost in their sockets, and his voice was rapier cold. 'Then while he was still in hospital at death's door she ransacked the safe, taking all the money and jewellery, and skedaddled across the ocean taking you with her. Your da could have coped with losing the use of his legs, terrible though that's been, but it was losing you that has made the last years hell for him. She might as well have finished the job she started and put a bullet in his heart. That'd have been kinder.'

He had always known there was something. Luke looked from his uncle to his mother. She had never talked much about his father except to say that he looked like him and he had been a businessman back in England. And according to her there had been no other family, the both of them being only children and both sets of parents having died. She had come to America with the little money she'd had, determined to make it work for her and give them both a future. He had always admired her for that. And all the time she had been telling him a pack of lies.

'Why did you leave him like that, my father?' he said stiffly, so many emotions coursing through him he couldn't have put a name to one.

'Because he had told everyone that I pushed him and caused him to fall. It was a lie, it was an accident, but I knew if I stayed his family would believe it and take their revenge. They would have killed me and taken you.' Josie gulped hard. 'You were just a little baby, you needed me, and I couldn't let that happen.'

'Is that true?' Luke looked straight at Bruce. 'Would you have done that?'

Bruce stared at his nephew. He could lie and the boy might or might not believe him, but instinct told him to tell the truth. This was Adam's son, a McGuigan, and there was something in Luke's eyes that made him feel that if he was honest with the boy he'd accept it. His mother had been lying to him for years and if he played his cards right, that would be her downfall. Quietly, he said, 'I love your da, lad, and whatever your mother says to the contrary he's a good man. So yes, I would have taken my revenge as she puts it but to my mind it would have been the right thing to do. She's ruined his life. Putting him in a wheelchair would have been enough for me to make sure she drew her last breath, but the cruelty of taking you away from him was worse. He loved you from the moment you were born – I've never seen a father so besotted with his son – and although he's suffered every day in his body it's been nothing to the suffering in his mind, not knowing where you were, if you were safe and well looked after.'

'He's twisting everything, Luke.' Josie wanted to reach out to him but something stopped her. 'The McGuigans are nothing more than gangsters, criminals, and they would have moulded you to be the same. You wouldn't have been able to escape their influence, they'd have brainwashed you from a child.'

'What if I didn't want to escape?'

There was a long silence following this remark, then Josie murmured, the catch of tears in her voice, 'What do you mean?'

'What if I had wanted to be like my father and his family? Would you still have loved me?'

'Of course I would still have loved you.'

'I don't think so. You want me to be perfect, that's why you're always going on at me, but as my uncle says, no one is perfect.'

'I don't want you to be perfect, I never have, just happy and doing the best you can in life. Everything I've done I've done for you because I love you.'

Bruce saw his chance and entered the conversation again: 'Is that including taking the boy halfway across the world and denying him his family? To my mind that's not love, that's domination and control.'

'*You*, to say that!' As she stared at Adam's brother, Josie knew if she'd got a knife in her hand she would have used it. 'Your father and the rest of you built your little empire on terror and intimidation. How many people have you had murdered in your time, Bruce?' She swung back to Luke. 'He had my own brother, Toby, beaten to death because Toby didn't want me to marry your father. That's what the McGuigans do if anyone gets in their way.'

How the devil had she come by that information? Bruce kept his face from revealing his surprise as he said, 'Now we're into the realms of fantasy. Your brother was set upon by the menfolk of a girl he was courting because he wasn't a Catholic. You know that as well as I do.'

'That's what you encouraged people to think but the O'Learys weren't responsible for Toby's death. The pity is I found that out too late.'

They stared at each other, their mutual hate vibrating in the air.

'Stop it.' Luke's voice was cracked. 'Just stop it.' Looking at Bruce, he said, 'Why have you come? To – to hurt her?'

'No, lad, no.' Bruce shook his head. 'When we found out where your mam and you were, I promised your da, your father, that I'd bring you to see him, that's all. He's— Well, he's not too good, the fall damaged his heart as well as his spine and lately he's been struggling.'

Luke's eyes widened. 'He's not going to die?'

'I don't know, lad.'

'I want to see him.'

'No.' The word was torn out of Josie. As Luke met her gaze, she said more softly, 'No, Luke, no. Don't you see what he's doing? He wants to get you back to England and he'll say or do anything to accomplish that.'

'I don't care, I want to see my father.' Looking at Bruce, he said, 'How soon can we leave?'

This had gone better than he could have imagined. Trying to keep his jubilation from showing, Bruce glanced at Josie. 'If you try and stop him he'll hate you for it, you know that, don't you? He's not a child, he's a young man. There's lads working down the mine back home at his age or doing other work to provide for their families and help their parents. You can't stop him—'

'I can, I'm his mother,' she bit back, but even as she said the words she knew she had lost. Bruce had manipulated Luke as he did everyone. Nothing would prevent Luke now from going to see the man who was his father – she could read it in her son's eyes.

And as if in confirmation of the thought, Luke said flatly, 'I'm going, Mother.'

She cast a desperate appeal for help towards Carmella but her friend was clearly stunned by what had happened and said nothing. Looking away, Josie said shakily, 'Then I'm coming with you. If you're determined to go, we'll go together.'

'That's up to you.' Now the satisfaction did show in Bruce's voice. 'There's an extra two passages booked on the return trip to England and the ship leaves tomorrow.'

'No.' She shook her head. 'I need time to put things in place here if I'm going to be out of the country for a while. Luke and I will follow as soon as I can make the necessary arrangements and—'

'I'm going with my uncle tomorrow.' Luke's voice was still quiet, flat. 'It's up to you whether you come with me or stay here, but I'm going.'

'We'll – we'll talk about it later, when we're alone.' She drew in a long deep breath, attempting to gain control. 'I can't just leave at a moment's notice, Luke. Surely you can understand that?'

'I don't understand anything about you.' His jaw muscles tightened and his mouth was set. For a moment it was as though Adam was sitting there, not her twelve-year-old son. 'You've lied to me my whole life and kept me from my father. You had no right to do that. I used to listen to the other boys talking about theirs and think that I would do anything for just one day with mine, and all the time—' His voice broke and he jumped up, dashing from the room into his bedroom and slamming the door.

Josie stood, her hand pressed tightly over her mouth, and then half-fell into a chair as her legs gave way.

As Larry got up and joined Bruce and the others, Carmella came and stood by Josie's chair, putting her hand on her shoulder as she said softly, 'He'll come round, it is the shock, that is all.'

'I don't think so.' Bruce made no effort to hide his jubilation. 'You've had your answer and he's coming with me tomorrow, with or without you.'

'You know I wouldn't let him go with you without me.'

'That's up to you. I'll be back at midday for him tomorrow and the ship sails at three.' He waited for her to reply and when she remained silent, he looked at Carmella. 'I dare say you've heard her side of the story but I can tell you she's not what she pretends to be, not by a long chalk. She came from scum and scum she remains—'

'Do not talk to me about my friend.' Carmella's voice was like the crack of a whip and so at odds with her usual quiet demeanour that Josie raised her head in surprise. 'Josie is a good woman, a woman of courage, but you are bad.' She said something in her native tongue, an insult by the way she virtually spat it out.

'Birds of a feather, eh?' Bruce said scornfully. He turned, clicking his fingers at the two men who'd been standing impassively either side of him, and they followed him like obedient dogs out of the apartment, Larry making up the rear.

Josie heard the front door close behind them but for the life of her she couldn't move. Luke had never told her how he had felt about not having a father but she should have known, she told herself wretchedly. But then, if she had, would it have altered anything? He would have done exactly what he was doing now and insisted on going to find him if she had admitted his father was alive. She'd had to try and protect him from the McGuigans. Hadn't she? But now, for the first time since she had left England, she wasn't sure.

It was early the following morning and she had gone to see Jack. He was still living in his attic apartment despite the generous wage she paid him because, as he had told her on more than one occasion when she'd suggested he move to something a little more luxurious, it suited him.

She had just related what had transpired the evening before and now he was staring at her, shock and horror etching his features. 'You can't be seriously considering going back? It's madness. You'll never leave England alive, you know that, don't you? This Bruce has admitted he still wants his revenge and over there you'll be completely at their mercy.'

'I have to go, I can't let Luke go alone.'

'Then make him stay, damn it. I'll talk to him, make him see reason.'

'That would only make things worse.' She closed her eyes for a moment. She hadn't slept a wink and was feeling sick and shaky. 'He won't talk to me except for repeating that he's going to England with Bruce today and that if I try and stop him he'll run away and find his own way there. And he would, Jack.'

'Then I'm coming with you. You're not walking into that viper's nest without some sort of protection.'

'Your presence would be like a red rag to a bull, you can surely see that? They'd think—' She stopped abruptly.

'That I love you? Well, they'd be right, wouldn't they,' he said softly. 'And don't shake your head like that. You know I love you, I've loved you practically from the moment I set eyes on you.'

'Don't, Jack.'

'Why not? I've kept quiet for twelve years but I'm damned if I will now. I love you so much it hurts, Josie Gray, and believe me I've done everything I can to rid myself of the way I feel but it's hopeless. And now you're talking about virtual suicide and you expect me to stand by and let you leave?'

'If – if you do love me you'll stay and look after everything while I'm gone. You know everything there is to know about the business—'

'Damn the business. This is your life we're talking about. Don't you realize how this will turn out?'

As she stared at him she knew she was about to cry. She put her hand across her mouth, telling herself she must leave or she would break down, but in the next moment he had pulled her into his arms and then the tears came in a flood. Somehow she found herself sitting on his lap in his old armchair and once her sobs had lessened, he said quietly, 'I can't let you do it, Josie. If Luke wants to go so badly then I can understand you might have to let him but there's no sense in you going too. They won't hurt him, you know that, he'll be safe, and once he returns here you can begin to rebuild your relationship again.'

She continued to lie against his chest, feeling his heart pounding as he held her close to him. She would have liked to stay there for ever, wrapped in his love and concern. But in spite of his love he didn't understand. How could he? He had never had a child. She sat up a little and when he offered her his handkerchief she wiped her eyes and blew her nose. Looking into his eyes, she said the words she'd told herself she must never say: 'I love you. I love you so much but I have to go and you must stay here.'

'No—'

'Please, Jack. I have to be with Luke whatever happens.'

She couldn't voice even to Jack her deepest fear, that once the McGuigans got their hands on Luke they would never let him go. If she wasn't there and they made him stay, how would she survive it? She wouldn't. She had to be with him or they'd ensnare him and turn him into a McGuigan, that's how she felt. 'You'd only endanger yourself and me if you tried to come with us and if anything happened to you because of me I wouldn't be able to bear it.'

His arms tightened around her and now when he crushed her to him it wasn't gently as before but savagely, his mouth taking hers with a hunger that had built for many long years. And she returned his kiss with a passion that told him more than any words could have done. How long the embrace lasted neither of them knew but when eventually she pulled away, she said shakily, 'Whatever happens, remember I love you.'

He pulled her in to him again as though he couldn't let her go, murmuring against her mouth, 'I can't let you do this, I can't.'

'I have to, so help me be strong. I can't stay here while Luke's in another country wondering what's happening—'

'But that's exactly what you're asking me to do.'

'I know.' She traced his dear face with one finger. 'And I'm sorry for asking so much of you, I really am.'

His face working, he said almost angrily, 'When you come home things are going to be different, all right?'

'All right.' She wasn't going to argue, not now, besides which she didn't want to spend another decade without his arms round her. She doubted Adam would agree to a divorce even if Bruce and the others let her leave England, but she'd cross that bridge when she came to it. She wanted to be with Jack and make up for all the years they'd wasted – years *she* had wasted, she admitted painfully. 'You'll look after Carmella when I'm gone? Her brother's a lot better now but she worries about him and her two nephews.'

'I'll look after everything – don't worry about anything or anyone but yourself.' He tightened his arms about her. He was terrified at what she was proposing to do but knowing Josie as he did he knew she'd made up her mind and nothing would dissuade her now. 'Write to me once you're there and let me know how things are and when you're coming back.' He'd already made up his mind that regardless of what she said, if she wasn't home when she said she would be he would go to England, and if he found out they'd hurt her . . . His arms tightened still more. He'd kill Bruce McGuigan and Adam too. He knew certain people in the Lower East Side, he thought grimly, the sort of men who would give the McGuigans a run for their money, and he could buy whatever he needed from them. He wouldn't go unarmed.

'I will, I promise,' she murmured, looking up at him.

The tenderness in her eyes caused Jack to groan inwardly. He didn't know how he was going to stand by and let her do this, it was an act of madness, and all for that little ingrate, Luke. He had tried to take to the kid over the years, he was Josie's son after all, but he saw very little of the woman he loved in the boy – not just in his looks but in his nature too. And he knew Luke didn't like him either, which was fine, he wouldn't lose sleep over that, except that now with what was happening he wished he'd had some influence over the kid.

Knowing it was useless but unable to stop himself, he said pleadingly, 'Don't go back, Josie, not by yourself. We'll find a way through this together. I'll do anything, anything, but don't go unprotected.'

The entreaty in his gaze and the brokenness in his voice allowed her weary mind to clutch at a fleeting hope for a moment. Could there be a way out that didn't involve her returning to England with Bruce today? Deep inside she knew what her fate could be at the hands of the McGuigans. They wouldn't do anything overtly, of course, not with wanting to keep Luke onside, but the chances were high that an accident would be engineered at some point. And then reality kicked in. There was no way out. She would rather die than let Luke go by himself.

Tears blinding her eyes again, she whispered, 'I love you and we'll have a life together when I come home, I promise. Just – just keep believing that, darling.'

The endearment cut him in two but knowing he had said all he was able to, he nodded. He had to make this as easy for her now as he could. 'I'll be waiting; however long it takes I'll be waiting.'

By the time Josie left the attic apartment some minutes later she felt calmer. She had been dreading saying goodbye to Jack, knowing it could be the last time she would see him, but it was done. Now she just had to get on with finishing their packing and preparing herself for the voyage to England. A shiver of fear went through her and she raised her chin and straightened her shoulders in answer to it. The McGuigans frightened her, it would be useless to deny it to herself, but they wouldn't crush her where it mattered, in her heart and her mind. She wouldn't let them.

Chapter Twenty-Five

Sadie McGuigan was severely out of sorts and furious with Bruce. According to the message which had been delivered by one of her son's hired hands nearly two weeks ago, he'd got business in the South somewhere that he had to see to and he'd gone before she could talk to him. He knew Adam was ailing; whatever this business was it could have waited and she'd give him the length of her tongue when he turned up. It was beyond her how Bruce could think anything was more important than his brother, especially when he knew how much Adam looked forward to seeing him every day when he was poorly. It broke Adam's day up when Bruce popped in, and made him feel he was still valued as part of the firm when Bruce discussed things with him.

She glanced at Arthur, who had opened the door to her knock some minutes ago and ushered her into the sitting room. He'd told her Adam was resting in his quarters and couldn't be disturbed. She wasn't sure about Arthur, she told herself grimly. There was no doubt the man had been good for Adam in some respects and served him well, but she thought Arthur was a sight too big for his boots at times, like today. Stopping her from seeing her own son, for goodness' sake. It wasn't good enough.

She compressed her lips as she took the cup of tea the maid had brought in, before she said, 'Well? How is he?'

Arthur was fully aware that Adam's mother considered him a mixed blessing but he always gave her the respect she was due, whilst being firm with the autocratic old lady. 'Mr Adam had a disturbed night, ma'am, but he's sleeping now.'

'He's been more tired lately, wouldn't you say?' Sadie didn't wait for a reply before continuing, 'And of course it doesn't help with Bruce having disappeared to goodness knows where. He knows full well that Adam likes to hear all the news from him. It makes him feel that he's still involved. You haven't heard from him at all?'

'Mr McGuigan? No, nothing.'

Sadie took another sip of tea, glancing round the room. It was festive, a large Christmas tree to one side of the roaring fire and paper chains hanging from the ceiling. As ever at this time, her thoughts turned to her youngest grandson. Luke had been born just before Christmas and since that woman had absconded with him this season had always been painful. Her thoughts making her voice even more brittle than usual, she said tightly, 'I shall have something to say if he's not back within the next day or so. Christmas is virtually upon us.'

She always had something to say, Arthur thought wryly.

Age had not diminished the lash of her tongue, more's the pity. His voice expressionless, he said, 'I don't think Mr McGuigan would miss being here with the family at Christmas.'

'You don't, do you?' Sadie sniffed. 'But then I'm sure you didn't think he would disappear on some whim or other either. According to Phyllis, she has no idea exactly where he is which is odd, don't you think?' Again she didn't pause as she continued, 'I don't hold with this cloak-and-dagger sort of going-on and I shall tell him so when I see him. Business indeed!' Another sniff followed. 'That can mean anything.'

How right you are, Arthur thought, and how right his master had been to insist that Mr McGuigan said nothing to their mother about his mission. She was bad enough at the best of times but she would have been beside herself if she'd caught a whiff of what was afoot.

Silence reigned while Sadie drank her tea and then she stood up. 'I shall pop by later to see my son. I trust he's not thinking of going into the office while he's under the weather?'

'I couldn't say, Mrs McGuigan.'

'Well, don't let him, man! The wind's enough to cut you in two and it's snowing again. The best place for him is in front of the fire. Tell Finnigan I'm ready to leave.'

Matt Finnigan was Sadie's long-suffering chauffeur-cum-jack-of-all-trades and was presently being entertained in the kitchen. Arthur went through to the back of the house and while the maid scurried to help Sadie on with her coat and hat, the chauffeur went out the back door and started the little car that Bruce had bought for his mother. At the time Sadie had objected strongly, saying her horse and carriage was good enough, but secretly she had been delighted with the prestige of owning a motor car that she could show off to her social circle.

Once Sadie had left, Arthur made his way to Adam's suite of rooms that were slightly separate from the rest of the house and situated overlooking the sweeping lawn and flower beds to the rear of the property. They comprised a small sitting room, bedroom and bathroom and had been built to his needs. Adam was awake when he entered the bedroom, sitting up in bed and reading, and his first words were, 'Has she gone?'

'Yes, sir.' Arthur grinned. Unless Adam was in the main part of the house they usually fielded off his mother – it wasn't unusual for her to 'pop round', as she called it, a couple of times a day if she knew her son was at home and it drove his master mad. When he was feeling well enough he knew Adam's days at the office were more to keep his mother at bay than anything else. 'Another nail in my coffin, I'm afraid.'

'I'm sorry, Arthur, but I just couldn't have coped with her this morning.'

Arthur understood perfectly. He was of the opinion you needed all your wits about you to deal with Sadie McGuigan at the best of times, and he knew Adam was beside himself about what Bruce's journey across the ocean would bring forth. The last couple of nights his master had barely slept at all. 'No problem, sir,' he said now, 'all part of the service. She did say she was going to call in later, though.'

Adam groaned.

'Would you like your lunch in here, sir?'

Adam shook his head. 'I'll get up now, I can't sleep anyway.'

It took a while, but once Adam was washed and dressed Arthur pushed him through to the main sitting room, or drawing room, as his mother insisted on calling it. It was a lovely room. The whole house had been built and furnished exactly how Adam had wanted it with wide doorways and easy access to the outside world, giving him as much independence as was possible in the circumstances. This had diminished in the last months, though, Arthur thought, as he settled Adam in his chair by the fire and went to see about some coffee. His master's health had declined; he knew it and he knew Adam realized too although it was never discussed, but increasingly Adam was able to do less and less. He just hoped and prayed that somehow Bruce would be able to bring Adam's son home soon. He didn't allow his mind to add 'before it was too late'; he believed in positive thinking and that one's state of mind had a huge impact on the body.

Adam was thinking along the same lines as he sat by the fire watching the red and gold flames leap up the chimney. The exhaustion that was with him day and night now made even lifting a cup to his lips an effort, but he had to believe that this spell would pass, he told himself wearily. Arthur's mantra was 'I am and therefore I can', and in the early days it had helped him. Lately it hadn't worked so well.

He sighed deeply. The thought of wanting to die had been in his mind again recently the way it had been before Arthur had come into his life. He was tired of being a prisoner of his own body. Then Bruce had come with the news about Luke and hope that he would see his son had infused him with expectation and optimism, but the last few days he'd begun to brood about what he would do if his brother returned home alone. He didn't doubt that Bruce would find them, but what if Luke refused to leave America? Josie had had years to work on the boy, after all, and no doubt she had brainwashed him into believing his father was a monster, damn her.

His gaze rested on his hands lying on his knees. They were limp and still, as if his being knew nothing of the hatred that ate him up when he thought of his wife, a hatred so intense that at times he could feel it clawing at his chest like a live thing. The urge to destroy her had been with him since the day Bruce had told him she'd vanished into thin air and taken Luke with her. The only thing that had given him any comfort was Bruce's promise that he would find them and bring Luke home, but the lad was no longer a baby or a toddler. His thirteenth birthday was tomorrow. *Thirteen*. Adam had been nearly thirteen years without seeing him, watching him grow, taking him places.

He groaned, the gnawing sense of loss as keen as ever. It had coloured every day of his existence, knowing his son was in the world somewhere, eating, sleeping, laughing, crying and living a life without him.

Arthur came in with the tray of coffee and sat down beside the wheelchair on a sofa. It was their custom to have coffee together when it was just the two of them. There was no master-and-servant formality, just two friends who were comfortable in each other's company. Arthur reached into his jacket pocket for the silver hip flask Adam had bought him for Christmas some years before, tipping a measure into each cup before handing his master his. 'Mr McGuigan will bring the lad home, sir, never fear,' he said softly as they sat in the quiet room scented with the sweet smell of pine from the Christmas tree. 'If ever I saw a man on a mission when he left that day, it was your brother.'

Adam had often wondered if Arthur could read his mind and today was no exception. 'I hope so,' he said after a moment. 'I do hope so, Arthur. He's thirteen years old tomorrow.'

'Aye, I know, sir.' Years ago just before Christmas, he had heard Adam crying in his bedroom late one night. The sound had been such that he had screwed up his eyes in protest, the rawness painful to hear. He had contemplated going in to see what was wrong and if he could help, but instinct had stopped him. It had been a few days later that he had heard Bruce and his mother talking about Adam's son and his birthday being at this time of the year, and then he had understood. It had been from then that the respect he'd had for Adam as his employer had deepened into genuine compassion and then liking. He knew the story, of course, and although he would never dream of voicing it to a soul he could appreciate why Adam's wife had disappeared the way she had. Her life wouldn't have been worth a fig if the McGuigans had got their hands on her, and she would have known that. But to take a man's son – no, he didn't agree with that. A boy should be raised by his da, it was only right and proper. And she'd written her own death warrant in the process.

The rest of the morning passed peacefully, and after a light lunch, Adam had a short nap. Sadie came and went in the early part of the afternoon and for once she didn't stay long, having some Christmas shopping to do. Arthur was relieved she kept her visit short; she didn't have a soothing effect on her son and he knew Adam was on edge.

As the snow thickened and the light vanished earlier than usual the night closed in. The sitting room took on a cosy feel with the Christmas tree lights and the roaring fire adding to the festive atmosphere. Adam had wheeled his chair by the French doors so he could watch the falling snow and sat without speaking, clearly lost in thought. Knowing how quickly his patient could fall into deep melancholy, Arthur had tried to interest him in a game of cards but to no avail.

It was just after five o'clock when they heard a knock at the front door, followed by Bruce's voice in the hall talking to the maid. Adam had turned and was looking towards the door when it opened and Bruce walked in, followed by a smaller figure.

Adam's heart was pounding. One of his fears had been that if he ever came across his son he wouldn't recognize him. Luke had only been a few months old when Josie had spirited him away. But the boy staring at him across the room was unmistakably his child; everything about him, his hair, his eyes, even the way he held himself proclaimed who he was. Unable to speak, he waited for whatever came next – rejection; distaste for what he was now, a cripple; blame for what had happened all those years ago or a dispassionate wariness for the stranger he must seem to be.

'Father? You're my father?'

The voice was flavoured with an American twang but that didn't disguise the note of wonder that rang through. Adam's face was drained of colour but suddenly he knew it was going to be all right. He held out his arms and like a moth to a flame his boy flew across the room and into them, half-falling onto his lap. As Adam felt thin arms go round his neck he closed his eyes, striving not to break down. He didn't want to frighten him but his arms, telling his hunger, crushed Luke to him as a mist of tears blinded his eyes. His son was home.

Josie sat in Phyllis's drawing room feeling sick with fear and dread. Not of the McGuigans or what they might do to her, but with thoughts of what might be happening in Adam's house.

The long journey to England had been turbulent in more ways than one. The seasickness that had begun immediately on leaving New York was one thing, but worse had been watching Luke's rapport with his uncle as the days had progressed. Luke genuinely liked Bruce and nothing she said made any difference. If anything, any criticism of Bruce or the McGuigans caused a defiant hardness to come over Luke's face. He had been cold towards her, and he had revealed his anger and bitterness in every word and gesture. His total withdrawal was terrifying her.

'It'll work out, lass.' Phyllis leaned forward, her voice sympathetic as she took Josie's hands in hers. 'You're Luke's mam and he loves you. He might be put out now but he'll come round. When he comes back from Adam's I'll have a word with him on the sly when Bruce isn't around and explain how it was before you left and why you had to go.'

'No, don't do that. If Luke says anything to Bruce you'll be in trouble.' Josie knew Phyllis was scared of her husband like everyone else was. This was difficult enough for her friend as it was. They had come straight from the port further down the coast, where the ship had docked, to Bruce's house and it had been a shock for Phyllis; Bruce had apparently told her he was away on business and that was all.

Phyllis bit her lip. She wanted to support Josie but she knew only too well how Bruce felt about her friend. She'd taken him aside when Josie had first arrived and said that rather than Josie and Luke staying in a hotel, it would look better to Luke if they offered them accommodation whilst they were in England. 'It would be more natural, Luke being your nephew,' she'd wheedled, 'and appear you're letting bygones be bygones. You want to keep the boy onside, don't you?' She could make sure Josie was safe if she was with her; it would be too easy for someone to go missing from a hotel. Bruce had agreed – reluctantly – but he hadn't been pleased. She knew she'd have to tread carefully over the next little while. Perhaps it would be better after all to say nothing to Luke. The boy had scarcely been able to wait to go and see his father with Bruce and they'd left immediately after offloading their luggage. Bruce hadn't asked Josie to accompany them.

Now, the catch of tears in her voice, Josie murmured, 'Luke's changed since Bruce turned up, Phyllis. He's different.' But was that entirely true? she asked herself in the next moment. Was it that Luke had changed, or more that meeting his uncle had brought the McGuigan side of him more to the fore?

Phyllis squeezed Josie's hands and then turned to the tea trolley the maid had wheeled in a few minutes before. 'Have something to eat, it'll make you feel better, lass. And you're safe here with me if you're worried about Bruce. He wants to keep in Luke's good books anyway, he wouldn't dare hurt you.'

She didn't think Phyllis believed that any more than she did but there was no point in saying so. Changing the subject, she said, 'Do you think Sadie knew Bruce was going to America to find me?'

Phyllis shook her head. 'He told his mam the same story he told me. She's been hopping mad at him disappearing.' Lowering her voice even though it was just the two of them, she whispered, 'I saw your mam a few times after you'd gone and she said she'd heard from you and that you were all right but she wouldn't say where you'd gone. I suppose with me being married to Bruce she didn't know if I'd say anything, not that I would have, of course. So, why America, lass, and how did you get there?'

'It was a sea captain who used to come in the Fiddler's Elbow who took me. He knew someone in America I could stay with at first, a friend of his, till I sorted myself out. I've seen him a few times since, when he comes to New York and we'll have a meal together for old times' sake. He's a lovely man.'

Phyllis raised her eyebrows and Josie smiled. 'No, nothing like that. He's very happily married and getting on for sixty now. It was Mrs Mullen who came up with the idea of America actually so I could get as far away as possible.'

'There's far away and then there's the other side of the world. Weren't you scared?'

'Not as scared as the thought of staying.'

'Aye, well, I can understand that. So, you've done all right for yourself then? Tell me everything.'

Josie filled her in as much as she could, but she was careful to make no mention of Jack. She trusted Phyllis but as her friend had said herself, she was married to Bruce. A careless word or something like that could mean disaster because Bruce would be furious if he thought she loved someone else. Jack's anonymity was his protection. She could say quite truthfully that she lived alone with Carmella and Luke and that was all anyone connected with the McGuigans needed to know.

'By, lass.' Phyllis sat back in her seat, shaking her head when Josie stopped speaking. 'You're one on your own and no mistake. But you haven't said how Bruce found out where you were?'

'I don't know, he wouldn't say. Perhaps you could find that out?'

'I could try,' Phyllis said doubtfully, 'but you know Bruce. He's a closed book when he wants to be. I tell you one thing, though, he was like a man possessed when they found out you'd gone. He had his men scour the town and then further afield, and offered a huge reward. He was determined to find you and get Luke back for Adam, and he would definitely have done for you if you had stayed, Josie. You did the right thing in getting away, you know that, don't you?'

Josie nodded. Bruce would still do for her if he got the chance. 'He said Adam's ill, really ill, I mean, and that the fall did something to his heart as well as his spine. Is that true?'

'Aye, it's true. Adam wasn't too bad at first with his chest. He couldn't walk, of course, but his heart seemed all right although the doctor from London said things might change as time went on, and he was right. He's had a couple of seizure things in the last year and he's not too grand, truth be told.'

There had been no accusation in her friend's voice but Josie felt she had to say, 'I didn't push him that night, Phyllis.'

'I believe you, lass.'

'I've gone over it a thousand times since. He came after me onto the landing and we were near the top of the stairs when he lost his footing.'

'Like I said, I believe you.'

'The others won't, though.'

Phyllis lowered her eyes to the cup of tea in her hands and said nothing, which was an answer in itself. Josie found herself wondering exactly what had been said over the years as Phyllis took another sandwich and bit into it.

No, no one would believe her but that wouldn't matter if Luke accepted her version of events on that fateful night. But would he? If Adam kept to his story that she had deliberately pushed him down the stairs, would their son believe her or the father he had recently found?

She forced down a couple of sandwiches and drank the tea before Phyllis showed her upstairs to one of the guest rooms, Luke being next door. Phyllis and Bruce's children had all married and left home although they were living close by as seemed to be the McGuigan tradition. Phyllis was a grandmother twice over, she'd told Josie, both little boys, and Bruce was far more indulgent with his grandchildren than he had ever been with his children.

Once Phyllis had left her alone to freshen up before

dinner, Josie sank down in a chair by the large bay window. It was a beautiful room decorated in pastel shades but although the fire had been lit in the small ornate fireplace it hadn't had time to warm the room through and it was cold. She shivered as she gazed at the winter wonderland outside, but it was more a chill in her soul than her body. Whether Luke wanted to listen or not, she would have a talk with him tonight once the household was asleep, she told herself. She wanted to tell him everything that had happened all those years ago, quietly and without any hysterics or exaggeration. She had no doubt that Bruce had been whispering in the boy's ear throughout the journey from America and painting her as the villain of the piece, but when she had tried to put her case he'd have none of it and she'd felt too ill with the seasickness to persist.

She was downstairs again with Phyllis when Bruce came home, and immediately he entered the drawing room where they were sitting quietly talking she looked for Luke. Bruce walked over to the cocktail cabinet and poured himself a large whisky without glancing towards his wife and sister-in-law, and it was Phyllis who said, 'Where's Luke? Has he gone upstairs?'

Bruce turned, deliberately taking a long swallow of whisky and swilling it around his mouth before he swallowed, and then another, before he said, 'The lad's with his da, where else?' There was a cruel satisfaction in his voice. 'He wanted to stay the night with Adam, they've got a lot of catching-up to do.'

Josie was well aware that he was waiting for her reaction, savouring the moment. He wanted her to protest, perhaps even say that she was going to fetch him, and it took every ounce of willpower she possessed to sit and calmly take a sip of the sherry that Phyllis had poured for them earlier.

Phyllis looked hard at her husband but she, too, said nothing although one of her hands reached out and covered Josie's, causing Bruce's eyes to narrow. She knew he wanted her to ask how the meeting had gone but she wasn't going to give him the satisfaction.

A taut silence ensued for a few minutes until Cissy put her head round the door to announce that dinner was ready, her eyes flashing over Josie. There had been great excitement in the kitchen over the day's happenings.

Whether it was the sherry – she wasn't used to alcohol – or exhaustion, Josie didn't know, but she felt something akin to hysteria sweeping over her as she sat at the dining-room table with Phyllis and Bruce. A few days ago the most she'd had to worry about was Luke's school report, and now here she was seated at the table of her most bitter enemy with her son virtually estranged from her and in the company of his father. She had never longed for Jack more, or so strongly regretted all the years she had wasted when she could have been with him.

Aware of Bruce's dark gaze on her face she forced herself to eat the food placed in front of her with every appearance of enjoyment, even though every mouthful threatened to choke her. Eventually the meal was over.

She made her excuses that she was tired from the journey and retired to the privacy of her room, but even there she had to stifle her sobs in her pillow for fear of Bruce hearing her.

When the storm of weeping was over she lay for hours in the shadowed darkness, too heartbroken for sleep. She'd pulled the curtains back before she'd retired and the snowy night provided natural illumination once her eyes adjusted. She felt no fear of being at Bruce's mercy here in his home, the agony about Luke consuming her. How she was going to get through the next days without going mad, she didn't know. She felt as though she wanted to scream and shout and beat her hands against something, but she knew if she started she wouldn't be able to stop and she'd lose her reason altogether.

In hindsight, she wished with all her heart that she had told Luke about his father and the McGuigans and her reasons for fleeing England when he was old enough to understand. At least he wouldn't have been able to accuse her of being a liar, as he'd done frequently on the journey to England. But she had thought they were safe so far away in America, that by choosing the path she'd taken she was giving her son the best possible chance of fulfilling his own destiny free of the McGuigan curse.

But Luke hated her for it. Her baby, her boy, hated her. Again she stifled her moans with the pillow and it was like that, curled into a little ball, that she eventually drifted into a troubled sleep.

Chapter Twenty-Six

When Josie came downstairs the next morning Bruce had already left the house and Phyllis was sitting having breakfast in the dining room. She looked up as Josie entered, taking in her white face and puffy eyes. 'Did you manage to get any sleep?'

'A little.' Josie sat down at the table, refusing the cooked breakfast the maid offered and asking for toast. Once the girl had left the room, she said quietly, 'I need to go to Adam's house and see Luke and then call at my mam's.'

Phyllis nodded. 'Aye, all right. I'll come with you to Adam's, lass.' She hesitated, and then said softly, 'I need to tell you something. I was going to say it last night but you looked done in after the journey and everything.'

'What is it?' A sudden stab of fear made itself felt. 'Is my mam all right?'

'She's fine as far as I know. It's not her, it's your da. He went missing a while ago and then they found him floating in the river, lass. He – well, he'd been stabbed, they say.'

Josie's eyes opened wider. 'Murdered?'

'Aye, that's what I heard. I'm sorry, lass, this on top of everything else.'

Josie stared at her friend. 'He wasn't a nice man, Phyllis, in fact he was horrible but – but he was my da.'

'I know, I know.'

'To end up like that . . .' Josie took a deep breath. 'Do they know who did it?'

Phyllis shook her head. 'You know what the docks are like and the pubs round there. There's always fights and when it's pay day and the men drink too much things happen. A sailor had his head cleaved almost in two just the other night—' She stopped abruptly, realizing that was less than helpful in the circumstances. 'I'm sorry,' she said again.

Josie took a sip of hot tea to combat the shock that had her stomach churning. There had been times in the past when she had hated her da and he had been a nasty piece of work, but for his life to end in such violence and horror . . .

Phyllis sat looking at the pale beautiful face and wondered how much more Josie could take. For the first time in her married life she'd stood up to Bruce last night when he'd been ranting on about Josie and calling her every name under the sun. She'd let him have his say before she'd stopped brushing her hair and turned from the dressing table to look straight at him. 'She's told me she didn't push Adam down the stairs, that it was an accident, and I believe her,' she'd said quietly.

'Then why did she scarper?' he'd growled.

'You know full well why. How long would she have remained alive if she'd stayed, Bruce? She ran for her life and I'd have done the same in her position. Adam was carrying on with other women and leading her a hell of a life with the drink and all, but she didn't try and do him in. She wanted the marriage to work, for Luke's sake as much as anything.'

'Well, she's taken you in, that's for sure.' He'd glared at her. 'And I'm not discussing this further.'

They had slept as far away from each other as they could and Bruce had risen early and left the house before she was even awake, but she found she didn't regret what she'd said. She had owed it to herself as much as Josie; in a strange sort of way she'd found she'd needed to pin her colours to the mast when she had heard him swearing and cursing about her friend. He probably wouldn't forgive her for it but that didn't matter.

Josie cut into her thoughts, saying, 'Thank you for breaking the news about my da. I'd rather have heard it from you than anyone else. Oh, Phyllis, I feel I'm standing on sinking sand now I'm back. It was different in America.'

'Aye, I can imagine. Take it one day at a time and you'll get through, lass. Are you sure you want to see Adam? Why don't you wait and see if Luke comes here later on?'

'But what if he doesn't? It's his birthday today and I need to see him and talk to him. I – I can't wait.'

'Well, you know best. We'll finish breakfast and go then.'

Josie nodded. She had to face Adam sooner or later even though the thought of seeing him made her flesh creep.

Once they were ready and the car had been brought round from the back of the house they stepped outside. Josie stood at the top of the steps for a moment looking up into the pale winter sky. She prayed silently for strength. Adam wouldn't make this meeting easy for her, she knew that, and she had no idea how Luke would be. Her world had fallen apart in just a few days and she didn't know how to make things right with Luke.

Phyllis glanced at Josie as they climbed out of the motor car, which had just drawn up on the wide circular drive of Adam's residence. Josie was as white as a sheet, her face tense. She slipped her arm through her friend's in silent support.

Norman, who was now married to Cissy and living in the servants' quarters, stared at Adam McGuigan's wife too through the car mirror. She looked bad, he thought. She'd been daft to come back here. He wouldn't want to be in her shoes for all the tea in China.

Phyllis paused before she rang the bell. 'Don't be drawn into an argument in front of Luke because you won't win. You know what Adam's like,' she said quietly.

Josie nodded. Oh, yes, she knew what Adam was like. That charm, the same charm that Luke had inherited, was as persuasive as it was deadly. It could make you believe that black was white.

The door was opened by a maid but a man appeared in the hall from a room some yards away and came towards them smiling. It was he who ushered them into the warmth of the house, saying, 'Good morning, Mrs McGuigan,' and nodding courteously to Josie as the maid took their coats and hats. 'It's good to see that the snow is letting up, for a while at least.'

'Good morning, Arthur.' Phyllis took Josie's arm. 'This is Mrs McGuigan, Adam's wife.'

A pair of keen hazel eyes in a rugged face that wasn't unfriendly met Josie's gaze as he said, 'Aye, I thought so. I'm pleased to meet you, Mrs McGuigan. Mr Adam and the young master are in the main drawing room if you'd like to follow me. Shall I order coffee to be served there?'

Phyllis nodded. 'Thank you, Arthur.'

It was all very civilized, Josie thought, the hysteria she'd felt at the dinner table last night rising up. As though they were playing a game. She took hold of herself, breathing in deeply through her nose. She had dressed carefully for this meeting. Her suit was plain and a dark charcoal colour, but the pink blouse beneath had a frill at the neck and the gold brooch in the shape of a butterfly attached to her lapel had been expensive. The outfit was from a shop on Fifth Avenue and she had felt guilty about the price when she'd bought it but it was worth every dollar for the boost it was giving this morning.

They followed Arthur across the light, wide hall. The

door that he had emerged from moments earlier was slightly ajar and as they approached, a sound from within the room pierced Josie's heart like a knife. Luke was laughing in the way he did sometimes when he was really happy. A man's voice – Adam's voice – said, 'I don't believe it, you've thrashed me again. Where did you learn to play cards so well?'

'Irwin's father's real good at cards and he taught Irwin and Irwin taught me so—' Luke stopped abruptly as they entered the room, the laughter dying from his face.

Josie took in the scene in front of her – the beautiful room, the Christmas tree, the roaring fire and the card table pulled close to the wheelchair – but she kept her eyes on Luke's face as she said softly, 'Happy birthday, darling.'

Luke stared at her warily without replying.

They walked further into the room and she forced herself to meet Adam's gaze. He didn't speak and neither did she and it was Arthur who broke into what had become a charged atmosphere by saying cheerfully, 'Sit yourselves down, ladies, and I'll see about that coffee.'

The man in the wheelchair was Adam but not as she had expected to see him. She had prepared herself that he'd look older – it had been well over a decade, after all – but she was shocked at the change in him. He could have been fifty, even sixty years old. His hair was still thick but heavily streaked with silver and he was so thin that his bone structure was sharply defined, making his nose appear more tapered and his lips narrower. He was gaunt and hollow-cheeked but still handsome, but it was his eyes that held her gaze. They had always been his best feature, dark and velvety with thick lashes, but now they were emitting a black light as they stared at her and she knew that if he'd had the power she'd be struck dead on the spot.

Luke had stood up from his stool in front of the card table and had placed one hand on his father's arm. The action was both proprietorial and protective, and it hurt her more than any words could have done. After a moment, she managed to say, 'Hello, Adam,' and was surprised how normal her voice sounded, considering the turmoil inside.

Adam stared at his wife. If he'd hated her before, he hated her even more for the way she looked – beautiful and young, full of life and vitality. She knew how to dress too, he thought bitterly. That outfit she was wearing had clearly cost a penny or two, but then from what he'd gleaned from Luke she wasn't short of money. Who would have thought that the little chit he'd married from the waterfront would have done so well without him? But then she'd got her start from what she'd stolen from him, damn her. Aware of Luke at his side, he allowed no trace of what he was feeling to show in his voice when he said quietly, 'Hello, Josie. It's been a long time.'

Phyllis had sat down on a sofa and Josie joined her, her heart thumping so hard she wondered if it was audible. She had Luke's birthday card and present in her handbag and had been hoping for a private moment or two to give him her gift. It was an expensive wristwatch that she'd bought some weeks before and brought with her from America. Luke had spotted the watch in one of the jewellery stores in Upper Fifth Avenue when they'd been out together, and she had returned the next day when he was at school and bought it for a surprise on his birthday. She didn't know if he would be returning with them to Bruce's so she could give it then or whether he intended to stay longer with Adam, so she had brought it with her.

As though he'd read her mind, Luke looked straight at her. 'Did you bring my things?'

'Your things?'

'My suitcase and everything I brought with me,' he said impatiently.

Phyllis intervened, saying quickly, 'We thought you'd be returning home with us, Luke.'

He shook his head, his shiny black curls flopping on his forehead. 'Father says I can stay here with him if I want to.'

Josie saw Adam place a hand over his son's, and for a moment her anger rose in a spiral before she warned herself to go steady. Losing control was the last thing she must do. Keeping her voice pleasant, she said, 'I'm sure your uncle would be only too pleased to bring your things later.' Phyllis shot her a quick look – she had caught the underlying sarcasm.

'Luke has decided to spend Christmas here,' Adam said smoothly. 'Of course you're welcome to join us. A family gathering with all the relatives would be nice, don't you think?'

No, she did not, but she wasn't about to fall into the trap of saying so. 'That would be up to Bruce and Phyllis,' she said calmly, 'as I'm staying with them. I don't know what arrangements they've already made.'

'None that can't be changed, I'm sure.' Adam glanced at Phyllis, who nodded. 'Good, that's settled then.' He turned his head and smiled at Luke. 'This will be the best Christmas your grandma's ever had, you know that, don't you?'

In answer, Luke put his arms round his father's neck in a bear hug.

Over the boy's head, Adam smiled a smile that wasn't a smile at Josie, relishing her pain. 'Have you shown your mother the birthday present from me?' he said softly, as Arthur entered the room once more, opening the door for the maid, who was carrying a coffee tray, the cook bustling behind her with another full of pastries and little cakes.

Luke rolled up the sleeve of the shirt he was wearing to reveal a wristwatch. 'It was Father's,' he said proudly. 'Grandma bought it for him on his twenty-first birthday but he wants me to have it.'

'It's a little big at the moment,' Adam interposed, 'but we're going to get the strap adjusted tomorrow, aren't we.' Luke nodded enthusiastically. 'And I think while we're about it a nice pair of cufflinks might be in order, now you're a young man of thirteen.'

He wanted to destroy her and he was using their son

to do it. Josie sat in numb silence. She didn't ask herself at this moment what she could do about it because deep down in her she knew the answer. She glanced at the card table. Adam held all the aces now.

They left the house an hour after they had arrived, possibly the worst hour of Josie's life. Luke had barely spoken to her unless he had to and then only in monosyllables. When they were making their goodbyes it was Adam who said, his voice a low purr of poisonous reasonableness, 'Kiss your mother goodbye, Luke.'

The kiss had been a swift grudging peck on the cheek and even his lips had been cold. She had handed him the card and present as they'd taken their leave, saying as she did so, 'It will do as a spare,' her voice flat.

Norman had had a cup of tea and half a dozen girdle scones oozing with melted butter in the kitchen while he was waiting, along with a good gossip with the cook and maid about the events of the last twenty-four hours. As he said to Cissy when he got home, Adam McGuigan had no intention of letting his son leave now he'd got his hands on him again. He was in England for good.

Phyllis was thinking much the same thing and once Bruce got in for his lunch, she whisked him into the drawing room and shut the door. 'Josie's resting in her room,' she said without preamble, 'and I want to know what's going on. What have you and Adam got planned regarding Luke?'

'Planned?' Bruce narrowed his eyes. 'What are you on about?'

'You know full well what I'm on about. The way that lad treated his mam this morning was disgusting and you can't tell me that Adam didn't put him up to it.'

'I don't know if he did or not but I wouldn't blame him anyway. The lad was thirteen today, *thirteen*, and Adam hasn't seen him since he was a baby. That time's gone for ever and there's no getting it back.'

'I know that—'

'Then stop your harping on about poor Josie this and poor Josie that. She deserves everything she gets and if Luke turns against her that's his business.'

'And of course you've helped that process on.'

He glared at her and for a moment she thought he was going to shout and carry on, but after a pause he sighed, shaking his head. 'You're a good woman, Phyllis,' he said, surprising her both by the words and by the soft tone in which they were spoken, 'and that woman doesn't deserve your concern, I tell you that. And I'll tell you something else an' all, if you'd been there when the lad saw his da for the first time you'd know how the land lies. He loves Adam, it's as simple as that.'

'And Josie? What about her?'

Bruce shrugged. 'She don't know how to handle the lad, that's for sure. And don't frown at me like that, it's the truth. She gets his back up. According to Luke she's always been on at him to do better at school no matter how high his marks are and blaming him for things that aren't his fault. Now, they're his words, not mine.'

'Aye, I can imagine they are Luke's words.'

'What does that mean?'

Phyllis sighed. Luke was his father's son in every respect and this had been evident today. She didn't like him and that was awful because he was Josie's son and the lad was only thirteen years old after all, but nevertheless, she didn't like him. She could imagine that, like Adam, he could charm the birds out of the trees when he wanted to and that as long as everything was going his way he'd be sweetness and light, but disagree with him or try to reprimand him and there would be another side to the lad. She shook her head slowly as she said, 'I can see you're for him no matter what so I won't waste my breath. Suffice to say the lad's a McGuigan through and through.'

There was a telling silence as Bruce glared at her again and the soft tone had gone when he growled, 'Aye, you're right, an' if our lads were the same I'd be a happy man. Oh, to hell with it, I'll get me lunch in town,' and with that he slammed out of the room.

Luke was sitting quietly by his father's wheelchair. They'd had lunch and retired to the drawing room for coffee but Adam had dozed off almost immediately and Luke hadn't tried to wake him. He glanced at Arthur, who was sitting opposite drinking his coffee, and his voice was low when he said, 'How – how ill is he?'

Arthur didn't try to prevaricate. 'He's not too good at the moment but he's had other spells like this.' He didn't add that with each successive attack Adam had got weaker.

Luke bit down hard on his bottom lip to stop it from

trembling. He had liked Arthur instantly; there was something about the older man that was warm and welcoming and he was clearly devoted to his father, his da. He liked the North-East word, it was softer than 'father' but he felt self-conscious about saying it. After a moment, he said, 'I'm not going to go back to America. She can't make me, can she?'

'What about your life there, all your friends and your school and so on?' Arthur didn't mention Josie; the lad wasn't too pleased with his mam and he could understand why, and the word 'she' had expressed a lot.

'I can go to school here and make new friends. I want to stay with my father and the rest of my family.' He knew his grandma was coming round later with all his uncles and aunties and cousins so they could meet him. His father had arranged a birthday tea and a special cake but he didn't care about all that. He just wanted to be with his father.

'Well, that's something that will have to be discussed,' Arthur said diplomatically.

'Father wants me to stay, he's already said so, and I could live here with you and him and go to a school nearby. I'm good at my lessons and I make friends easily so that won't be a problem, and American is the same language as English – well, there's a few words that are different but not many – so that's good, isn't it. Father would be happy and I'd be happy and everything would be just fine.'

For a moment his quick-fire talk halted, but only for

a second. Then he went on, 'I won't go back, I mean it, and Father said that the courts would be on his side, not hers. She stole me away as a baby and has kept him from seeing me for years and all my family are here, not in America. The law would back Father.'

'Aye, I daresay he's right about that. But it would mean saying goodbye to your mam, perhaps for a long time. Have you considered that?'

'I don't care about her. Not after what she did to my father, and she's lied to me all my life. I hate her.'

Arthur let a few moments elapse before he said quietly, 'Hate is a strong word, lad, especially when applied to your mam.'

Luke shrugged, picking up his coffee cup and drinking, and as Arthur looked at him the likeness to Adam was remarkable. *He's a chip off the old block*, Arthur thought to himself, *that's for sure*. He wouldn't want to be in Josie McGuigan's shoes right now. If she'd scarpered all those years ago and left the child behind she wouldn't be in this mess now, but there, mother love was a funny thing. His own mam had been as rough as old boots and as hard as nails, but she'd always fought for her bairns and he and his siblings had known they came first with her when the chips were down. He'd daresay Josie was the same. Whatever, the lass was going to have a rough ride in the days ahead.

Chapter Twenty-Seven

Maggie Gray heard the tap at her back door and closed her eyes for a moment, sighing. It was early afternoon, about the time that Flo sometimes popped in for a cuppa but for once she didn't feel like chatting. She'd had a feeling on her the last week or two since they'd dragged Ralph's body from the river, a bad feeling. She couldn't explain it but she knew it was nothing to do with him being gone. That was a relief, may God forgive her.

As the back door opened she stitched a smile on her face and turned from the table where she was making some dumplings to go in the rabbit stew cooking in the range. Joe had dropped the rabbit in last night on his way home from work; although he was married now with a couple of bairns he never forgot his old mam, she thought fondly.

For a moment she stared at the tall, well-dressed woman standing on the threshold, flakes of snow on her hat and shoulders, wondering if she was seeing things, and then Josie said, 'Mam, it's me,' and Maggie gave a cry that came from her soul. It brought the two of them together, holding each other tightly, and their faces were wet with tears when they eventually drew apart.

'Lass, lass, I can't believe it.' Maggie let Josie go only to draw her to her again and once more they clung together for long moments. 'Come and sit down by the fire, you're frozen,' Maggie said when she pressed Josie from her, 'and I'll make a cuppa.' But when Josie was sitting she made no effort to make the tea, saying again, 'I can't believe it, lass, you being here, but whatever made you come back? It's not safe.'

Josie smiled a watery smile. She had been away for twelve and a half years but everything was the same, right down to the smell of the dinner cooking in the range. 'It's a long story, Mam,' she said softly. 'Make the tea and I'll tell you. Bruce found us. He turned up at my apartment in America.'

'Bruce? But how? You've not been in contact with Phyllis, have you?'

Josie shook her head. 'She wouldn't have told him anyway.'

'Then how could he have known where you were, lass?'

'I don't know.'

'And Luke? Is he with you?'

'Once he met Bruce wild horses wouldn't have stopped him coming to see Adam. He's with him now at Adam's house. We got here late yesterday afternoon and he's been with his father ever since. He – he won't leave him.'

'Oh, lass.' Maggie said no more. The look on Josie's

face made her want to cry again but in a different way and that wouldn't help things. She busied herself at the stove and once she had poured them both a mug of tea, she sat down opposite Josie at the table where she could feast her eyes on her bairn.

'I know about Da, Mam,' Josie said as she took her mug. 'Phyllis told me. Are you all right about it?'

Maggie nodded. 'It was a shock, him being murdered and having the constable call and all that but, God forgive me, I feel lighter with him gone if you know what I mean? I know you shouldn't speak ill of the dead but he wasn't a good man—' She stopped suddenly, staring at Josie as though she had seen a ghost. 'It was him,' she said faintly. 'He told Bruce.'

'What?'

'Your da, he must have found your letters, lass. I noticed the other day they were out of order but I put it down to me not knowing if I was on foot or horseback what with the shock of your da and the funeral and all and muddling them up, but I hadn't. It was him. He found them and went to tell Bruce McGuigan, I'd bet me life on it. He went on and on about the reward for information about you and the bairn after you'd first took off – he was after that, I'll be bound. It's too much of a coincidence, him being done in and then McGuigan turning up on your doorstep.'

Josie's mind was racing. 'But if he went to Bruce, why would they have him killed? That doesn't make any sense. He helped them, didn't he?'

'Bruce McGuigan is nobody's fool. I reckon he'd got the measure of your da and couldn't trust him to keep his mouth shut,' Maggie said grimly. 'It all fits, doesn't it, him going missing when he did and turning up in the river.'

Yes, it fitted. In fact, it had the McGuigan stamp all over it. Josie let the full import sink in. First Toby and now her da. She'd loved Toby and disliked her da but that wasn't the point. Bruce and the rest of the McGuigans had wreaked havoc on her family one way or another. Because of Adam and his determination to have her as his wife, her mother had lost her firstborn and she had been separated from her mam and her sisters and Joe for years.

'Lass, you have to get away.' Maggie was distraught. 'Now, today. You should never have come back. The McGuigans will stop at nothing, they're not like normal folk.' She gazed at the beloved bairn she'd never thought to see again this side of heaven, and the irony of the fact that she was trying to make Josie leave her when she'd only just got back wasn't lost on Maggie. 'You're in danger every minute you're in England, hinny. Go to America as fast as you can and then sell up and move again, it's the only way that you'll be safe. Bruce is too powerful and he has too much control in this town, you know that. You need to go back home and lose yourself. America's a big country.'

'No, Mam,' Josie said gently. 'I won't do that. I'm not going to let Bruce and Adam force me out of my home, not again. Besides, Luke wouldn't come back with me at the moment. He wants to have more time with his da and I'd never persuade him to leave.'

'But Luke is safe here, hinny. You're not.'

Josie took her mother's hand. The skin was fragile and wrinkled and spoke of a lifetime of hard work. She kissed it before she said, 'Mam, I'm staying for the time being, all right? I'll be careful, I promise. Now let's talk about something else, something nice. How's Joe and the girls? You said in your last letter that Ellen's expecting again and Kate's first will be born about the same time. That'll be lovely, two new babbies in the family.'

Maggie wasn't going to be deflected so easily. 'I'm worried, Josie, won't you think again? Please, hinny, for me.'

'I shall stay till after Christmas and then I'll see. Talking of Christmas, can I come here and spend it with you and Nelly? I don't want to stay at Phyllis's another night; she's lovely but it's Bruce's house and I hate being there. Luke will be with Adam and apparently all the McGuigans will congregate there, according to Phyllis. It's the same tonight. Adam's invited everyone for Luke's birthday and you can imagine what Sadie will be like.' She pulled a face.

'You're not thinking of going, are you?' said Maggie in alarm.

'I wasn't going to, no, but actually . . .' Josie's chin raised a notch. 'It's my son's birthday and why should I let them put me off seeing him? Sadie can do her worst but if she starts then she'll hear some home truths and I shan't hold back. I've had enough of the lot of them, Mam. I remember those endless dinners when I was first married to Adam, and Sadie holding court as queen bee.'

Maggie didn't find this reassuring. 'That woman'll play you like a violin, hinny. You know what she's like.'

'She can try,' Josie said grimly.

She'd changed, Maggie thought, before reprimanding herself. Of course the lass had changed; twelve years was a long time and she'd had to be strong to make a new life for herself and the bairn in a different country, so far from everything she'd ever known. Josie was her own woman now.

Far from comforting her, the realization made Maggie more anxious. If Josie stood up to the McGuigans, any of them, she would never win. They were the Devil's own spawn and played by their own rules. She'd lost one bairn to them and she still grieved every day for her lad and the shocking manner of his death. She didn't want to lose Josie too, but she'd said all she could say, she could see that from the look on the lass's face.

She poured them both another cup of tea before she said softly, 'Just go canny with them tonight, hinny. I know you think a bit of Phyllis but don't forget she's married to Bruce McGuigan and that says something, doesn't it? There's a badness in the lot of 'em and they might act like other folk when it suits them but at bottom not one of them can be trusted.'

* * *

Josie was thinking of her mother's words later that afternoon as she sat in Adam's dining room amid an almost frenzied atmosphere of merriment. The whole McGuigan clan had gathered, and everyone was intent on pretending that this birthday tea was just like any other of the numerous celebrations they had together.

Luke had been made much of, and he was sitting at the head of the long table next to Adam, his cheeks rosy with excitement and his eyes bright. Sadie had fawned over the boy, there was no other word for it, and had bought him an armful of expensive presents that she must have spent hours acquiring in the town today, saying, as she gave them to him, 'They're to make up for all the years I have missed your birthday, darling.' It had been the only time anyone referred to the issue they were all avoiding, and Bruce had sent his mother a warning look after which she'd said nothing more.

It had told Josie what she'd suspected. Bruce was determined to present the family as the injured party, who were big enough to forgive and forget the terrible thing that had been done to them. In front of Luke, anyway.

When she had got back to Phyllis's after seeing her mother she'd told her friend about the letters and what she thought concerning her father's death. Phyllis had been shocked but had put forth another possibility; that if Ralph *had* taken the letters from their hiding place and shown them to Bruce, he would have been paid for his trouble. 'Perhaps your da was in one of the pubs flashing the money about and showing off and someone mugged him for it? Not everything that happens has to be laid at Bruce's door.'

Josie had nodded and said nothing more. She appreciated the fact that Phyllis was married to Bruce and that she must have some feeling for him – they'd got a family and a lovely home and Bruce wasn't mean with his money – but she didn't think for a moment that it had happened as her friend had suggested. He'd had her father murdered just as he'd had Toby done away with; she was sure of it although of course she could never prove it.

She was sitting next to Phyllis with Hilda, David's wife, on her other side, and as she looked round the table she thought what an unreal life the women of the McGuigans led, even Sadie. Because of what their menfolk provided and the way they were treated, the women shut their eyes to where the money came from and what the men were involved in. They knew, of course, but it was never mentioned. At home the brothers were good husbands and fathers on the whole, and equally good sons to Sadie. Not only that, with their influence with some of the leading lights in the town and the legitimate businesses they owned as a cover for their widespread criminal activities, the McGuigans had managed to inveigle their way into polite society. Or, she thought, more often than not *buy* their way in. It enabled the women to continue their pretence.

If Adam had treated her the way Bruce or David and the others treated their wives, would she have become like that? It was a sobering thought. If she was completely honest she didn't know the answer. She had certainly loved Adam once and believed in him, and she had wanted to continue believing in him even when the truth had become glaringly obvious.

Josie suddenly became aware that Adam was staring at her from the other end of the table. He had one arm around Luke's shoulders and the boy was leaning in to him, his hand lying on the armrest of his father's wheelchair as he talked to one of his cousins a few feet away. It was a father-and-son pose, one of intimacy and comfortableness. As her lips tightened, Adam smiled, his dark eyes malevolent.

Luke had said hello dutifully to her when she had arrived at the house and allowed her to kiss him on the cheek, but there had been no warmth in his face. In spite of his American accent he had slotted into the family as though he'd always been here, one of the clan, she thought painfully as Arthur came into the room carrying an enormous fancy birthday cake blazing with candles. Everyone oohed and aahed. After Luke had blown out the candles he sat beaming, his face alight. Arthur cut the cake and served them all a slice with the help of the maid, but before they ate it Adam tapped his fork against his wine glass. 'I want to propose a toast,' he announced as all eyes turned to him.

Luke turned in his chair as his father spoke, looking at Adam with adoring eyes as Adam smiled at him.

'You are thirteen today, a young man. Young enough to have the rest of your life in front of you, but old enough to be able to choose your own path from this day forth. I couldn't be more proud of you if I tried, and words can't express how much I love you, son. To Luke,' he added, raising his glass and glancing round the table as everyone did the same, echoing, 'To Luke.'

Josie lifted her glass and drank but she didn't taste the wine. Adam's words had been a message to her, a bullet aimed at her heart. He was telling her that he'd see to it that the path Luke chose was with him, here in England, and that she had lost her son.

The following morning she told Phyllis that she wanted to spend Christmas with her mother. She thanked her friend for her hospitality and packed her things, and Norman drove her to the East End. As she was leaving Adam's house the night before she'd asked Luke if he would like to visit his other grandmother and see her side of the family at some point in the next little while. A disdainful expression had come over his face and he'd looked more like his father than ever when he'd said, 'No, not really. They don't like my father, do they.'

'I don't know, Luke,' she'd replied quietly.

'Of course they don't, they're on your side.' He had glared at her, turning away before she could say anything more. Not that there would have been any point, she told herself, looking out of the car window at the big fat snowflakes falling from a laden white sky. She just hoped that once Christmas was over and she had a chance to talk to Luke properly on his own, she could get through to him. At the moment he had built a wall between them as real as any brick one and it was impenetrable.

She had written a letter to Jack before going to sleep the night before, a long letter saying how much she missed him and how things were. She'd explained that she would probably be staying a few weeks in England until she could persuade Luke to leave, and had asked him to be patient.

Once she had left Phyllis's house she asked Norman if they could stop in town for a bit before they went to her mother's as she had some errands to do. She'd gone straight to the bank and asked them to change some American dollars into English currency, and then on to the post office. She felt slightly better once the letter was on its way; it brought Jack nearer somehow.

After buying some bags of groceries including a whole cooked ham, a huge slab of cheese, butter, nuts and fruit she took them back to the car, before venturing off again. She wanted to buy her mother some new clothes and in Fawcett Street at Binns drapery she found what she was looking for: a thick winter coat and hat in a matching shade of deep blue, a warm scarf and gloves, and a thick navy-blue woollen dress with a lace collar for Christmas Day. Walking back to the car she passed a jeweller's and a small gold brooch in the window caught her eye. It was in the shape of a flower basket, each bloom a tiny twinkling gem, and on impulse she purchased that too. She knew her mother would think it was a terrible extravagance but that didn't matter. Her mam had never owned any jewellery except for her thin gold wedding band and that had denoted a lifetime of servitude, poverty and misery being married to her da, she thought grimly.

Once Josie was back in the car she decided that she would give her mother the new clothes as soon as she arrived at the house. The brooch she'd keep for Christmas Day as a surprise. And tomorrow she'd take her mam out to buy whatever else they needed for a grand Christmas. Now there was no need for secrecy she could go ahead with what she'd been longing to do for years and open a bank account for her mother. She could transfer money to her every month so her mam need never again worry about paying the rent or making ends meet. It would give her mother security in her old age as she couldn't be here helping her in person, although she knew Joe and her sisters would always be on hand.

At least something good would come out of all this, she told herself as the car stopped outside her mother's house. Her mam would have some peace in her old age and money in her pocket to do with as she chose.

There was a horde of snotty-nosed ragamuffins pelting snowballs at each other in the street and they paused in their game to eye the car. They didn't see motor cars in this part of town. The children watched with big eyes as she and Norman staggered to the front door loaded with bags, and her mother's eyes were just as big when she opened the door to see Josie surrounded by them on the doorstep. It was unusual for anyone to use the front door, and for a moment when Maggie had heard the knock her heart had jumped into her mouth that it might be the police constable bearing bad news. Josie was in danger every time she left the house.

Once they were alone, Maggie stared in wonder at all the food and then shed a few tears when Josie presented her with the new clothes. 'Everything is beautiful, just beautiful, lass, but you must have spent a fortune,' she protested, wiping her eyes on her pinny before fingering the thick tweed of the coat. 'This lot'll set the tongues wagging and no mistake. If I was a few years younger they'd be saying I was on the game,' she added, the light dancing in her eyes as she giggled an almost girlish giggle. And then they were both laughing, something Josie hadn't expected to do when she'd awoken that morning, and as they hugged each other, Josie thought, *Oh, it's good to be home.* The McGuigans' houses with all their grand furniture and silver and expensive carpets and the like weren't a patch on her mam's.

Chapter Twenty-Eight

Josie stood outside the front door of Adam's residence, summoning up the courage to ring the bell. She had visited the house several times since Christmas without much success. Twice in a row she'd been told by the maid that Adam and Luke were out: once, Sadie had been sitting with them in the drawing room and she had only stayed a few minutes; and on another occasion Adam's manservant had informed her that his master was unwell in bed and Luke was with him and they were not to be disturbed.

Taking a deep breath, Josie pressed the bell and waited. It was some moments before the door was opened by the maid. 'I've come to see my husband and son,' she said with far more authoritativeness than she was feeling inside.

The girl hesitated. It was beginning to rain, and whether that had some bearing on her decision Josie didn't know, but after a moment the maid said, 'I – I've been told not to let anyone in but you'd better come into the hall while

I find Arthur, Mrs McGuigan. The master's had a turn and the doctor's with him.'

'A turn?' Josie asked as she stepped into the hall, but the girl seemed not to hear her, shutting the door and scurrying off.

The house was quiet, almost unnaturally so, and when Arthur appeared from a door at the end of the hall his face was grave. She watched the manservant approach, getting ready for more excuses as to why she couldn't see Luke, but when he reached her his voice was gentle as he said, 'Your husband has suffered a seizure after lunch, Mrs McGuigan, and is quite poorly. I think it would be better if you came back another day.'

'I didn't come to see Adam, I came to see my son. Is he with his father?'

There was a moment's silence. 'The young master is in the drawing room with his grandmother and Mr Bruce.'

'Then could I see him, please?'

'I really don't think that's wise.'

'I'm sorry, I want to see my son.' The conspiracy to keep her from Luke had had her nerves jangling for days and she'd had just about enough. Her voice had risen slightly as she had spoken and she swallowed hard before saying more quietly, 'I won't stay long if it's a difficult time but I want to see Luke.'

'The boy is upset, Mrs McGuigan. They all are.'

'I understand that but I'd still like to have a minute or two with Luke.'

Arthur stared at her for another moment and then

nodded, turning and leading the way to the drawing room. After knocking he opened it and stood aside for her to pass him, saying, 'Mrs McGuigan, sir. She insisted on seeing Master Luke.'

Luke was sitting between his uncle and grandmother on one of the sofas dotted about the room. No one moved but the three of them looked at her with such naked hostility it was palpable.

Her voice sounded weak even to herself when she said, 'I called to have a word with Luke but I understand that Adam's been taken ill this afternoon?'

What happened next took her completely by surprise. Sadie sprang up, her face contorted, looking like a madwoman. '*Taken* ill? He's been ill since the day you tried to murder him. You didn't expect him to survive the fall, did you? You thought you'd be sitting pretty in a fine house with plenty of money, but my boy did survive and he was able to tell us what you'd done. He gave you everything and you repaid him by trying to kill him, you witch. When you realized you hadn't succeeded you robbed him and took the one thing you knew he loved beyond life, his boy, his son.'

The last words had been said on a scream and now Sadie leaped towards her but Bruce moved quicker, grabbing his mother from behind and holding her as Sadie's hands clawed the air. She was shrieking abuse and Luke, from appearing frozen, now jumped up and tried to help his uncle as he cried, 'Grandma, Grandma, stop, you'll hurt yourself. Please, Grandma.'

It was taking all Bruce's strength to keep a grip on his mother, who was writhing and twisting in her determination to reach her prey, and it was into this screaming melee that Dr Preston walked.

When she saw the doctor Sadie collapsed, and now Bruce was holding his mother up rather than trying to prevent her reaching Josie. He eased her back on the sofa and sat down beside her with Luke on his grandmother's other side as Dr Preston said grimly, 'I don't know what is going on here but you should all be ashamed of yourselves. Adam needs rest and quiet, don't you understand that?'

He turned to Josie, who was standing tense and white-faced, shocked beyond measure at what had occurred. 'Sit down, Mrs McGuigan. I need to talk to all of you,' he said sternly.

She complied, perching on the edge of an armchair, but the doctor remained standing as he addressed them. 'Adam is a very sick man as you all know. His heart has been failing for years and I'm afraid the attack today was a serious one and has weakened it still further.'

'She did this to him, *her*.' Sadie was crying now and shaking. 'She wanted him dead.'

Luke put his arm round his grandmother, drawing her against him in the manner of a man rather than a thirteen-year-old boy. His voice didn't sound like a young lad's either as he said painfully, 'How long has my father got, Dr Preston?'

The doctor cleared his throat. 'It's difficult to say in

cases like this, Luke, but possibly days rather than weeks. I'm very sorry.'

Luke nodded, and as he did so he glanced at his mother. Josie recoiled from the look in his eyes. She stared at them – Luke, Bruce and Sadie – and it came to her that the three of them were joined in thought and purpose and their love for Adam, as well as their hatred of her. She had always known how Bruce and Sadie felt about her, but when had Luke turned so completely?

For the last minute or so Bruce had been sitting like a boxer who was stunned by a knockout blow, but now he said, 'I see. Thank you, Doctor. I suppose Arthur knows about the medication and so on?'

'Absolutely.' The doctor hesitated. 'You understand that your brother mustn't be left alone from this point on?'

It was Luke who spoke: 'He won't be.'

'Good, good. I'll leave you to it then but don't hesitate to call if you need me.'

When the doctor turned and left the room, Bruce looked at Josie. 'Get out,' he said softly.

She stood up. Sadie was making pitiful little sounds against Luke's shoulder and he still had his arms round his grandmother. She knew it was useless to try and defend herself against what had been said right now and she left the room without a word. The maid was hovering in the hall but she let herself out and once outside, careless of the rain which was now pouring down, she stood for a moment breathing in the icy air. The atmosphere in the house had been deadly, toxic.

Dr Preston had just started his car but now he wound down the window and called to her. 'May I offer you a lift, Mrs McGuigan?'

She opened her mouth to reply but strangely she found she couldn't speak, and it was only then that she realized she was shaking. In the next moment the doctor jumped out of the car and came across to where she stood, taking her arm and leading her over to the vehicle. In a daze she allowed him to help her into the front passenger seat, but as he slid into the driver's seat beside her and they moved off, she managed to say, 'I'm sorry, I don't want to delay you for your next patient.'

'Nonsense.' His voice was kind. 'I understand you are staying with your mother at present in Long Bank?'

She nodded. She didn't know how he knew that but it didn't matter anyway.

'My next home visit is near Mowbray Park – it won't take more than a minute or two to drop you off first.'

She sat in numb misery and they had reached the East End before Dr Preston spoke again. His voice was conversational, matter-of-fact even. 'I have known your husband all his life, Mrs McGuigan. In fact, I delivered him in the master bedroom of the house his mother still lives in. Adam was the apple of her eye from the moment he drew breath but I'm sure you are aware of that only too well. Unfortunately, certain aspects of his nature were never challenged and he grew up believing himself to be above the normal codes and morals of society. I believe this has had a severe detrimental effect on his personality from a young boy. I'm sure one of my psychologist associates would find him most interesting but that's by the by. Suffice to say that Adam has little conscience and is adept at creating his own version of the truth in any given situation. Believing it, even.'

She turned and stared at him. They had reached Long Bank and due to the appalling weather no one was about. 'I didn't push him down the stairs that night, Dr Preston. He was drunk and he fell.'

He nodded but didn't comment. 'May I give you some advice, Mrs McGuigan?' Without waiting for her to reply, he went on, 'Leave here as soon as you can because every minute you stay you're endangering yourself. Once Adam dies, and I believe that will be soon, any restraint that's been shown thus far will disappear. You saw how his mother was tonight. She will want her pound of flesh.'

'I can't go without my son.'

'M'dear, you may have to. Forgive me, but Luke seems very attached to his father.'

'He doesn't know what Adam's really like,' she said bitterly. 'What he's capable of.'

'That may be so but it doesn't change the situation you find yourself in. The thing is—' He paused.

'Yes?'

He sighed wearily. 'You love your son and that is perfectly right and proper, but perhaps now is the time to face the truth? From what I've seen of Luke – and yes, I admit that isn't much – I fear he's more like his father than you may want to believe.'

'But if Adam dies, he'd go home with me. There would be nothing to stay for in England.' Even as Josie said the words she knew she was fooling herself. Bruce and Adam and the others too had drawn Luke into their web like determined spiders. They wouldn't want him to leave and they'd do anything to keep him here.

'Blood is thicker than water, and the blood that flows through Luke's veins is McGuigan, m'dear. Go back to America while you can, with or without him. There has been too much tragedy as it is.' He patted her hand. 'The boy will be cared for, you know that, and perhaps after everything settles he will seek you out.'

'Thank you for the lift, Dr Preston.' She managed a smile before she slid out of the car, feeling even worse than when she had got in. The doctor had been trying to be kind but he'd voiced her deepest fears about leaving England without Luke.

What was she going to do? she asked herself wretchedly as she stood and watched the car drive away, making no effort to get out of the pouring rain. What *could* she do? She stood, a lone figure in the deserted street, her tears mingling with the raindrops.

Maggie stood at the kitchen table preparing the evening meal. She was stuffing pieces of cod with a mixture of sage, chopped onions, egg and breadcrumbs that she'd made the night before, and once the fish was ready she placed it in a dish with two tablespoonfuls of dripping and stock and put it in the range to cook beside the baked taties. It was one of Josie's favourite meals and she wanted to encourage her daughter to eat something; she'd barely had a bite in the last few days.

She sighed heavily. She was always on edge when the lass left the house but Josie had been determined to go and see Luke again and try to talk to the lad. She could understand it, Luke was her world, but she could wring the boy's neck for what he was putting his mam through.

After clearing the table she made a pot of tea and sat down with a cup in the rocking chair Josie had bought her. It was a fine affair with thick flock cushions to nurse her aches and pains. She'd always had a mind for a rocking chair but she hadn't known her lass had cottoned on to that. And Josie had set her up for the future too. There'd be no more going to the slag heap to scratch for cinders to eke out the coal for the range or worrying about putting food on the table. Josie had even tried to persuade her to move to a two-up, two-down house in the more respectable part of town but she didn't want that. She'd been in Long Bank all her married life. It was where the bairns had been born and she had good neighbours, Flo especially. She wouldn't want to start afresh at her time of life.

The kitchen was as warm as toast and as she sat gently rocking her thoughts meandered on. She might buy a double bed for the front room now she could afford it with what Josie was giving her. She and Nelly could do away with the mattresses on the floor. It'd be grand to sleep in a proper bed.

She finished her tea and got up and poured another, settling down again as she waited for Josie to come back.

It was getting on for five o'clock and she had lit the oil lamp some time ago due to the lack of light. The snow of Christmas had disappeared over the last days and a thaw had set in, turning everything to grey mush. It was miserable outside, she thought, as a gust of rain battered against the kitchen window, and there was Josie out in all this. The wind was howling down the chimney and in spite of the warmth Maggie shivered. It sounded like a banshee, one of those female spirits whose wailings warned of a death in the house. She wished Josie would come home.

She got up and walked over to look out of the kitchen window. Much as she'd sorrow when her lass went back to America, she wished her gone, and even then she'd worry. The McGuigans' reach was long. At least there Josie would have this man Jack she'd talked about to look after her, though. From what her lass had confided the two of them would get together, and even though it meant her daughter would be living in sin, she hoped it would happen.

It was a few minutes later when Josie walked in, water dripping off her hat and coat. 'Eeeh, lass, what a night and you out in it,' Maggie said, as she helped Josie out of her things. 'Come and sit down and I'll make a fresh pot of tea while we wait for Nelly to come home.' Then, taking in her daughter's strained face, she said, 'How did it go at Adam's? Were they in?'

Josie nodded. 'Adam's had a seizure. Dr Preston was there when I called.'

'Is he bad?'

Josie nodded again. 'Dr Preston doesn't think he's got long. Days, probably.' She sat down at the table. 'Bruce and Sadie were there. It was awful, Mam.'

Maggie joined her at the table, putting one of her hands over Josie's. It was stone cold. 'Tell me, hinny,' she said quietly. 'But first I'll make that tea. You need something hot inside you – you look like death warmed up.'

As Josie related what had happened Maggie listened without interrupting, but as she finished, Maggie said grimly, 'That woman is the Devil incarnate, lass, but Luke's a bright lad. He won't believe her.'

'He will, Mam. He does. I could see that today. Unless Adam tells him the truth about that night I don't think Luke will go back to America with me and I can't leave him here. I just can't.' She began to cry, shuddering sobs, and Maggie rose and patted her back, not knowing what to do.

Nelly came in a few minutes later and the three of them ate dinner together, but later that night, as Josie lay beside her sister on the mattress in the front room, she came to a decision. She would go back to the house tomorrow and insist on seeing Adam, and she would ask him to tell Luke what had really happened that night.

If Dr Preston was right and Adam was dying, he would soon be meeting his Maker; surely he would see that now was the time to tell the truth? That was all she wanted from him, to tell Luke the truth.

*   *   *

Adam was lying propped up in bed by a swathe of pillows behind him to help his breathing. Apart from a feeling of total exhaustion and difficulty in drawing air into his lungs he didn't feel too bad, he thought. The crippling pain in his chest when he'd collapsed the day before had gone and he was comfortable enough.

He glanced at Luke, who was sitting in a chair by the bed reading out loud to him from a Dickens novel, and the boy, sensing his gaze, looked up from the book and smiled before continuing. Such was the surge of love he felt for his son that for a moment it made him even more breathless. All the years he'd missed, all the good times they could have shared, and now, when Luke was finally home again, he himself was going to be the one who would have to leave. Not that Dr Preston had indicated his death was imminent – the doctor had been his usual calm and professional self – but he knew nevertheless, and if he hadn't, one look at his mother's face when she'd come to see him after Dr Preston had left the day before would have told him.

He closed his eyes again, listening to the sound of Luke's voice but without taking in the content of what was being said as thoughts swirled in his head. The day after Luke had come home he had called his solicitor and made sure his will was in order; everything would be straightforward as far as his affairs were concerned. Luke would inherit everything, lock, stock and barrel, including this house and a substantial amount in the bank along with stocks and shares. Arthur had agreed that in the event of his passing, he would stay on and be an unofficial guardian of the boy if Luke wanted to remain living in the house, and Bruce would take his nephew under his wing, he knew that. Luke would be well cared for and his future would be secure. Would his son choose to stay in England, though? He thought so, but he wasn't entirely sure, and the thought of Josie getting her hands on his son again was eating him up. If he was alive he felt that wild horses wouldn't have dragged Luke from his side, but if he died would Josie talk him round?

Arthur came into the room and he opened his eyes, saying, 'I told you to get some sleep, man. Luke's with me.' Arthur hadn't left his side since the heart attack and he'd had to force him to go and rest an hour or so ago when he'd noticed him dozing in his chair by the window.

'Mr McGuigan is going to sit with you tonight, I'll sleep then.' Arthur came close to the bed, his voice scarcely above a whisper and he glanced at Luke, who had stopped reading. 'The thing is, your wife's called and she wants to see you.'

'Josie?' Come to gloat, had she? He was about to say he didn't want to see her when something stopped him. This might prove the opportunity to put a spoke in her wheels concerning Luke for good. He had been careful what he'd said to the lad about his mother or more *how* he'd phrased things, never letting his bitterness and hatred have free rein and presenting himself as the victim; the grieving husband and father who had been ill-used and abandoned. 'All right, let her come in, Arthur.'

'Are you sure? Dr Preston said you weren't to get upset, sir.'

'Send her through.' The command was quiet but firm and brooked no argument.

'Shall I take the lad with me?'

'I'm not going anywhere,' Luke said quickly, looking at his father.

'No, Luke can stay.'

In the few moments before Arthur showed Josie into the room the two of them said nothing, but Luke stood up and came to stand next to the bed by his father's shoulder, one hand resting on Adam's arm. Adam's mind was like a battlefield of love and hate – love for his son, and hate and bitterness towards his wife – but he was warning himself to go steady. There was too much at stake for him to lose his temper.

As soon as Josie entered the bedroom Luke's stance hit her like a physical blow, along with the stiffness in his face as he looked at her. Their eyes held for a moment and then she transferred her gaze to the figure in the bed and she had to admit she was shocked. Adam hadn't looked well the last time she had seen him but since then his skin had taken on the appearance of old grey parchment and his eyes had sunk deeper into their sockets. Before she had left Long Bank her mother had warned her that Adam might be exaggerating how ill he was to gain Luke's sympathy, but she saw now that wasn't the case. Her voice low, she said, 'I'm sorry to hear you're so unwell, Adam.'

He drew in a long draught of breath. 'Thank you.'

She hesitated, unsure of what to say next.

After an uncomfortable moment or two, Adam said, 'Why have you come here, Josie? What do you want?'

Straight away she felt he had put her in the wrong. Colour flushing her cheeks, she swallowed hard. 'Yesterday, when I came and Dr Preston was with you, your mother and Bruce were in the drawing room and your mother said some things in front of Luke that weren't true. Bad – bad things about me.'

'Bad things?'

'She said I tried to murder you, that I did it for your money, but we both know that isn't true. When you fell that night it was an accident and you had attacked me first because I had objected to you – you sleeping with other women.'

'*Stop it.*' Luke's voice was loud and angry. 'You'll make him upset and he mustn't be.'

'It's all right, son.' Adam lifted his hand and placed it over Luke's. 'I'm not upset, just sad that even now your mother is persisting with this travesty when she knows full well I never looked at another woman from the day I met her. There was no attack that night, Josie, not by me anyway. I knew you were annoyed at me because I'd objected to you continuing to sing in low common establishments once we were married, but I was trying to protect you from yourself by stopping that. Because I loved you and I didn't want the sort of men who frequent such places taking advantage of you.' He shook his head.

'I just didn't realize how angry you were so perhaps in that respect, yes, I am guilty.'

She stared into the gaunt face in which only the eyes seemed alive, eyes that were emitting a dark light. 'Adam, please, don't do this. Tell him the truth.'

'You pushed me, I fell, and when you knew I was going to live and would say what had happened you raided the safe and took money and jewellery and disappeared with our son, the son you've lied to for years and kept from me and his family. The truth, Josie. Satisfied?' Adam lay back against the pillows and closed his eyes. 'I'm very tired. Please go now.'

She stood, shaking, her hands gripped together. 'Luke, I swear that's not how it happened. Please believe me. That's all lies—'

'You, to talk about lies.' Luke's voice was trembling but clear. 'You're my mother but I don't know you. I don't think I ever knew you. This singing, it's what you wanted more than anything, that's why you started again as soon as you got to America.'

'No, it was a means of earning money for us both, that's all. I had to keep a roof over our heads and—'

'Well, you won't have to keep a roof over my head any more because I'm not going back, I'm staying here.'

'You can't stay here—'

'Yes, I can.' He glared at her, looking so like Adam in the early days that she caught her breath. 'Father says I can and Uncle Bruce too. I'm staying here with Father and Arthur, and Uncle Bruce said he'll get a court order if he needs to. I'm not going back, not ever. This is my home, my real home.' He glanced at Adam, who still had his eyes closed. 'You're making him worse, you've upset him.' His face was burning; the colour suffusing it was almost scarlet. 'I don't want to see you again so don't come back,' he said, his voice vehement. 'Go back to your singing and your businesses, that's all you've ever really cared about anyway, not me.'

She had to leave. She had made everything ten times worse by coming here but she had never dreamed that with Adam knowing he was dying, he would take the stand he had. She looked at him and then her son and they seemed like a combating force, linked not just by their looks but in every way; and it was in that moment she knew that although she felt she had just lost Luke over the last weeks, the reality was that she had never truly had him. He was her boy, her baby, but he had always been first and foremost Adam's son, a McGuigan, and she couldn't fight that any more. The McGuigans had won and she had lost. It was over.

Chapter Twenty-Nine

Adam died peacefully in his sleep just as dawn was breaking a week later, the day before Josie had made arrangements to leave England for New York. She hadn't returned to Adam's house in that time, neither had she made any attempt to see Luke, although he filled her thoughts every waking moment. In the last meeting with him and Adam, hope had died within her. She knew now that whatever she said or did, she couldn't reach her son. Nevertheless, she'd written Luke a letter which she'd asked Phyllis to deliver into his hands. She had detailed exactly what had happened from the day she met Adam. Toby's murder on Adam's say-so; his associations with other women and neglect of her; his attempted rape on the night he'd had the accident; all of it.

She had been careful to be factual and unemotional for most of the letter, but she had finished by saying that from the moment he was born he had become her reason for living and that she would always love him beyond words. Her singing, the businesses, had been a means to an end, and that end had been providing a good secure future for him whether he believed it or not.

She had asked Phyllis to tell Luke that she was returning to New York, and she hoped with all her heart that he would contact her in the future and that her door would always be open to him. In the days that had followed she had heard nothing but she hadn't expected to. Maybe at some point in the years ahead Luke would rethink things but at the moment he was so under the McGuigan spell he believed his father and Bruce implicitly.

She knew her mother was frightened for her but in a strange way she no longer lived in fear of Bruce McGuigan. What could he do to her that was worse than losing her son? She wouldn't have said to her mother but there were times when she thought death would be preferable to the torment in her mind. Even the fact that Jack was waiting for her was of little comfort, her loss was so raw and painful. Her life had been so wrapped up in Luke that she could barely imagine how she would manage to go on without him.

The weather had turned bitterly cold again and it was snowing in the wind when she opened the door to Phyllis on the afternoon before she was due to leave for America. Norman was in the car and to her surprise she noticed Bruce was sitting in the back seat. Phyllis stared at her and immediately Josie knew, even before her friend murmured, 'He died early this morning. Can I come in?'

Josie opened the door wide in answer. She'd known it

was going to happen sooner or later but now it had, shock was foremost.

Once in the kitchen Maggie made the inevitable pot of tea and Phyllis and Josie sat at the table. Hesitantly, Phyllis said, 'I can't be long, Bruce's waiting, but we've just come from Adam's and I wanted to tell you myself. They're all there, the lot of them, you can imagine.'

Josie nodded. 'Yes, I can imagine. How's Sadie?'

'Bad.' Phyllis took the cup of tea Maggie handed her with a smile of thanks. 'She wasn't there when he went and she's blaming Arthur for not sending for her. Bruce had to tell her what for, so that didn't go down very well.'

'Was Luke with him?'

'Aye. Arthur knew the last couple of days it was drawing close, Adam wasn't awake much and he'd seen it all before with the man he'd worked for years back. Luke made Arthur promise to wake him if he thought it was going to happen and so he did. It was just the three of them, there was no point in sending for the doctor or anything. Lass, are you all right?'

Josie raised her eyes to her friend's face. 'Not really, Phyllis.'

Maggie had seated herself at the table now beside Josie and her voice was bitter when she said, 'I hope he burns in hell for what he's done to my lass, Phyllis.'

'Mam, stop. There's no point.' Josie's voice was weary. Adam was dead, she was rid of him and she was free. She should be glad, and she *was* glad but then why was there this pain in her? Ever since she had come back to England she had been trying to fight the feeling of pity that had assailed her when she had seen him, what he'd become, and the guilt that had accompanied it. Not for his injuries – he had brought those on himself when he had attacked her and caused her to fight back and his falling had been an accident. No, the guilt was for separating him from his son all these years, and Luke from his father.

Phyllis leaned forward and took one of Josie's hands in hers. It was cold despite the warmth of the kitchen. 'Lass, I wouldn't be able to say this if Bruce was here but I know the life Adam led you once you were wed and it wasn't right. And after the accident you had no choice but to get away, we all know that.'

'But I took his son, Phyllis.'

'Aye, you did, and I'd have done the same in your place. There's many a time I've wished my lads didn't have McGuigan blood running through 'em but they're not like—' She stopped abruptly. In her effort to sympathize she'd been in danger of saying too much.

'Like Luke?' Josie finished for her flatly.

'I was going to say like the McGuigans,' Phyllis lied.

Josie shook her head. 'No, you weren't, and you're right. Your boys aren't like Luke but the thing is, I love him, Phyllis, whatever he's like. I thought in taking him away he'd be able to grow up free of the McGuigans, that I could steer him in the right paths, but all I did was delay the inevitable and make him hate me into the bargain. He's Adam, isn't he, through and through.'

She couldn't go on, and as she began to weep, Phyllis exchanged a helpless glance with Maggie over her friend's head. She stayed a few more minutes trying to console Josie before leaving to join Bruce in the car. Once they were under way, he said, 'And how did your dear friend take the news?'

'She was upset, obviously.'

'Upset? Huh. She'd be dancing on his grave if she got the chance.' He ground his teeth, his jaw rigid. 'Did she ask after the lad?'

Phyllis nodded.

'And did you tell her that Luke doesn't want her anywhere near the funeral, that he never wants to see her again, in fact?'

'She knows that, Bruce. Anyway, she's leaving tomorrow, *you* know that.'

'So this hasn't made her change her mind?'

'What for? As you pointed out, she wouldn't be welcome at Adam's funeral.'

'Too damn right.' He said no more, his reason for letting Phyllis come and break the news to Josie accomplished. He wanted to make sure she would still be on that ship to America tomorrow; he'd got two men primed to board and their tickets were already bought and paid for. Somewhere on the journey a tragic accident would befall the lately widowed Josie McGuigan. Man overboard, or in this case, woman. He would have liked to have taken care of the matter himself but had realized that was too dangerous in the circumstances. He needed to be as far away as possible when Josie met her unfortunate end. Nevertheless, it rankled that he couldn't be there, and once home he found it impossible to settle, images of the day flashing through his mind. Adam, his thin body barely making a mound under the covers and looking as though he was just asleep; his mam demented with grief and trying to shake him awake so they had to restrain her, whereupon she'd fainted away on the spot; his brothers in a huddle crying – the first time he'd seen that since they were bairns – and Arthur trying to comfort Luke, who was distraught but insisting he wanted to stay close to the body of his father. It had been the worst day of his life and he'd had a few of those in his time.

After a dinner which he couldn't eat he took himself off to his study with a bottle of whisky, sitting at his desk and looking out into the dark night. He had gone through three-quarters of the bottle when Phyllis came into the room two hours later, standing and looking at him for a moment before coming over and putting her arms round his shoulders as she kissed the top of his head. It was unusual for her to show any affection and it touched him deeply, making his voice husky as he said, 'You go to bed, lass. I won't be able to sleep yet. I'll come up later.'

'For what it's worth he died happy, Bruce. He'd got Luke back and that meant the world to him.'

'Aye, but after twelve-odd years without seeing him or knowing if he was dead or alive. I could wring her neck, I could straight.'

449

'I know, I know.' Phyllis couldn't wait for Josie to get on that ship tomorrow. After a moment she said, 'I'm going up then, don't sit down here all night.'

Once he was alone again he sat a while longer, his rage and frustration mounting. He needed to see her one last time and put the fear of God into her before his men did the job on the ship. He opened the desk drawer and took out a knife he kept there, an evil-looking thing with a razor-sharp blade. He didn't intend to use it but he wanted the satisfaction of seeing her fear.

He left the house quietly. He wanted to walk and clear his head rather than take the car. There had been a sprinkling of snow during the night but now the sky was high and clear but bitterly cold, with the biting tang of frost in the air. He could remember other nights like this, he thought, when he and Adam and his other brothers had gone drinking together; happy times before Adam had come across Josie Gray, damn her. The chit had cast a blight over their lives and nothing would be the same again.

He nearly skidded on a patch of black ice and swore to himself before walking on more warily, his mind turning to Adam's son. Luke had fitted into the fold like he'd always been here, and he intended to make sure he never left again. In truth, the lad felt more like his than his own sons ever had. He didn't doubt that in the years ahead, when the time was right, Luke could step into his shoes and run the whole caboodle when he retired. Adam would have liked that. There was nothing namby-pamby about Luke; already, even at thirteen, he had the McGuigan traits that would serve him well.

When he reached Long Bank the normal smell, one of poverty and smoke and fish, wasn't so strong as usual due to the freezing conditions, but the overall grime of the area couldn't be offset even by the layer of snow on the roofs and windowsills. Adam had brought her out of this, he thought, as he turned into the back lane. He'd given her a fine house, servants, jewellery, and she'd thrown it all back in his face.

A big rat shot past him with a cat in hot pursuit and he grimaced. He didn't like rats; of all the creatures on God's earth they were the ones who turned his stomach.

It was nearly midnight when he walked into Josie's mother's back yard. The neighbourhood was mostly in darkness but as he looked towards the kitchen window there was a light glowing from behind the curtains. His fingers tightened on the knife in his pocket. It could be her mam or the sister who still lived at home in there, of course, but he'd make sure he saw Josie. He wanted to see her grovel for her life. He needed that satisfaction even if he wasn't there to put an end to her at sea.

Josie had retired to bed with her mother and Nelly but she had been unable to sleep. After listening to the cacophony of snores for what seemed like hours, she had slid out from under the covers, taking care not to disturb Nelly, and left the front room. Once in the kitchen she had lit the lamp and made herself a cup of cocoa before curling up in the rocking chair by the range, pulling her mother's shawl which Maggie had left on the back of the chair round her.

All day she had tortured herself with thoughts of boarding the ship without Luke. It was so final, so terrifying, and she didn't know if she could do it. At least here he was just a couple of miles away but once she went back to New York there would be an ocean between them, a world, a universe.

She stared into the glow of the fire, seeking an answer when she knew there wasn't any besides the one she had made. She had to go and staying would serve no useful purpose.

When she heard the back door open she turned her head and saw Bruce standing looking straight at her. In that moment she knew she'd been expecting him to make an appearance sooner or later. She stood up, her voice steady when she said, 'It's customary to knock.'

Her calmness took him aback. 'Is that so? Well, I make a habit of not doing what's expected of me.' He took the knife out of his pocket, its blade gleaming in the flickering light.

She looked from the knife to his face, and again he was nonplussed at her lack of fear when she said, 'On the contrary, you coming here like this is not at all unexpected.'

'So why wasn't the door bolted?'

'Would a bolted door stop you?'

He smiled grimly. 'No.'

'Well then.'

She looked like a young lass of eighteen, no more, standing there in her nightdress with a shawl about her shoulders and her bare feet buried in the clippy mat, but she was no young girl. She'd been a married woman for years, she'd borne a child and now she was a widow. Adam was dead and she was alive. His fingers tightened on the knife. 'I'm going to cut your throat,' he said almost conversationally, his voice low. 'Did you expect that too?'

'Something of the kind. I wasn't sure if it would be you who'd kill me or your hired thugs like you arranged for Toby.'

'Ah, yes, your dear brother. How did you find out about that, by the way?'

'That's none of your concern.'

'I beg to differ. I could make you tell me.' He raised the knife higher.

'No, you couldn't.'

Their gaze held, their mutual hate throbbing between them, and what he read in her face increased his pent-up fury. She should be weeping and pleading with him by now, damn her. He glared at her, his eyes narrowing, and then, his voice still low, he said, 'You think I won't do it? Is that it?'

'I think you and your family are capable of anything, being the dregs of humanity that you are.'

His eyes narrowed still more until they became black slits as he tried to make sense of what she was about; the kitchen weighed in a silence like that which follows the announcement of something terrible. After some moments, he said, 'And do you include your son in that?'

'You leave Luke out of this.'

For the first time since he had entered the kitchen he saw life come into her face. 'How can I when he is more of a McGuigan than most of them put together? I've great plans for him, I can assure you of that, and with Adam gone no doubt we'll get even closer. The lad needs a father —'

'You're not his father,' she shot back, her hands clenching into fists as she spoke, 'and one day he'll see you for exactly what you are.'

'He knows what I am. Unlike you, I've never lied to him. He hates you for what you did, do you know that? I mean, *really* hates you, the sort of hate that will only get stronger, not weaker in time.' She'd gone white; his words were hitting home in a way that physical blows could never have done, he realized with a burst of joy. This, then, was her Achilles heel, the boy. It was losing him that could destroy her. 'You'll never see him again,' he said softly, 'and every day of your life will be lived knowing he hates you for what you did. When he marries, has bairns, moves on with his life you'll never know, never be part of it.'

In spite of herself, Josie couldn't stop the tears from raining down her face as he spoke the very things that had been tormenting her. The thought of being in the world and not knowing when he was happy or sad, when he laughed or cried, who his friends were, what he was doing and if he was being cared for, was like the knife Bruce was holding being plunged into her chest over and over again except that no physical pain could come close. 'He'll understand one day,' she said, choking on her tears. 'When he's older he'll understand.'

'No, he'll forget you for days, weeks, months at a time, and when he remembers it will just be a bad memory of the woman who lied to him for years, who killed his father, who never really loved him.' He smiled again, the same grim smile. 'And do you know what the real beauty of that is, the ultimate justice for what you did to Adam? It's that you've made Luke think that way. Not me, not his father, not any of us. You did it all yourself. Do you know what he said to me the other day? That even his name wasn't real because he isn't Luke Gray, he's Luke McGuigan, and he's proud to be a McGuigan.'

She shook her head, words beyond her.

'So go back to your fancy life on the other side of the world with my blessing,' he said quietly, relishing the pain she couldn't hide. 'Back to your bars and your singing and making money, a life that's empty of love. You might get through in the day but each night you'll be alone with your thoughts and it'll be then that the demons come.' He drew in a deep breath and then let it out slowly as he put the knife back in his pocket. 'It'll be a life sentence, even worse than the one you gave Adam.'

He turned, walking across the room and opening the door, which he shut quietly behind him once he was outside. He didn't look behind him as he crossed the yard into the back lane, and once on his way he walked briskly, the dead weight that had been on his chest since he had looked at his brother's lifeless face lifting. He would call his men off tomorrow; he didn't want Josie Gray dead, that would be too easy. He wanted her to suffer, every day that she lived, however long or short it was he wanted her to suffer the torments of the damned, and she would. Oh aye, she would. He'd seen that tonight.

He stopped at the corner of Long Bank, lifting his face to the black velvet sky in which hundreds of stars twinkled and shone. 'Rest in peace, little brother,' he said softly. 'Rest in peace.'

Chapter Thirty

'I've had enough of this waiting, Carmella. I'm going to book a passage to England this afternoon and be done with it. I need to know she's OK.'

Jack had called in to see Carmella as he had every day since Josie had been gone to check that the older woman was all right. They'd taken to having lunch together before Carmella left for the afternoon to prepare the dinner at her brother's house for him and the boys. He knew Carmella was missing Josie and Luke and that she didn't like the empty apartment; furthermore she had been distraught about the situation as a whole and had confided to Jack that she thought Bruce McGuigan was a dreadful man.

'Josie didn't want you to do that,' Carmella said quietly. 'You know this. They'll be back soon, be patient.'

'I'm done with being patient.' Jack pushed his plate aside and stood up, beginning to pace about the dining room. 'She played into their hands going to England, you know that.'

'She had no choice. Luke was set on going as soon as he heard his father was alive.'

'I know.' He stopped and ran his hand through his hair. 'It's a hell of a fix.' If only she'd told Luke the truth about why she had come to America from day one, the boy would have been prepared for what had happened. No, no, that wasn't fair; knowing Luke as he did that would have meant trouble in a different way, because he'd had a feeling from when the boy was old enough to walk and talk that he would have stopped at nothing to find his father. Josie had been intent on protecting him from the McGuigans and their way of life and he could understand that.

'Luke, he seemed to like this man who was his uncle,' Carmella said slowly. 'I don't understand this.'

He did. There was very little of Josie in her son as far as he had been able to determine. He'd always felt guilty that he couldn't take to the boy, he admitted silently, but the man who had fathered him was always in evidence and not just in his looks. There was a lack of feeling for others, a supreme arrogance about Luke that was unusual in one so young. Oh, the boy was clever enough to conceal it most of the time with his charm and wit, but it was always there, looking out from behind his eyes.

'He will settle again once he is home.' Carmella looked at him for affirmation. 'He is a good boy.'

There was no reply Jack could make to this. Carmella looked on the boy with blind adoration, she always had done, ignoring the fact that Luke didn't like to be challenged in any way and always giving in to his whims and fancies. He had often thought that the set-up here did Josie no favours; because of Carmella's indulgence with the boy Josie was always put in the frame as the bad guy, and this had become more apparent in the last couple of years.

'Come and finish your meal,' Carmella said, her tone motherly. She didn't think Jack ate enough and was always trying to feed him up.

He had just sat down again when they heard a noise from the hall and the next moment Josie was standing in the doorway of the dining room. Jack reached her in a second and careless of Carmella pulled her into his arms, whereupon to his great surprise she burst into tears. Controlled pandemonium ensued for the next few minutes but then eventually they were all seated in the sitting room, Josie and Jack together on the sofa and Carmella facing them in an armchair. Jack's arm was tightly round her and she was leaning in to him, still hiccupping with the occasional sob. Carmella had made coffee while Jack had tried to calm Josie down, and now she poured them all a cup, her face pale and serious. She had realized Luke wasn't with Josie and that could only mean one thing.

After Josie had taken a few sips of her coffee, she said shakily, 'I'm sorry, it was seeing you . . .' Her voice trailed away and she swallowed hard.

Softly, Jack said, 'Tell us.'

And so she did, leaving nothing out. When she came to a halt Carmella was crying, and Josie leaned forward and touched her hand. 'I'm sorry,' she said again. 'I know how much you love him.'

'You have nothing to be sorry for.' Jack would have done murder if Bruce was in front of him and he would have liked to get his hands on Luke and shake the boy till his teeth rattled.

'Luke doesn't see it that way.' Josie sighed, feeling totally exhausted and drained. The journey home had been as horrendous as ever and she had come to the conclusion that she simply wasn't a good traveller because no one else had seemed to suffer with seasickness as badly as she had. The only good thing about it was that she had felt so ill she hadn't been able to dwell on losing Luke so much. When she had got off the boat and hired a cab the eight-, ten- and eleven-storey structures that shadowed the streets had been comforting in a strange sort of way, her surroundings so different to the North-East where all the tragedy in her life had taken place.

Jack held his tongue when he would have liked to rant and rail against the boy, knowing that wasn't what she needed right at this moment. Instead he said softly, 'He's young, Josie. Still wet behind the ears. Give him time.'

'He hates me, Jack.'

'No.' He stroked her cheek softly. 'He might think he does but he doesn't hate you, my love. The McGuigans have presented themselves in a certain way but sooner or later he will see them for what they are and understand that what you did was because you had no choice.'

'I wish I could believe that. Adam kept to his story

right to the end even when he knew he was going to die and that must carry some weight. I don't understand how he could do that.'

'Because you are intrinsically good and he was intrinsically bad. How could you understand?'

'And Luke?' She turned, staring into his face. 'What is he?'

'Your son.'

'But Adam's son as well.'

As her eyes filled with tears again he took her in his arms, pressing her close. He wanted to make it better; he had never thought to see the strong, independent woman he'd known and loved for so many years crushed and broken like this, but all he could do was to be here for her, and he would be. For the rest of his life. 'You need to rest, you're exhausted. I'll come back later and we'll have dinner together and—'

'Don't go.'

Her voice didn't sound like Josie, it was small and filled with pain. 'Stay with me.'

'Only if you try to sleep. Come on.' He stood up, drawing her with him, and to Carmella's surprise and secret disquiet led her to her bedroom, whereupon he made her lie down on the coverlet and then lay down himself, taking her in his arms again as he gently soothed her, whispering soft endearments until her regular breathing told him that she had fallen asleep.

Carmella left the apartment for her brother's after a little while but he stayed where he was, thinking over everything that Josie had told him. When the time was right – later today or tomorrow – he would ask her to marry him. She was free now. And they wouldn't wait for a conventional amount of time either. People here knew her as a widow anyway. He would obtain a special licence and she could be his within days.

His blood raced through his veins and he kissed the top of her head, his lips lingering on the softness of her hair.

She was heartbroken now, at the end of herself, without hope, and exhausted mentally and physically after doing battle with the McGuigans, but he would make her happy again. His eyes narrowed in determination. Bruce McGuigan had said that she would live a life empty of love and when she had repeated that to him her voice had trembled and broken, but he would make sure the opposite was true. He would fill her life with love, every moment of every day and night; oh, yes, especially the nights.

It was growing dark outside when she awoke and Carmella had arrived back and was busy in the kitchen after putting her head round the door, which he'd left open, and asking if he needed anything. 'Just Josie,' he'd replied softly. 'I'm going to ask her to marry me, Carmella.'

The Italian woman had beamed her delight, whispering, 'This is good, Jack. It is what she needs.'

When Josie began to stir he kissed her lightly on her brow. She opened her eyes, looking at him dazedly for a moment and then smiling.

'Hello,' he said gently, kissing her again but on the lips this time. 'My sleeping beauty.'

'How long have I been asleep?'

'All afternoon.'

'And you stayed with me? Oh, I'm sorry, you must have had things to do.'

'Stop saying you're sorry,' he chided softly, 'and I had nothing to do that's more important than looking after you. In fact, that's what I want to do for the rest of my life – if you'll let me, being the bossy, independent woman that you are.' He grinned at her, propping himself on one elbow as he said, his face straightening, 'Will you marry me, Josie? Soon? As soon as I can arrange a special licence? I think we've waited long enough, don't you?'

She lay looking at him, her eyes moving over every feature of his face before she simply said, 'Yes, please.'

He had expected that he would have to persuade her to put convention aside, that she would want time to get used to the idea of committing herself to a man again after what she'd been through, and now his face lit up and he slowly and firmly drew her in to him. This moment was the start of her new life and he was going to love her as a woman had never been loved before.

They only invited Carmella and Jack's parents to the short service at the register office and to the meal at the Fifth Avenue Hotel, the grandest and most glamorous hotel in New York. Located near luxurious residential enclaves and in the middle of the city's entertainment district, its giltwood public rooms made it ideal, according to Jack, who had insisted on paying for the reception himself.

Josie had worn a simple ivory dress and a matching coat with a fur-lined hood and Jack said she had never looked more beautiful . . .

He had arranged for them to spend the wedding night in the sumptuous honeymoon suite, and when they entered it later that evening after saying goodbye to their guests, Josie stood amazed in the doorway. The sitting room was filled with white roses and lilies and the perfume of hundreds of blooms was heady.

Ridiculously, considering that she had known and loved Jack for years and had been married before, she suddenly felt shy, stammering a little as she murmured, 'It's – it's lovely. Th-thank you.'

'You're lovely,' he said, his voice husky and deep. 'So lovely I can't believe you're mine at last. You could have any man you want—'

She turned, putting her arms round his neck, the shyness evaporating. 'You're all I want, all I'll ever want.' He had been so good to her in the days before the marriage, holding her when the sorrow about Luke welled up and became unbearable, and soothing her with endearments. When she had left England she had imagined that the future would be for ever dark and meaningless but now, with Jack by her side, she could face it. She didn't know if she would ever be truly happy again but she would settle for being content with moments of joy and be thankful for that. She kept telling herself that it wasn't as if Luke had died and she was mourning him; he was alive and healthy and with folk who loved him in their own way. She had to let go. Jack had told her that countless times and it was true. She had to let her son go and just hope that one day he would allow her into his life again.

Jack led her over to a small table where a bottle of champagne on ice and two flutes were waiting for them. Filling the glasses he handed her one, his vivid blue eyes drinking her in as he murmured, 'To us, my darling. To us and the years ahead, which will be good ones, I promise you that.'

'I know.' And she did know, she told herself, fighting back the tears that fell so readily these days, determined not to cry at such a moment. 'I love you with all my heart.'

'And I you, my love.'

They drank with their arms entwined and then he whisked her up into his arms, making her squeal as the champagne spilled over the edges of the glasses. He carried her into the huge bedroom with silk covers and drapes and yet more flowers, and as he undressed her and then himself his eyes worshipped and adored her, banishing all thoughts of that first wedding night so long ago.

Their lovemaking was all that Josie had dreamed it would be and afterwards, when they lay wrapped in each other's arms, her head on his chest, he whispered, 'We'll never be apart again, my love,' as his arms tightened round her. She drifted off to sleep enclosed in love in the scented room, and for the first time in years her slumber was deep and dreamless. She was safe and she was home because home was where Jack was.

Epilogue

1906

It was a balmy soft day in late August and Josie was sitting in the garden of her Staten Island home. They had moved to New York's most attractive suburb not long after Josie had discovered she was pregnant at the beginning of the year. In the last decades Staten Island had transitioned from a rural county of oyster fishermen and vegetable farmers to a place where industry, commerce and a substantial community of middle-class Americans now lived. The contrast between the bustle of lower Broadway and the quiet beauty of the villages at the other end of the ferry was remarkable, and Josie had fallen in love with the Island the first time they'd visited it.

They had chosen to live in the southernmost town on the Staten Island railroad, Tottenville. Unlike the North Shore of the island, which was becoming more industrial, Tottenville was still countrified in its wide stretches of hills and valleys, its lawns and gardens and its attractive houses, whilst remaining close to the city with many urban comforts.

They had purchased a pretty, six-bedroomed house with a substantial garden to the rear complete with fruit trees, and the front garden had boasted well-tended flower beds and bushes surrounded by a quaint picket fence. Carmella had moved with them and continued in her chosen role as housekeeper and cook, but now they also employed a maid, the daughter of a local oyster fisherman, who came every morning at six o'clock and left late evening.

Jack caught the ferry to Lower Manhattan several times a week, continuing to manage their business of bars and restaurants which grew from strength to strength each year, and until her pregnancy had slowed her down Josie had gone with him most days. The last two months she had concentrated on getting the house just as she wanted it though, especially the nursery which was waiting for its new occupants. She was expecting twins, which had been something of a shock at first. Jack's mother, a homely, motherly woman who was delighted to have Josie as a daughter-in-law, had told her that twins ran in their side of the family, and everyone had been thrilled at the news, Josie less so as the pregnancy had advanced and she'd become as big as a house with a waddle rather than a walk.

She was sitting in a big, cushioned cane chair under the shade of a cherry tree, a cup of coffee that the maid, Grace, had brought her at her elbow, and Jack was dozing in an identical chair a few feet away. The babies were due in a week and for the last couple of days she had

had niggling backache on and off and Jack had refused to leave her. Josie had been adamant that she didn't want to go into hospital to have the twins. The local doctor was a middle-aged man of considerable experience and his wife was a midwife, and after meeting them it had been decided that Josie would have the babies at home, with the proviso that if the doctor or his wife were concerned at any point she would be taken to hospital.

She had just reached for her cup when she paused in mid-stretch as a familiar cramping pain in her stomach caused her breath to catch. When it subsided she drank her coffee but within fifteen minutes she'd had three more and she knew the babies were on the way. She put her hand on her stomach, enjoying the last hours when the twins were still solely hers, and as ever her thoughts turned to Luke. Despite writing to him lots of times, she had received nothing in return, but since she had become pregnant her resolve to keep trying had strengthened rather than weakened. One day the twins would meet their big brother, she was determined about that; when and how it happened wasn't important, but happen it would. She refused to accept that Luke was lost to her for ever. She hadn't told him in her letters about her marriage to Jack or that she was pregnant, though. She didn't know if he showed them to Bruce or talked about the contents, but the instinct to protect Jack and now her unborn children was still strong.

The next contraction made her gasp and once it was over she woke Jack and told him that he needed to fetch

Mrs Parsons. He didn't need to be told twice, helping her into the house and up the stairs to their bedroom, which overlooked the rear garden and all summer was scented by climbing roses. Leaving her in Carmella's care, he rushed off to fetch the midwife, returning with her in just a few minutes.

Mrs Parsons was a nice woman but she was disapproving about Jack's determination to stay with his wife at the birth. She'd told Josie and Jack that but they had gently insisted and she'd had to give way. Josie had wanted her husband with her and once Jack had realized that, wild horses wouldn't have dragged him from her side. Whenever possible they did everything together so why would the long-awaited birth of the twins be any different?

Things progressed quickly. She had wondered if this confinement would be the long drawn-out affair it had been with Luke, but it appeared not, for which she was thankful.

Just three hours after the first pains their daughter made her entrance into the world, crying in protest as she was expelled from the nice warm place where she'd been happy for the last nine months. Once the cord was cut and the baby was wrapped in a soft blanket, the midwife handed the child to Jack before she continued seeing to Josie, who still had more work to do.

'You have a beautiful daughter, Mr Kane,' she'd said softly and Jack had taken the small bundle gingerly. The baby was so tiny but as he gazed down into the little face he fell instantly and completely in love, emotion flooding over him. When they'd been told that Josie was expecting twins, he'd hoped that at least one of the babies would be a girl, a little Josie he could spoil and indulge. He sat down on the edge of the bed, his eyes wet as he murmured huskily, 'Look what we've made, my love. She's exquisite,' as he showed Josie their daughter.

As the baby yawned, showing tiny pink gums, Josie stared at her in wonder, and Carmella, who'd been assisting the midwife, whispered, 'She looks like her mother, yes?'

She was so small, Josie thought, so small and perfect, with wisps of fair hair and a tiny button of a nose. 'Hello, Abigail,' she said softly, 'your daddy has been waiting to meet you.' She smiled tenderly at Jack, who had tears streaming down his face. They had chosen the name because it meant 'father rejoiced' or 'father's joy', both of which Jack had said would apply to him if they were blessed with a girl.

As another strong contraction gathered steam, Jack handed the baby to Carmella and took Josie's hand again. He couldn't believe what hard work it was to bring a baby into the world, or how painful, but the amazing thing was that Josie didn't seem to mind. She had put up with the first few months of being sick during the pregnancy without complaint, and even when her stomach had got so huge and as tight as a drum, she had been serene about it all. She was born to be a mother, which must have made it so much harder when she had lost Luke. Bending close, he whispered, 'One out and one to go. You're halfway there, my love,' wishing he could take some of the pain for her.

It was another ten minutes before Abigail's brother was born and he had the same feathery blonde hair as his twin and an identical little button nose, along with a good pair of lungs if his cries were anything to go by.

Once the cord was cut and the baby was cocooned in a blanket like his twin, Mrs Parsons handed him to Josie. 'They're like two peas in a pod,' she said, smiling, 'even though this one is a boy.'

Their first choice of a name for a son had been Alexander, with Toby as a second name. Again, the meaning had been the important thing to Josie. Alexander was from the Greek and it meant 'defender of men'. It suggested to her someone who was brave but compassionate towards his fellow man, a person who would protect and stand up for those weaker and more vulnerable than himself. She hadn't delved into her mind as to why that was of significance; it was too painful.

She gazed down into the tiny face and as she did so the baby opened his eyes. The grey-blue gaze travelled over her features as though he was searching for something. And then he smiled, a sweet quirk of the tiny rosebud mouth. Josie knew it was just a reflex action, one of the things that newborn babies did, but that was head knowledge. Her heart told her that somehow her son had expressed his approval of the woman who was his mother, and it touched her to the very core of her being.

She hadn't even mentioned it to Jack but she had been frightened that if one of the twins was a boy, she'd be unable to love him as he deserved, grieving as she was about Luke. But instead, she found herself experiencing the acute throb of incredulity that accompanies any feeling bordering on unbelievable joy.

'Hello, Alexander,' she whispered into the little face still watching her so intently. 'I'm your mam.'

Dancing in the Moonlight

By Rita Bradshaw

As her mother lies dying, twelve-year-old Lucy Fallow promises to look after her younger siblings and keep house for her father and two older brothers.

Over the following years the Depression tightens its grip. Times are hard and Lucy's situation is made more difficult by the ominous presence of Tom Crawford, the eldest son of her mother's lifelong friend, who lives next door.

Lucy's growing friendship with Tom's younger brother, Jacob, only fuels Tom's obsession with her. He persuades Lucy's father and brothers to work for him on the wrong side of the law as part of his plan to force Lucy to marry him.

Tom sees Lucy and Jacob dancing together one night and a chain of heartbreaking events is set in motion. Torn apart from the boy she loves, Lucy wonders if she and Jacob will ever dance in the moonlight again . . .

Beyond the Veil of Tears

By Rita Bradshaw

Fifteen-year-old Angeline Stewart is heartbroken when her beloved parents are killed in a coaching accident, leaving her an only child in the care of her uncle.

Naive and innocent, Angeline is easy prey for the handsome and ruthless Oswald Golding. He is looking for a rich heiress to solve the money troubles his gambling and womanizing have caused.

On her wedding night, Angeline enters a nightmare from which there is no awakening. Oswald proves to be more sadistic and violent than she could ever have imagined. When she finds out she is expecting a child, Angeline makes plans to run away and decides to take her chances fending for herself and her baby. But then tragedy strikes again . . .

The Colours of Love

By Rita Bradshaw

England is at war, but nothing can dim land girl Esther Wynford's happiness at marrying the love of her life – fighter pilot Monty Grant. But months later, on the birth of her daughter Joy, Esther's world falls apart.

Esther's dying mother confesses to a dark secret that she has kept to herself for twenty years: Esther is not her natural daughter. Esther's real mother was forced to give up her baby to an orphanage – and now Joy's birth makes the reason for this clear, as Esther's true parentage is revealed.

Harshly rejected by Monty, and with the man Esther believed was her father breathing fire and damnation, she takes her precious baby and leaves everything and every-one she's ever known, determined to fend for herself and her child. But her fight is just beginning . . .

Snowflakes in the Wind

By Rita Bradshaw

It's Christmas Eve 1920 when nine-year-old Abby Kirby's family is ripped apart by a terrible tragedy. Leaving everything she's ever known, Abby takes her younger brother and runs away to the tough existence of the Border farming community.

Years pass. Abby becomes a beautiful young woman and falls in love, but her past haunts her, casting dark shadows. Furthermore, in the very place she's taken refuge is someone who wishes her harm.

With her heart broken, Abby decides to make a new life as a nurse. When the Second World War breaks out, she volunteers as a QA nurse and is sent overseas. However, life takes another unexpected and dangerous turn when she becomes a prisoner of the Japanese. It is then that Abby realizes that whatever has gone before is nothing compared to what lies ahead . . .

A Winter Love Song

By Rita Bradshaw

Bonnie Lindsay is born into a travelling fair community in the north-east of England in 1918, and when her mother dies just months later Bonnie's beloved father becomes everything to her. Then, at the tender age of ten years old, disaster strikes. Heartbroken, Bonnie's left at the mercy of her embittered grandmother and her lecherous step-grandfather.

Five years later, the events of one terrible night cause Bonnie to flee to London, where she starts to earn her living as a singer. She changes her name and cuts all links with the past.

Time passes. Bonnie falls in love, but just when she dares to hope for a rosy future, the Second World War is declared. She does her bit for the war effort, singing for the troops and travelling to Burma to boost morale, but heartache and pain are just around the corner, and she begins to ask herself if she will ever find happiness again.

Beneath a Frosty Moon

By Rita Bradshaw

It's 1940 and Britain is at war with Germany. For Cora Stubbs and her younger siblings this means being evacuated to the safety of the English countryside. But little does Cora know that Hitler's bombs are nothing compared to the danger she will face in her new home, and she is forced to grow up fast.

However, Cora is a fighter and she strives to carve out a new life for herself and her siblings. Time passes, and in the midst of grief and loss she falls in love, but what other tragedies lie around the corner?

As womanhood beckons, can Cora ever escape her troubled past and the lost love who continues to haunt her dreams and cast shadows over her days?

One Snowy Night

By Rita Bradshaw

It's 1922 and the Depression is just beginning to rear its head in Britain, but Ruby Morgan is about to marry her childhood sweetheart and nothing can mar her happiness. Or so she thinks. An unimaginable betrayal by those she loves causes her to flee her home and family one snowy night.

Crushed and heartbroken, Ruby vows that, despite the odds stacked against her, she will not only survive but one day will show the ones she left behind that she's succeeded in making something of herself. Brave words, but the reality is far from easy.

Dangers Ruby could never have foreseen and more tragedy threaten her new life, and love always seems just out of reach. Can a happy ending ever be hers?

'Catherine Cookson would have been proud to put her name to this heartfelt and moving saga'

Peterborough Evening Telegraph

The Storm Child

By Rita Bradshaw

It's midwinter, and in the throes of a fierce blizzard Elsie Redfern and her husband discover an unknown girl in their hay barn about to give birth. After the young mother dies, Elsie takes the infant in and raises her as her own daughter, her precious storm child.

Gina grows into a beautiful little girl, but her safe haven turns out to be anything but. Torn away from her home and family, the child finds herself in a nightmare from which there's no waking. But despite her misery and bewilderment, Gina's determined to survive.

Years pass. With womanhood comes the Second World War, along with more heartbreak, grief and betrayal. Then, a new but dangerous love beckons; can Gina ever escape the dark legacy of the storm child?

'Expect the unexpected in this enthralling story with a wealth of colourful characters'

Coventry Evening Telegraph

The Winter Rose

By Rita Bradshaw

It's December 1902 and Rose O'Leary is looking forward to her baby girl's first Christmas. But then tragedy strikes: her husband dies at the shipyard where he works and within days his friend, Nathaniel, makes it plain he's determined to have her.

Rose flees with her child, but soon finds the world is a cruel place for a beautiful woman with no protection. More tragedy ensues and yet, although she's bruised and broken, Rose is a fighter.

Then, when she least expects it, love enters her life again, but she cannot escape her past and now it threatens not only her happiness but her very life. Will she ever find a safe haven?

'Raw passion and power on every page'

Northern Echo

Believing in Tomorrow

by Rita Bradshaw

Molly McKenzie is only eleven years old when her abusive father beats her to within an inch of her life. Escaping from the hovel she calls home, Molly is found by kind fisherfolk, sick and near death. With them she experiences the love of a family for the first time and, even though life is hard, she is content.

Time passes and Molly's looking ahead to a future with the boy she loves, but then a terrible tragedy rips her life apart. Once again she's cast adrift in an uncaring world, but Molly is made of stern stuff and is determined to survive.

In the male-dominated society of the early 1900s, Molly has to fight prejudice and hatred, and rejection comes from all sides. Can she hold fast and become the woman she is destined to be?